## WE DIDN'T KNOW WHAT TO EXPECT.
## WE JUST KNEW IT WOULD BE BAD. . . .

I had six men besides myself. They crowded around as I came through. Bob Casey said, "What the hell's the deal?"

"There's a raiding party on the way," I said.

"How the hell you know that? You got spies?"

I told them briefly about the rockets. It left a few open-mouthed, but Casey asked, "What they coming here for?"

I looked at him. I didn't like the man one little bit, and the feeling was growing. "They're coming to kill cattle. When they find there ain't no cattle to kill, they'll do what devilment they can. Your job is to make sure they don't."

After that, I told them their positions. I put Bob Casey and Arnie Welch in the middle. I put two of my regular hands down with Lew and kept one beside me at my corner. "Now get this straight," I said. "Nobody fires until I do. And keep your heads below the top of the corral. Fire through one of the lower openings."

The cowboy beside me, a young man named Slayto_____ we about to k_____ He sounded plenty _____

I s_____ shoot well enoug_____t, why, you are w_____s—they are going to be shooting to kill y___

*Books by Giles Tippette*

# Cross Fire

## GILES TIPPETTE

JOVE BOOKS, NEW YORK

CROSS FIRE

A Jove Book / published by arrangement with
the author

PRINTING HISTORY
Jove edition / July 1990

ISBN: 0-515-10391-8

Jove Books are published by The Berkley Publishing Group,
200 Madison Avenue, New York, New York 10016.
The name "JOVE" and the "J" logo
are trademarks belonging to Jove Publications, Inc.

PRINTED IN THE UNITED STATES OF AMERICA

10  9  8  7  6  5  4  3  2  1

To Peter Hawthorne,

who was stupid enough to get caught
in a cross fire of birdshot, wearing my shirt.

Naturally, the shirt was ruined.

# CHAPTER
# 1

My youngest brother, Ben, said, "Justa, they're driving a herd of Mexican cattle down through our range."

I said, "What the hell do I care?"

I was sitting in my office in our ranch house in Matagorda County, Texas, and I was feeling pretty low. The woman I'd been planning on marrying had just run away with another man. I wasn't that deep in the bottle, because that ain't my style, but I was working on it.

Ben said with some intensity, "Justa, wake up! Dammit! Mexican cattle coming through our range mean tick fever. Mexican tick fever! You got to do something about it."

"The hell I do."

I was the eldest of three brothers, so when my father became incapacitated through bad luck and a gun shot, it became my lot to run the family business.

And I was tired of it.

I wasn't but twenty-eight years old and I was a hard six-foot-tall, hundred-and-ninety-pound man, but I'd been carrying the load for nearly eight years.

And for once, I thought someone else ought to get their shoulder under the wagon that was stuck in the ditch.

That was why I was a little cool to my brother when he wanted me to jump up and solve all the problems that were presented to our family.

"The hell with it. And the hell with you," I said.

"Why you big crybaby," he blurted out. "You're just sitting there feeling sorry for yourself over some damn woman."

I got up and hit him. It was only the second time in my life that I'd ever hit my little brother. He went reeling back and hit the wall of my office and sat there blinking, a little blood running out of his mouth.

If you took me and Ben and painted an outline of us against a white wall, all you'd get between us was about twenty pounds' difference. We both had the same build we'd inherited from our father: the wide shoulders and the slim hips; the wide hands and the big biceps. We got them from our dad and from hard work; we didn't go down to the mercantile and purchase any part.

The only problem with Ben was that he was about the fastest gun I'd ever seen. He was four years younger than I was, and he could shoot fast and he could shoot straight. He'd hit the wall after I'd punched him, slid down, and sat there looking at me. I was towering over him, in a rage. I watched for his hand to make the slightest motion toward his holster. Of course, it didn't. I was his big brother. He got up slowly and backhanded the blood off his mouth. "This ain't like you, Justa."

"What is like me? Tell me!" I yelled at him.

He turned toward the door and looked back at me. "Hitting your brother."

"You had it coming. You don't talk to me like that."

"What about those Mexican cattle?" he asked.

"Fuck those Mexican cattle! Can't you folks handle anything?"

And then he was gone, my hard-nosed younger brother that could damn near get any girl he wanted.

Next my middle brother, the banker, who wore suits and was always so logical, came in and said, "Am I disturbing you?"

"Hell yes. Get out of here."

But Norris, who had the patience of a piece of granite, said, "Let me talk with you."

"No."

But he sat down anyway and folded his hands across his lap like he always did. "Justa, if we let those Mexican cattle through our herds it will wipe us out. Think about that breeding program you put in, upgrading our beef. All that would be gone."

I took a drink out of the bottle of whiskey I had sitting on my desk. "Norris, why the hell don't you unfold your hands? You look like a Baptist preacher on a proselytizing mission. But you ain't going to convert me. I intend to sit here and drink this bottle of whiskey. If you want those cattle stopped, you and Ben go out and do it. If you can't reason them out of it, then Ben can blow off enough heads that they'll get discouraged and turn back."

Of course I knew what his concern was about. We lived along the coastal plains, the best grazing country in Texas. And in the year of 1892, beef prices were clear out of sight. So if I'd been some saddle-bound entrepreneur who'd just bought a herd of cheap Mexican cattle and somehow managed to get them across the border and by the customs inspectors, either by bribe or stealth, I'd have been driving them through our plains for the sheer purpose of fattening them up and getting a better price. Sounded like a solid business proposition to me.

Except we had five thousand head of blooded cattle that wouldn't last a week if they got mixed in with those maverick cattle from Mexico.

Cattle coming up from Mexico had to be held in quarantine for forty days to make sure they didn't have Mexican tick fever. Those Mexican cattle were immune to it, but that little tick bug would kill our cattle faster than if you shot them in the heads with a rifle slug.

"How the hell you know those cattle have been brought in here illegally?" I asked. "The man running those cattle might be an honest businessman."

Norris said, with that calmness I wasn't in the mood for, "Justa, we had a telegram five days ago that those cattle were brought through without inspection. I told you about it, but you chose not to listen. We have friends in Brownsville and we were advised. Now, they are only a hundred miles away. We have had rancher friends beating on this door for the last three days. When are you going to act?"

"I haven't heard anybody beating on this door."

"That was because you didn't want to hear them. But they are worried. As we all are."

I said, with a little more heat than I meant, "What are they coming over here for? I ain't their wet nurse. I ain't their sugar tit."

"Because you are the leader around here. And you know it."

I turned back to my desk and picked up the bottle. With it I gestured to the door. "Get out of here," I said. "Or I'll hit you like I just did Ben."

He got up. Before he turned for the door he looked at me coldly. "Yes, I know. That was very brave of you, considering he wouldn't hit you back."

"Get out of here. Now! Solve your own goddamn problems any way you can. I got my own," I said.

"Of course. Nora."

I threw the bottle, but he'd already shut the door behind him, and all it did was break harmlessly on the wood.

Then I put my face in my hands. I had to do something; I just didn't know what.

It was always Justa, Justa, Justa.

And I was sick of Justa, Justa, Justa.

Hell, let them handle it for a change. I was sick of being shot at, shooting and getting shot up. If there was anybody I wanted to shoot it was that sonofabitch that had run off with my Nora.

My Nora. Some joke.

I took another drink, and then I wandered out into the ranch yard. The first person I saw was Ray Hays. He was coming toward me with that worried look I think had been branded on his face. "Boss," he said, "we got to do something 'bout those cattle coming down."

Now, Ray was a different drink of water for me. Normally I treated most of the ranch employees with a pretty hard hand, but Hays was a different case. Something close to a year back I'd been in just a shade more than bad trouble up in the hard rock country around Bandera, Texas. Hays had been working for the man that meant me no good, but when he saw the error of his ways, he'd come over to my side and was pretty well instrumental in saving my life.

So even though I gave him a hard time on occasion in a vain attempt to make him remember who was boss, he was privileged and—the worst part about it—he knew it.

"Hays, I am going to feed the next man that mentions those cattle to the hogs," I replied.

"But Boss, we got to do something here and mighty quick."

I fixed him with a look. "You gone hard of hearing?"

"Well, no. Whatever in the world do you mean?"

"You are drawing wages here, aren't you?" I asked.

He got a sort of bewildered look on his face. Hays was never going to win any prizes in school for smarts. "Of course I am," he said. "Ain't that understood?"

"Are you drawing wages for arguing with me?"

Comprehension began to dawn. "Well, I reckon not."

I said, with plenty of sarcasm, "Then I *reckon* you had better get back to what you're drawing wages for before I forget how to write checks with your name on them. Last time I looked, you and Ben were supposed to be working horses. Smoothing out that rough string we just brought in. But all the both of you have been doing is bothering me. Now, you want to get to it or you want to seek employment somewhere besides the Half-Moon?"

He got a hurt look on his face. "Well, you don't have to take a man's head off. I was just thinking about the good of the ranch."

Then he turned around and walked off with a gait that suggested he was the injured party.

Oh, I was getting everyone straightened up that morning.

Everyone except me.

My daddy did that for me that evening in his own quiet way. Since he'd been shot and nicked in the lungs he didn't get around so good, so I was surprised when he came into my room. I still had that same brand of whiskey in my hand and I was brooding. He came in slowly, using both his canes and wheezing a little, and he sat down. He nodded his head at the bottle I was holding. "Got any of that to spare?"

"You ain't supposed to drink whiskey. You know that."

"Well," he said, "if you can give up, then I suppose I've got the right to do the same. So hand over the bottle."

I'm not all that dense. I said, "Don't come that game on me. You know it's not the same."

"Oh? Fine. Give me the bottle."

In settling and founding our ranch, my daddy had battled weather, bad luck, Comanche Indians, carpetbaggers and scalawags, dishonest people, and a few desperate people with guns in their hands, and now it looked like I was giving him a battle.

And he didn't deserve that.

But I wasn't going down without somewhat of a fight. "Listen, cut this out," I said. "We ain't the only people that live on this range. Let a few of them go out there and handle this one. I need a rest."

"Give me the bottle."

"It's not just the woman," I said. "I'm tired."

"Give me the bottle."

"Just tell me why it has to be me?"

"Because you took the job," he said.

I threw up my hands. "All right, old man, all right. You win. But at least let me pout till morning. A man's got a right to a little private grief."

He laughed, which was good to hear. But then he got up so slowly that it hurt me to watch. "Son," he said, "that's just the way it goes."

"Yeah, first your money and then your clothes," I answered bitterly.

"Drink up. I'm going to enjoy watching you with that hangover in the morning."

The old man always did have a way about him.

• • •

I absented myself from everyone that evening, but next morning right after breakfast, I called a meeting of Ray Hays, my two brothers, and Bob Harley, our ranch foreman. "Norris," I began, "I want you to go into Blessing and get off a telegram to Brownsville—whoever we know down there—and make sure those cattle that are being driven through are illegal. I'm not about to go off half cocked into another man's business."

Ben said, "Justa, I done told you—"

"Shut up, Ben. You take orders, you understand?"

He still bore the marks about his face where I'd hit him, but he looked so glad to see me back working that he didn't even bother to sull up. "And as for you two," I said, indicating him and Hays, "you'll get on your horses this very morning and ride south until you strike that herd. Then bring me back a full report."

Ben said, with that gleam in his eye I didn't like, "Suits me."

"I said for you to look them over. That's all. You understand me?"

He looked away a little. "Of course I understand you. What do you think I am, deaf?"

"No, you're hotheaded. You don't need to talk to a single one of the drovers. All you've got to do is get close enough to see if they're wearing a trail brand. If they're not then we'll know they're illegals."

In those days, since you might have a herd with mixed permanent brands, it was common for a trail herd that was traveling overland to put one hair brand on all the cattle. It was a brand issued by the state of Texas, and it was recognized that all the cattle in the drive belonged to that drive. Of course, the hair brand grew out by the time you reached trail's end, and the price the cattle brought was then apportioned out to the individual ranchers that owned the cattle with the permanent brands. This was done because a lot of different ranchers might participate in one big drive, each not having enough cattle or enough drovers to make a thousand-mile drive on their own. It was just a sensible practice that allowed a lot of smaller ranchers to get their cattle to the better markets without the trouble and expense of trying it on their own.

Hays said, "Boss, that's a good idea."

I fixed him with a look. "And your job is to keep Ben out of trouble. You don't let him go near those drovers, you understand?"

"Huh!" And he looked over at Ben. It was another way of saying "You think me or anybody else can stop Ben from doing what he's a mind to do?"

"You just do it," I said.

Ben said, "I won't go near a soul, Justa. I swear it."

"Don't 'swear' it," I said. "Just keep one thought in mind: You start trouble before I'm ready for it, you warn that bunch before I've got this thought out, and I'll have you *and* Hays for breakfast."

I knew that would do him. He might risk my wrath, but he wouldn't risk it for Hays. They were pretty good friends.

He just said, "Yessir."

I turned to Harley. "Bob, I want you to get every hand we can spare and get them out gathering cattle and start moving them back toward the coast. Let's stay out of the main line of fire."

Our ranch extended to the coastline of Matagorda Bay. Ordinarily we didn't graze our good, blooded cattle back there because it was mostly salt grass, and that's none too nutritious at its best. But, of course, this seemed like an unusual time and called for unusual methods.

Harley frowned. He didn't like it, putting those good cattle on such poor grass, but he wasn't one to argue. He nodded. "Justa, I can get about ten men started in the morning."

"No. This afternoon," I said. "I don't know how close that Mexican herd is, and I can't take a chance. We've got cattle scattered five miles in every direction and we've got to get a move on."

He shrugged. "All right, Justa. But it will mean leaving off on some other chores."

"So be it," I said. "Those cattle come first."

Down in our part of the country, every rancher had run

Longhorn cattle for years. But some time past I'd gotten sick of those wild, skinny, hard-to-handle, horse-killing sonofa-bitches and begun to interbreed them with blooded Hereford and Whitefaced bulls and cows, and the result was the finest herd on the coastal plains. My neighboring ranchers had hoorahed the hell out of me when I'd started my plan, saying that those delicate little northern cattle would never make it on the hot plains of Texas, that they were used to a different kind of grass and would die off on our coastal Bermuda.

Now every one of them was trying the same program. And every one of them was looking for me to save their herds from those Mexican cattle.

Well, I was going to try and save our cattle. If their cattle got saved in the bargain, so much the better.

After the meeting broke up and everybody set out about their tasks, I went into the house to tell Dad what I'd done. We had a big old whitewashed, stucco ranch house. All the houses in the area were made out of stucco because, as one of our neighbors had remarked, "They's barely enough wood to cook with, and you damn sure don't want to go wasting what little there is on a damn house."

Well, that wasn't exactly right. We could now import lumber and most of our outbuildings were wooden, but it was true that we had a serious shortage of trees. Oh, we had some copses of stunted post oak and mesquite, the kind of trees that someone from timber country would call bushes, but mostly what we had was rolling grasslands. Nora, who was a relative new-comer to Matagorda County, had said the monotony of the place was driving her crazy. I'd asked her if that included me. Apparently it had, because she'd chosen a dry-goods drummer who called on her daddy's store over me. I hoped she wouldn't find Kansas City equally monotonous.

But that was country behind me. Never look over your shoulder.

I found my dad in the study, dozing over a book. When he got good and awake, I told him what I'd done.

Now, I didn't go to him for approval and damn seldom for advice. When I took over the ranch, I took over the ranch. But

I liked to keep him apprised of what was happening, just so he wouldn't feel left out. He was getting awfully old, and what little I could do to ease his burden was a pleasure for me.

When I finished telling him, he just nodded. Then he said, "But don't you think you ought to let our southern neighbors, the ones that will be exposed first, know what is happening?"

"Well, I could do that," I answered. "I've got riders heading in that direction to drift our cattle back this way. I'll let them advise everybody along their route, but I won't let them go off our range. I don't have the time."

"Son, what are you going to do if that herd is headed this way?"

"If they're illegal, I'll stop them," I said.

"How?"

"Any way I have to."

"Give me a for instance."

I looked at him. Sometimes he tested me, and I figured this was one of those times. "Paw, you of all people ain't proposing to ask me how I'll fight an enemy I ain't never seen and don't know the first thing about, are you?"

He just kind of chuckled.

# CHAPTER 2

I had never wanted the job of running the ranch in the first place. But after our mother had died and Dad had started going down, he'd called me in and told me he wanted me to take over some of his duties. I'd argued that Norris, who'd had university schooling, was much better equipped for the job. But Dad had said I was the eldest and the best suited, and that was that.

So that had been that.

He'd also said that Norris couldn't control Ben and that I could, and that was true. Ben was a handful, and no mistake. He could get into more trouble in five minutes than I could get him out of in a month of Sundays. But in a gunfight, there was no other man I could think of that I'd rather have by my side.

But that didn't keep me from getting up early next morning and walking over to the horse corral with an anxious eye peeled on the horizon, looking for Ben and Hays. I knew they shouldn't be back until noon, not even if they rode hard, but I was anxious for word.

Ben, along with the help of Hays and one other cowboy, ran our *remuda*, our horse herd. On a ranch as far flung as ours, with as many cattle as we had to work, we used up a lot of horses. And Ben was as good with horses as he was with a gun.

11

So I wasn't that surprised, about ten that morning, to see them coming hard off in the distance. They'd each taken an extra mount, ridden one hard, switched, and then left their spare horses to make their own way back to the barn.

I walked out into the ranch yard and waited. In a moment, coming like the wind, they rode in and pulled their horses up hard, their mounts lathered up and sweating. Before he even got down, Ben said, "Justa, them damn cattle ain't fifty miles from here! And they ain't a trail brand on a one of them."

Hays added a little breathlessly, as if it had been him and not the horse that had been doing the running, "Not a one, Boss! Not a one!"

I said, mildly, "You boys trying to kill these horses?"

They got down and walked their horses to cool them out. I followed along while they talked. Ben said, "Man that is bringing in the cattle is named Flood, J.C. Flood. But he ain't the one to watch out for. He's hired a man named Clarence Wooley to run the outfit, and he's supposed to be one tough hombre. He's got about fifteen gun hands with him. Justa, these ain't just drovers, they're gun hands. It's plain that man means to get these cattle through, and he ain't planning on nobody stopping him."

"I see," I said. "Now then, *you* tell me something: How'd you find out all this from long range like I ordered you to do?"

Hays had the good grace to look shamefaced, but Ben just sort of glanced away. "Oh, we happened up on some of their men," he said.

"I see. And exactly how did that happen?"

Ben looked down at the ground. "Well, we kind of went in and applied for jobs."

Hays said, "I tried to stop him, Boss. Swear I did!"

"Shut up, Hays. You *kind* of went in and applied for jobs?"

"Weell . . . I guess that's what we done."

"You pup!" I said. "Don't you reckon they might have recognized the Half-Moon brand on your horses and figured out what you were doing? That brand ain't exactly unknown, you know, in this part of the country. And don't you reckon they've already figured out their biggest opposition is going to come from the Half-Moon? Do you think they thought they could just run that herd of Mexican fever cattle through this country and everybody would just back off and take it? Of course you didn't think. You've never had a thought in your life."

"Boss, we thought of that," Hays put in. "We kind of rubbed a little mud over the brands on our horses so it weren't so clear."

"Oh, that was smart!" I was getting plenty worked up. "Why didn't you just put up a sign that said 'We're here on a scouting mission, but we don't want you to know it.' You two beat anything I've ever seen. Now you've given them fair warning and put them on their guard." I was disgusted.

Ben said, "Justa, we done it for the best. We was trying to get you all the information we could."

"Yes," I said, with some heat. "I sent you down there to get information, not *give* it. I swear, Ben, if you weren't my brother I'd run you off."

Hays said, as if he were trying to draw some of the fire onto himself, "Boss, it's lucky we found out they is gun hands. They ain't cowboys like our'n."

I turned on him. "Ours?"

He looked away. "Well, yours."

"Shit!" I said and kicked the ground with my boot. "Well, I might as well get some good out of this. How big is the herd?"

"We reckoned it to be about four thousand head," Ben said. "Rough guess."

Hays added, eagerly, "Them ol' skinny Mexican cattle, Boss. Hard to get a count on them."

I gave him a sour look. "How fast they moving them?"

Ben said, "They're lettin' 'em graze along. About seven or eight miles a day, I'd reckon."

"Tryin' to fatten up them ol' skinny Mexican cattle," Hays said. "On our grass!"

I would have given him another look, but it would have been a wasted effort. "And somewhere around fifteen hard men?"

"That or better," Ben said. "We wasn't in exactly no

position to ask. We took as good a count as we could. It might be twenty."

"All right," I said. "Go see to those horses."

As they turned to lead their mounts away, I asked, "By the way, what did they say when you applied for jobs?"

Over his shoulder, Ben said, "Said they couldn't use us."

I said, dryly, "I can understand that."

From a few steps away, I could hear Hays asking Ben: "Now what did he mean by that?"

Ben answered, "Shut up, Ray. He's mad enough as it is. Don't make him no madder."

Norris rode in that afternoon from the telegraph office in Blessing, our nearest little town, some seven miles away. And also the site of Nora's father's store. He came into my office and sat down, knocking the dust off his pants with his hat, which was unusual for Norris: Even in dusty country he never seemed to collect any.

"I sent off fifteen telegrams and got replies to every one," he said. "Justa, there is no record of a large herd being held in quarantine for the last year. And the best I could find out, they didn't bribe anyone. They'd have had to have bribed half the border inspectors to get that many cattle through. I think what they did was crossed them upstream on the Rio Grande and then swung down our way to keep from having to go through that hard country around Uvalde and Kerrville. They are heading our way deliberately. And whoever is doing it knows this country and knows our grass and knows it's the softest way. I'm betting they are intending to sell those cattle in Houston."

"Why?"

"Because they could never reach a northern market, not without quarantine records, and not through all those range inspectors in Oklahoma and Kansas and Nebraska. And they could never get the railroads to take them. I'm betting they've got a buyer in Houston. Else they'd never take this kind of a gamble. They might have a buyer who can turn these into legitimate cattle. Then he could ship them north. But I'm just guessing."

"What are cattle bringing in Houston?" I asked.

He shrugged. "Ours would weigh out to about fifty dollars a head. Those little Mexican cattle, depending on how much weight they could put on them between here and there . . . Maybe twenty-five to thirty dollars a head."

I thought a moment. It came to somewhere between a hundred thousand dollars and a hundred and twenty. That was a lot of money. I was trying to figure just how desperate these men would be and just how much of a fight they'd put up. Likely they'd put up a hell of a fight for that kind of money. I told Norris what Ben and Hays had found out.

He sighed. "Well, that sort of fits, doesn't it. Justa, I'm afraid we're in for a rough time."

"Damn, Norris," I said, "I'd have never figured that out if you hadn't told me."

"Don't be sarcastic with me," he said. "Save that for those who can appreciate it." He paused, then asked, "What are you going to do?"

"I've already done it," I said. "I've sent a rider out to the next three ranches down the line—the Browns, the Smalleys, and the Osgoods. I've asked them all three to be here for a meeting tomorrow night. I figure we've got about four to five days to get ready. We've got to meet that herd somewheres around ten miles south of here."

Norris gave me a disgusted look. "The Browns, the Smalleys, and the Osgoods. You better not mention Ben's report— that these are gunmen disguised as drovers. Not if you want their help."

"It's their cattle too," I said.

"They'll find business elsewhere. I can just hear Old Man Smalley saying he's suddenly been called to Galveston on urgent business. He'd love to stay and help, but . . ."

"I can't send them in there blind. Them or their men."

"Men? They hear about this, they won't have any men left." Norris stood up. "I've got to get something to eat. I'm famished."

I asked casually, as he headed for the door, "Any word of Nora in Blessing?"

He looked back. "I didn't ask." Then he added, "Justa, you might as well make up your mind. You can call all the meetings you want, but in the final analysis, it's got to be us that stops that herd."

I raised my eyebrows. "Final analysis? What the hell does that mean?"

"You know what it means. Now I have *got* to get something to eat. And don't be too hard on Ben and Hays. Sounds like to me they did good work."

Which showed what Norris knew. "They have been appreciated," I said. "Does that satisfy you about my fairness? *Duly* appreciated."

He hesitated another second. "Justa, I wouldn't take whoever is behind this drive too lightly. I know you think you can whip the world . . ."

Too lightly? Here was a man—or men—proposing to drive tick-fever cattle through twelve or fifteen ranches, exposing the ranchers involved to disaster. You don't take men like that lightly. I say twelve or fifteen but I didn't really know the number all up and down the coast. All I knew was that there were three or four ranches now between us and that herd. What was up north of the Half-Moon was immaterial to me if they got through us. "I believe I'll give the whole matter pretty serious consideration," I said simply.

"Somebody has thought this out well," he said. "Think of that."

"You think on finding yourself something to eat. You may need your strength."

Norris is not normally given to under- or overstatement, but to me him saying that somebody had planned and thought out the drive was an example of the former.

So, on his instructions, I sat and thought about it.

What I thought about it was that we were in a hell of a jam. I had fourteen hands on the place, outside of myself and my brothers. Of those I figured that no more than seven or eight would be any good in a serious gunfight. I didn't figure, as Norris had so strongly indicated, to get a great deal of help from my fellow ranchers. They were just stockmen, and the men that worked for them were just cowboys—cowboys who only carried a revolver in case of the occasional rattlesnake or to fire into the air to turn cattle. To put those kind up against hardened gunmen was to send them to their deaths. They wouldn't have a chance.

So I kept sitting there and thinking about it, and the more I thought, the bleaker the picture got.

Now, we had law in that part of the country. We had a sheriff in Blessing and a deputy in Markham. But I was friendly with them and I didn't see no point in forcing their courage to take them into an impossible situation. My dad had friends in the state legislature, but by the time they got through arguing and passing bills and filibustering, that herd would be on down to Houston and slaughtered and shipped to God knows where. There was the army and there was the state militia, but they couldn't act in civilian matters except on direct government orders, and that put us right back in the same old quandary.

We had range inspectors, but they didn't operate much down in our part of the country. Most of the illegal drives from Mexico went through the northern part of the state, that being the most direct route to the markets in Kansas City and Omaha. So those inspectors were usually stationed up in that part of the country.

Yes, whoever had devised the drive knew the coastal plains and had thought it out well.

So it looked like, to me, that what it came down to was Williams and Co. and what other little help we could get.

Up against a hardcase bunch of fifteen or better gunmen and a man that was playing for at least a hundred thousand dollars.

It was not the most appealing prospect I'd ever faced.

But face it I would have to. I went in and joined Norris to get something to eat. I figured *I* was going to need all the strength I could get.

But getting something to eat around our house wasn't as easy a proposition as you might have thought. We had an old cowboy that Dad had kept on as a cook when he'd got so stove up from getting bucked off tame horses that he couldn't sit a horse anymore. Well, one thing for sure, he couldn't sit a stove any better than he'd ever sat a horse. But he'd been with Dad back in the old days, and Dad wouldn't let me put him out to pasture.

So we got stuck with him in the kitchen so he'd feel useful. His last name was Butterfield, but we called him Buttercup just to infuriate him because he infuriated us so bad with his cooking. I'd hired him two assistants, two Mexican women, but they mostly cooked for the bunkhouse. But Buttercup— either out of loyalty or vengeance, and I was never sure which—insisted on cooking for the family. I tell you, there was many an evening that any one of us would slip off down to the bunkhouse to eat with the hired hands, just so you could get something in your mouth you could chew.

The steak he set in front of me was just about up to his norm. I took one bite and said, "Buttercup, you have got to quit slaughtering our riding stock. I swear I was on this horse just last week. You've got to learn to tell the difference between a horse and a beef."

He stood there looking like I was joshing him and said, "Aw, Mr. Justa, that ain't no hoss. That's a mule."

If we'd had any mules on the place I would have believed him.

Buttercup had one talent, as wore out as he was, which is one of the reasons Dad valued him: He was about as fine a long-distance rifle shot as there was around the country. Even at his age, which I reckoned to be about sixty. Just a few years younger than our dad, he could still make a hell of a shot with his old buffalo rifle at distances up to five hundred yards. In years past it had amazed us brothers. He'd once hit a scarecrow we'd erected at a distance of five hundred and sixty yards. We'd never understood how he'd done it, but he'd just said, nonchalantly, "Boys, some got it, some ain't."

Which didn't make a damn bit of sense for a stove-up old cockeyed cowboy like him to say, except he could do it. And it hadn't been that big of a scarecrow neither.

When he got my steak served up, he sat down in one of the chairs with his cup of coffee. We never could convince him he wasn't one of the family. He didn't eat with us, though, and with good reason. I think he ate back in the kitchen, so we wouldn't catch him eating the grub the Mexican women had fixed.

"Careful there, Buttercup," I said. "That chair you're setting in has been known to buck."

"Harrh, harrh," he said, making what he thought was a laugh with his near toothless mouth. "Lissen, whippersnapper," he said, "wadn't fer me they wouldn't be no ranch here. Was me broke the rough stock nobody else could handle. You ast yore daddy. Without no horses you ain't got no ranch."

I said, chewing with an effort, "I heard that they weren't rough stock until you got your hands on them. Dad said you were the only man he knew that could take a perfectly good saddle horse and ruin him within a week."

"Aw, he never said no sech thing. You just hoorahing me."

I looked over at Norris, who was looking relieved that he was nearly through with his steak. "Ain't that right, Norris?"

Norris got up, wiping his mouth with his napkin. "I'm not talking," he said. "Don't try to get me in bad with the cook."

That made me laugh. "Bad with the cook? How could it get any worse?"

"It could," Norris said as he was going out the door. "He might cook four meals a day instead of three."

"Harrh, harrh," said Buttercup. "Thet Mr. Norris is shore a cut-up."

If Buttercup thought Norris was a cut-up, it was a good sign the old man's mind was finally gone.

Buttercup said, "Mr. Justa, what's all this here talk I hear about some Mexican cattle comin' through here? We can't 'low thet."

"We'll try not to," I said. "But they seem determined to come through."

"Wahl, if you need another gun, you know where they's a good'n."

I was getting up from the table. "I'll keep that in mind."

As I was starting for the door, he called, "Hey, wait jest a minute! You ain't finished yore meal."

"Oh yes I have," I said. "It was starting to fight back."

"Harrh, harrh."

The old boy was sure some cut-up.

"Now, I ain't got no quarrel with we got to do somethin',
Justa," said Alf Osgood. "But I ain't seein' us going up against
a bunch of hired gunsels. Hell, we got laws in this country. Let
them do somethin'."

I glanced over at Norris, and he just shrugged as if to say "I
told you so."

The meeting had been going on for an hour, and other than
a lot of whiskey and coffee getting drunk, nothing had happened. Once I'd explained what Ben and Hays had found out,
a sort of pall had settled over the room. Only Tom Brown
showed any sign of siding with me.

But he was younger than Smalley and Osgood, being somewhere just below forty. He also had the second-biggest spread
in the area and had made the most progress toward upgrading
his cattle. Consequently, he had nearly as much to lose as we
did.

George Smalley had made the point that, since he was
running straight Longhorns, he didn't think his herd would be
that affected.

I'd said, "George, that's sort of a selfish attitude. And one
that might be remembered by the rest of us in this room."

He'd backed down quickly. "Justa, I didn't mean it that way.
Don't get on yore high horse. I was just pointin' out that we
ought to each contribute as to what each had to lose. Now that's
fair, ain't it?"

But the prevailing opinion in the room seemed to be that one
of two parties ought to do something about the matter—either
the law or the Williamses.

"Hell, Justa," said Osgood, "I ain't sayin' I ain't willin' to
help, but what am I supposed to tell what few riders I got? That
we're going out against gun hands? Hell, ever' one of 'em
would roll their gear and head out. They hired on to work
cattle, not get shot."

"Alf, you've got six men," I said. "Can't any of them
fight?"

"Can any of your'n? You got fifteen. You guarantee ever' one of them?"

He had me there. "A few." I shrugged. "Not all."

Tom Brown said, "I think I've got about two I could count on. I'd have to pay them extra, of course. And then there's me. That makes three."

I gave him a grateful look and then fixed Smalley with a question. "George?"

George Smalley was an old man who'd grown up in the country. He'd once worked for my father when he was in need of cash money to keep his place going. He shrugged. "Justa, I don't see how I kin be much he'p. I only got the four regular hands. I can't speak for them, but they might be one, was you to give him a little money could he'p out."

Ben, who had been quiet so far, said, "*We* give him money to protect *your* cattle?"

Smalley looked down. "I ain't been doin' as well as I might here lately," he said.

I gave Ben a severe look. There was no use in embarrassing the man. I said to Smalley, "Speak to him for me, George, will you? It would be worth fifty dollars to me to have an extra gun."

Alf Osgood said, querulously, "I still say it ain't our affair. I still say it's an affair for the law."

"One sheriff and one deputy, Alf?" said Norris, dryly. "And the sheriff is as old as you?"

"Then we send for the state officials. Hell, don't we pay taxes?"

Ben laughed, and Norris said, "Alf, by the time we got any help down here, those cattle would have come through us like a host of locusts."

Osgood got up. "Wahl, I got the furtherest to ride, so I got to git goin'. I'll go along with whatever ya'll decide."

"You mean as long as it don't involve you," said Ben.

"Shut up, Ben," I said. To Osgood, I said, "I appreciate you coming, Alf. I'll keep you posted."

George Smalley also got up. "Reckon I better git, too," he

said. "My ol' woman's been poorly lately. I'll talk to thet man fer you, Justa, and send word."

I thanked him for coming, and then it was just my brothers and Tom Brown. We sat and looked at each other for a moment. "Well," I said, "I reckon the next step is to call a meeting of the hands in the morning. Ben, you see to that. We're going to have to get a head count as to who we can count on."

"You want me and my two men here?" asked Brown.

I shook my head. "Not as long as I know I can count on you."

"I can guarantee that," he said. "We all got a stake in this. You figured out yet what you're going to do?"

I sighed. I had a tumbler of whiskey on the table by me, and I took it up and had a sip. "A lot of it will depend on how many men I can raise," I said. "But I figure to try and have the showdown about twelve miles down the coast. Right on the other side of Osgood's place."

Ben said, with a little heat, "Osgood's place? What the fuck you want to protect that bastard for? He won't lift a finger."

I looked at Norris, and he looked at Ben. He said, pityingly, "Little Brother, don't act any dumber than you already are. Osgood's cattle get infected, it's the same as having ours infected. Haven't you ever noticed his brand mixed in with ours?"

"Oh," said Ben.

"Besides," I said, "there's a piece of ground up there that I like. A little knoll with some swampy ground off to the right, which would force them to drive off to our left."

"If it comes to that," Norris said.

"Yes," I agreed, "if it comes to that."

"So is that about it?" asked Brown.

"Yes," I said. "I'm planning on going into Blessing sometime tomorrow, after I meet with my cowboys, and look up Sheriff Ward and tell him what I'm planning."

"If you can find him," Ben said. "He's already heard about the trouble and has taken a train for Dallas."

"Ben," I said, "don't you ever shut up?"

"Well, you know it's true."

"Vic Ward has been a good friend to this family."

"He's just too old to be sheriff."

"And you're too young to speak ill of your betters," said Norris.

Ben reared up. "Who says he's my better?"

"I do," I said. "Now shut up."

"Well, I reckon I'll be going," said Brown.

We shook hands, and he left. I sat back down, sipping at my whiskey. "It's quite a problem, isn't it," Norris said.

"Yeah," I said. "It's kind of a life's work problem." I was tired, discouraged, and worried. "We could damn near lose everything. And that Mexican herd is close—oh so close."

"Shit!" cried Ben. "It wouldn't have been if you hadn't sat around here for three days suckin' on a whiskey bottle and moonin' over some damn worthless girl."

Norris looked at him in amazement. "Do you like having your mouth busted open? You keep up that line of talk, Justa might not stop with just the one punch."

"No, let him be," I said. "He's right. I must have gone to sleep. He's got full right to say it."

"Not to his brother."

"Let it go. I'm in charge, and I should have been more responsible. It's late. Let's go to bed."

Ben hung back until Norris had left the study, then he came up and said, "Justa, I'm sorry I said that. It was a mighty poor remark."

I put my hand on his shoulder. "It's all right. You didn't say anything more than I've been saying to myself."

He looked grateful. He was a good kid, and I knew I was going to have to depend on him heavily in the days to come.

I met with our hired hands about an hour after dawn. They assembled in the ranch yard, shuffling around and looking uncomfortable, some of them yawning, some of them drinking coffee and smoking. I didn't know how much they knew, but I could see they were worried, because it was an uncommon

thing for me to do. I think some of them expected I was going
to fire the whole lot on the spot.

We had fourteen riders. Bob Harley made fifteen, and me
and my brothers brought the total up to eighteen. But how
many I was going to be able to count on was anybody's guess.

I didn't keep them waiting long. As simply and as directly as
I could, I laid the situation out for them. I wound up by saying,
"Now men, I'm well aware that you're being paid to work
cattle, not fight gun battles. I'm going to ask for volunteers
who will be willing to stand by me and my family in this
trouble. But I want to say that any man that doesn't want to get
involved will be thought none the less of. He'll still have his
job, and he'll keep it as long as his work satisfies me and Bob
Harley. Whatever you decide this morning will have nothing to
do with your future on this ranch. I just want to make sure you
understand that. But I will offer you this: Any man that's got
the stomach for it and thinks he's good enough—and I want to
bear down on that 'good enough,' because my brother reports
that these drovers are hard folks who look like they've used a
gun before—any man who wants in and can help will get a
hundred-dollar bonus at the end of this trouble."

That made them stir a little. A hundred dollars in one sum
was a lot of money to most of them. But Hays had to say,
"Hell, Boss, I don't need no hunnert dollars to do my duty. I'm
with you."

"I wasn't talking about you, Ray," I said. "You're already
overpaid for whatever it is you're supposed to be doing around
here."

Well, that made them laugh. Ben and Norris were standing
right behind me, and I was about to turn around and ask them
if they had anything to say, when old Buttercup came hobbling
out of his kitchen, wiping his hands on his filthy apron. "By
Gawd, me too!" he was saying.

The old fool had been listening the whole time. I was just
surprised he hadn't come out carrying that monstrous .50
caliber Sharps of his. I waited until he'd fell in with the rest of
the hands, and then I said, "I want it understood that you could
get killed. I'm going to do my best to see that that doesn't

happen, but I want you to understand that it can. Now, raise your hand if you want in on this fight."

Twelve hands went up. Behind me, Norris counted them slowly and methodically. Unfortunately, two of the hands belonged to Harley and Buttercup. "Buttercup," I said, "as bad as I'd like to see you killed before you kill somebody with your cooking, I'm going to have to save you for a later day."

"What day would that be, sonny?" He didn't look or sound happy.

"When they're driving those cattle through the front door of the ranch house," I said.

It got a good laugh, but Buttercup didn't think it was so funny. He just gave me a look. Didn't bother me. What the hell was he going to do, poison me?

"And Harley," I said, "I appreciate it, but I can't spare you. Somebody has got to stay and run the ranch, and that would be you. And I'm glad all of you didn't volunteer, for the same reason. If you had, I'd have had to have turned some of you down, because the ranch business has got to go on. I got ten men, which is just about what I was looking for." I turned around. "Ben, Norris, either one of you want to say anything?"

They just shook their heads. I turned back to my crowd and said, "You volunteers give your names to my brother Norris, so we don't get mixed up about who gets the bonus. Later on today, my brother Ben is going to work with you on your shooting. He'll let you know." I looked back. I'd kind of taken Ben off guard with that one, but I could see it pleased him. Well, it was one way of saying I was sorry about hitting him. "That's all," I said. "I'll be gone the balance of the day, but go to my brothers with any questions you've got. Harley, put them to work. We've still got cattle to gather."

Later, Ben, Norris, and I went into the kitchen and sat around the table. Buttercup slammed a cup of coffee down in front of me and went off muttering, "Damn whippersnapper! Thinks I'm too old. Dern him!"

Norris raised his eyebrows, but I just shook my head. Wasn't a thing I could do about it. I stirred my coffee and said, "Ten of our men and us three. And three with Tom Brown. That makes sixteen." I shook my head. "And maybe one from Smalley. Seventeen. I don't much like those odds."

"It ought to be just about even," said Ben.

"Huh!" I said. "We know about those drovers, according to you. And you ought to know. But we don't know anything about the caliber of our own people. Ben, that will be up to you to find out. If they get back in this evening with enough light, you get that ten out somewhere and find out who can shoot and who can't. I know they all think they can. All cowboys think they can shoot. But I mean, really shoot."

"Yessir," he said. He was taking it serious.

"What do you want me to be doing?" asked Norris.

I just shook my head. "Thinking, I guess. There's really nothing for any of us to be doing, except trying to think of a plan."

"Shoot the damn lead steer, you dern whippersnapper!"

I looked around. Buttercup was glowering near his stove. Naturally, he'd been listening to every word. "I'm going to shoot you if this coffee doesn't improve," I said.

I got up. "Ben," I said, "for the time being, you've got the most important job. I know you can't turn them into gun hands overnight, but do your best."

"I will, Justa," he said.

He was growing up fast.

"I expect to be back tonight," I said, "but if I'm not, don't worry. I might have trouble finding Sheriff Ward. If I do, I'll board up somewhere."

Riding into Blessing, I was speculating on what I was going to say to Norris and how. If it came to a fight, I was going to have to hold him out—not only for his own sake, but for the sake of the family.

And he wasn't going to like that.

It wasn't that Norris wasn't a fair gun hand; he was. But that was the problem: He was just fair. And I had a feeling that if we had to fight, the men we'd be fighting would be better than fair. Norris had always resented the fact that he was not quite as good as Ben or I, and he was constantly trying to make up for it with misplaced courage—a mistake that could get him killed if I didn't keep a close eye on him.

Norris took after our mother. He was fair, as she had been, while both Ben and I were dark, like our father, and built very much like him. Not that Norris wasn't tough—he was plenty tough—but his mind just ran a different way. It ran to books and to analytical thinking and to business and to a hundred other things that Ben and I—or Dad, for that matter—didn't understand.

Which was the other reason I'd have to hold him out. Norris looked after our banking affairs, our other business interests, our property interests; in short, he handled everything but the day-to-day running of the ranch, which was the cornerstone of our holdings. The fact was, he was just too valuable to the family and to the ranch to risk in a gunfight.

But that still didn't mean he was going to like it. He might understand it, yes, but like it? No. I'd done it to him several times before in the past when there'd been trouble, and he'd resented the hell out of it.

I thought of sending him off on some errand when it came time for the confrontation, but then I realized that would be pissing into the wind. You didn't fool Norris that easy. No, if it came down to it, I was just going to have to tell him the same way I always had.

And then never hear the end of it.

Blessing was a town of about a thousand souls. Well, nearly a thousand souls—there was a question about some of the people living there. But it was a good town. Dad said you could always tell a good town if the saloons didn't outnumber the churches and the school by more than four to one.

It was the rail terminus and had been put in for the convenience of the ranchers down in our part of the country, who shipped out a considerable number of cattle. Dad had been one of those responsible for talking the railroads into extending a spur line on down to us from the main branch going down to Galveston. It had been a blessing, and that's the way the name of the town had come about. Because from Blessing we could ship cattle all over the country, even to the big markets up north. It had saved us many a hard drive, and the cost of shipping was more than made up by the cattle we didn't lose or the flesh that didn't walk off on the drives.

I rode into town on the main street, which was practically the only street, past the stores, past Nora's daddy's mercantile, past saloons, a church or two, and pulled up in front of the sheriff's office. I tied off my horse and went on inside. Sheriff Ward had a half-grown boy named Harvey Something-or-Other that did part-time duty as his caretaker and coffee maker. When I went in, Harvey was sitting at Ward's desk, so I knew the sheriff wasn't there.

Harvey said, "Shur'ff gone fer his noonin'."

Well, that could mean a considerable wait, if Vic had decided to take a nap. I hadn't realized it was lunchtime since I'd had, for me, a late breakfast and wasn't particularly hungry. There was no point in waiting around for the sheriff, so I told Harvey that I'd be down at Crook's having a beer in case the sheriff got back before I did. I said to tell him that it was urgent.

He said he would.

Which I doubted. I didn't figure ol' Harvey could remember that long.

I stepped out the door and headed up the little wooden sidewalk toward Crook's, which was a kind of combination cafe and saloon. I was just sauntering along, thinking that maybe I'd have a steak along with the beer—maybe a big enough steak that I wouldn't be hungry that evening and could avoid Buttercup's cooking.

Then the first person I run into is Nora.

# CHAPTER
# 3

She was just coming out of the grocery store with her shopping basket over her arm. Then she turned and saw me. She stopped, and her free hand flew up to her mouth. I came up to her. "Hello, Nora," I said. "How are you?"

I said it pretty nonchalantly, but my free hand had flown up, too, and grabbed at the pit in my stomach. Damn, she looked good. She was wearing a gray frock that went with her hazel eyes and light brown hair. She had nice round cheekbones and pouty little lips and breasts that I knew all about. Though that was all I knew about her body. Firsthand, that is.

Not that I didn't want to know more, but when she'd said "Stop," I'd always stopped. And now some other man had solved that mystery between her legs.

She was flustered. "Oh, oh,—Justa," she said.

I took off my hat. "Yeah, it's me. Good old Justa. How are you getting along?"

She was regaining some of her composure, although there was still a flush on her pretty face. "Uh, fine," she said. "Just fine. And you?"

"The same." I was studying her face. She was only twenty-two, but there was a tiredness about her eyes that I'd never seen before. "Home for a visit?" I asked her.

It made her look exceedingly uncomfortable. She hesitated before saying, "No, not exactly."

Now what was that supposed to mean? "You mean you and your husband are going to headquarter here?" I said. It seemed like a strange place for a Kansas City drummer to operate out of.

She said something so quietly that I couldn't catch it. "What?"

She colored up again. "I don't have a husband. I was never married."

Well, that nearly floored me. "What are you talking about? I understood you left here to get married in Kansas City."

"I did," she said. She looked down and shifted her market basket from one arm to the other. "Really, Justa," she said, "I don't want to talk about it out on the street."

"Then let me walk you home," I said. "I find this mighty interesting."

"I'm sure you do. But I'm not sure I want to tell you about it."

I saw right quick what she was afraid of. She was afraid I was going to gloat. "Look, Nora," I said, "whatever happened is none of my business. I'm just glad to see you. Now, can I walk you home?"

Without saying anything, she handed me her basket. I turned, and we started down the street. As we passed the sheriff's office, I glanced in and saw that Harvey was still sitting at Ward's desk, so I knew he wasn't back.

We walked in silence for a time. Her parents lived in a pretty little white frame house just at the edge of town. It had a big wide porch all around on three sides, with a swing.

A swing I knew mighty well.

"Hot for this time of year, ain't it?" I said.

"Yes, it certainly is."

"You going back into school teaching?" I asked.

"Of course, they replaced me when I gave notice. I'll have to look for a position somewhere else," she answered.

"Town's growing," I said. "Might be they'd need another one."

Norris was on the school board.

"That would be nice," she said.

"How's your daddy's business?"

"Fine, I guess. He never discusses it."

We had arrived at her gate. We both stopped, and I held out the basket to her. She hesitated. "Why not sit on the porch for a few minutes. I'll make us some lemonade. Like you say, it's hot for this time of year."

She took the basket, and I followed her to the house. While she went in, I sat down on the swing and lit one of the little cigars I sometimes smoked and wondered what had happened to her. I also examined my heart to see what I felt.

I didn't think I felt any bitterness. I think that was all past me. But I also didn't think I felt that consuming passion that had once lit me up every time I laid eyes on her. I decided I'd wait and find out what had happened before I came to any conclusions.

After a time, she came out with a pitcher and two glasses and set them on the little wicker stand beside the swing. She poured out a glass for me and then one for herself. She handed me mine and then sat down beside me. She didn't sit close, but neither did she sit clear over to the other end.

For a few minutes we sort of sipped and swung gently. I'm not a great hand for lemonade, but it seemed like every girl I'd ever courted had insisted on shoving a gallon of it down my throat. I used to carry a flask for such occasions and I'd always managed to slip a little whiskey in my glass to make the stuff somewhat more palatable. Once, when I was considerably younger and considerably more reckless, I'd poured the flask into the pitcher, thinking it would do wonders for this eighteen-year-old girl's attitude that I was courting. But her mother had come out, drank two glasses, and got tipsy as hell, and the upshot had been that the old man had ordered me off the place with instructions never to come back.

Which had been all right with me, since the girl was about as ugly as homemade sin.

Finally Nora said, hesitantly, "I probably have no right to say this, but if I hurt you I'm sorry. I made a mistake, that's all."

I started to lie and then decided the hell with it. "Well, it wasn't the most pleasant shock I've ever had," I said. "I guess it was the suddenness that took me off guard. No word, no nothing. Just one day you were gone and your mother was telling me about it."

"I know," she said. She sounded miserable. "I made a mistake."

"Of course, it was your right," I said. "It really wasn't as if we had an understanding."

"Maybe that was it."

"What was?"

"That we really didn't have an understanding." She started to say something else but then stopped.

I looked over at the street and thought. Finally, I said, "I guess that was my fault. I had an understanding in myself. I guess I just never got around to telling you about it."

"It would have helped," she said.

I set my lemonade glass on the table and turned to her. "Nora, what the hell happened?"

She shook her head slowly. "I don't really know. One day I got so frustrated I couldn't stand it anymore. There were you and I, and nothing was happening. You were always so busy running your ranch. Time for everyone else." She sighed. "And I kept getting older. Day by day."

I said, dryly, "And then this handsome stranger came along with a glib tongue, promising you an exciting life in the big cities."

She half smiled. "Don't rub it in."

"God knows you rubbed it in me hard enough," I said. "My chest is still sore from wearing a hair shirt after you left."

She laughed and slapped me lightly on the thigh. "Oh, I don't believe that. Justa Williams, you never pined for any woman in your whole life."

"No," I said, "but it makes a good story." I was damned if I was going to tell her the whole truth on the square.

"Well," I said, "you going to tell me what happened? How come you're back? How come you didn't get married?"

She shrugged. "Since I have to, there's really nothing to tell. I got off the train in Texarkana and came back."

"Just like that?"

"Just like that."

"What about what's-his-name?"

"Charles. I sent him a wire."

"And he just took it?"

"He wired he was coming down here."

"Good for him," I said. "I'd like to meet the man."

She looked around at me. "Oh no, Justa! Don't get that tone in your voice. I wired him not to come. You stop thinking what you're thinking. You are not a bully."

Well, she had me there. I have never fought a man in my life that didn't have a chance against me. In fact, I've walked away from fights when I knew the other man was completely outmatched. It was a code we'd all learned from our father. "So, I guess you just got back," I said.

"I've been home a week."

I looked at her in some astonishment, thinking about the week I'd spent drinking and brooding and not tending to the family business. I wanted to tell her how much money she might have cost us by what she'd done to me, but then I thought better of it. She hadn't done anything to me; I'd done it to myself. But I did ask, "Couldn't you at least have sent me a note?"

She looked away. "I started to, Justa. I started to a hundred times. But I was afraid you'd be bitter or wouldn't care anymore and just ignore it. And I couldn't have stood the pain."

Well, I guessed I could understand that. But I didn't tell her so. Instead, I stood up. "Well, thanks for the lemonade, though whiskey would improve the taste wonderfully," I confessed. "But I got business up the street." I put on my hat. "I'll be seeing you, Nora. Glad to have you back."

She looked up at me anxiously. "Won't you come for supper?"

"No, I reckon not," I said. "My business here won't take long, and then I'd better get back to the ranch. We got some things going on."

She made a wry face. "You always have things going on back at the ranch."

I left her with that and started back to town. As I walked, I got to thinking that Norris must have known that Nora was back in town. He hadn't told me she was or wasn't, he just hadn't told me anything. I wondered about that, and then I decided that Norris had figured to let me work it out on my own. Well, I thought grimly, I might just work Mr. Norris out.

The sheriff still wasn't in, so I went on down to Crook's and ate a steak and drank a couple of beers to get the lemonade taste out of my mouth. By the time I'd finished and got back down to the jail, Vic Ward was there. He was sitting behind his desk, looking well fed from his lunch and well rested from his nap.

"Hello, Justa," he said. "Heard you was looking for me."

Vic was a pleasant-faced man in his midfifties. Some said he was past his prime, but then there wasn't all that much for a sheriff to do in Matagorda County. Oh, you had your occasional drunken fight or your occasional dispute over property lines or the brand on a head of beef or a husband-wife squabble, but mainly the two jail cells collected more dust than they did prisoners.

I sat down and took off my hat. "Vic, I've got a little problem and I think you ought to know about it."

He put his head in his hands. "Do I have to? I just ate."

I laughed. "It won't ruin your appetite for supper."

"Tell me," he said.

So I did. And then I told him what we were planning on doing about the problem. I ended up saying, "Vic, I don't want to involve you and your deputy in this, because it ain't really within your province of the law. It's more state law. But I don't have time for them to act."

He swiveled around in his chair and stared off for a second. Then he came back to me, and his plump, pink face had gone serious. "Justa," he said, "I understand what you have to do and I don't blame you. But I am the law around here, and I've got to take some sort of a hand in this. I can't just have you come in here and tell me about this and act like I never heard of it. This sounds like a killing mess to me, and I've got to do what I can to stop it."

"Vic, I don't see where you can do anything."

"What say you and I ride out there and meet that herd," he said. "It's too late to start this evening, but we could get off first thing in the morning."

"It's not going to do a damn bit of good, Vic," I told him. "These people are going to know the law. God knows they've done a good enough job of getting around it. They're going to know you don't have any jurisdiction."

"I've got to try. Maybe they'll listen to reason. Maybe they'll strike a bargain."

"Sure," I said, "and next you'll be telling me the train's on time."

"But will you go?"

I looked at him, deliberating. It'd be one more warning I'd be giving whoever was running the herd, one more view of what he'd be up against. And that wasn't good tactics. And hell, I ought to know about tactics. After all, I was a lieutenant colonel in the Texas militia, an office that carried about as much weight as a riderless horse. But here was Vic asking me for a favor, and I could see his point. He couldn't very well have a range war in his county without being able to say that he'd done what he could to stop it.

And he'd been a friend a long time. I said, reluctantly, "All right, Vic. I'll lay over tonight and we'll take off at first light."

He said, as if by way of thanks, "Will you come to supper?"

I shook my head, thinking of Nora. "No thanks, Vic. I've got some other business I need to be thinking on."

He looked at me as if he understood, but I hoped that he didn't. As I was heading for the door, he said, "One thing I wonder . . ."

"What?"

"Why," he asked, "am I always the last to know what the hell is going on around here? I bet half the people in this county know about that herd."

I opened the door. "They don't want to interrupt your nap, Vic."

I went on down to the hotel and got a room. Well, actually, I got a key to our room. We were in Blessing so constantly that we just kept a permanent room at the hotel. Besides which, we owned the hotel.

I told our desk clerk, Freeman, that I wanted a bath and I wanted it fixed up in about half an hour. He said he thought he could handle that. Freeman was a middle-aged man who'd once worked in a hotel in Chicago, and he was a little bit snobbish. I never could figure out what he was doing in our part of the country, but from time to time, he gave me dark hints that it had to do with a woman.

We all kept a few clean clothes in the room, so I got a clean shirt and some clean socks and went on down the hall and took my bath. After that, I examined my chin and determined I could do with a shave. So after I'd dressed, I sauntered outside and went to the barbershop. I had a trim and a shave and got my boots blacked and my hat brushed, and I come out feeling pretty presentable.

And also pretty much like a fool.

I killed a little more time and then, just after four o'clock, I wandered down to Parker's Mercantile. Lonnie Parker's face lit up when I came through the door. He was Nora's dad, and I knew he'd been dead set against her running off with that drummer, and I also knew why. Our ranch did considerable business with his store, and I reckoned he'd thought we'd discontinue our custom out of my disappointment. Well, all that meant was that he didn't know the Williams family very well.

But I also knew that her mother had been upset about what Nora had done, and it had nothing to do with the fact that we had a little money. I believed it was because she thought that Nora and I would have made a good match.

"Hello, Lonnie," I said. "How's trade?"

"Could be better," he said.

"You always say that."

"What brings you to town?" he asked.

"Oh, not much. Just enough to keep me overnight."

He was behind his counter, with the yard goods behind him. He leaned forward, resting his elbows on the countertop. "Reckon you ain't heard that Nora come on back. Come to her senses in time."

Mr. Parker was a harmless little man with his sleeve garters and his slightly balding head. He was a merchant, and he didn't mean any harm. Nevertheless, I sort of resented him dangling his daughter out like that. But I just said, mildly, "Yes, I saw her this afternoon. She don't look none the worse for the experiment."

"If you're going to be in town tonight," he said, "how about coming to supper."

Of course, that was the reason I was in the mercantile. But I said, "Nora done asked me and I said I couldn't."

"How about if I was to ask you?"

I sort of hesitated. "Weeell, if I thought there was fried chicken in it . . ."

Mr. Parker immediately straightened up and yelled, "Yoddie! Yoddie!"

In about five seconds, a fourteen- or fifteen-year-old boy came racing in from the back and skidded to a halt in front of Mr. Parker. "Yessir!"

"Yoddie, you git on to my house and tell Miz Parker we got a special guest for dinner. Tell her to kill two chickens."

Before he could say anything else, the boy was already nearly out the door, so he had to yell the last: "AN' YOU STAY THERE AND HELP HER PICK 'EM AND CLEAN 'EM! YOU HEAR?"

"Yessir!" But it was just the faint echo of a body that was outrunning its own voice.

"Boy's attentive," I said.

Mr. Parker just shook his head. "You've got to be careful what you say to him. First thing that sounds like instructions, he's off like a rocket. You got to get your main points in first."

Which struck me as what I might have to do on the morrow with that bunch of drovers. I figured I was going to have to convince someone that the price might be a little higher than they wanted to pay. That would be my main point.

But then there was the matter of Mrs. Parker's fried chicken, which was much more pleasant to contemplate. She could fry chicken in such a way that it would damn near make you give up cussing. Nora's presence notwithstanding, I would have accepted the invitation and accepted an evening of being bored silly by Lonnie Parker just for that fried chicken.

As I was going out, Mr. Parker said. "Supper's at six."

Like I needed reminding.

With time to kill I wandered back to Crook's, intending to take on a few whiskeys and listen to see if anyone else had heard about those Mexican cattle. But just as I got in the place and got myself seated, I recognized a man at the bar that I'd hoped I'd never see again. My heart sank. I'd been looking forward to a pleasant supper and a pleasant evening, and now it could all be ruined by one man turning around from a bar and seeing me.

His name was Lew Vara and he was a hard piece of work. He was good with a gun and good with his fists. Some year and a half past, he and I had had about a thirty-minute fight in Crook's that had pretty nearly killed both of us. I'd fought him fair for as long as I could, right up to the point where it looked like he was going to finish me, then I'd come reeling up off the floor with a beer mug in my hand and got him a hell of a crack over the head. I'd hit him again as he was going down, just to make sure he stayed there, because I wasn't sure what I could do if he got up.

But he'd stayed down, mainly because I'd damn near split his skull. He was laid up for quite a while, but when he come to well enough to think, he'd sent word that he was going to kill me on sight when he was able. But by the time he was up and around, I was off on a cattle-buying trip; and by the time I got back, I'd heard he'd quit the country.

To my somewhat relief. I wasn't afraid of him, but I figured it would be a rough fight and I figured to get hurt—even just a little—because he was a man that struck me as requiring quite a bit of killing.

And now here he was, standing at the bar with his back to me. Even as I thought on the consequences, he turned and looked straight at me. There could be no questioning him seeing me and none of him remembering me. But he just turned back to the bar and went on with his drink.

I slid my chair back from the table a little and straightened my right leg to better clear my draw. I figured his plan was to lull me to sleep and then suddenly whirl, drawing as he did, and fire. I planned to draw and fire under the table. I didn't think there'd be time to get my revolver over the top.

One of the waiters yelled over to see what I'd have. "Whiskey," I said. "A bottle."

Enough time passed for the waiter to bring me the whiskey and a glass. All the time, my eyes were riveted steadily on Lew's back. I was looking for that first muscle twitch. There was a bad second when the waiter got in the way, but I ordered him aside with a rough word or two. He gave me a startled look because I was not known to speak that way. But I had no time to apologize then; that would have to come later.

And then Lew did turn. But he did it so slow and easy that he was around and leaning back against the bar before I could get alarmed. He had a glass of whiskey in his gun hand and his left elbow was resting on the bar. He looked over at me for a long moment. Then he pushed away from the bar and started my way.

I watched, on the ready. His gun was holstered on the right and the drink was in his right hand, but there was nothing to stop him from dropping the glass and drawing. He came up to the table. I looked up. "Hello, Justa," he said.

I nodded. "Howdy, Lew."

"Mind if I set down and jaw a minute?"

"That all you got in mind?"

"That's all."

With my left boot, I shoved a chair out for him across from me. But my right hand was still on my thigh, close to the butt of my revolver.

Lew sat down. He held up his drink and said, "Luck."

With my left hand, I poured myself out a drink. I lifted my glass and said, "Luck." Then we both knocked them back.

I reached over with the bottle, still with my left hand, and poured both of our glasses full. Lew half smiled. "I swear, Justa, I don't recollect you being left-handed."

"I alternate," I said. "Keeps one from getting too much work."

He fiddled with his glass. I noted that he was carefully keeping both hands in sight. Finally he said, "What I wanted to talk to you about . . . that business that passed between us some time back . . . As far as I'm concerned, that's done with."

"You ended it with a threat," I said.

He grimaced slightly. "I know I did. But I didn't mean it. Man gets angry, sometimes he says things he don't mean."

"Bad habit."

"Yeah," he agreed. "I used to be eat up with it. But not so much anymore. Tell you the truth, I got out of this part of the country to let things cool down. Hell, I don't even remember what we were fighting about."

I looked at him appraisingly, wondering if he was telling the truth. Lew was dark and swarthy, and he had a sort of Mexican-sounding last name, but he didn't look so much Mexican as Indian, and he didn't have any accent at all that my ear could hear. "You passed a few remarks about people who didn't have to work for what they had," I reminded him.

"Yeah," he said. "Now I remember." He rubbed his chin. "I must have been drunk."

"You didn't fight drunk. That was probably the hardest fight I ever had in my life. And I think I'd've got whipped if that beer mug hadn't come to my hand. Which wasn't exactly clean fighting."

He shrugged. "I'd've probably used it if I could have got hold of it."

Lew was about my height, but he outweighed me about ten pounds. He had big thick shoulders and powerful arms. I knew how hard his belly was, because I'd given up hitting him there after about four or five licks. But he'd nearly lifted me off the floor with uppercuts to the body.

"I've forgot—how come guns didn't get into it?" he asked.

"We started scuffling and punching, and they got scattered out of our holsters. I think Crook had the good sense to collect them off the floor before one of us got any ideas. It was bad enough as it was."

He laughed again. "Well," he said, "that was one more time I got lucky. I've heard about you and guns. Was much damage done?"

"About a hundred and fifty dollars worth. I paid it."

He grimaced. "Well, I'm beholden to you. I ain't got my half right now, but when I get it, I'll get it to you."

I was getting an idea, but I wanted to see how much further we'd drift before I said anything.

He said, "Uh, I'd be willing to shake and drop the whole matter, if you was of a like mind."

"Suits me."

He put out his hand, and I slowly brought my right up and shook. He looked a little embarrassed. He immediately picked up his drink and lofted another toast. "Luck."

"Luck," I said.

We knocked them back.

After the whiskey had settled, I said casually, "You wouldn't be looking for work, would you?"

"I might," he answered. "Ain't been back in town but three or four days and ain't had time to look around. But I ain't interested in no straight cowpunching job."

"It ain't cow work at all," I said. "We've got a little problem coming at us and I could use another good hand. I reckon it might turn into rough work. The job might take a week, might take ten days. It would pay a hundred and seventy-five dollars. That would leave you a hundred clear after paying your half of the damages. You'd stay at the ranch, so you'd get room and board."

"Sounds pretty good," he said. "I really wasn't looking for nothin' permanent anyhow. Just come back to see my folks. I'm thinking of heading west."

"I got to warn you," I said. "We're likely to be outgunned. And these are rough folks."

He shrugged. "Suits me. When do I start?"

"You just did. Be at the hotel at first light. Me and you and the sheriff are going to take a little ride."

"All right." He got up. But he paused before he walked away. "If it's in your mind that I might be playing you false to get your guard down, you can forget it. That ain't my style."

"I know that," I said. "And I'm glad you do, too."


Supper was a pretty quiet affair. Nora and Mrs. Parker served, while me and Lonnie bore in on the fried chicken and mashed potatoes and garden peas. Lord, was it a relief from Buttercup's idea of what food was. I'd had a good steak lunch and now this supper. I calculated that if I could get a good breakfast down me in the morning, I might not have to eat for two days after I got back to the ranch.

After supper Mrs. Parker shooed me and Nora out to the front porch. Lonnie looked like he was going to come along to be sociable, but Mrs. Parker laid a gimlet eye on him and put a stop to that foolishness.

For a time Nora and I just swung back and forth, gently. "I'm mighty glad you changed your mind and came to supper," she said.

"I didn't change my mind; you just didn't tell me your mother was making fried chicken."

She gave me a nudge in the ribs. "I've got some news for you, Mr. Smarty. *I* fixed that chicken."

I was that astonished. "The hell you say!"

"Yes," she said primly. "You never bothered to ask, but a lot of meals you've eaten over here I've fixed."

"Well, I'm damned," I said.

"You keep talking like that and I've no doubt you will be."

After a time I kissed her. But I did it so softly and gently that it was just a whisper against her lips. She didn't put her arms around me, but neither did she pull her head back when it was over. Her face stayed there as if expecting more.

But I stood up and put on my hat. "I'm off at dawn tomorrow so I better get to bed." I told her. "Got a long ride."

"Will you be back soon, Justa?"

"Soon as I can," I said. "And when I do, I want to take you out to the ranch. I've got something I want to show you."

"What?"

"It has to do with this business of an understanding between us."

"Tell me."

"No, I'll show you."

Then I was down the steps and out the front gate. On the walk back to the hotel, I pondered my own foolishness. Without an understanding with Nora, I had staked off where I intended to build us a separate house on the ranch. Maybe if I had shown her that, she'd never have run off with the drummer. But I'd wanted to get it a little way under construction before surprising her with it. Well, that just proved a man ought not to count his chickens before they'd hatched or his wife before she'd married.

I hadn't been able to look at that plot since I got word she'd left. Now I figured I could. I planned to take her out and show it to her and ask her if she thought I ought to start building.

If she said yes, that ought to count for a pretty good understanding.

We got off pretty early the next morning. Sheriff Ward gave me a questioning look when I showed up with Lew Vara, but when I didn't offer any explanation he didn't ask any questions.

I figured we had about a twenty-five-mile ride to the herd. Blessing was south of our ranch and, consequently, back toward those Mexican cattle. Still, it would be a pretty good round trip for all concerned. I'd gotten the hotel kitchen to put me up a half a dozen roast-beef sandwiches and a big pot of beans. On top of that, I had some onions and apples and a cook pot. If we had to overnight, I figured we could make it.

As we rode I explained the whole proposition to Lew. "I agree with you," he said. "There's a lot of money involved here. Them ol' boys ain't gonna give in too easy. Not if the head honcho is smart enough to be paying them good wages."

"I figure," I said, "he's paying them good and he's giving them a bonus if they get the cattle through. That's what I'd do."

"Yeah," said Lew, "but you got one advantage in a fight that he don't have: He's got to worry about fighting you and holding those cattle together at the same time."

Vic Ward laughed at that.

"Lew, I can see you have been off the range a long time," I explained. "I'm more interested in holding those cattle together than anybody. The last thing I want them to do is scatter and get mixed in with our domestic herds."

"I never thought of that," he said. "Guess that's why I ain't never made much of a hand around cattle."

But still, I was feeling good about Lew. First about having him with me and then about having settled our dispute. I could sure use a man like Lew—an experienced gunfighter. So far as I knew, Ben and I were the only ones I could count on in that category. I hoped some of the rest would turn out to be pleasant surprises, but I wasn't holding my breath.

We rode hard for four hours and then made a nooning under a willow tree by a little shallow creek. Lew and I took a roast-beef sandwich, but Sheriff Ward had some biscuits and bacon with him and he preferred that. We made do with water, having nothing stronger along.

When we were finished eating and after taking a quick rest, Sheriff Ward said, "Tell me, Lew, where you been this past year since you lit out?"

"Oh, here and there," answered Lew vaguely. "Up around Fort Worth, mainly."

"Cattle work?"

"Well, no, not all told. Just odds and ends. First one thing and then the other."

"I see," the sheriff said. He kept looking hard at Lew as if he'd never seen him before. Which was strange, because I knew he'd known Lew and his family at least five years, maybe more.

We got away and rode hard for another two or three hours,

and then, about midafternoon, we topped a rise and there was
the herd in front of us, about a mile distant.

For a few minutes we sat and watched. They had the cattle
well strung out and were moving them slowly, letting them
graze along and fatten up on that good grass. I took as good a
count of the drovers as I could, but there were so many cattle
and such dust as a drive will raise that it was hard to be
accurate. But I counted at least eighteen riders in the saddle,
not counting whoever was in the cook wagon.

Lew said, flinging out an arm, "Look yonder. Up at the front
on this side, up in front of the point."

I looked, and damned if there wasn't a man driving a buggy.
He was staying well up front and well to the windward side, so
that he wasn't catching any of the dust. It was the first time I'd
ever seen a man driving a cattle herd out of a buggy.

"That," I said, "ought to just about be Mr. J.C. Flood. And
I believe those are his cattle."

"Now Justa, let me start in on the talking," Vic said. "We're
going to be inquiring about the legality of the man's business,
and it will sound better coming from an officer of the law."

Well, I was willing to do that. But I was going to be damn
certain that Mr. J.C. Flood got my message that his cattle were
not coming through our range.

We kicked off down the side of the rise and rode straight for
the buggy. It was early June, so the grass was green and lush
and halfway up a horse's leg.

As we rode I speculated on that buggy. Mr. Flood had
planned this route all the way. You could take a buggy from the
border to Houston if you hugged the coast, because it was easy
going. But you could never get over the rough country up north
near Uvalde in such a contraption. The man had never had a
doubt about what he was doing.

We rode at a gallop, and as we closed the distance, the
buggy stopped. We came up to it at a canter and pulled up just
as we came alongside. In the buggy was a fat, cheerful-looking
man, wearing a suit with a vest and tie. All he needed to
complete the outfit was one of those black rounded hats. It was
the damnedest sight I'd ever seen on a cattle drive.

"Afternoon, gentlemen," the man said. Then he seemed to take notice of Vic's badge and added, "And Sheriff."

"I'm Sheriff Ward of Matagorda County. Who am I addressing, sir?"

"You are addressing J.C. Flood, Sheriff. Of Houston."

He was so genial looking and cheerful speaking that you'd have never thought he could be a man of a nature to bring ruin to other cattlemen. But that's what he was doing. While Vic Ward had been talking, I'd been looking around at the stream of cattle moving slowly past. They were strictly *corrientes*— small cattle with big horns. That came of poor nutrition at an early age. Most Mexican cattle were stunted, because most of the northern part of Mexico was just damn poor land.

"Do you own these cattle, Mr. Flood?" asked Vic.

"I do indeed, sir. Is there some question about that? I have the bills of sale."

"I was more interested in your quarantine clearance, Mr. Flood."

"Oh, I have that," he replied. "Yes, indeed. Indeed I do, sir." He began to rummage around in a valise. After a second, he came out with some documents and handed them to Vic. The sheriff examined them for a moment and then turned to me with a puzzled look. "Justa, these look all right to me."

"Let me see them."

I scanned the documents quickly. They had been signed by a border inspector that both Norris and I knew of. He had been fired over six months past for several illegal acts, such as taking bribes. I handed the papers back to Mr. Flood. "S. Perkins has not been on the boarder in six months," I said. "Looks like he took some spare forms with him. But it still won't wash."

Mr. Flood's eyes twinkled. "And now it's my turn to ask to whom I have the honor of speaking?"

I said, "I don't know about the honor, but my name is Justa Williams."

"Ah, yes," said Mr. Flood. "Of the famous Half-Moon Ranch. You would be the scion of the family."

"I'm the boss, if that means the same thing," I said. "Look

here, Mr. Flood, I don't generally interfere in anybody else's business until they go to interfering in mine. And it appears to me that that's what you're about to do."

"How is that, Mr. Williams?"

"You are planning on driving some cattle through my range that have not been quarantined and of which every one could be carrying Mexican fever. I reckon that's my business, wouldn't you say?"

"I'd say yes, if it was so. But I assure you these cattle have been quarantined, Mr. Williams."

Now, of course, the reason nobody wanted to quarantine large numbers of cattle for that period of time was that they had to be kept in enclosed feed lots, which meant no grazing. To feed four thousand cattle for forty days would just about break most men and certainly wipe out any chance for profit. So this man was talking to me like I'd just fell off a turnip wagon. "I won't debate the point with you, Mr. Flood," I said. "But we know for certain that no large herds have been quarantined in Matamoras, Reyanosa, or anywhere else along the border for the last year. And certainly no herd this big."

Mr. Flood smiled. He was the most pleasant sort. "Perhaps I held smaller bunches at several locations," he said.

"Then how come your entry papers only mention Browns-ville?"

"Well, we can argue this some other time, Mr. Williams," he said cheerfully. "As you can see, I'm a busy man."

"You ain't half as busy as you're gonna get, you keep driving those cattle in my direction."

A quiet voice suddenly said, "Some trouble here?"

# CHAPTER
# 4

I'd been so intent in talking to J.C. Flood that I hadn't heard him come up. I looked around quickly. He was sitting his horse just off to my left, resting his arms on his saddle horn. He was wearing a flat-crowned black hat with a black vest and black gloves and sleeve garters to hold his cuffs off his hands. He had a flat, mean-looking face and flat, mean-looking eyes. It didn't take long to figure I was looking at Clarence Wooley, a man that certainly didn't match his name.

Mr. Flood said, "Oh my, no, Clarence. Nothing to concern yourself about. Mr. Williams and I were just having a little discussion."

But he still sat there, relaxed in the saddle, staring at me with those flat eyes, not even seeming to blink. He had his left side to me so I couldn't see how his gun was set up, but I thought I could guess. He didn't look to me like a man who knew one breed of cattle from the next, but I had no doubt he knew which end of the gun the bullet came out of.

And where it was going when he let it off.

"Mr. Flood," I said, "this discussion ain't quite closed. You say these cattle are legitimate. I notice none of them are wearing a trail brand. Want to tell me why? That's range law."

"Quite honestly, Mr. Williams, we've been too pressed for time. We've got a marketing schedule to meet."

"I bet you do," I said. I glanced over at Clarence Wooley and noticed he was no longer giving me the benefit of his stare. He was looking at something to my left and behind me. He had the faintest of smiles on his face, but his eyes held steady, still not seeming to blink. I glanced back. Lew Vara was sitting his horse just behind me. He was staring back at Clarence Wooley with almost the same look on his face. Except he wasn't wearing even the trace of a smile. I said, coming back to Flood, "All right, then show me the trail brand issued you by the Cattlemen's Association. That's law, too—that you have that."

He chuckled slightly. "Happens I've misplaced that, Mr. Williams."

"Yeah, I bet you have. That and a few other things. Like your sanity, if you think we're letting you bring these tick-infested cattle through our herds."

Some of the twinkle went out of his eyes. "Oh, I don't much like the sound of that, Mr. Williams."

"And I don't much like what you're trying to do."

"Not trying, Mr. Williams. Doing."

"Mr. Flood," I said, "you are not driving those cattle through our range."

He gave me a mild look. "Oh, I think I will be, Mr. Williams. I have men I'm paying to see that they get through."

"You better also be paying them to fight, Mr. Flood," I said.

"Are you threatening us, Mr. Williams?"

"Justa, take it easy," Vic said. "This ain't the time or the place."

Clarence Wooley suddenly said, softly, "We can make it the time and the place."

I brought my attention around to him, shifting slightly in my saddle so as to better clear my revolver. "That might simplify matters."

But Vic said, "Hold on! I'll arrest the first man that draws a gun. There's to be none of that in front of an officer of the law."

"No, indeed!" said Mr. Flood. "We are going about law-abiding business."

Wooley just kept staring at me, that little smile on his face. "Another time, Mr. Williams."

"Yes, Mr. Wooley, another time," I promised. "And soon."

Mr. Flood said, "Well, if you gentlemen will excuse us."

"Flood, this is my last warning," I said. "Don't try and bring those cattle through our range."

He turned to the sheriff and raised his hands as if he was the most cooperative man in the world. But even though he was looking at Vic, he was speaking to me. "What would you have us do, Mr. Williams? You're a cattleman. You can see I have a considerable investment here. Would you have me throw it away?"

"Turn north," I said, "and take them through Kerrville. That's sparsely populated country with damn few cattle to infect. Not like down here, where you could wipe out ten thousand head in a week."

"For that very reason that it is sparsely populated with cattle," he said, "we don't choose to go that way. That is inhospitable country, Mr. Williams, and I'd lose what little flesh my poor little cattle are carrying now. No, I'm afraid I have to reject that suggestion, sir."

"Then drive them back to the border and put them under honest quarantine."

"Impossible."

I gathered up my reins. For some time my horse had been stamping his feet in impatience. He acted about as tired of the conversation as I was. "Then this is my last warning. Drive those cattle back or we'll drive them back for you."

"Is that a threat, Mr. Williams?"

"Call it what you want to." I reined my horse around. "I'm just telling you we're going to protect our property. You figure it out from there." To Vic and Lew I said, "Let's go."

We turned and rode off at a slow lope. It was a mile before we reached the head of the line of slow-moving cattle.

After we'd ridden another mile, we all pulled up and let our horses blow a minute. They'd been ridden pretty hard that day.

But I was riding a big bay gelding that was hard as iron and could stay at a steady lope all day and half the night. I said to Vic, "Well, Sheriff, you can't say I didn't try."

Vic rubbed his chin. "I don't know what we can do, Justa. As close as they are, it would be too late to try and get official help down here. I guess you'll have to do what you have to do."

"I don't see any choice."

"The man is determined. And from the looks of the men he has with him, he came expecting trouble."

"He's going to get it. Well, Vic, I guess Lew and I will head for the ranch. No use us going back to Blessing. I've got a wonder of things to do."

"Oh, is Lew going with you?" Vic asked, glancing at Lew.

"Yeah. I thought you understood. He's going to help out in this little situation."

"I see," said the sheriff. He gathered up his reins. "Well, I'll be seeing you in a couple of days, Justa. Probably."

"Vic, you don't want to get mixed up in this."

"Oh, I may just drop in. Now, you take it easy."

"Adios."

I figured it was a little better than thirty miles to the ranch. We weren't going to make it that day, but it wouldn't be the first time, by a hell of a long shot, that I'd bedded down on the prairie. We'd ride until it came nearly dark and then make a camp at the first good spot we could find. Naturally, we both had a bed roll tied behind our saddles. That was something a man just always had, because he never knew when night might overtake him in some unlikely spot.

Just before twilight we made Caney Creek, which, at that time of the year, was running nearly full. Not that that was saying much, but it was lined with willows and was the coolest spot around, and it meant water for the horses. Lew gathered up downed wood for a fire, while I unsaddled the horses and turned them out with hobbles on and laid out the grub. We got a fire going just as dark came on and warmed up the beans and made a pretty good supper out of them, along with the roast-beef sandwiches and onions and apples. Except Lew said, as we were finishing, "I wish I had a drink of whiskey. That or a cup of coffee."

"I forgot both," I said. "Or you did. Or we did."

He laughed. "I guess we both did. You blame me and I'll blame you."

When you didn't have to fight him, Lew was a downright likable guy.

We got settled down on our bed rolls, both of us lighting up the same kind of little cigarillo I smoked from time to time. We stared into the fire for some time, and then Lew said, "I'd watch Clarence Wooley if I was you, Justa."

"Lew, his name was never mentioned," I said quietly. "Not his whole name; just Clarence."

He didn't say anything.

"You know him, don't you?" I asked.

"I might," he said.

"No 'might' about it. I caught you two staring at each other. I think you know him pretty good, Lew."

He said, roughly, "I know him well enough to tell you to watch yourself at all times around him. Including when your back is turned."

I kept quiet for a moment, thinking. "You ain't been running with the likes of him, have you, Lew?"

"Justa, let's leave off on this. I've been doing what I've been doing. If you don't want to hire me on account of it, then we're still square."

"I never said I didn't want to keep you," I said. "I was just gently inquiring about something I thought might be my business. That man Wooley is my enemy. I was trying to find out how friendly you might be with him. That's all. I wasn't sticking my nose in your business."

"Friendly?" he said. "Shiit! Boy, have you got your foot in the wrong stirrup. If I'd knowed Wooley was on the other side, I'd've taken this job for nothing!"

"That's all I wanted to know," I said. "Let's get some shut-eye."

• • •

We rode into the ranch about noon, and just as we came up to the house, Ray Hays came bolting out of the cook shed. I swung out of the saddle, glaring at him, and said, "How come every time I see you lately, you are either lallygagging around or trying to give me advice? Don't you ever work?"

"I was told to keep a watch for you," he said, stiffly. "Ben and Norris want to see you soon's you come in. Where the hell you been, anyway?"

I ignored the question and said, "This is Lew Vara. He's going to help us out. Take care of my horse, and then take Lew over to the bunkhouse and get him settled. Introduce him around."

He looked disappointed. "Looks like they is a war council shapin' up in there," he said. "Reckon you don't want me along?"

"No, I certainly don't. Now, reckon you could do what I just told you to do?"

"I guess, Boss," he said.

I just shook my head and went into the house. I found Dad and Ben and Norris sitting in the study, looking worried. "Where the hell you been?" asked Norris.

I took off my hat and hung it up and then sat down in my usual chair. There was a bottle of whiskey sitting on the side table, and I poured out a tumbler of that and took a sip before I answered. "I rode out with Vic Ward to take a look at the opposition. I didn't much like what I saw."

"Well, you're going to like what we've got to tell you a whole lot less," said Norris gloomily.

"Tell me."

"Smalley, Osgood, and Tom Brown have been here since you left," said Ben.

"And?"

"And they said they didn't want no truck with the opposition. Said to tell you they were sorry, but they were just small fish and they couldn't do anything."

I glanced over at Dad, and he cocked his head and smiled partially.

"What about Tom Brown?"

Ben glanced at Norris, who said, "Tom came in very apologetic. He said the two hands he'd promised us didn't want to fight. And that he was wavering." Norris leaned forward and put his hands together. "He said this man Flood sent an emissary to him, offering to indemnify any cattle he might lose. Pay him for any loss he might sustain."

The whiskey suddenly felt sour in my stomach. "So that's it," I said slowly. "He got to Smalley and Osgood with the same story. Don't they have sense enough to know this man Flood is no more going to keep his word than a dead horse can run?"

"They're operating on hope, not logic," Norris said. "Hope and fear."

"Divide and conquer," said Dad.

I glanced over at him. He looked terribly old and shriveled up in his chair. "So that's his game. Wonder why he didn't try it on me yesterday when I saw him?"

Dad said, "What would have been the point? You'd have had to have looked awful dumb to have believed a story like that. To indemnify us against loss would cost twice as much as his herd is worth. So he wouldn't expect you to fall for a story like that. Smalley and Osgood, yes. They don't have much to lose and they're afraid. But I'm surprised at Tom Brown being that gullible."

"I doubt if he's so much gullible as afraid," I said glumly. "Maybe they sent Mr. Clarence Wooley to see him."

"You see him?" Ben asked.

"Oh yes. We had a staring match."

Then I told them the gist of what had happened on my trip, deliberately leaving out the part about Nora. It didn't seem the right time to discuss it.

Ben said, marveling, "And you mean to tell me that you and Lew Vara made up? Lord, I never thought I'd hear that. Not after that fight you and him had."

"He's a good man," I said.

"But can we trust him?" asked Norris. "This man Flood seems to be covering all angles. Perhaps he's deliberately planted Vara in our camp to report back on our plans."

"I don't think so."

"But how do you know?"

"Dammit, Norris, I don't know anything for sure right now," I said, with irritation, "except we got a lot of trouble. Now, what other good news do ya'll have for me?" I turned to Ben. "What about our ten men? Did you try them out?"

"Yeah," he answered gloomily. "Four can't shoot a lick and six think they can. I don't know which is the most dangerous. And I don't mean to what they're aiming at."

"You mean they ain't worth a damn?"

"That would be bragging on them."

"Well, that's just great," I said. "Damn!"

A voice suddenly came through the door of the study that led to the dining room. "Drop the damn lead steer!"

It was Buttercup. He'd been listening from the dining room. "I'm gonna drop you if you don't mind your own damn business!" I said, loudly.

"It are my business."

"Listen, you old fool!" I yelled back. "You drop the damn lead steer and those cattle would scatter all over the place. Which is the last thing I can have. Now, can you figure that out or do you want me to draw you a picture?"

In every trail herd there was one steer that walked firmly forward and established himself at the head of the pack. Once he'd taken up his position, the rest of the cattle would follow him like he was a guide. A wise herdsman protected his lead steer at all costs. If you could turn the lead steer in a stampede, you could turn the whole herd.

Buttercup grumbled to himself, "Smart aleck whippersnapper. Thanks he knows it all."

I ignored him and turned to Dad. "Howard, I reckon I need to ask you to draft a telegram to your friends at the Cattlemen's Association in Austin. Ask them to send a range inspector down here as fast as they can. I know it'll be too late, but I don't know what else to do right now."

Dad nodded. I didn't often call him by his given name, but sometimes I did because it made him feel more a part of matters. I saw him take up pen and paper.

"Anybody got any other suggestions?" I asked.

"If it was fall and the wind was right," Ben said, "we could fire the grass."

I didn't even bother to answer him. I just looked at Norris, who shook his head. "I have no ideas. Ten years from now this wouldn't be allowed to happen, but, sadly, it's not ten years from now."

"Maybe I could go to San Antonio and hire some gun hands," Ben suggested. "I hear that place is crawling with them."

I thought about it for a moment and then rejected the idea. "That herd will be at the limit I put on them in three days at the most. We'll have to be in position a day ahead of time. That only allows two days. You'd never have time to find the men and get back here in time, much less weed out the ones who just say they're gun hands. And I don't want to go into a fight with a bunch of riffraff I don't know anything about." I slapped my knee in frustration. "Dammit, what we need is time. Time to get some help. Time to get better organized."

"Here," said Dad quietly. I got up and took the draft from his hand. It was addressed to the president of the Cattlemen's Association:

UNINSPECTED HERD OF MEXICAN CATTLE COMING THROUGH OUR RANGE UNDER HEAVY GUARD STOP NEED HELP DESPERATELY STOP SEND RANGE INSPECTOR SOON AS POSSIBLE STOP

"Thanks." I didn't look at Dad. I'd hated to ask him to write it, because I knew that Howard Williams hadn't very often asked for help. And for him to have to admit that we had a situation on our hands that we couldn't handle was, I knew, a heavy load for him. I said, "I'm sorry about this, Dad."

He shrugged. "They're stacking the deck on us. Looks like we got to try and stack it back the right way."

I gave the draft to Ben, with instructions for him to dispatch a rider with it to Blessing lickety-split. "And don't send Hays. He'd just go in a saloon and forget what he was sent for."

"Aw, Hays ain't that bad," said Ben. "You're too hard on him, Justa."

"Yeah, just like I'm too hard on you."

Then we just sat and drank whiskey until time for supper. It was always a good idea to get a little tight before you went into one of Buttercup's meals. I thought about Nora a little, but without much resolve or definition. I had too much on my mind trying to think of some way to get out of the box we were in. And that herd was getting closer and closer with every passing daylight hour.

And there was nothing in the way to slow them up—no natural barrier, no grass fire, not even a few neighbors.

It was just a hell of a mess. And even Dad didn't have any suggestions. I was outgunned and outmanned, and it looked like I'd been outthought.

It was galling. And I still had supper to get through. I thought of Mrs. Parker's fried chicken—or really Nora's—and it just made matters worse. Dad looked at me sympathetically, but that wasn't much help. He seemed to be saying "It'll be all right, Son," but that wasn't necessarily always the case. Sometimes things weren't all right; sometimes the worst did happen.

I came bolt upright in the middle of the night with a sudden thought that had hit me in my sleep. Fumbling around in the dark, I located my pocket watch. By squinting and by benefit of the moonlight streaming through my bedside window, I made out that it was just a little after midnight. "Ben!" I yelled, jumping out of bed. Struggling with my trousers, I yelled again. "Ben!" Then I raced down the hall, yelling his name. I pounded on his door. "BEN!"

The door was suddenly jerked back and Ben met me, gun in hand. "What the hell!" he said.

"Get dressed," I said. "Then get Hays and Lew Vara up. Have them saddle horses for you, me, and Lew. Then hitch up the lightest buckboard to the two fastest wagon horses we got."

He stared blankly at me. "What the hell is going on?"

"I ain't got time to explain," I said. "Just do it and be damn fast. We got no time to lose."

By now the commotion had woken Norris, and he came staggering out into the hall, rubbing his eyes. "What is happening here?"

"Go back to bed, Norris. We're in a hurry."

"But Justa, what are we doing?" asked Ben. "Hell, it's the middle of the night."

"Hurry up, dammit!"

Then I raced off to another part of the house. Buttercup lived in a little room just off the cook shack. Since his door was open, I rushed in without bothering to knock. The old man was lying on his back, snoring like a buzz saw. I took him by the shoulders and began shaking him awake. "Buttercup!" I said. "BUTTERCUP!"

He came awake snorting and snuffling and looking wide eyed and frightened. I suddenly realized that in the dark, he couldn't tell it was me. "Buttercup," I said, "it's Justa! Wake up, dammit!"

It took a moment or two, but I finally got him conscious and aware of who I was. He mouthed out something that sounded like "Vash da helsh!"

"Put your teeth in and get dressed," I said. "I've got a job for you. A big job."

He sat up, still blinking, while I lit a lantern. Then he found his teeth and slipped them in. "Mr. Justa, have you taken complete leave of yore senses?"

"Old man," I said grimly, "you been yammering to do something. Well, now I'm going to give you that chance. How many cartridges you still got for that Sharps rifle of yours?"

He had to think. "I dunno. Twenty or thirty, I reckon. Maybe more."

"Well, get them all. And get some grub and water together and be outside as soon as you can. We've got to hurry."

It was taking me so much time to get people moving that I began to fear for the feasibility of my plan. I figured we had, at the most, six to six and a half hours to get into position. Much more than that and they'd be too close.

I went on back to my room, finished dressing, and then strapped on my gun belt and took my saddle rifle and a box of cartridges and went outside. The moon was up good and nearly full. That would help. For a few minutes I stamped about impatiently, and then Ben came out of the barn, leading two horses. Lew was right behind him, and in a moment, I heard the light rumble of the buckboard with Hays driving.

"Set up back o' the cook shack," I said. "We're picking up Buttercup."

Ben gave me a startled look. "We're doing what?"

"Ben, just do what you're told. I ain't got time to explain every little thing."

In a moment Buttercup came stumping out, carrying his big old Sharps rifle that was damn near as tall as he was. I told him to get in the wagon.

"What?" He had the sack of grub in his other hand. It made me shudder.

"GET IN THE GODDAMN WAGON, YOU OLD FOOL!"

Well, he scurried then. I mounted up and said, "Follow me. We're going to be moving fast."

With the moon to help us, I set off in double quick time over the smooth prairie. Lew and Ben rode side-wheelers on the buckboard while I led. Behind me I could hear the steady grumbling of Buttercup over the sound of the buckboard.

I figured we had something over twenty and less than twenty-five miles to go and about six hours to do it in. But I had to be careful of the horses. They would have to make the long trip and then have something left for a quick getaway if we needed it.

We went hard for three hours and then I called a halt at that same Caney Creek Lew and I had camped at to let the horses blow and take on a little water.

As I swung down from the saddle, Ben said, "Now will you tell us what the hell is going on? I've damn near had to hold Buttercup in the buckboard. He's about ready to walk back."

For answer I said, "Let's see what kind of grub he's got in that sack. I went to the end of the wagon, where Buttercup was grumbling a mile a minute. "Jes' some way to treat an ol' man!

Jerk him outen bed at God knows what hour and fling him inna damn wagon an' trundle him off to God knows where an' his ol' bones jes' a achin' from the cold. An' not a word of reason to it! Not one! No, by God, sir, not one! It ain't right, I tell you! It ain't right!"

"Oh, shut up!" I said. "And give me that grub sack. If I was to kill you, everybody that has to eat at that ranch would thank me."

I got the grub sack away from him. He'd packed cold biscuits and beef jerky. Either one would be a test for your teeth. I took some and passed the sack along. While we squatted down, eating, I said, "I know you're all wondering. Well, it come to me last night that what we really need is time—time to get help, time for a range inspector to arrive, time for our neighbors to come to their senses. So I'm going to try and buy us some time."

"How?" Ben asked.

It took me a long time to answer, because I was trying to chew a biscuit. Finally I said, "By scattering their herd. It ought to cost them a day or two to gather it back up."

Ben said, "But I thought you didn't want to do that, scatter their herd."

"I didn't," I said, "where I initially planned to intercept them. But where they are now it doesn't matter. There are no cattle around—no local cattle. It's that long stretch owned by that outfit out of Dallas, and they ain't stocked it yet. That's what the rush is all about—to catch them while they're still in that area."

From the wagon Buttercup hollered out, "Drop the goddamn lead steer."

I nodded. "For once you're right, old man."

"Buttercup?" said Hays, in some amazement.

I nodded. "Buttercup. We can't risk getting near enough for one of us to use a carbine. They'd be on us before we had a chance to run, and we can't fight fifteen or twenty of them. But Buttercup can make a shot at a distance that will give us time to get away." I raised my voice slightly. "You can still shoot, can't you, Buttercup?"

"Damn right I can still shoot," he said. "Some got it, boy, and some ain't."

I still wasn't sure he understood what was going on. But he damn sure would in another few hours.

"I hope to hell this works," said Lew, grimly. "You are about to piss off some serious men."

I looked across at him in the half light. "I'm a little serious myself." I stood up. "We've got to move it, but we've got to save the horses as much as we can. We might have a hard run getting away."

We kept going hard. Even though I knew the country like the back of my hand, it was hard to distinguish landmarks in such terrain with only the moon for light. It came false dawn and then real dawn began to show, and there was still no sign of the herd.

Which was gratifying. The further south I could catch them, the better I was going to like it. I was aiming for a little place I knew, a small mound that ought to be right in their path. It was only a little hummock, perhaps half an acre across and maybe only ten feet above the prairie at its highest, but it was dotted with a little copse of stunted oak trees. It would make the best defense and the best firing position for miles around.

I kept riding, peering ahead in the coming light for the little hill. Finally I rode on ahead and saw it, some half-mile distant. I put spurs to my horse and galloped up to it. I tied my horse off on one of the little stunted oaks, loosened his cinch so he could heave better, and then clambered up to the top. Peering through the oaks I could see, at least two miles off, the beginning of the herd.

I scrambled back down the little embankment and waved to the others to come on. They came with agonizing slowness, but finally Hays rattled up with the buckboard. I told them to tie the horses and loosen their girths. "I don't reckon anybody thought to bring any feed," I said.

"I did," said Hays. "Brought a sack of oats."

"I don't believe it," I said. "Well, give each horse a little bait. But not much, because they're going to be on the move again pretty damn quick. Everybody bring their rifles and all the shells they got. We're going up top."

Buttercup was getting out of the wagon, cussing a blue streak about being sore all over from such a ride in the middle of the night. I took him by the arm. "Come on, old man. It's time to quit grumbling and earn your keep for a change."

I helped him up through the oaks to the top of the hummock and then to the last line of trees. The herd was perceptibly closer. Wondering about his eyes because he didn't wear spectacles, I asked, "Can you see that herd, you old fool?"

"Of course I can see the damn herd. I can damn near pick out the lead steer from here."

I was impressed. Unless he was lying, it was more than I could do. I went back down the slope and told Hays to take the sack of feed up to Buttercup for a rifle rest as soon as he finished feeding the horses. Then I got his big Sharps out of the buckboard and his sack of shells. I took a look inside the bag as I climbed back up. I tell you, those shells looked more like they ought to be fired by an artillery piece. They were damn near as big as ten-cent cigars.

I got to the top. Lew and Ben and Buttercup were standing just inside the last line of trees, staring out at the herd. I estimated they were about a mile off.

About then Hays came puffing up behind me with the remains of the sack of oats. "Where you want this, Boss?"

"Where you want to fire from?" I asked Buttercup.

He didn't answer for a moment; he just moved from spot to spot, studying the oncoming herd. Finally he pointed to a narrow spot between two trees. "Right chere," he said.

I motioned to Hays to drop the sack where Buttercup had indicated. "What's that?" asked the old man.

"A firing rest."

He snorted. "Hell, I don't need no consarned rifle rest. I kin shoot off hand at something as big as a steer."

"Now listen, you damned old fool," I said, "you're going to be doing considerable shooting besides the lead steer. Our lives could depend on how well you shoot. So don't come the prima donna on me now. You understand? You fuck up and I'll make

you eat your own cooking the rest of your life." I handed him
his rifle and his bag of shells. "Now get down there and get
ready."

He did as he was told, though he grumbled about his
"rheumatiz" on the wet ground. I hunkered down beside him
and said, "Now, when they're in range, when you're sure you
can't miss, I want you to kill the lead steer. You got any idea
how far that might be?"

He raised the breech of the big rifle and put in one of those
huge shells. As he closed the breech, you could hear the
cocking mechanism. He pulled the hammer all the way back.
It went *clitch-clatch*. Then he sighted down the barrel for a
second or two. "Wahl," he said, "ain't no wind to speak of this
mornin'. I reckon 'round seven hundred yards."

I heard Lew whistle behind me. "Seven hundred yards!" I
said. "Are you sure?"

He looked around at me. "Lissen, sonny boy, I may not be
able to cook fer sour apples, but don't you be tellin' me 'bout
no rifle shootin'."

"So much the better," I said. "But listen, and this is
important. After you fire the first time, they are going to see
the smoke from your rifle. That thing looks like the church on
fire, the amount of smoke it puts out, so immediately some
riders are going to start our way. You've got to drop the first of
them. I don't care if you hit the man or his horse, but stop him.
Then try for the next. He ought to be closer. Then the next. If
you hit two or three of them, it ought to discourage them
enough they turn back. Meanwhile, the rest of us are going to
be firing into that herd with our carbines. At this range we may
not even draw blood, but it ought to spook those cattle. If we
can get them running in all directions, those drovers are going
to have to forget about us and try to turn that stampede. But
without that lead steer, they are going to have merry hell
trying."

Ben was getting excited. "Justa," he said, "this just might
work."

"It damn well better," I said grimly. "Else those Mexican
cattle are going to be in our lap day after tomorrow."

"Don't aim?" Lew asked.

"Don't aim. Just fire into the front of that herd as fast as you can lever another shell in the chamber."

About that time, Hays was on the point of striking a match to light a cigarette. I just gave him a look and slowly shook my head.

"Oh," he said. "I reckon not."

I said to Lew and Ben, "Now, when we go to getting away, us three will have to lag back to protect the wagon. Obviously it can't go as fast, and we're going to have to stop pursuit to give Hays and Buttercup a good lead."

From the ground, Buttercup bristled up. "Ain't nobody got to protect my ass. Them suckers chase me, they gonna wish they hadn't."

"Shut up, old man," I said. I squatted down beside him again. "Now listen, on your last shot: You'll see a gent driving a buggy. I want you to drop his horse."

He looked around at me. "Aw hell, Justa, I don't like shootin' no horse. Let me just plug the sonofabitch in the buggy."

"We can't do that just yet," I said. "But I don't want him able to drive around and organize matters. You've got to put him on foot."

It was all said, and then all we could do was wait, in anticipation, and watch as the herd slowly approached, growing bigger and bigger in the distance.

The smell of blood spooked cattle. I was hoping that Lew and I and Ben and Hays, by firing steadily into the mass of cattle, could wound enough animals to get the scent into the nostrils of the rest and cause them to run wild. Of course, I didn't know at that range. A carbine is really only effective up to about a hundred yards—that is, if you have any intention of hitting anything. What effect the bullets would have at such a range was something I didn't know.

The herd was close enough now that I was just about to decide that a big orange and white steer was on the lead, when such a boom came right next to me that I jumped nearly a foot off the ground. When I settled back to where I could see, the big steer was down and the other lead animals were milling all over the place. "Fire!" I yelled, and I began levering and shooting into the front of the herd just as fast as I could. Even as I fired, I became aware of three or four riders suddenly leaving the herd and heading our way at top speed. The first rider had gone perhaps fifty yards when the huge boom came again and the rider and horse both went down. I didn't know if Buttercup had hit man or animal and didn't much care.

Around me the others were firing and reloading as fast as they could. The cattle were milling and starting to dart here and there. Soon there was so much dust that we were just firing into where we thought they might be.

BOOM!

And I saw the second rider go down. The other two kept coming. Through the dust, I was trying to locate Flood in his buggy. Finally I saw him off to my right. He'd reined in and was standing up, and he appeared to be shouting at someone or something.

BOOM!

The shot was made at about four hundred yards, and this time I could see that Buttercup had clearly picked the rider out of the saddle. I reckoned he thought he'd been struck by a cannonball. The other rider hesitated, seeing the fate of his colleague, then reined up and started back.

He never made it. The big rifle said KA-BOOM again, and the rider went over his horse's head.

That's at least two less, I thought grimly.

It was time to go. There was such a pile of dust we couldn't see anything of the mass, but I could see individual cattle running in all directions, while frantic drovers tried to put them back together again. I knelt down beside Buttercup and yelled in his ear, pointing as I did, "The buggy horse! The buggy horse!"

I could see that Flood had sat back down and was whipping his horse up, heading for the midst of the confusion.

I saw Buttercup swivel around slightly, and then came that ear-splitting blast. I could see the buggy horse go down like a tree had fell on him. The buggy rolled another foot and then turned over, jerked over by the fall of the animal in the shanks. I saw Flood come spilling out and hit the ground, hard. I hoped the sonofabitch had broke his neck.

But there was no time for that. I grabbed Buttercup by the arm and lifted him up. "Wait jes' a cornsarned minute!" he said. "I ain't through yit!"

"Yes you are!" I said. I grabbed up the big rifle and his sack of shells. I yelled at Hays to quit firing and go down and get the horses cinched up and the buckboard ready.

Ben looked around at me questioningly. I yelled for him to keep firing for another minute and then for him and Lew to get mounted up.

I was yelling, because I was about half deafened from all the noise.

I got Buttercup down the slope and into the wagon, along with his Sharps and his shells. Hays was busy cinching up my horse, but I told him to leave off and get the wagon started for home. He untied the team and jumped on the seat, wheeled around and was gone.

I finished my horse and then checked Ben's and Lew's. They were done. I mounted my horse and then checked the load in my rifle. The magazine was full. I didn't expect a great deal of pursuit, expecting them to be pretty busy chasing cattle, but then I couldn't be sure.

About that time, Lew and Ben came scrambling down the slope. They were both grinning like fools. They got mounted, and we rode out from behind the little hummock. For a moment we looked back toward the Mexican herd. Of course, we couldn't see as well from prairie level, but what we could see looked mighty pleasing. It appeared it would be more than a day or two before Mr. Flood got his herd lined out again.

Ben came up beside me and clapped me on the shoulder. "That was a hell of an idea, Justa! And God, that Buttercup can still shoot! Lord if he can't!"

"It ain't over yet," I said. I glanced behind me. The wagon appeared to have made about half a mile. Hays looked to be taking it pretty easy on the team, which was what I had told him to do. We all had pretty tired horses and a long way to home. We'd have to take it mighty easy the rest of the way. But even as tired as they were, the horses were nervous and fidgety from all the noise. I imagined that every one of them had nearly had a fit each time that cannon of Buttercup's had gone off.

"Let's start back," I said. "But at a walk."

We proceeded that way about a mile, going slowly, keeping the distance between us and the wagon about the same. I glanced back from time to time but couldn't see anything. Of course, that didn't mean much. They'd have a world of fresh horses, and they could give us a five-mile head start and still catch us.

"Let's close it up a little," I said.

Accordingly, we put the horses in a slow lope and closed up to some two hundred yards behind the wagon. Then we drug down to a walk again. Caney Creek was some eight or nine miles ahead, and I figured we'd take a rest there and water and feed the horses and maybe have a bite ourselves.

About then I heard Lew sing out, "Look out! Here they come!"

I looked back. About a quarter of a mile away, I could see four horsemen riding hard, straight for us. There was no mistaking their intentions. I yelled at the buckboard to be on guard, then said to Lew and Ben, "Just wheel around and be at the ready. Let them come on. Shoot for their horses when they get in range."

We waited, watching them come on. At about two hundred yards, two of the riders stood up in their stirrups, having looped their reins around their saddle horns, and fired their rifles at us. The sound came distantly. We heard the whine of the bullets passing over our heads, saw the white puff from their rifles, and then heard the crack of the shells' explosions.

"Hold your fire," I said.

"They might get lucky," said Lew.

"Not at this range."

Then I suddenly felt something that sounded like an artillery shell come whistling right by me, heard that familiar BOOM, and saw the lead rider suddenly go backward off his horse, as if he'd been hit by some gigantic hand.

I looked behind me. Buttercup was on his back in the bed of the buckboard, with his legs and the barrel of his Sharps sticking straight up in the air. He'd fired it off hand from a sitting position, and the recoil had knocked him ass over tea kettle.

But I had business in front of me. The sudden loss of their compadre had given them some serious second thoughts about the wisdom of continuing. They were still a good hundred and fifty yards away, but I said, "Fire at the one on the far right!"

We all set up a lively fire at the one man. By now he'd practically stopped, but even though the range was a little too great, we were throwing enough lead his way that something had to hit home.

His horse got it first. I saw him stumble as the rider tried to turn him, then I saw the man sag in the saddle as he, too, caught a slug. One of the other riders came to his aid and it appeared that he might have taken a hit, too, because he suddenly jerked up in the saddle and clutched at his shoulder.

By now there were riding away as fast as the man on the wounded horse could move. We threw a few more shots at them and then let them go. I turned around and looked for the buckboard. Buttercup was sitting up in the bed of the buckboard, but he didn't have his rifle in his hands. Instead he was rubbing his shoulder. I imagined his old shoulder had taken a pretty good beating that day.

"Let's get on home," I said. "Nice and easy. We'll rest at Caney Creek and then go on. I reckon they won't be pursuing—at least not today."

We were a pretty jubilant group when we rode into ranch headquarters that evening. While the others put the horses and gear away, I went inside to give Dad and Norris the news. Norris was quietly enthusiastic and congratulatory, but Dad didn't have much to say. I finished up by saying, "At least it bought us some time. Dad, maybe that range inspector will have time to get down here now. But what I'm going to do, I'm going to try and send to San Antonio for some hired gun help. We got at least three of them—or Buttercup did—but it still ain't even. Now I figure I've picked up at least a day or two, and this ought to give me time to send for help."

He didn't say anything.

"Well, what do you think?" I asked him.

"I'm wondering if that's wise—to bring in outsiders. The men you hire might end up causing you more trouble than the kind we already got."

It sort of exasperated me. "What would you have me do?" I said. "It's too uneven a fight as it is right now. You want me to go up against hired gunmen with inexperienced cowboys? They might be willing, but Ben says they're damn sure not capable. I've got to even the sides."

He shrugged. "Seems like you did a pretty good job today with just four of you and an old man."

"That was from long distance," I said. "And it's a stunt that's not likely to work twice. By the time they get those cattle gathered and get started back our way, they'll be too close for me to scatter their herd again."

"Well, you asked what I thought," he said. "I told you. You don't have to listen. You are, after all, running this ranch."

It gave me kind of a sour feeling, probably because I wasn't too enthusiastic myself about bringing in the kind of men I'd have to hire. With those kind, they could jump sides before you knew it.

But I had to have some help.

"Justa, I'm with Dad," said Norris. "I don't really want that kind on the ranch."

"Oh?" I looked at him steadily. "What kind do you want on the ranch? Dead cattle? Because that's what we're going to have."

"We know there's five of us that are good," he said.

"Which five is that?"

"Why, you and me and Ben and Lew and Hays."

I wouldn't have said it in just that way if I hadn't been exasperated, but I was, so I said, "You got it wrong. There's four. Count yourself out. We're not keeping books here, we're shooting guns."

He jerked his head back like I'd slapped him. I got up and stalked out of the room.

We praised and bragged on Buttercup until we were plumb wore out from the activity. If one of us said "Best damn shot in the world!" we all said it a thousand times. And still it wasn't enough for him. We finally got him drunk enough late that night that he finally passed out and we could all get a rest.

There was one unexpected benefit that came from the foray. Next morning Buttercup's shoulder was so sore that he couldn't cook. I gratefully gave him the next few days off. As we went into breakfast Ben gave a look that said, eloquently, "You never know where your blessings are going to come from."

But that midmorning Dad said something to me that I already knew. "You know—don't you, Son?—that this man Flood is not going to stand still for that raid."

"I know," I replied.

"Are you making plans?"

"I'm thinking on it," I answered. "I figure it will take him twenty-four hours to get his stock rounded up and decide how he wants to hit us. It's not something I have to figure out right now."

"I wouldn't leave it too long," said Dad. "He now knows for certain that you mean to oppose him. Harshly."

"And there's a lot of money at stake. I know."

"All right, then I don't need to tell you."

I hated to see him take that attitude, but I had the faint feeling it was an offshoot of my determination to bring some less-than-savory help in.

I hunted up Lew Vara before he could get lost to sight. He was in the bunkhouse, cleaning his guns. The other hands having been put to work by Harley, he and I shared the place alone.

I sat down on the bunk next to his. "Lew, do you know where I could get any help? And you know the kind I mean. Three or four hard boys that would shoot for a price."

He gave me a glance. "What makes you think I'd know such men, Justa?"

"Just a guess," I said. "How about it?"

He went on oiling his revolver for a moment. Then he ran it in and out of its holster to make sure it was clearing easily. Finally he said, "I might. But I think you'd be making a mistake."

"Why?"

He kept his eyes on his work. "Oh, them kind are awful hard to get rid of once they get their feet under the grub table. They take a power of running off."

"But will they fight for you?"

He looked up. "They'll fight if you pay them enough. Be that whoever it is."

"How much is enough?"

"For this little shindig? I'd say about two hundred a man. Maybe a little less."

"Where would you find these men?"

He shrugged. "All over. But San Antonio is about the closest. Maybe a few in Houston."

"I think Flood has already got all those hired up." I took fifty dollars out of my pocket and handed it to him. "There's a noon train out of Blessing for San Antonio. Gets in there tonight. One gets back in here tomorrow night. Try and make it as fast as you can."

He stood up. "All right. But Justa, I've got to say this: You're the boss and it's your decision, but I think you're making a mistake."

I shrugged. "Lew, I ain't got no selection right now."

"I'm on my way," he said. "Quick's I can get saddled up."

# CHAPTER
# 5

Right after lunch, I said to Hays, "I want you to ride into Blessing and go to Parker's Mercantile and get twenty or thirty of the biggest rockets he's got. Also, I want you to get a bunch of strings of firecrackers." It was coming on for the middle of June, so I knew he'd be stocking up for the Fourth of July.

Naturally, Hays had to give me a blank look. "Boss, it ain't none of my business, but don't you reckon we're goin' to celebratin' a little too soon? I mean, them cattle is still comin'."

I said, tiredly, "Hays, why don't you surprise the hell out of me sometimes and do what you're told without an argument?"

He gave me a hurt look. "Boss, I'm just thinkin' of yore welfare."

"Just get the rockets," I said. "And the firecrackers. The firecrackers ain't real important, but don't you dare come back here without some rockets. Big ones."

"All right," he said, giving me a look to indicate he was convinced I'd finally overloaded my mind.

"And do not dally," I told him. "Get in, get those fireworks, and come straight back here. Do not go in the saloon. Do not talk to anyone. Do not tell anyone about these fireworks. Just go in and come back. I know how long it takes to ride to Blessing and back. And don't come back here two hours late with any stories about your horse throwing a shoe."

"Boss," he said earnestly, "that kind of hurts my feelings. You know you ain't got a more dependable hand on the place."

"Yeah, dependable: I can always depend on you to argue. Now get kicking."

Then I hunted up my foreman. "Harley," I said, "starting tonight, I want you to detail off two men to stand watch all night in that buffalo wallow about seven or eight miles south of here. I'm expecting company, and I'm going to need early warning. That will mean another man staying up here at the ranch."

He gave me a puzzled look. "How they going to get word back to the ranch? If that bunch strikes back like we all figure, they'll be in the chicken coop before we can close the door. You ain't expecting two men to make a fight out of it, are you, Justa?"

"It ain't all worked out, Harley," I told him. "Just do like you're told. I'll give you the final details when I can."

He shook his head. "All right, Justa. But you are stretching me mighty thin on men. We're moving cattle down to the coast as fast as we can, but they are scattered, sir, mighty scattered. I'd guess we ain't moved half."

"Harley," I said wearily, "we are all stretched thin, but we're just going to have to do the best we can. Now, call in three men right now and have them get some shut-eye so they can stay up all night." He started to turn away and I added, "And, starting tonight, every man sleeps with his gun. Them as don't want to fight might not have a choice."

"All right, Justa," he said. He turned away again.

And I stopped him again. "Never mind about detailing a man to watch here at the ranch. Me and my brothers will take turn about on that. Just have two men for that buffalo wallow. I can't take the chance on just using one. One might go to sleep, but if there's two, they can sleep turn and turn about."

"All right, Justa."

This time I let him go. I knew I was acting nervous and

undecided, and the reason I was, was because I was nervous and undecided.

By that time Hays was saddled and ready to go. He hollered out to ask me if there was anything else I wanted from town. I yelled back, "No! Just go, dammit!"

But there *was* something I wanted from town: Nora. But I had to put her out of mind for the time being. I'd wanted to go get those rockets myself, just so I'd have a chance to see her, but I knew I dared not leave the ranch any more than I absolutely had to. I watched Hays ride away with feelings of regret and envy.

Early that afternoon, I was coming back from one of the calf barns when I was surprised to see Sheriff Ward come riding into the ranch yard. I hollered at him just as he got down and tied off his horse. Even as we shook hands, I could see something was troubling him. I wondered if Flood had gone in and sworn out a complaint against me for the raid we'd pulled on him. But that hardly seemed likely. A man engaged in an illegal activity seldom complains about being treated in a like manner. Besides, I'd given Flood fair warning in front of Sheriff Ward.

But that wasn't it. Vic said, unhappily, "Justa, I'm looking for Lew Vara."

"He's not here." I started to say I'd sent him to San Antonio, but something about the look on Vic's face stopped me.

"When will he be back?" Vic asked.

"I don't rightly know," I said. "Vic, what's this all about?"

He looked distressed. "Justa, I've got papers on Lew. He's wanted up in north Texas. Waxahachie."

Well, it didn't surprise me overly much. "What for?" I asked.

He looked down at the ground. "Murder."

"Murder!" That didn't much sound like Lew, and I said so. "He might have killed a man in a fair fight, but he ain't the kind to do murder. You sure you got the right man, Vic?"

He was looking more and more unhappy. "I'm afraid so, Justa. I've had the papers for about two months. I never connected it to Lew until that morning we rode out to the

Mexican herd. Then I got to studying Lew and thinking about that description, and it fits to a T. I'm afraid he's the man. You know he's always been a hardcase."

"Hardcase, yes," I said with a little heat, "but a murderer, no."

"Justa, I ain't enjoying this, believe me. I know his folks. I know him. But I got to do my job. I've got to bring him in and notify the authorities in Ellis County that I'm holding him."

"Well, he ain't here," I said roughly. I waved my hand toward the range. "He's out riding picket. I don't know when he'll be back in. You're welcome to go look for him."

He said sadly, "Justa, they ain't no use trying to conceal him. I'll get him sooner or later."

"Then make it later," I said. "Right now I need him. I need him bad. You know how outgunned I am. Lew is one of the few men I've got I can depend on. You may want him, but I need him."

"Justa, I dreaded coming out here."

"Then go on back. Look, I'll make you a deal. Leave him alone until this trouble is over and I'll convince him I'll get him the best lawyer money can buy and get him to surrender himself. Because I don't believe Lew Vara ever done murder."

He studied me for a moment. Then he sighed. "All right, I'll go on back into town. And I'll wait seven days before I come out again. But when I come, I'm coming to take him back with me."

"That ain't a lot of time, Vic. It might not be over in seven days. I scattered Flood's cattle yesterday."

"Yeah," he said, "I heard about that. Osgood and Smalley were in my office this morning at first light. Seems Flood sent word to them that they'd pay if you pulled that stunt again. Not that I blame you. Which is what I told them."

It stunned me. "Why them chicken-livered sonsofbitches! Instead of standing with their neighbors, they go to the law to complain."

"They're scared, Justa," said Vic. "They think they're caught between you and Flood. They don't know what to do."

"Not but one thing to do: fight. But by the time they realize that, it will be too late. Well, if they think I'm going to back off of Mr. Flood for their sakes, they got another thing coming. I'm expecting Mr. Flood to pay me back any night now. Or at least try. Now, what about Lew? How about a little more time?"

He hesitated, thinking. Then he said, slowly, "I'll put my mind to thinking about something else. I'll study that paper and maybe begin to get some doubts. I know you're in a bind right now, and I don't want to throw nothing else on you to make it worse."

"I appreciate it, Vic," I said. "Now, come in the house and have a drink or some coffee and pie before you start back."

"Buttercup's coffee?"

It brought a smile to my face, but it brought an even bigger one to his when I told him about Buttercup's temporary retirement and why. I ended by saying, "And for God's sake, act like you already know every detail or he'll insist on telling the story again and again, from beginning to end."

But I wasn't smiling later that evening when Tom Brown rode in. He got off his horse and came stomping up to the house with fury on his face. I saw him ride up from the window of my office, and I met him at the door. "Tom, howdy. Come in and make yourself at home."

He said, spitting the words out, "No thank you, Justa Williams. I just come to tell you I been a good neighbor to you for nearly eight years and I damn sure don't appreciate what you just done to me."

It stunned me, so I didn't have speech for a second. When I finally recovered, I said, "I don't know what in the hell you are talking about. Exactly what have I done to you?"

"Don't come the dumb act with me, you bastard!"

I let it pass. He was overwrought and he didn't stand a chance against me with either gun or fist. "If anybody is coming the dumb act it's you," I said. "I can't read your mind. Now, you want to simmer down and tell me what's got in your craw?"

"You know damn good and well what's in my craw. I had a visit from several of that fellow Flood's men, one of them that

Clarence Wooley. They made threats about reprisals against me for that stunt you pulled yesterday. Said if you done anything like that again, they'd start shooting my cattle."

I said, dryly, "Well Tom, they're going to kill them anyway, one way or the other. Might as well be by shooting. At least that way you can beef them out."

"Now you listen here, Williams," he said, and he commenced shaking his finger under my nose. "You sit up here high and mighty on your big spread and you don't think about any of the rest of us. Well, I want to tell—"

I cut him off. "Oh, shut up, Tom. I already know about this business. Smalley and Osgood went into the sheriff this morning. I've already talked to him. They didn't go in to complain about Flood, they went in to complain about me. Me, protecting my property. Well, I expected that of them, but I didn't expect it of you. Now, I told you men all along that I intended to fight, and fight is exactly what I'll do."

He said, "I took notice you didn't do it on your range— fight, that is."

"No, nor on yours nor Smalley's nor Osgood's. Now look, Flood is not going to shoot your cattle. He starts that, it goes out of the range jurisdiction and comes under local law, and the sheriff will arrest his ass."

"Vic Ward? That ain't even funny."

"Yes, Vic Ward," I said calmly. "With our help. He can't do it single-handedly, but he could if we all got behind him. But whether Wooley and Flood scare you or not, I'm going to stop that herd. One way or the other. Be it on your range or Smalley's or whoever's. It ain't coming through here. Now, you can crawl in a hole and watch everything you've built up go straight to hell, or you can try to help. It's up to you. But don't come whining to me. Hell, Tom, can't you see what the man's trying to do? He's trying to set us at one another. I've got him worried, and he's striking back. This time at you three and next at me. Don't be sap enough to fall for his bullshit."

He was starting to cool down. He stared at me for a long time and then he heaved a sigh. "I reckon you're right," he said. "I reckon I'm just scared."

"So am I," I said. "We got a right to be."

"Well, what are we going to do?"

"I don't know." I held the door wide. "Right now, why don't you come on in and have a drink and let's talk things over. I'd like you to stick around until this evening. I've sent a man into town for some things, and I'd like you to wait here until he gets back."

Amazingly enough, Hays made it back in good time, arriving a good two hours before dark. He came into the house with his package, acting as if he'd done something good because he'd followed orders. I just took the package and told him to put his horse away and see what Harley had for him to do.

He gave me an unbelieving look, as if to say "I just nearly kilt myself and a good horse going hell-for-leather and now you want me to work out the rest of the day?" But he said, "When did I start workin' for Harley? I was under the distinct impression I worked for Ben."

"All right, Ben, then," I said with irritation. "Just go find something to do. And where did you learn to say 'distinct impression'? You been hanging around Norris again?"

"Huh!" was all he would say as he stalked out of the room. Oh, Hays was a great hand for stalking. "It's still too early for no celebration," he said.

I unwrapped the package. There were about twenty long strings of firecrackers and thirty rockets. The rockets were big suckers with a head on them about the size of a big banana. Maybe bigger. Tom Brown whistled. "What the hell are those for?" he asked.

I handed him three of the rockets. "You know how to make these work?"

"I reckon," he said. "Fired off enough of 'em when I was younger. An' then later for the kids."

"Set these up where you can get at them," I said. "If you get trouble, fire a couple off. You're only five miles away, and these suckers will go about half a mile in the air. We're going to be keeping a night watch for reasons of our own. We'll see your rockets and come to help. But be sure and fire two.

Otherwise it might get confused with the signals from my own men."

He asked me what I meant, and I explained. "I expect to get raided in retaliation for that stunt I pulled on Flood. I figure he's been busy thus far getting his herd back together and licking his wounds, but he'll send a night party—you can bet on it. I've studied on a way to get some early warning, and I've hit on this plan. I'm going to station a couple of men about two miles south of you in that big buffalo wallow. Any raiding party will have to go right by there. When the party is good and past, I'm going to have my men fire off signal rockets at about five-minute intervals. Maybe three or four of them. That ought to give us at least an hour's warning. With that much time, we ought to be more than ready for them."

Tom looked impressed. "That's a hell of an idea, Justa. What made you think of that?"

"I remembered reading somewhere that that's how they used to communicate sometimes during the Civil War, when there wasn't no telegraph handy and they needed to pass on word faster than a post rider could."

"But won't the raiders see the rockets?" he asked.

"They might," I said. "If they're looking behind them. But I don't think they'll understand. Or care."

"Yeah, but what if they're not coming for you, or to burn you out? What if they're coming to shoot your cattle?"

"Won't do them any good. We've been moving cattle down to the coast for the last five or six days. My foreman has got the south range swept nearly clean. Most of our cattle still on this range are north of here. And to get at them, they'll have to go right by the ranch house. And that ain't going to be real healthy."

He got up looking bemused. "Justa, maybe I ain't been thinking so good. Maybe Flood can be fought." He looked down at the floor. "Maybe I spooked a little soon."

"It ain't too late, Tom," I said.

He said, "What can I do?"

I handed him four strings of the firecrackers, each one about two foot long, and then told him what he could do, if and when the opportunity presented itself.

He smiled. "I'm gonna have another talk with those hands of mine. Maybe I can put a little backbone in them."

After he'd left, I carried the rockets outside and hollered up Harley. When he showed up, I told him to rout out the two hands who'd be standing watch in the buffalo wallow. "That would be Boyd and Charlie," he said.

They came out of the bunkhouse, yawning and rubbing the sleep out of their eyes. It was only about an hour to dusk, so they were going to have to hurry.

Harley brought them up to where I was standing in the middle of the yard. "Now, you men pay close attention here," I said. "The safety of this ranch could depend on how well you do your job. You understand?"

"Yessir," they said.

I showed them the rockets. "Know what these are?"

Boyd, who was a little man in his midthirties with big ears and a cautious look on his face, said, "Yessir, them is explosives."

"No, they're not," I said. "They're skyrockets. We're going to use them for a warning signal." I then explained about my fears that the Mexican-herd bunch would try to raid us, perhaps as early as that night. "If they come," I said, "there ought to be a good number of them—maybe six, seven, ten, maybe more. But they have to come right by you. You let them get about a mile on down the road, and then you light off one of these rockets. Wait awhile, about five minutes, and then light off another one."

"What if they see us?"

"They ain't going to see you. But if they do, get on your horses and ride like hell. You know the country and they don't."

They were both still looking uneasy. I thought it was out of fear of the raiders, but that wasn't the case. It was the rockets. When I started to hand over a bundle to Charlie, he sort of backed away. "Look here," I said, "what's the matter with you?"

"Boss, them things is likely to 'splode."

"Oh, bullshit!" I said. "Little kids fire these things off. Quit acting silly."

He looked over at Boyd and kind of worked his long neck around. He was a young stringbean of a cowboy who wasn't afraid of a bad bull or a mean bronc, but these little powder-packed red rockets were scaring him to death. I said, in some disgust, "All right, I'll show you."

I sent to the barn for a crowbar. With that I made a hole in the ground and stuck the wooden stick of the rocket down in that. Then I lit the fuse with a match. As the fuse burned up toward the business part of the rocket, the two cowboys, and even Harley, began to shrink backward. Then it caught and took off with a loud WHOOSH! All three men jumped. Then, when they realized they hadn't been killed, they tilted their heads back and watched the rocket flying straight up in the sky, trailing a spiral of smoke. Finally it reached its apex, and there was a little puff of smoke and sound and then it was no more. I estimated it had gone at least half a mile high. It would be easy to see from six or seven miles away. I looked around, half expecting to see Boyd and Charlie gone. But they were standing there transfixed, still staring up at the sky.

"Goolleeee!" cried Charlie. "Did you see that thang?"

Boyd said, "It lit out of here like its ass was on far."

"See?" I said. "They can't hurt you. You just light the fuse and step back. But be sure and make your hole where the rocket points straight up."

"Golly!" said Charlie. "This gonna be fun. Kin we do another'n right now?"

"No," I said. I handed Boyd four rockets. "Now, you boys had better get going. You got matches?"

"Aw, yeah," Charlie said. "I chew, but Boyd smokes. He's got a pocketful."

"No smoking," I said. "Understand? No smoking. No fires, no lights of any kind until that raiding party is past you. You make a light, and you'll have that whole bunch in your lap. You understand that?"

They said they did, and I gave them the crowbar and sent

them on their way. Watching them ride off, I said to Harley, "I'm going to have to get to know some of our hands better. Where are you getting people like that?"

Harley spit. "Hell, that's a couple of the smarter ones."

"Oh, shit!" I turned around and walked into the house.

At supper that night, I explained what I was doing to Norris and Ben. Dad wasn't feeling well and was taking his dinner in his room. My brothers liked the idea. "But it's going to mean someone on this end staying up to watch," I said. "Harley says I'm stretching him thin on his cattle moving and he can't spare any more men, so I reckon it's got to be us. Ben, you take the first shift from eight until midnight. I'll take it from there to four, and Norris can finish it out."

Naturally, Norris protested. "Hell, it's light by six-thirty, seven o'clock. That's not a fair share."

"All right," I said wearily. "Back it all up an hour. I'll pick it up at eleven and take it until three. *Then* you can have it, Norris. You happy now?"

"It's more equitable," he said.

"So is this meal," Ben said. "Whatever that means."

"I agree," I said. "Maybe we can get Buttercup to shoot every day and keep him sore."

Norris cornered me in the study just like I knew he would. "Now what's all this about holding me out of this fight?" he asked.

I sat down and poured myself out a drink of whiskey. "Just what I said."

He sat down across from me. "Justa, you ain't doing this to me."

"I'm not doing anything to you, Norris. We have been over this in the past and the reasons haven't changed. You are too valuable to this ranch and this family to risk you in a gunfight. You are the only one who knows how about seventy-five percent of our business works."

"No, what you're saying is that I'm not any good in a gunfight."

I looked at him for a long moment, not quite sure how I

wanted to put it. Finally I admitted, "Well, you're not the best I've ever seen."

"I'm better than most of those hands out there," he said stubbornly.

"Yes, but they can't keep books or do banking. Let me say that you are not a good enough gunfighter to risk your other skills. Does that make sense to you, or do I need to put it another way?"

He said, with some heat, "I'm getting tired of you babying me."

It was the same old argument and the one I'd been dreading. Well, I wasn't going to discuss it further. "Norris," I said, "when they get to the front door you can take gun in hand. Until that time you are going to stay out of it. Now, that's final and we'll say no more about it."

"You mean *you'll* say no more about it. You're getting just a little too arbitrary for my tastes."

I didn't answer him. I just picked up a book and began leafing through it. I wasn't even sure which book it was. But holding the book made me think of school, and school made me think of Nora. I suddenly had a powerful hankering to see her. I wondered if I could dare risk a quick ride into Blessing. But then I dismissed the thought. It was coming on for seven o'clock, and even though I didn't expect Flood's raiders so soon, they still might come that very night.

Ben came in and asked where I thought he ought to take up his station. "Why don't you get up in the door of the hayloft of that south barn," I suggested. "Nothing in between. Ought to be as good a place as any, unless you got on the roof."

"I may do that." He went out.

Norris was still sitting, still staring at me intently. "Are you going to change your mind?" he asked.

"No." I didn't even bother to look up.

"All right." He stood up. "I'm going to talk to Dad."

"You leave Dad alone," I said sharply. "He's not feeling well. Dammit, Norris, grow up. I thought Ben was supposed to be the baby of this family. But sometimes you act like it."

"Aw, the hell with you!" he said disgustedly. He walked out of the room.

I tell you, sometimes I felt like I was the ringmaster at some kind of circus. If it wasn't one thing, it was another. I couldn't get but few people in the county to join me in a gunfight, and yet here was my bookish brother pouting because I wouldn't let him get himself killed. It was enough to drive a man to strong drink.

Which I did.

A little after eight, I went in and laid down, bothering only to take my boots off and loosen my belt. I figured we were in for several long nights, and a man was going to need all the rest he could get.

I didn't figure to go to sleep, but I must have, because the next thing I knew Ben was shaking me. "Justa," he said. "Justa."

I came straight awake and sat bolt upright. "Is it the signal?"

"No," he said. "It's eleven o'clock. Little after."

"Oh." I swung around on the bed and set my feet on the floor, yawning and rubbing my eyes.

"Justa, you better get out there. Ain't nobody watching right now. That signal could come while we're both in the house."

"You're right." I hurried into my boots, strapped on my gun belt, and then hurried out of the house. As I went through the door, I glanced anxiously toward the night sky. It was clear and a velvet blue, with the only lights showing being the tiny twinkle of the stars.

I made my way to the south barn, entered, climbed to the loft, and installed myself in the door, propping my legs up comfortably. Too late I realized I'd forgotten my pocket watch, but I wasn't much bothered. I could generally tell, just by the position of the stars, what time it was within fifteen minutes. Years of night herding had taught me that.

I just sat there, keeping a watch on the southern sky and waiting. After a time I got out a cigarillo and lit up. I was wishing I'd thought to have brought along a bottle to have a little nip off of every once in a while. There is nothing more monotonous than standing watch. But this was one time it had to be done.

I let my mind stray from one subject to another; from Nora to wondering how Lew Vara was doing on his recruiting trip to San Antonio and what kind of men he might show back up with.

On that subject it suddenly struck me he'd be arriving in Blessing with three or four men and only his own horse. Well, likely he'd have sense enough to rent a buckboard to bring them back out to the ranch. Then it struck me he'd be getting in at night and the livery would be closed. It appeared that I was going to have to send a man in to stand by and wait, since I couldn't be sure which night Lew would be getting in.

Another man. And us stretched as thin as a piano wire already. Maybe, I thought, I could send Buttercup in. Surely his shoulder wouldn't be too sore to drive a buckboard. He'd say it was if he didn't want to go, but I'd find some threat to convince him he should.

But there was still the matter of Sheriff Ward. If he saw Lew in town, he'd be honor-bound to arrest him. Yes, I decided, I'd have to send a man in to meet the train and hustle all of them out of town.

God, if Flood would just give us another night after this one. If he hit the next night, I wasn't going to be ready.

I was thinking like that when I heard the stairs behind me creak. I whirled, drawing my gun as I did. Then I reholstered it. It was a very angry Norris.

"Some more of your babying?" he said.

"Now what are you talking about? And what are you doing here?"

"It's four o'clock. Now ain't I even good enough to stand guard?"

"Oh hell, Norris," I said. "I didn't bring my pocket watch and I got to thinking and the time just passed. I wasn't trying to slight you."

"Of course not," he said bitterly. "It just happened that way."

"Yes, it did," I said. "Whether you choose to believe it or

not." I stood up and stretched. I was stiff from staying in one position so long. I was also amazed how the time had flown by. I knew Norris wasn't going to believe me, but I'd gotten so deep in all the problems I had to deal with that I'd plumb forgot to keep watch on the stars.

Norris said, taking my place in the door, "Well, this is just another example of your high regard for me."

"Oh, go to hell, Norris. I've explained what happened."

"Sure."

Imagine a man being hurt because he didn't get called for watch duty. Well, that was Norris for you. He didn't just want to be the business brains of the outfit, he wanted to be as tough and hard as Ben and I. Which was funny, because I envied him what he had, but I had the good sense to know I couldn't have it.

I went back to the house and went instantly to sleep.

Nothing much happened the next day. Charlie and Boyd surprised me by not forgetting to bring their rockets back. They didn't seem quite as frightened of the fireworks, handling them almost casually. They said nothing had happened, that they hadn't seen anything except some curious cattle of either Tom Brown or Osgood. They looked sleepy enough that I figured they hadn't laid down on the job. I told them to get some breakfast and then get some sleep, that they were going back on duty that night and that they'd need to be especially alert.

After that I called Harley to me and we took a walk around the ranch, discussing the defensive positions I'd want the hired hands to go to if there was an alarm.

There was no pattern to our ranch. It had just sort of grown like topsy. Contrary to the way most places were set up, our outbuildings were not behind the house but more out in front and to the sides, like wings.

As Harley and I walked, I pointed out where I wanted men placed: three in the south barn, perhaps on the roof for a better firing angle, two in the calving barn; two in the tack and harness room; and so on. We had one defensive feature that I particularly liked. This was a big, branding, horsebreaking, general-purpose corral that was set out some fifty yards in front of the other buildings and more or less on the south side. If raiders came from the south, it would be the first defense they contacted. The corral was about fifty yards long and about thirty wide. But what was good about it was that it was constructed of big, heavy planks, set close together so that a calf couldn't get its head in between and get caught. And the fence was about five feet high. No horse was going to jump that and put a raider in our midst. I said, "I'm going to station myself here, along with Lew Vara and whatever men he can bring back."

"If he comes back," Harley said. "And I ain't sure I hope he does."

I looked at him. It was an amazing thing for the soft-spoken Harley to say. "What?" I asked.

He looked away. "Nuthin'."

"Harley. Tell me."

He scuffled the ground with his boot toe. "Well, Justa, he ain't a good'n. That's all I want to say."

"Has he caused trouble in the bunkhouse?"

"Well, no. Not prezactly."

"What does that mean?"

"Well, the other boys are a little afraid of him. Mind you, he ain't done nothin'. It's just . . . Well, it's just you get the feelin' he might."

I laughed. "Harley, that ain't like you. That's old woman's talk. He might do something. Now that's downright silly."

"I was jus' sayin'," Harley said. "It kind of popped out of my mouth."

"Well, pop it back in."

We finished our tour. I told Harley I was going to have Ben anchor the south flank from the loft window of the south barn. "In case they try to get around us that way." Then I said I planned to have Hays and two men hold the first of the north running barns. "They might try to go around that way, so I want you to ask Ben who the best men you've got with a gun are and put them with Hays. And I want you and the rest of the men to take up your positions inside the house in case they get through us. And use Buttercup. Don't discount that old man.

But for God's sake, make sure he doesn't get one of us confused with the enemy. I don't want one of those cannonballs of his up my ass."

"Well, we've got the southern range nearly clear," Harley said. "I'm only sending out two men today to catch what stragglers we might have missed. Give me one more day and I ought to have the biggest part of the cattle up north back toward the coast. I hope you realize, Justa, that this is costin' us a good deal of trouble and they's a bunch of work ain't gettin' done that ought to get done on account of it."

"I know," I said wearily. Harley was a first-class foreman, but he did like to cover his tracks. I said, "I thought we already had this conversation, Harley."

"Just wanted to make it clear."

I had done everything I could think to do. Now it was mainly a question of waiting, and I wandered around restlessly, trying vainly to occupy my mind with other matters.

About two in the afternoon, I got a little excitement when I told Buttercup he was going to have to drive the buckboard in and meet the six o'clock train from San Antonio. He reared back like I'd slapped him and said, "Wahl, if thet don't beat all! You'd take the hero of the Mexican ambush an' make a delivery boy outen him?"

"Oh, damn, Buttercup, that ain't the point at all. It's just that there's nobody else. I've got every spare hand out moving cattle, and I can't go and neither can Ben or Norris."

"An' me hurt," he said. He shook his head. "Ain't a drap of thanks left in this world. I liked to have taken the shoulder offen myself, and this is the thanks I get."

I said, calculatingly, "Well, if you can't, you can't. I just didn't know you was so puny. Little rifle shooting get you down that much."

"Puny!" He started sputtering. "You young whippersnapper, you half the man I am when you git my age you can damn well be proud. Puny! Why . . . why . . ."

"I'll get somebody else," I said. "Though it will short the ranch."

"Never you damn mind!" he said. He got up from the table

where he'd been sitting, drinking coffee. He went stumping toward the door, favoring his bad hip. Or what he said was his bad hip. "I'll just hitch up."

He was about halfway out the door when I called after him, "You still remember how?"

That stirred him up. He showered me with a pretty good assortment of cusswords. I let him run down and then said, "But you be careful. They don't call it a buckboard for nothing. And you know how you and bucking get along. You try and stay aboard."

That brought on another stream, but I had quietly left the kitchen with him standing outside, cussing me through the door.

Before he could leave, I caught him coming out of the barn leading his team, and I told him the situation, carefully leaving out the part about the sheriff looking for Lew Vara. I just said, "Now Buttercup, they might not get in tonight. If they don't, you've got to lay over and meet the train tomorrow night. But whatever you do, don't do any talking about what's going on. Just have a few beers and keep your mouth shut."

He gave me a severe look. "Listen, you young whelp, I been tortured by wild, savage Comanches and never opened my yap. You reckon I was born yestiday?"

"Well, whenever you was born—and I privately think it was about a hundred years ago—you just collect Lew and whoever he's got with him and hightail it straight back to the ranch. Tell them I said there was a reason to hurry. Now, can you handle that, Buttercup?"

"One thang we is gonna discuss when I gets back," he said. "An' that is this here 'Buttercup' bid'ness."

"On your way or I'll make you start eating your own cooking," I threatened.

Then there really wasn't anything left to do. Ben and Hays were out moving the *remuda* closer to the coast, and Dad was still in his room. His rheumatism was acting up pretty badly. Norris was in the office, going over some books. I looked in on him, but the cold reception I got convinced me to leave before I got froze out.

It wore on toward late afternoon. The day was only middling hot, but I didn't like the look of some thunderclouds that were building up to the southwest. I was standing out in the ranch yard, looking in that direction, when I saw a funny-looking little thread of white arching up across the sky. If it hadn't been for the dark background of the thunderclouds, I would have never noticed it, because it wouldn't have been visible against the light sky. I stood there, watching, wondering; then I saw another streak of thin white smoke rising. It suddenly hit me: It was the rockets I'd given Tom Brown. Either he was in trouble or we were. Either way, I had to have some help. I went racing into the house, yelling for Norris. He got up from his desk, a startled look on his face. "What is it?"

"We got trouble," I said. "Hays and Ben are about half a mile toward the coast, working horses. Ride like hell and get them. We ain't got a minute."

Then I raced outside and ran over to the bunkhouse and woke Boyd and Charlie. "Get your rifles and saddle your horses and get over to the branding corral," I told them. "Where is Harley?"

Boyd was rubbing his face with one hand and pulling on his boots with the other. "Reckon just up north of here," he said. "Some of the boys said thet's whar they'd be workin' today."

I went out of the bunkhouse at a fast walk. I had my horse loose-cinched in front of the house. I pulled the cinch up tight, swung aboard, and then wheeled and spurred him toward the north range as fast as he could run.

It was luck that Harley had just turned back toward the ranch headquarters to check on any stray they might have missed. He had two men with him. I pulled up short and yelled for them to come on. They put spurs to their horses and came at a run. I stayed at a lope until they caught me, and then I clapped on the spurs and we fairly flew over the low ground, heading for the ranch. As we rode in, I tried hurriedly to tell Harley what I thought was happening. "Get ammunition and rifles and get to the branding corral. We're going to fort up there. Spread the men around. I've got to get my brothers."

I rode around the ranch house and headed for the coast.

Within half a mile, I saw Hays and Ben and Norris coming fast.
I waved an arm at them and then turned back for the ranch.

At the house, I tied my horse off and ran inside and got my
rifle and all the ammunition I could find. Just as I was coming
out of my room, Dad came shuffling out into the hall. "What's
the commotion, Justa?"

As much of a hurry as I was in, I couldn't tell him much, just
what I had surmised. "Didn't you give those rockets to Tom for
him to warn you if he got raided?" he asked.

"More or less," I said. "Or to let me know if he saw trouble
heading our way."

"Well, reckon I better get my rifle loaded."

"You better load yourself back in that bed," I said. "Now
Dad, don't give me no trouble. You stay in this house. I ain't
got time to worry about you."

He coughed a wracking cough that made me wince and said,
"You be careful, Son."

As I went outside, Ben and Norris and Hays were just riding
up. I explained quickly what had happened. "I don't reckon
we've got much time," I said. "We'll take a stand in the
branding corral. Everybody get their rifle and plenty of
ammunition."

"Shall I bring my books?" asked Norris sarcastically. "Or
don't I get to come at all?"

I was tempted to tell him to stay in the house and look after
Dad, but I needed every gun I could get. I just swung aboard
my horse, not bothering to answer him.

Once in the corral I got my men spread out, putting myself
at the most southerly end, Ben in the middle, Hays at the far
side, and spreading the rest out in between. Counting Norris
and Harley, who was no great shakes with a gun himself, we
were nine. I didn't know how many raiders might be on the
way, but I figured we ought to be able to give them a pretty
warm time of it from such a fortified position. One of the good
points about the corral was that it also afforded us an open field
of fire back toward the house, in case any raiders went for it.
It was a scant eighty or ninety yards away.

I alternated between cursing myself for being so certain the
marauders would come at night and congratulating myself for

having given Tom the rockets. And thanking my lucky stars for the thundercloud that had allowed me to see them.

Time passed. I stared over the weathered top plank of the corral, my eyes roving over the grassy prairie. It was blank of any moving object. Of course, we had cleared it of cattle and horses, and we should have been able to see anything coming our way from a long way off.

Nothing did. The prairie stayed as still and empty as a barren field. The only motion was the heat waves rising.

I looked at the sun. It was lowering in the sky. There was perhaps two hours of light left. And at least an hour had passed since I'd seen the rockets. A sinking sense of foreboding was coming over me. I waited fifteen minutes more and then said, "Ben, you and Hays mount up. We're going down to Tom Brown's. Harley, Norris, the rest of you, stay where you are until we get back."

As we rode away Ben asked, "What the hell?"

"I'm afraid Tom was signaling he was under attack," I said. "It's been better than an hour. If they were heading our way they'd have been here by now."

As we rode, I thought of Tom signaling and me not answering. But it had stuck so certain in my mind that they'd decided to hit during working hours, when all the hands would be out working cattle, that I hadn't given much thought to anything else. Besides, it made no sense for them to jump on Tom. He hadn't done anything.

"I hope I haven't let a friend down," I said uneasily.

"At best it had to be a guess, Justa," said Ben. "Don't go to blaming yourself. Tom ain't exactly been a pillar of strength so far."

"He was coming around," I said grimly.

"Boss, reckon it's all right to be leaving the ranch?" asked Hays. "We be the only real gun hands."

I gave him a look. Depend on Hays to find an opportunity to pat himself on the back in any situation. "If they're heading our way, we'll run into them and we can turn back."

It wasn't long before we began to see cattle—spooked cattle—wearing Tom's brand. You could tell they'd been scared by something the way they were running around, wringing their tails and not bothering to graze.

"Something has got into these cattle," said Ben.

"Yes," I said, "and I reckon I can guess what."

A few minutes' ride on further and we spotted Tom Brown and one of his hands. They were just sitting their horses, staring. As we neared, I could see what they were staring at. The prairie was littered with his cattle. Twenty, thirty head; I couldn't be sure how many. We came riding up alongside. Tom barely turned his head. There was no use asking what happened; it was plain to see. "How many jumped you, Tom?" I asked.

He shook his head bleakly. "I don't know. They were all over the place. Could have been eight, could have been ten. Could have been more."

"How many cattle you figure you lost?"

He shook his head again. "I don't know. We're trying to figure it out now. We were out trying to move them back to the coast like you done, and the next thing those raiders were in amongst us. They just came shooting, dropping everything in sight."

"Tom, I'm sorry as hell," I said. "I would've got here sooner, but I wasn't sure what your rockets meant."

He just looked sad. "It wouldn't have mattered. They were here and gone in a matter of minutes. I went back and shot off the rockets to warn you. I didn't know if they'd be heading your way or not. They hit one of my men. Grover Leeland."

"Bad?"

"A gunshot wound ain't ever good. Got him high in the shoulder. I think it broke the bone. I've sent him into town in the buckboard with Bob Chambers."

"Were you trying to fight, or did they just plug him?"

"I don't know." He sighed. "We got off a few shots, but then I seen it was pointless and yelled for everybody to ride for the ranch. That's when Grover got hit."

I looked around at the dead cattle. "Damn!" I said. "That sonofabitch."

"Yeah," Tom said.

I looked at him. All the fight had gone out of him. All he could do was stare at his dead cattle. "What I don't understand, Tom, is you was going to go along with Smalley and Osgood. . . . Why would they take after you?"

"There was a man here last night," he said dully. "Not that Wooley. He said they'd be here in two days and they didn't want any trouble. I told him they'd better not come through my herd."

Ben whistled softly. "Yeah, that would do it," he said.

"Did they hit Smalley or Osgood?"

"I don't know," said Tom. "I didn't hear any shots."

"Two days," I said. "That means they're about fifteen to twenty miles south of here."

Tom looked at me. "I'd watch out now, Justa. These people ain't even civilized. Shooting a man's cattle . . ."

There wasn't any point in discussing what had just happened. "Tom," I said, "it's a local-law matter now. You better get word to Vic Ward."

"I have," he said. "Bob Chambers is going to take him word when he gets Grover to the doctor." He leaned out of the saddle slightly and spit on the ground. "Not that I reckon it's going to do much good. Flood will just deny any of his men had anything to do with it. Where's the proof?"

"That's a point," I said. I looked around again and just shook my head. "Tom, when all this mess gets straightened out, maybe we can help you get back on your feet." I figured at, say fifty dollars a head, that he'd lost at least twenty-five hundred dollars. That was a grievous loss for a rancher his size.

"Well, much obliged, Justa. But I should have stood in with you from the first. Instead of crawfishing."

"Like Smalley and Osgood," said Ben.

Tom looked at him. "He didn't kill their cattle."

"Not yet," Ben said. "And not with bullets. But it will be the same."

"Tom," I said, "you better get busy hazing the rest of your cattle back to the coast. I figure a showdown is coming up pretty quick."

As we rode back, I was pleased to meet Boyd and Charlie on

the way to their station at the buffalo wallow. We stopped and I said, "Be alert tonight, men. You'll see dead cattle on your way, and that's what can happen to us if we don't get early warning."

We rode on to the ranch, and I dismissed the men who were still manning the branding corral.

# CHAPTER
# 6

About eight o'clock that night, Buttercup pulled in with his passengers. I was sitting out on the porch smoking, when I saw them turn in at the ranch gate. I got up and sauntered out into the yard, signaling for Buttercup to come to me. As they neared, I could see that there were four men in the back of the buckboard. That meant that Lew had been able to scare up three extra hands.

Buttercup pulled up in front of me. He looked and sounded cranky as hell. Or as cranky as Buttercup. "Wahl, I done it. An' I hope you is satisfied. Dern ride damn near kilt me. I'm down in the back, my arms is near wore off fightin' these iron-mouthed brutes an'—"

"Thanks for doing your job," I said. "Now put the team up and go to bed."

The four men were climbing down from the back, bringing what little gear they had with them. "I done the best I could, Justa," Lew said. "But I didn't have a whole hell of a lot of time."

"I'm sure you done fine, Lew. I appreciate it."

He gestured as the three men came up. "This is Bob Casey,

Arnie Welch, and Joe Thibbedoux. They're from all over. They already know your name."

I shook hands with each one and welcomed him to the ranch. "In a minute I'm going to send you into the cookhouse to get something to eat," I said. "I imagine a meal wouldn't go amiss right now. But first I want to fill you in about what we're up against."

"I already told them, Justa," said Lew. "By the way, you're paying them two hundred a man."

The one named Bob Casey, a tall, well-set-up man with a knife scar on his cheek, said, "Them's pretty poor wages for our line of work. How long is this supposed to last?"

Well, I wasn't exactly taken with his attitude, but I really hadn't expected much different. I said evenly, "A lot of that question will depend on how good you are. But it should be over in three or four days. I can't see it going any longer."

Casey, who they seemed to have elected as their spokesman, said, "We gen'lly git half in advance."

I nodded. "That's reasonable enough, though I don't know where you're going to spend it around here. I'll get you your money while you're eating. Lew, take them to the bunkhouse and I'll go stir the cooks up. They can eat in the house cookshed tonight. Just bring them back here after they stow their gear and get settled in."

They left, and I went into the house and to the safe. We didn't keep a great deal of money at the ranch—just a matter of a couple of thousand dollars. Times had progressed, and most of your bigger transactions were done by bank draft. But the hands still liked to be paid in cash and there were other piddling outlays, so we did try and keep some cash money on hand.

I opened the safe and got out three hundred dollars, mostly in fives and tens. I separated it into three stacks and then went into the kitchen and told the two Mexican women to fix up a big batch of steak and eggs and coffee for four men. Then I went in and had a drink and stared out the window at the southern sky. Ben was on watch, but my turn would come at eleven. I had to remind myself to take my pocket watch. I couldn't afford to anger Norris further.

I heard the men coming into the kitchen, the sound of boots on the wooden floor, the sound of chairs being pulled back. I went in. They were all sitting around the big table. I put a hundred dollars in front of each man and said, "You're on duty twenty-four hours a day. You don't get out of the sound of my voice. We could, for instance, have visitors within the next twenty-four hours. Maybe within the next hour. So sleep with your guns handy." I said to the one named Joe Thibbedoux— who I figured must be from Louisiana, judging from his name—"I see you didn't bring a rifle with you. I'll see you get one, along with some ammunition."

He shook his head. "Don't need one."

"There could be some long-distance shooting," I told him.

"Sounds damn good to me," he said. He put his hand down and came up with the longest-barreled six-shooter I'd ever seen. The damn barrel must have been a foot long.

"Suit yourself," I said. "Long as you get the job done."

"Ah'll git the job done," he said. "You jest look out fer the money."

They didn't look any better in the light. If anything, they looked considerably worse. Wasn't a one of them looked as if he'd had a bath in a month—or wanted one. And their clothes looked like they'd been sleeping in them. But from what I could see, their weapons reflected the care of their profession. If they'd taken as good a care of themselves as they took of their guns, they'd have been sleek and shining.

"Lew," I said, "your defensive position is going to be the branding corral. And when you get the call, you ain't going to have long to get there. So don't bother to shave."

Casey looked up at me just as one of the Mexican women put a plate in front of him. "I thought," he said, "this was supposed to be some kind of *rancho grande*. Where the hell is all yore cattle?"

"We moved them down to the coast," I said. "Get them out of the way. Give you a clear line of fire."

The one called Arnie Welch said, "What about some whiskey? I ain't had a drink in two days."

I shook my head. "No drinking right now. Not until this is over."

"That ain't lilac water I smell on yore breath," he said.

I looked at him steadily. They all three gave off a calculated air of menace. I'd figured they'd test me sooner or later, and it was best to have it over with. "When you start paying me, you can make the rules," I said. "Until then, I make them. Understand?"

We had a staring contest for a good fifteen seconds, but then he dropped his eyes to his plate and began eating.

"Now, you're hired on Lew Vara's word," I said, "but if I see you can't do the job, I'm going to pay you off in a hurry. And the one thing you better be careful to not do is cause trouble among the regular ranch hands. They're just cowboys. They'll do their job an you do yours, and I'll stay happy."

Casey looked up at me defiantly. "That would be of inter'st to us? How happy you wuz?"

"You'd just be surprised." I turned toward the door. "Lew," I said, "come see me in my office when you're done."

He nodded.

I sat in my office, smoking and debating whether to tell Lew about Sheriff Ward's visit or not. I knew he deserved to know, but I was half afraid he wouldn't believe that Vic would hold off for a week and would break and hightail it. And I needed his gun badly. I was still thinking on it when he came in, patting his stomach and smoking a cigarillo.

"Boy, my stomach was sticking to my backbone," he said. "I don't believe I got a square meal that whole trip."

I nodded my head toward the kitchen. "Where'd you get them three? Out of the drunk tank at the county jail?"

He shrugged and sat down. "I told you it was going to be slim pickings. You didn't give me much time to shop around, Justa, so I grabbed what I could find as quick as I could and caught the train."

"Are they any good?"

"They say they are. And word is, what little time I had to ask, that they are."

"You ever work with any of them?"

He got a guarded look on his face. "I don't know what you mean by 'work with them.'"

"Come on, Lew, let's don't kid each other. Do you know firsthand that any of them are any good?"

He cleared his throat and looked at the glowing end of his cigarillo. "Well, I've been around Bob Casey enough to know that he's good. Plenty good. And I've heard about the Cajun Kid. That's Joe Thibbedoux. Don't know much about Arnie Welch, except the others vouch for him." He looked up at me. "Justa, I wish you wouldn't ask me too much, if you don't mind."

"All right," I said. "Man's entitled to his privacy."

He said, "You understand that these ain't choirboys. I wouldn't be a bit surprised if they didn't have friends on the other side."

"Men like that have friends?"

"After their fashion. But I wouldn't go to turning my back on them."

"I'm going to depend on you to keep an eye on them," I said. "If they start any trouble in the bunkhouse, I want to hear about it pronto. Try and keep them in line yourself. If you can't, come straight to me."

He got up. "All right, Justa. You always played straight with me. I'll do my best for you."

That gave me a twinge because, in point of fact, I wasn't playing straight with him. As we'd talked I'd made the decision to hold off telling him about Sheriff Ward until I saw what Flood was going to get up to. It was another way of saying I didn't trust him not to run out on me. But I said, with ashes in my mouth, "I appreciate that, Lew. I just hope they can shoot better than they look."

He laughed. "They'd have to."

After he was gone, I parked myself in front of the south-facing window and stared at the sky. It was almost nine-thirty, and there didn't seem to be any point in going to bed for just an hour.

So I just sat there, smoking and taking an occasional nip of whiskey and thinking mostly about Nora. She was as good a reason as any for me to want this mess over with in a hurry. One of her biggest complaints against me had been that I could never give her any time, that I was always busy with some crisis on the ranch. Well, it was true. A ranch, any ranch, just seemed to operate from one crisis to another. And ours was no exception.

Still, if we ever got married, she'd at least be on hand for the crises and be able to share them with me. Then maybe she'd understand what ranch life was like. And it wasn't anything like keeping store.

I let my mind wander around, playing with the thought of being married to Nora. Some of the thoughts I had made me get a little thicknecked and get that copper taste in my mouth. Thoughts about solving that juicy mystery between her legs.

Oh, I'd had plenty of women in my life, and a goodly number of them were real ladies. Not in Blessing to speak of, but then I traveled a lot on ranch business to Galveston and Houston and Dallas and Fort Worth, and I'd been received by some good families and even better received by some of the daughters. I'd even managed to plumb the depths of the daughter of a man who'd been trying to kill me when I'd been passing through the hard rock country up around Bandera on my way to San Antonio on a cattle-buying trip. She'd been a red-haired beauty that I'd taken on several occasions in her own private coach. She'd later got shot as a result of my dispute with her father, but that was another matter.

So it wasn't as if I lusted after Nora out of frantic need. It was just that there was something so cool and reserved about her that she set me ablaze every time I got around her. I'd tried every trick on her through our years of courtship that I knew, but nothing had worked. She could stop me with a cool look or an even cooler word. It seemed like I'd make progress on one occasion, only to lose back the ground I'd gained on the next.

But there was no more time for such thinking. It was coming on eleven o'clock. Time to go and relieve Ben.

The first rocket went up around two-thirty. I was just in the midst of a yawn and had my eyes kind of narrowed, but they came wide open quick enough as soon as I saw that bright streak heading straight up in the sky. I swung around in the loft door, all attention, waiting for the next flare. It was an agonizing wait. I didn't know if either Charlie or Boyd had a watch. For that matter, I wasn't sure they could even tell time. I didn't wait for the third. Instead I jumped up and raced across to the stairs and went down them two at a time. I wasn't exactly sure how long we had, because I wasn't sure how long Boyd and Charlie would have waited once the raiders passed. If I was any judge of men, I figured they waited a good long while, long enough to make sure they could get hid in case the marauders saw the flares and came back to find out who'd lit them off.

I hit the ground running. First I went to Harley's little cabin, which was just off the end of the bunkhouse. I pounded on his door until he finally swung it back. "They're coming," I said. "Arouse the bunkhouse and put the men where they're supposed to go. Make sure they understand that they are not to fire until I do. I'll be at the south-corner fencepost in the corral. Tell every man that can to keep his eye on me. Don't let anybody forget their rifle."

Harley stared at me blankly. I guess it was a good deal to take in when you've just been waked up. But he said, "I'll see to it, Justa."

Then I ran for the house. First I pounded on Ben's door, then stepped down the hall and hammered on Norris's. By the time I got back to Ben's, he was awake and had his door open and was in the midst of pulling on his boots. He looked up as I came in. "They here?"

"Boyd and Charlie did their jobs," I said. "I figure they're five miles away. Riding at night, probably saving their horses for the ride back, I figure they're about an hour away. But no more. With this bunch of jugheads we've got to get in place, we ain't got a minute to spare. I want you at the south end of the south barn. If they try and get at the house, they'll come that way."

"Right," he said. He stood up and buckled on his gun belt.

Norris came in then. He'd already dressed and was wearing a gun. "Where do you want me?" he asked.

"Here in this house," I said.

He gave me a look. "I might have known."

It made me angry and I lashed out. "Goddammit, Norris, in some ways you are the biggest baby of all! Always wanting to go out and play guns. Well, this ain't play. Listen, somebody has got to stay here and watch over Dad. If you think that ain't an important job, why just say so and I'll do it. You go out and plan and lead the defense."

He looked down at the floor. "All right," he said. "As long as you put it that way."

"And get Buttercup up and have him in the cook-shack window with that cannon of his," I said. "If they get by us, they are coming straight for the house. You might get to play guns a little more than you care to."

Ben and I grabbed our rifles and a pocketful of ammunition and ran out the door. As we trotted toward the branding corral, I could see shadowy figures flitting back and forth, getting to their stations as Harley directed them. Up on top of the south barn, which had a very gentle slope to its roof, I could see a couple of cowboys, rifles in hand, slowly making their way to the crest.

"I saw the buckboard come in last night," said Ben. "Those new men get here?"

"Yeah."

"They any good?"

"We're about to find out," I said. "God knows they are sleazy enough."

"How many you reckon he's sending?"

"Now how the hell should I know that, Ben? Here, here's the south barn. For God's sake, don't let them get around you, Ben."

"I won't." He branched off at a trot.

I went on to the corral, going through the gate and then closing it behind me. I had six men besides myself. They crowded around as I came through. Bob Casey said, "What the hell's the deal?"

"There's a raiding party on the way," I said.

"How the hell you know that? You got spies?"

I told them briefly about the rockets. It left a few open-mouthed, but Casey asked, "What they coming here for?"

I looked at him. I didn't like the man one little bit, and the feeling was growing. "They're coming to kill cattle. When they find there ain't no cattle to kill, they'll do what devilment they can. Your job is to make sure they don't."

Arnie Welch laughed. "Likely we'll know some of them ol' boys. I hate shootin' friends."

I faced him. "You want out? Give me the money back and take off. Right now."

His face straightened somewhat, and he said, "Oh, I jest said I hated shootin' friends. I didn't say I wouldn't do it."

I shook my head. After that I told them their positions. I put Lew at the north corner—a vulnerable spot that led straight toward the house if they could turn the corner. Of course, they'd still have to ride directly past the bunkhouse, where I had two rifles stationed. And if they got by them, they'd have to face Norris and Buttercup.

I put Bob Casey and Arnie Welch in the middle. I put two of my regular hands down with Lew and kept one beside me at my corner. "Now get this straight," I said. "I don't want any premature firing. Nobody fires until I do. And keep your heads below the top of the corral. Fire through one of the lower openings."

The cowboy beside me, a young man named Slayton, asked, "Do we shoot to kill?" He sounded plenty nervous.

I said, "Well, Slayton, if you can shoot well enough to wing a man in the dark of night, why, you are welcome to try. But I'll tell you this—they are going to be shooting to kill you."

Casey called down, "Hey, you paying a head bounty?"

"Shut up, Casey," I said. "Do your job. And I don't want to hear anymore talk out of anyone. They could be closer than I think."

I heard Casey mumble to Welch, "Sum'bitch thinks he's tough. We may just have to see about that."

But I had other things to worry about besides one of Casey's kind.

We waited. The minutes went by like small crawling bugs. It seemed as if hours were passing. Up and down the line I could hear men growing restless, shifting from one booted foot to another. I heard a whisper from Welch and Casey. I said fiercely, "Sssh! Sound carries on this prairie for miles."

Another period of time went by—how long, I was unable to say. I was beginning to wonder if Boyd and Charlie had gotten their signals crossed or if the raiders had seen the rockets and taken heed and turned back. If they had, Boyd and Charlie were to have fired another rocket after they'd passed in the other direction. I'd seen none.

I even got to playing with the thought that they might have stopped short and hit Tom Brown again, but then I hadn't heard any firing.

Just then I saw them, barely silhouetted against the dark sky. They appeared to be no more than a half mile away. I hissed, and heads turned. I pointed, and men peered between the slats.

I watched them coming on. It was impossible to tell how many; they were just a large dark mass. Then, unaccountably, they pulled up. For a second it had me mystified, and then I saw little pinpricks of light. Then big blossoms of fire. They were lighting torchs. They meant to burn us out.

Now it was easy to tell how many they were. I counted ten torches. I was surprised that Flood would risk so many men, unless he figured we would be that easy. They started up again. Even in the dark, it would be easy shooting. Figuring that most men are right-handed and that they would be carrying the torches in their right hand, all we had to do was shoot just to the right of the torch.

Now they were a quarter of a mile away and coming fast. I planned to let them get within fifty yards and then cut them down with one volley. I slowly eased the hammer of my rifle back and took a sight down the barrel. They were closing in a hurry. I calculated they were no more than two hundred yards away. Well, we were fixing to teach Mr. Wooley and Mr. Flood a fairly painful lesson.

And then it happened. From behind me and above, a shot suddenly rang out. I looked up at the top of the south barn. One of my fool cowhands had fired way too soon. When I switched my head back to the marauders, I could see that the one shot had been enough to alert them. They immediately split ranks and began to scatter. There was no longer any point to silence. I yelled, "FIRE!" and then sighted down my rifle at the first torch I could see. I fired, and nothing happened. I fired again and then again, and finally the torch went down. I didn't know if I'd hit the raider or if he'd just thrown the torch to the ground.

They were throwing a few shots our way, but it was nothing to the hail of bullets we were pouring at them. By now most of them had dropped their torches and we could see them riding back and forth, holding their distance at a couple of hundred yards, firing spasmodically back at us.

I fired and cursed, fired and cursed. I was going to have the balls off whoever it was had fired that early shot. Because of him we'd missed a chance to break Flood's back. If they'd have come on to a reasonable distance, we wouldn't have left him with enough drovers to move a hundred cattle.

The drovers did not last long. They made one half-hearted attempt to get around us to the south, but steady fire from Ben and the men he had with him drove them back. Now that they'd dropped their torches, you couldn't really see if the fire was having any effect, but I was sure I'd seen at least two riderless horses galloping away.

Their fire, as near as I could tell, was having absolutely no effect, not as well forted up as we were. We kept shooting, at nearly anything that moved, and before we knew it, they were there no more. The only sound to be heard was an occasional final gunshot from our side and the sound of their horses' hooves as they galloped south.

"Every man hold his place," I said. "Nobody moves. They could be waiting for us to come out from cover and then double back."

We waited. I'd fired so many shells that the barrel of my gun was too hot to touch. I looked at the sky. There was a faint glow in the sky to the east, but I knew it was a false dawn. Sunrise was still a good hour away.

And I didn't intend to move until then.

After a time I heard Ben calling from his position. "Justa! Justa! What now?"

"Stay put!" I yelled back.

Down the corral line I heard Bob Casey say, "Aw, this is horseshit! Hidin' out like a bunch of schoolgirls. Who the fuck we working for?"

Oh yes, he was going to be a problem that would have to be tended to.

I called out, "Anybody hit?"

There was no answer.

Finally Harley called back: "I'll go around and see, Justa."

"No. Stay where you are."

I had been aware of a slight sound from the prairie, but now as things grew quiet, the sound became more and more distinct. Someone was lying out there groaning. Wounded, most likely.

Hays yelled from his position at the north barn, "Boss! They is somebody hurt out there!"

"I got ears," I said.

"Want me to go out and see?"

"No, I don't want you to go out and see."

"He sounds bad hurt to me."

"Nobody invited him to come calling."

Finally dawn came, and we could see. A light fog had rolled in, but it wasn't much. I stood up and opened the corral gate. I said, "Lew, come with me." Then I raised my voice and called, "Hays, Ben. Come on with me. We're going out." Before I stepped through the gate I told the others, "Ya'll go on to breakfast. It ought to be ready soon."

Arnie Welch said, "I could use a drink."

I ignored him and started out on the prairie, followed by Lew. He said as we walked, "That was some trick with the Fourth of July doodads. Whoever would have thought of that."

"When is Bob Casey going to try me?" I asked him. "He seems to be working his way up to it."

"Aw, I wouldn't put no stock in Casey. He does a lot of mouthing off just to hear himself talk tough."

I said, "Well, I'm getting tired of it. And that kind of insubordination can spread."

Just then Ben and Hays came up. We stopped, as the moaning was just ahead. I drew my gun. "Careful," I said.

"Hell, he's hurt, Justa," said Hays.

"Maybe."

As we walked toward the moans, I saw two more bodies lying on the prairie. I said to Ben, "You and Lew check those two. Hays and I will see to this one."

He was lying on his back, his mouth half open, breathing in short pants. His shoulder was all over blood and his right arm lay limp, lifeless, like it didn't belong to the rest of his body.

He didn't appear to have a gun, and he didn't appear to be in any shape to use one if he'd had it. I knelt down beside him. He was a mean-looking hombre, unshaven, long stringy hair, some scabs on his face from either a fight or a fall. He had a long hooked nose and bad teeth. His eyes fluttered open. "I'm hit," he said.

"No shit," I said sarcastically.

"Where the other'ns?"

"The other'ns," I said, "have left you to die out on this prairie. They hightailed it back to Mr. Food. Tell me, was Clarence Wooley on this raid?"

He licked his lips. "Dunno."

I stood up. "Then I dunno if I can help you."

"Hold up," he said. He breathed for a moment. "Naw, he didn't come."

"Lew," I said, "go back and get a buckboard and tell Harley to set up in the bunkhouse to do a little doctoring."

Harley was our resident physician. In his time he'd worked on just about everything from broken bones to gunshot wounds to horn gorings. I said to the man on the ground, "We're going to fix you up, but just barely. And I don't even know why we're doing that."

Then I went over to Ben and Hays and told Hays to catch up

the loose horses that were running around, stepping on their bridles. "Should be three. Take them to the bunkhouse."

Ben and I walked around, looking over the scene while Hays and Lew were gone. We didn't find any more bodies. I figured as I walked. "We know Buttercup got three," I said. "And I think me and you and Lew got that fourth one on that ambush. And we got three here. That's seven. If we figured right and Flood started with twenty, he's only got thirteen men left."

"Plus Clarence Wooley."

"Plus Wooley," I said. "Not counting Flood, that makes fourteen. The sides are getting evener."

Ben gave me a look. "Yeah, if we can be certain which side those three Lew brought in are on. I've gotten a good look at them. Justa, mark me, we will have trouble with them before it's over."

I sighed. "One thing at a time, Ben. Please."

"All right. I'm just saying."

"This raid should have slowed Flood up some more," I said. "He sent ten men. They can't be back to his herd yet. And I can't see him moving many cattle with just four men. Not that many cattle."

We walked and looked, thinking. I wondered how much more it was going to take to convince Flood we were serious, that he was not going to bring his diseased cattle through our range.

But it was useless speculation. No man can figure what's in another man's mind or what drives him. For all I knew, Flood no longer cared about his investment in his herd; maybe now all he cared about was wreaking vengeance on me.

Lew came with the buckboard, and Ben and I went over and helped him load the wounded man in the back. He groaned with our every movement. "Does that hurt?" I asked him.

"Yeah."

"Good." I shoved him up in the bed of the buckboard a little harder than I meant to. "I guess ya'll brought them torches to give us a house warming, right?"

He just groaned.

Ben and I climbed up on the seat with Lew, and we drove to

the bunkhouse. I could see Hays and another cowboy running down the marauders' loose horses. When we got to the bunkhouse, Harley came out and helped us carry the man in. Some of the cowboys were coming back from breakfast, and I detailed two of them to go back out with Lew and pick up the dead bodies.

"You ain't going to bury them here, are you?" cried Ben. "On our land?"

"I ain't going to bury them at all. Let's go get some breakfast, while Harley does what he can for Jesse James here."

We ate in the house kitchen, served by one of the Mexican women. Fortunately, Buttercup still couldn't cook. But he was seated at the kitchen table, drinking coffee and complaining that he hadn't gotten a single shot. He said, "Couldn't you have let one of them sonsabitches get through? Jest one?"

"Oh, shut up," I said. "You sound worse than Norris. Besides, one more kick of that rifle would have killed you."

"How many you get?"

"Forty," I said.

Ben laughed.

Buttercup gave me the eye. "Aaaw," he said, "I don't believe that. Yo're joshing me."

"All right—thirty."

"That's more like it."

Ben laughed again.

After breakfast, I went to see how Dad was. Norris was in the study, which was on the way to Dad's room. He looked up and said, "Have fun?"

I just shook my head. "Norris, contrary to your heartfelt belief, this sort of foolishness is not fun."

"How would I know?" he said.

"You beat anything," I said. "You know that? Anything. I don't guess we've had any word about that range inspector?"

He shook his head. "Too soon to hope for."

"Yeah." I went on into Dad's room. He was out of bed and dressed. I noticed his carbine leaning against the wall right beside the opened window. I jerked a thumb at it. "Was you planning on doing a little hunting?"

"Crows been in the corn again. I was figuring on scaring them off."

"Yeah." I sat down and gave him a brief account of the morning's activity.

He nodded slowly. "It was good planning, Justa. A good plan and well carried out. You think this might end it?"

I shook my head. "I don't think so. I think this Mr. Flood is in too deep to back off. It might not even be the money anymore."

"What's your plan now?"

"I'm going to send him word. One final warning. After that . . . Well, it's up to him. But those cattle are not coming through this range."

He was quiet for a second, thinking. Then he said, "But if you've got all our cattle back out of the way, why not send him word, asking him to go just a little northwest and you'll let him pass. Save a lot of trouble. Maybe a few lives."

I stood up. I was a little surprised to hear Howard Williams talk like that. "Dad, those cattle are illegal. And they're also infectious. Osgood and Smalley don't have their cattle back. And if they get mixed in with that Mexican herd, we'll have to hold our cattle back on the coast for God knows how long—maybe sixty days to be on the safe side. But that still ain't the point. That sonofabitch was trying to ram something down our throat with his hired guns and his high-handed ways. We were just supposed to buckle under. Well, I'm not going to buckle under. I'm going to stop that herd before it gets to Osgood's range. Stop it once and for all."

"You are determined about this?"

"Damn right." I told him about seeing Tom Brown out on his range and looking at his slaughtered cattle. "And they'd've done the same thing to us if there'd been cattle to shoot. But they also came equipped to burn us out."

"Then do a good job of it, Son," Dad said slowly. "If you set out to say *no* to a man, make sure he doesn't misunderstand and think you might have said *maybe*."

I said grimly, "He won't misunderstand."

I walked out of the house and went down to the bunkhouse.

It was crowded with a gang of cowboys, standing around and watching while Harley was bandaging the wounded man. "What the hell is this?" I said. "A free show? You men can't find something to do, I'll find it for you. Hays, you and Lew stay here."

They scattered, and I went up to the man. Harley had his shirt off. He was sitting on the edge of the bunk, looking weak and gray-faced. Harley turned as I came up. "Bullet knocked a chunk off his shoulderbone. Broke something, I reckon, thought I can't exactly say what. Ain't got a lot of use in his arm."

"Gimme a drank of whiskey," the man said thickly.

Harley looked around at me. "Hell no," I said. "What does this look like—a saloon?"

"Ya won't give a feller that be hurtin' a little drank of whiskey?"

"Listen, you dumb sonofabitch," I said, "I'm just sorry we didn't kill you. You come down here to do us harm and you want me to serve you refreshments? Hell, next you'll be wanting to be fed."

"I could do with a bite," he said.

I looked at him, considering. I had a chore for him, and I figured he'd need a little strength. I told Hays to run to the cook shack and fetch him a plate of steak and eggs.

Hays give me a look, as if to say "You expect me to wait on this outlaw?"

I said sarcastically, "I'd go myself, but I'm fixing to get busy writing out paychecks."

"I'm goin', I'm goin'," he said. "Never said I wouldn't, did I?"

I stepped outside. The two dead raiders were lying on the ground on their backs. There wasn't much to choose between them and the one that Harley was bandaging, except they weren't doing much talking or eating our food. I yelled up a couple of ranch hands and told them to get some rope and drape the two dead men over their horses and tie them on secure. "And get a move on," I said. "Likely they'll stiffen up in a few more minutes, and then it won't be such pretty work."

Hays came with the man's breakfast. I stood by and watched, as he tried to eat awkwardly with his left hand. Harley finally cut his steak up for him. I wouldn't have done it, and I was surprised he hadn't just picked it up in his hand and gnawed at the bone.

"The bullet come out," said Harley. "I dug around in the hole a little, but they wasn't nothin' in there. Reckon it hit the point of his shoulder, broke that, and then come out the back. Bullet must have split, because they is three holes where it come out up top of his shoulder."

"You reckon he's strong enough to ride maybe fifteen, twenty miles?"

Harley shrugged. "Beats the hell out of me. He got any choice?"

I shook my head.

When the man was finished eating, I stood in front of him. "Does Flood still owe you wages?"

He nodded. "Two months."

"You want to go back and get them?"

"Yeah." His face brightened. "You thinkin' of lettin' me go?"

"I'm not letting you go. I'm sending you on an errand. And if you don't do it, I'll know. You understand?"

"Yeah."

"You crossed a creek coming here last night," I said, "a creek lined with willows. It's called Caney Creek. You can't miss it—it's the only fair-sized creek in this part of the country."

"I 'member it," he said.

"Well, I want you to go back to Mr. Flood, and I want you to tell him that if he crosses that creek with that herd of Mexican cattle he is fair game. Tell him I'll stop at nothing. Now, have you got all that?"

He nodded slowly. The food had taken some of the gray out of his face, but he wouldn't be going on any raids for quite some time.

"And tell Wooley I'm looking forward to that 'right here and now' he spoke about the last time we met."

That got a startled look out of him. "You shore you want me to tell him thet?"

"Yes," I said. "And just who is Mr. Clarence Wooley?"

He shook his head. "I don't know much about him. Except I ain't messing with him. One of the other hands tried him out we first got started on the drive. He come off second best."

"Just how many hands you got left?" I asked him.

He thought a minute and then shook his head. "I don't rightly know. We had five new ones come in right after ya'll busted into us the other morning. Say, what was ya'll shootin'? A cannon? One of the boys had a hole through him you coulda put your arm in."

My heart sunk at the thought of reinforcements. It was another indication of how dead set Flood was. Well, it looked like he thought I was still saying *maybe* instead of *no*.

"Ya'll help this man on his horse," I ordered. "Hays, those bodies are loaded on their horses. I want you to tie their bridles to this man's saddle horn. Do it with a piece of rope so they'll trail all right. But tie them tight, so he can't undo the knot with one hand."

When they had him mounted, he turned and looked at the two horses he'd be leading. He didn't like it very much. "I'm gonna have a hell of a hard enough time makin' it on my own, 'thout pullin' them two spooked broncs."

It was true the horses didn't much like their load, either. Horses are about the same as cattle when it comes to smelling blood, and these two were shuffling around and acting mighty uneasy.

"Well, that would be your problem, wouldn't it," I said. "But it'll get to be more of a problem if you try to shuck loose of your load on our range. You take them boys home to Mr. Flood. They belong to him. Savvy?"

He didn't look happy, but he nodded. I detailed off a couple of riders to accompany him. "Go along with him for a few miles and help him get lined out. If he gets confused about which way to go, why, shoot the sonofabitch. Now, ya'll get going."

We watched them ride away. Standing beside me, Harley

said plaintively, "Ain't we ever going to get back to gettin' a little work done around here? My God, it'll take us a month to catch up."

I would have laughed if it hadn't been so damn serious. "I guess it's all part of it, Harley," I said. "Dad said in the early days they used to get in one day of ranch work to three days of fighting Indians. But he might have exaggerated. Might have been only two days fighting Indians."

Ben and I walked back up to the house and went into the study with Norris. Dad was there, trying to conceal the condition of his arthritic hands by cupping them together. I uncorked a bottle. "Anybody want a morning whiskey?"

Ben and Norris shook their heads. "I'll have one with you," Dad said.

"Sure you will," I said. I poured myself out a drink and downed it.

"Give me a weak one, Justa," said Dad.

"Aw, Dad, you know what the doctor said."

"The hell with the doctor. He has his drink when he wants to. The old bastard is trying to get back at me because I used to take his money at poker. Now fix me a weak one."

Over the disapproval of Ben and Norris, I dribbled a little whiskey in a glass and filled it up with water. He had to pry his fingers open with his off hand, but he got hold of the glass and took a sip. "Aaaah," he said. "Tastes good. And I hate to see a son of mine drinking alone. Bad habit."

He seemed uncommonly cheerful. I couldn't account for it, other than to figure he'd had a good rest. But then he said, "Justa, how soon you figure you got to hit that herd?"

I thought for a moment. "Well, if he keeps coming—and I've got no reason to think he won't—I think he'll be crossing Caney Creek some time tomorrow. I've sent word he's not to cross it with that herd or I'm coming after him."

"Where you going to take up your position?"

"There's a pretty good-sized mound about two miles this side of Caney," I said. "Just beyond Osgood's range. Well, hell, you know it. Damon's Mound."

"Of course. I knew Old Man Damon. He was about as early

a settler as there was around here. He built him an adobe cabin up there when the Indians was real bad."

"Some of the foundation is still there," Ben said.

"It's a good place," Dad said. "But I got another idea for you. You figure to be in position when?"

"At the latest, tomorrow afternoon. It's a little better than a three-hour ride."

"Then you've got time to send to town."

"For what?"

"Dynamite. Give him a real welcome. Dynamite and a hell of a long run of primer cord so you can be way the hell back."

I'd been thinking the same way as Dad, except I was thinking too small. I'd been thinking firecrackers; he was talking dynamite.

Real big firecrackers.

I said slowly, "Dad, I don't know about dynamite. That's a stretch further than I'd been thinking."

"You blow off about twenty sticks of dynamite in front of those cattle," he said, "and they won't quit running until they get to the border."

"Yeah," I said, "and I might blow up some men and horses at the same time."

He sipped at his drink, obviously enjoying participating in the war council. "Was it you started this fight?"

"No. But there's a few places I stick at. And this dynamite idea might be one of them."

"I'm for it," Ben said.

"I'm not," said Norris.

Dad said, "Look here, Son, when you attack that herd, do you not intend to shoot to kill those men if they try to come on with those cattle?"

"That's different," I said stubbornly.

"How different?"

"They can shoot back. But they can't plant dynamite charges under our ass. No, Dad, I thank you for the suggestion, but I believe I'll pass."

"How many men has this feller Flood got?"

I sighed. I hated to argue with Dad. He was like a dog with

a bone when he got an idea into his head. I said reluctantly, "About twenty. Unless he's brought more in that I don't know about."

"And how many have we got?"

I answered, again reluctantly, "Not counting on any help from the neighbors, I'd say fifteen."

"How many experienced?"

I fell silent at that, but Ben had to put in his two cents' worth. "Not near half," he said. "And that's counting that three that Lew Vara brought in that don't appear to be nothing but trash. We get in a fight, I'm gonna make damn sure they are not behind me."

Dad just sat and looked at me. His meaning was clear: We were heavily outgunned, and I needed to do something to even the odds.

I got up. A thought had just occurred to me. In the business of the morning, I'd forgotten all about getting the identity of the yahoo who'd fired that early shot. I meant to have the hide off him, whoever he was.

Besides, I wanted to get away from Dad and his persuasive argument about dynamite.

But he had the last word before I could get out the door. "I wouldn't put off too long sending to town for a case of the stuff and a lot of cord," he said. "And one of those plungers you use to set it off. You may change your mind. By then it might be too late."

I didn't answer; I just went outside and ran down Harley. I found him in the barn, supervising the movement of some hay that was about to go moldy. I drew him aside and said, "Harley, some one of our hands fired early this morning. I am plenty hot about it. If that fool hadn't let off that round when they were still so far away, we could have drawn them close and cut them to pieces. Now, I want you to find out who it was and fire him. I don't want no damn fools working for me."

Harley looked away. "I already know who it was," he said. "And I've had the whole story and read him out good."

"I don't want him chewed out, I want him fired."

He coughed—something he did when he was nervous. "Uh, Justa, it was that young Hawkins kid."

The Hawkinses were our near neighbors to the north. They were good people, but they were trying to operate on a shoestring and were having a tough time getting started. I'd given their oldest boy, who was barely eighteen, a job to help them with some cash money. "Oh," I said. But then I hardened my heart. "It can't be helped. He ruined a damn good chance for us."

"Justa, it was an accident. He's got an old carbine that only has one cock on it. And he was nervous. He went to cock his piece when they were coming toward us, and the hammer slipped out from his thumb. He never meant to shoot. Wasn't even aiming. I talked to the man next to him. His rifle was pointing off at an angle. The boy feels mighty bad about it. He come to me without me seeking him out and told me straight off it was him. He expected to be fired, but I said I'd talk to you about it."

I glared at him. "Well dammit, Harley! You take a lot on yourself, don't you? Did you read him out good?"

"Damn good."

"Well, all right then," I said. "That's that. But for God's sake, get the boy a decent rifle so it don't happen again."

I started to walk away, still seething, but my teeth had been pulled. Another thought occurred to me. "Say, where are Boyd and Charlie?" I asked. "I want to tell them they done a good job."

Harley looked blank. "I haven't seen them. Don't you reckon they'd be in the bunkhouse? Sleeping?"

"Let's go see."

But they weren't in the bunkhouse, and their beds hadn't been slept in. Harley sent a cowboy to ask around the ranch. He came back shaking his head. "Nobody's seen 'em," he said. "Likely they ain't come back yet."

# CHAPTER 7

I felt a sudden sense of foreboding. I said to Harley, "Send two men as fast as they can ride to that buffalo wallow I had Boyd and Charlie hid out in. Have them take a couple of extra horses, just in case they let theirs get away from them and they had to walk back. Maybe that's what happened. Maybe they've done a damn fool thing and paid for it with a long walk."

But even as I said it, I knew it wouldn't be the case.

Harley tried to reassure me. "They're damn fools," he said, "but they ain't damn fool enough to let themselves get taken on the bald-ass prairie. After they let off them rockets, they more'n likely got on their horses and made a big circle to make sure they wadn't in the path of them raiders when they was headed back. Likely that's what is delaying them."

I looked at my watch. It was going on ten o'clock. "They fired the rockets around two-thirty. Seven and a half hours to make it back seven miles?"

"Well, you know cowhands," said Harley. "Maybe they taken it into their heads to go into town. You give one of these jugheads a halfway chance to get to a saloon, and they'll do it."

I shut my watch and put it back in my pocket. "I hope you're right. I hope all I have to do is dock their pay."

Back in the house I was too restless to sit. I alternately paced and worried. Hell, I told myself, there was no need to worry. All they had to do was fire the rockets and hide. How could they have come to grief?

Ben waited with me, saying the same things.

Then Harley came in with a new worry. The hands that I'd kept close to the ranch were lining up for their noon meal, which was being served off a table outside, when Casey and Thibbedoux and Welch had insisted on shouldering their way to the front. There had been some pushing and shoving but no real damage until Arnie Welch had drawn his gun. Naturally my cowhands backed off; nobody wanted to get shot over the timing of a meal.

"Come on, Ben," I said.

We went outside. The hands were sitting all around, eating off plates held in their laps. I spotted Welch and Casey on the bunkhouse steps. Thibbedoux was a few paces away, sitting with his back against Harley's cabin. "Looks like they are trying to see how far they can push us," Ben said.

"You watch the Cajun," I said. "I can handle the two in front of me."

I walked up and stood in front of Arnie Welch. He looked up after I'd stared down at him for a few seconds. "Wahl, here's the high mucky muck."

I held out my hand. "Give me your revolver, Welch."

"Like hell I will."

"I'm not going to ask you again."

"Fuck you. Who the hell you think you are?"

In one move I drew my revolver and stuck the barrel against his forehead. "I'm the man who's going to blow your fucking head off in ten seconds if you don't hand me your revolver." Out of the corner of my eye I was monitoring Bob Casey. He just sat there, holding his plate and chewing slowly. All around me I could hear the men, who'd been talking away, suddenly go quiet.

Welch swallowed. "You don't appear to be giving me much of a chance."

"I warned all three of you about causing trouble. You did it, now you pay for it."

All of a sudden I was aware that someone was right at my shoulder. It was Lew Vara. For a second I was apprehensive, wondering which way he'd go. Then he said, "You better do it, Arnie. This hombre ain't somebody to prank around with."

"Do it careful," I said. "Just use two fingers."

Like he was handling glass, he carefully set his tin plate on the step beside him and then carefully, with his right hand, pulled the revolver out of its holster with thumb and forefinger. He held it out, and I took it. He said, in a kind of whining voice, "Hell, I was jus' funnin'. I never meant no harm." He looked up at me, and I could see the hate of the have-nots for the haves in his eyes. There are a lot of have-nots, but they don't all hate. This one hated because he was just plain mean.

"We don't think pointing guns around here is a joke," I said. "Especially loaded guns. Now get your gear and get out."

"I ain't got no horse," he said sullenly.

Ben said, "It's only about a seven-mile walk to town. Off yonder ways." He pointed. "Start now and you'll get there while the beer is still cold. Ice all melts around four o'clock."

"You owe me another hunnert dollars."

I uncocked my revolver and holstered it. "I don't owe you nothing but a bullet in the brain pan if you ain't outta here in fifteen minutes. Now move." I stepped aside to let him get up.

"What about my iron?" he said.

I said, "You lost that when you pulled it on my ranch hands. You were warned."

"That there gun cost me thirty dollars," he protested.

I looked at it. It was a Colt .44/40, a caliber a lot of gunfighters carried. A .44/40 was a .40 caliber revolver on a .44 caliber frame. The heavier frame allowed for good stability in the hand and less barrel deviation when it was fired, and the .40 caliber bullet was plenty heavy to stop anything you could hit. I myself preferred a .44/42 for pretty much the same reasons, except I liked a little more power.

But then I was bigger and stronger than Arnie Welch.

I said, about his gun, "I'm sure it did. And you'd still have it if you hadn't acted the fool. Now get your gear and get moving."

He stood up and walked past me a step. I shifted his gun to my left hand. I knew what was coming. Just as he started to take the second step, he wheeled around off his left foot and flung a roundhouse right hand at me. I hit him with a short, jolting right directly in the mouth. He went staggering back a step or two and then fell flat on his back. For a second he lay still, then he slowly began to shake his head, trying to clear the fog out of his brain. Then he sat up, still shaking his head. He looked up at me. There wasn't a sound from anyone.

"Want to get up and try some more?" I said evenly.

One of the hands laughed. I looked over at him and he shut his mouth.

I had broken a rule about not fighting a man that didn't have a chance with me. But in Welch's case I didn't feel a bit sorry.

He said, "You sucker punched me."

"Then get up and try and sucker punch me."

He worked his mouth for a second and then spit out some blood. A little was trickling down his chin from a split lip. He said, in that whining voice I didn't much care for, "I thank you busted a tooth."

"Then the sooner you get it to town and to a dentist, the better off you are," said Ben.

From behind me, Bob Casey said, "Mr. Williams, what about giving him another chance? I reckon he's learned his lesson. He'll stay in line. Arnie was always one of them kind had to push until somebody shoved back. I reckon you can count on him now. We're kind of together, an' if he leaves I'm honor-bound to leave with him."

Honor-bound, I thought. I figured these two knew as much about honor as a pig knows about table manners. Still, I needed their guns. That was why I'd hired them in the first place. I hesitated, looking down at Welch. He didn't look a bit different from the wounded raider I'd sent off that morning. He was wearing a beat-up old black hat and dirty clothes and scuffed boots. He could have used a shave and a wash and a haircut. But he was still a gun hand and I was paying him because I needed him. I hated to lose two of them over a silly incident. I said, looking at him hard, "I give you another chance, you going to give any more trouble?"

He looked down. "Naw."

"What?"

"Naw, sir."

"Be sure of it. Next time I point a gun at you, you won't get off with just a lick in the mouth. You understand?"

"Yes sir," he said. But there was a sullenness in his voice that I didn't like.

"All right. Get up and wash your mouth out and then finish your meal."

He got slowly to his feet. "What about my iron?"

"I'll keep it until you need it. You won't be needing it around here. And don't be picking up anybody else's gun. I see you with a gun around here and I'll figure you plan to use it. You understand me?"

"Yeah," he said.

Lew Vara caught up with me halfway back to the house. "Justa, I warned them about you. But nothing would do—they had to test you. It ought to be all right now."

"I hope so," I said.

I went on into the house, and Ben and I joined Dad and Norris for lunch. We were having chicken in some kind of rather warm sauce the Mexican women served it in. I said to Norris, "What's the latest along the banking front?"

He looked up from his plate. This was his area of interest. "The city of Houston is offering some municipal bonds. They're paying four percent on a thirty-year obligation."

"Does that mean you can't cash them in for thirty years?"

He gave me a pitying look. "Municipal bonds are traded just like stocks on the exchange. You can buy them one day and sell them the next. If interest rates go down from their present level you make money; if they go up you generally lose money. But right now prime interest—the kind we get—is three and a half percent. We've got around forty thousand dollars at the bank, drawing that three and a half. I think we should take that money and put it into the Houston bonds."

"What happens if Houston goes broke?"

He gave me another look. "I hardly expect that to happen."

"You can never tell," I said. "Now, if they were Galveston bonds I could see it. Galveston is going to be the biggest city around. They got the port."

"But Houston is a rail center. That's where all the commerce is taking place. Saying Houston won't make it is like saying Dallas won't survive because they don't have a port either."

I sat back in my chair and fanned my mouth. Then I took a drink of water. "Whew! That sauce is some hot! They must have spilled the jalapeños in there."

Dad said, "Tastes pretty mild to me."

"Aw, Justa always did have a tender mouth," said Ben, and his eyes glinted maliciously. "At least that's what Nora told me."

I was about to take him up sharp when Harley suddenly appeared in the dining-room door. I saw Dad look up and I twisted around in my chair. Harley coughed. "Sorry to disturb you, Justa, but I reckon you better come outside."

I didn't question him; I just wiped my mouth with my napkin and got up. My heart was sinking. From the expression on his face, I knew it was going to be bad.

As we walked to the door he said, "It's Boyd and Charlie."

I stepped out into the sunlight. The two cowboys I'd sent to see about them were sitting their horses just off the porch. Behind them, and tied belly down over their saddles, were the two men whom I'd assured would be in no danger. "Take them down and lay them out," I said.

Several cowboys came forward. They cut the ropes holding the two men and gently lifted them off and laid them on their backs on the ground. The fronts of their shirts were all over blood. I knelt down to examine them. The holes in their shirts didn't appear to be bullet holes, they looked to be stab wounds. I looked up at the two cowboys questioningly. The oldest of the pair, Max Remmick, said grimly, "We found them about four miles south. Their horses was right around handy, just grazing. Both of 'em still had their guns in their holsters. Not a shot fired. Neither one of 'em had fired their rifles, neither."

"Looks like they were stabbed to death," I said.

Max nodded. "That's what we figured. They wadn't no signs of no trouble. Near as we could figure, the remains of that raiding party come up on 'em as they was headed back."

I looked down at the two dead young men—not much more than boys, really—and slowly shook my head. "The damn fools," I said. "They headed straight back. Didn't even try and go around. I guess they thought we'd wiped them out. The damn miserable fools."

"Looks like they run slam into them," Max said. "I reckon they surrendered. Reckon that bunch could have seen them rockets and knowed to be on the lookout for somebody?"

"I don't know." I stood up.

Max said, "We figured they were stabbed to death so you wouldn't hear no gunshots and give chase. The fact is they was murdered, wadn't they?"

"Yes," I said. "They were. Now I'm fixing to do a little murdering myself." I yelled for Hays.

He was at the back of the crowd, and he came forward. "Yessir?"

"Is that new horse of mine ready?"

"Yessir."

"He got plenty of run in him?"

"I reckon."

Even Hays didn't sound like his usual smart-aleck self. What was laying on the ground in front of us had sobered and hardened us all. "Well, saddle him up," I said. "And put a pack saddle on another horse."

"Yessir."

I turned around and started up on the porch. Dad and Ben and Norris were all standing there. "Where are you going?" Ben asked.

"To town," I said.

"You want me to go with you?"

"No. I want you to stay here and tend to matters. I might be late getting back. Get everybody set for in the morning. We'll be leaving right after breakfast. And it'll be an early breakfast."

I went into my room and changed my shirt. Norris and Ben came in. Ben asked, "What are you going into town for?"

"Dynamite."

"It thought you were against it," said Norris.

"I was."

"What changed your mind?"

"Take a look outside."

"I don't think that's a good enough reason," said Norris. "You knew they were that kind of men before. You going to stoop to that level?"

"Aw shit, Norris!" said Ben. "Don't start sounding like the Bible."

"That's not in the Bible, Ben. It's a question of morals."

"Shut up, both of you!" I said. "Norris, in this heat those bodies won't last long. I don't think we got time to try and find their families, even if they got any. I reckon you better go ahead and see to them being buried this afternoon. Pick 'em a good spot. And say a few words over them."

"All right," he said. "I see you are determined on your course."

"Dammit, Norris," Ben said, "save your preaching for the burying. This is Dad's idea, and I'm for it and Justa is too. You're outvoted."

As I went out the door, I said to Ben, "I want you to keep Hays close to you until I get back. I don't reckon those three will get up to anything while I'm gone, but don't take any chances."

"They do and I won't go as easy as you," he said.

Hays had my horse saddled and waiting for me as I came out on the porch. As I mounted, I told him what I'd told Ben. He raised his hand in acknowledgment. "You ain't got to worry about nothing, Boss. We'll tend to this place."

I rode hard—or as hard as I could, trailing the pack horse on a lead rope. But Hays had picked a pack horse that was plenty fast, so we made good time. I was in a hurry, because I hated to be gone from the ranch any longer than was necessary. And I was going myself, because I didn't know enough about dynamite to tell anyone else what to get.

And I also wanted to see Nora. There was going to be a hell of a gunfight on the open prairie on the next day and I wasn't, after all, immortal. There was a time in my life when I thought that the bullet hadn't been made with my name on it, but the older I got the less sure I was.

I got into town about four o'clock and went immediately to the mercantile. Lonnie Parker gave me his usual effusive greeting as I came in the door, but I didn't have time to visit. "Lonnie," I said, "I need a case of dynamite and all the stuff that goes with it. And I don't know what that is. But I want to get off as far away from it as I can and use one of those gizmos like people in a rock quarry use. Where you push down on a handle and it blows up."

"You want a *detonator*," he said. "And you want some wire and some blasting caps. How much wire you want?"

"All you got."

That kind of took him aback. "Well, I got three or four reels. That's a buncha wire, Justa."

"I want to be a buncha ways back," I said. "I want to set the dynamite in five or six locations, maybe fifty yards apart, and then run one wire back to that thing, whatever you call it. Can that be done?"

"It can," he said. "I could probably help you better if you'd tell me what you plan to use it for."

I said tersely, "Lonnie, this is one time you don't want to know. Now, show me how to use this stuff."

He took me in the back. First he asked if I planned to shoot off single sticks. When I said no, that I figured on wrapping them in bundles of four or five, he gave me a look, but he showed me how to wrap the bundles and then insert the blasting caps. "You attach yore detonator wire to the cap. Now, if you're gonna run it into another batch, you take the wire outen that one and run it to the next and latch on to that blasting cap. Then so on until you get through. Then you run that wire on back to your detonator. This gadget here." He took a little wooden box off a shelf that had a couple of brass screws stuck in the top, along with a little handle you could push up and down. "Now, when you get the wire up to this here detonator, you split it and bare the ends and wrap them around these two little connections here. Then you screw them down tight. Then you raise yore handle all the way up. When you're ready to blast, you shove the handle down, and up she goes."

"What makes the dynamite go off?" I asked.

"An electrical current. Just like you got in a telegraph wire. When you shove this handle down you make something spin—I don't know exactly what, 'cause I never seen inside one—but that sets up this 'lectrical current, an' it goes rushing through the wire and sets off them blasting caps and they sets off the dynamite."

"Does it work every time?"

He shrugged. "I hear it does. Jim Fowler—lives about ten miles north of here—has been clearing his land with one of these gadgets, blasting out tree stumps, an' he swears by it. An' I sold a set to a couple of fellers was working a salt dome over near Markham. Ain't had no complaints."

"Well," I said, "I reckon I can work it."

"You ever seen four or five sticks of dynamite go up?"

I said I hadn't.

"Wahl, I reckon you're in for a surprise. It's a power of noise and a power of explosion. You want to be as far away as you can get and behind something solid."

"Just give me all the wire you've got."

"Anything else?"

"Yeah, would you load that on the pack horse I got tied up outside? I'd like to go down and see Nora if she's at home."

"Far as I know," he said. "You'll be staying for supper?"

I shook my head. "Afraid I can't. But if I ain't picked up that pack horse by the time you head home, will you bring him with you? I'd like to water both horses."

"We'll be having beef stew."

It was a powerful incentive, but I just smiled and shook my head and walked out of the mercantile.

I was about half afraid of running into Sheriff Ward, but he didn't seem to be anywhere about. I stopped off first at the telegraph office to see if we might have word about the range inspector, but there was nothing for us except a wire for Norris, which I knew had to do with the damn municipal bonds he'd been talking about. I tucked it in my back pocket, got on my horse, and loped down to Nora's.

She herself answered the door, holding it wide as soon as she saw who it was. It appeared she was pleased to see me. "Justa, what a nice surprise!"

I took off my hat and entered the dim, cool hallway. She was standing in front of me, and I impulsively bent and kissed the lips of her upturned face. For an instant it felt like she was responding, but then I heard footsteps and I pulled back. Her mother hove into sight, coming from the kitchen. She said, "Why Justa Williams, what a nice surprise! And just when I was wondering what I was going to do with all this beef stew I'd made."

"I can't stay long, Mrs. Parker, but thank you."

"Nonsense," she said. "You and Nora go into the parlor. I've got to get back to my cooking."

It was her way of saying she wouldn't be disturbing us and we could get into some heavy courting if we were of a mind.

Nora took my hand as we walked into the parlor and sat down on the settee. "I've heard there's trouble out on the range," she said. "Something about some Mexican cattle." She looked at me and her eyes were troubled. "Is it going to be bad?"

"I don't think so," I said. "We're negotiating with the parties involved right now."

"That's not what I heard. I heard there's already been shooting. I heard they shot a lot of Tom Brown's cattle."

I said, trying to get the worried look off her face, "Well, you can hear a lot of things. That don't make them true."

"I've heard there's men been killed. Is that true?"

Besides not wanting to worry her, I didn't much want to talk about it. Tomorrow would be on hand soon enough. Right then I just wanted to be with Nora. "Why don't we just skip over the subject?" I said. "It ain't worth our time to talk about it."

She was still looking at me with concern in her eyes. "I find it strange that you would come in to see me with trouble afoot. Unless it was going to be real bad trouble."

She was getting uncomfortably close to home. "I had to come to town for some supplies."

"When did you start fetching your own supplies?"

"Well, I had to send a telegram also."

"Justa," she said, "will you please tell me what's going on? I'm not a little girl. I'd rather know if you're in some kind of danger."

When I leaned over to kiss her, so as to shut her up, she unexpectedly put her arms around me and clung tight. It was a rare display of emotion for her and took me somewhat off guard. I kissed her for a long moment and then held her back and looked into her eyes. I said, trying to make her laugh, "So that's what it takes. Getting you to worrying about me."

But she didn't laugh. She just said, "Justa, I want to know."

I sighed. She was going to worry it to death. "Nora, there ain't much to it. We've got a disagreement with a man who wants to drive some cattle through our range. We don't want him to do it. We've discouraged him to the point where we believe he's ready to turn back. We've sent for a state range inspector. He ought to be here any day. Now, that's all there is to it. What else can I tell you?"

She eyed me suspiciously. "Are you sure?"

I said, in exasperation, "Well, if I ain't, who can be?"

"You're answering a question with a question."

"All right, Schoolteacher," I said. "Make me stand in the corner."

Just then her mother called from the kitchen. She got up and went to the summons. I lit a cigarillo and sat there thinking about the next day, trying to formulate some plans for the attack. But I didn't get very far. Nora came back in and said, "Mother said that dinner is almost ready and that if you can stay we'll eat early. Daddy ought to be home in a few minutes."

I got out my watch and looked at it. It was a little after five. Well, I had to eat somewhere, and it might as well be Mrs. Parker's cooking. "Well, tell her if it's no bother. I don't want to upset the routine. I know your daddy likes supper at six."

"Daddy likes supper whenever it's ready," she said. "I'll go help Mother get it on the table."

Lonnie Parker got home a few minutes later. He came in the front door and said, "I brung yore pack animal. They's a watering trough right behind the house. But you know that. Same place as it's always been. I'll just git washed up."

I went outside and led both my animals around to the back and watered them good. I was wishing I had a little grain for them, but I knew they'd been well fed that morning and they could hold off until I got back to the ranch that night.

When they were finished drinking, I took them back to the front and tied them off and went on into the house. From the middle of the hall I could see into the dining room, and I stopped for a moment to admire the way Nora looked bustling around, setting the table. She was certainly a shapely woman and a woman a man could be proud to have on his arm.

But, looking at her, I had a great hunger to have her someplace besides on my arm. Well, maybe that would come about when our present trouble was done.

As always, supper was a treat that made you wish you had a bigger stomach. I ate beef stew and rolls until I thought I was going to bust. But when I pushed my plate back finally, here come Mrs. Parker with a big apple pie and coffee. Well, you can't insult your hostess by not eating her dessert, so I pitched into that. I did, however, show considerable restraint by not having any whipped cream on my pie, pleading that I still had a long ride and only one horse. "I'm liable to founder him as it is," I said.

Then I asked Mrs. Parker if Nora would ever make as good a cook as she was. She said, "Why, Nora's already as good a cook as I am," she replied. "If not better."

I accused her of being a proud mother.

"Why, Nora cooks the biggest part of the meals. Doesn't she, Lonnie?"

But Lonnie had his head down over a piece of apple pie that would have choked a heifer. "Huh?"

"Doesn't Nora cook a big part of the meals?"

He looked at her and swallowed. "How would I know that? I ain't here when supper's getting fixed."

That got him a big frown from Mrs. Parker.

But then he turned to me and said, "Now Justa, don't be fretting about that dynamite suddenly going off. Dynamite don't just explode, you got to set it off. An' I got the dynamite on one side of the pack saddle and the blasting caps on the other. So don't worry about it getting jiggled around."

That got him a frown from me.

But it was too late. Nora looked from one of us to the other and said, "What dynamite? What do you need dynamite for, Justa?"

Well, that was the hell of it. On our range we didn't have any big stumps or rocks to blast out, so there was no need for a rancher like me to be using dynamite. All I could do was fumble around, trying to think of a reason. Finally I said, "We think we found a fresh-water spring in that island we own. We're going to try and blast out a pond and winter some cattle there next season."

We owned an island of some three thousand acres that was just a few hundred yards off our shore. I had actually used it when I began my breeding program so that I could selectively breed the Longhorns I wanted, mixed in with my purebred cattle. And there was a fresh-water spring on the island, but it didn't need to be made into a lake.

Nora gave me a look that told me she knew I was lying. "Right now?" she asked. "Right now when you got other troubles, you are getting a pasture ready for next winter?"

It sounded a little thin even to my own ears. "I told you that trouble didn't amount to anything." Then, before a discussion could get started, I put my napkin down and got up. "Mrs. Parker, that was as good as always. I hate to eat and run, but I got a long ride to the ranch. Reckon I'd better go, if you folks will excuse me."

Nora followed me out the front door and out to where my horses were tied. She came close and leaned against my chest. I put my arms around her. "I almost lost you once through my own stupidity," she said. "Don't let me risk losing you again by you doing something foolish."

I kissed her, briefly and tenderly, and then I swung aboard my horse. I took the lead rope of the pack horse in hand and looked down at her. "Nora, when this is all over, you and I are going to have a long talk. Get some understandings made."

I rode off, leaving her standing there in the dark, staring after me.

I got home a little after nine. After I'd unloaded the dynamite and wire and stuff and stored it in a safe place, I fed the horses and then turned them loose in the little corral that bordered the horse barn. Walking toward the house, I chanced to spy Lew Vara, sitting on the bunkhouse steps and smoking a cigarillo. I veered over his way. "What are you still doing up?" I asked. "We're getting out early in the morning."

He just shook his head. "Couldn't sleep." Then he appeared to hesitate for a moment. Finally he said, "Justa, I ought not to be hanging around here."

Of course I knew the reason, but he didn't know I knew.

He glanced up at me. "Don't worry. I ain't gonna run out on you before tomorrow, but I might not come back to the ranch."

"Why?" I asked, mainly just to see if he'd tell me.

But he didn't. He drew on his cigarillo and blew out a lungful of smoke. "Personal reasons. I might head on down to Mexico. Reason I mention it is I ain't real heavy on cash and I wondered if you might not let me have that hundred I got coming before we leave."

"Sure, Lew. But I'm paying them other hands two hundred, and you're better than they are and have done more. Why don't I give you a hundred and a half? And still figure you've satisfied your half of the damages we done to Crook's?"

"I'd appreciate it," he said. "If you got it to spare."

I turned away, feeling a little guilty for not telling him he had plenty of time. But to do that I'd have to explain why I hadn't told him before about Vic Ward's visit.

And I couldn't do that.

Ben and Norris were still up when I came in the house. They

were in the study, Norris at the desk going over some figures, Ben having a drink of whiskey and cleaning his guns. I took the telegram for Norris out of my pocket and dropped it on the desk and then fixed myself a drink.

"Get what you went after?" Ben asked.

"I think so."

"Find out how to use it?"

"I hope so."

He looked up from his work. "For some reason," he said, "hope and dynamite don't seem to go together no better than women and jealousy. Either one sounds like it could get you blown up."

"All right, I *know*. Ain't that much to it."

"Well, well, well," Norris put in. I glanced over at him. He was reading the telegram I'd brought him.

"What?" I asked him.

"This is from a friend of ours in Brownsville. Denny O'Shea—you know, he trades a lot down in Mexico, buying horses and hides and whatnot. He just got back from a trip, so that's why he's late sending this telegram. Sounds like he knows all about J.C. Flood. He says he's pretty sure the majority of that herd is stolen, gathered up from a number of rancheros along the border."

I sighed. "Well, that's just dandy. What we got is a stolen, unquarantined, diseased Mexican herd. No wonder Mr. Flood is balking about taking them back to Mexico. And I can see why he's so insistent on getting those cattle through to Houston. It's all net profit."

"I reckon that's what caused him to be so set in his ways," Ben said. "But where you reckon he got them bills of sale?"

I looked at him. "Bills of sale from Mexico?"

"Yeah, I guess that was a pretty dumb question."

I swallowed the last of my whiskey and got up. "Did anybody tell the cooks we'd be wanting breakfast extra early?"

"I did," Norris said. "Happy to help any way I can, unsuited as I am for the real work."

"Save it, Norris. I'm going to bed."

• • •

I came awake at four o'clock, groping toward my watch in the dim light. I awoke with a sense of foreboding and worry, but I was still so dazed from sleep that I had to come full awake before I could identify it. I reckoned myself to be as brave as the next man, but I figured unless a fellow was crazy or drunk, he'd have to feel some apprehension about going into a range war on the open prairie. There would be plenty of bullets flying, and all that a man would have to be was unlucky enough to be in the wrong place at the wrong time. I was never much afraid in gunfights where it was just me and another hombre—I always felt I was better. But that business of being in a running fight where you mostly couldn't see where the fire was coming from or who was shooting at you . . . Well, I never cared for that. I'd always been a man that liked to be in control of what was happening around him, and the kind of fight we were fixing to have that morning wasn't fitted out for that kind of luxury.

But I went ahead and got dressed and washed my face and shaved and then went into the kitchen for breakfast. Buttercup was the only one at the table. As one of the Mexican women brought me a cup of coffee, he indicated his big Sharps rifle leaning against the wall. "Wahl, I reckon we be ready."

I just gave him a look. I wasn't ready to get into a Norris-like discussion with him. I said, merely, "You're staying here. This is going to probably be a running gunfight, and we ain't got no buggy horses that can walk that fast."

"You could maybe set me up in a persition an' I could thin 'em out fer you."

"Buttercup," I said, "you have been thinning out my ranch crew with your cooking for years. Let's leave well enough alone. Your job is to stay here and look after Dad and guard the ranch in case any of them break through and come this way."

He took it, but he didn't like it. That last flickering flame of glory when he'd thought his best days were over had spoiled him rotten.

I finished my breakfast and then went outside to see what the weather was going to be like. I was no more than out on the porch when Welch and Casey and Thibbedoux confronted me. "We come to get the rest of our money," said Casey.

I looked at him. Over their heads I could see Lew Vara hanging back. I figured he'd come for his money as he'd asked; that he wasn't with the three. I said, "You ain't got any money coming. Not yet."

"Happens we ain't going to want to come all the way back here," said Casey. "So we thought we'd get it now."

I glanced toward Lew, wondering if he'd sounded off to the others about going on to Mexico. He understood my look and shook his head emphatically. "Happens I don't want to pay you before the fight," I said. "You might decide you don't want to fight."

"Now look here," Welch said belligerently, "you sayin' we ain't men of our word? Er cowarts? 'Cause if you is . . ."

"I'm not saying anything, except I'm not going to pay you until this matter with the Mexican herd gets settled. That's what you hired on to help with and you'll get paid when it's over. You savvy?"

"Well, we ain't goin' then," said Casey.

"Fine," I said. "I'm about sick of you anyway. Roll your gear and hit the prairie."

"Lend us horses. We'll leave 'em in town."

"Like hell. I wouldn't lend you a plank if the world was water. Now get off this ranch." I wasn't wearing a gun, but Lew was and he was behind them. Besides, I'd just heard Ben's familiar step at the door.

But the Cajun Kid, Thibbedoux, said, "Hey, this sum'bitch ain't goin' nowheres. I say I fight, I fight."

It was the first words I'd heard him speak. They sounded strange with his Louisiana accent. "You're not demanding your money?" I asked.

"Fuck naw. After the fight, damn right. Not now. Hell, I might get keeled. How I gonna spent it then?"

"All right, Cajun, you stay." I motioned toward the prairie with my chin. "You other two, get off my ranch. Right now. If you're in sight within the hour, you'll be treated like common trespassers."

Casey had a mean-enough-looking face at the best of times, but when it was filled with anger it was a sight to behold. He said, jabbing out his finger at me, "You thank you is mighty high and mighty now, don't you, bub? Well, one of these days it'll jus' be me an' you, an' you'll come to be sorry for this. I gurantee you."

"I doubt it," I said.

"Just wait, you sum'bitch!" Welch blustered. "You gonna git yores. Cheatin' us. By God, we won't stand fer it!"

"Get!" I said.

They went off, calling threats and insults over their shoulders.

From behind me Ben asked, "Want me to escort them off the place?"

I shook my head. "Naw. They'll go. But go to getting everybody saddled up. We're leaving as soon as we can. And make sure they've all got plenty of ammunition."

I went into the house and talked to Dad and Norris. "We should hit them some time after noon. My intention is to get them started back toward Mexico and stay after them until I'm sure they're on their way. I intend to scatter their cattle and kill as many of their men as I can."

Dad just nodded. Norris wished us good luck. I said, "I'm only leaving two hands here, and one of those because he's down sick with the grippe. The other one is that Hawkins kid. You can use him for a messenger if need be. But you shouldn't have any trouble. I don't think they'll get through us. And if they do, we'll be on their heels every step of the way."

As I left, Dad said, "Remember what I told you. Make sure the man understands you mean *no*."

"He will," I said.

Within the hour we were riding out onto the prairie. We were fourteen: ten ranch hands—including Harley, who I'd decided I had to have at the last minute—and me and Ben and Lew Vara and Thibbedoux. In reality we were only five experienced gun hands, counting Ray Hays. The rest had had a little practice when we'd been raided, but they were still question marks.

I'd loaded the dynamite myself. The pack horse was being trailed by a very nervous cowboy at the rear of our group. The rest were giving him plenty of room.

In the confusion with Casey and Welch, I had forgotten to get Lew Vara his money, but he hadn't said a word. Now I rode over next to him and explained what had happened.

"It's all right," he said. "I reckon I can go back."

I said, "I ain't got much on me—maybe thirty dollars. Ben might have some. Would you want to take that and go on, and I can wire the balance to you wherever you say?"

"Aw, that's all right," he said. "I'll just string along." He laughed a little. "Maybe it's best it worked out this way. Man ought not to go to spending his money before a gunfight. Might be bad luck. May turn out you won't have to pay me after all."

"May turn out I won't be around to pay you," I said grimly.

We rode, setting a pace that would cover the twelve miles in about three hours, a pace that would leave the horses plenty for the chase that I felt was sure to come.

Some time around nine o'clock, we fetched up to Damon's Mound. It wasn't really a mound—just a big swelling in the middle of the prairie, covered with low bushes and a few stunted trees. I told Harley to have the men dismount, loosen their horses' cinches, take the bits out of their mouths, and let them graze. "Tell the men to just rest up. Shouldn't be any action for a time."

Then I took the pack horse on lead and told Ben to come with me. We rode out a little over a quarter of a mile and then dismounted and began looking, like cattlemen, for the most likely area Flood would direct his herd through. It wasn't hard to figure out. The land sort of sloped off toward the coast, and there was some reedy marshland toward that direction. In the other was some bumpy land with trees. The only smooth route was between the two, a span of some six or seven hundred yards. "We can't cover it all," Ben said.

"We'll get a bunch of it," I said. "Unload that wire and get me four sticks of dynamite and that twine."

We'd brought a shovel, and I used that to dig a hole about two feet deep on the coast side of the trail. I took the four sticks that Ben handed me, wrapped them together with twine, tied it off, cut the twine, and then shoved a blasting cap in the middle of the bundle.

"Careful," warned Ben.

I looked around at him. "You want to do it?"

"I don't know how."

"What makes you think I do?"

I was nervous, but I was trying not to show it. I took the end of the wire off the reel that Ben had unloaded, wrapped it around the bundle several times so it wouldn't pull loose, then got out my jackknife and bared the end of the wire and stuck it in the blasting cap. I heard Ben suck in his breath when I did it, so I said, "Whew! Got away with that one! I thought it was going up for sure."

Then I carefully planted the bundle in the hole and then shoveled the dirt back on top of it, tamping it firm. After that, Ben and I set off on a line straight across the trail, unreeling wire as we did. We went what I figured was about fifty or sixty yards and then repeated the procedure. The only difference was I had to bare a strip in the middle of the wire, double it, and then stick it in the blasting cap. We did that until we'd planted six bundles over what I figured was a distance exceeding three hundred yards. It nearly encompassed the width of what we'd judged would be the trail they'd take. The only problem was that we'd used considerable wire. We had three reels with two hundred yards on each, and I figured we'd used better than half of our supply. That meant I wouldn't be able to be much more than two hundred yards away when I set off the blast.

We started toward Damon's Mound, unreeling wire as we went. Of course, I knew we'd never get that far—or anywhere close—but I wanted to be as near as possible.

We came to the end of our wire a few yards past a little clump of low cedar trees and bushes. I looked around. It was the nearest thing to cover I could see, but I kept remembering what Lonnie Parker had said about getting as far away as possible and behind something solid. Well, that little clump of cedars sure as hell weren't solid, but that might could be fixed. It would at least hide me from the eyes of the riders as they came on. I got the shovel and waded into the bushes and began scooping out a hole. Ben wanted to know what I was doing. I answered sarcastically, because I was a little nervous, "We need water for the horses, don't we?"

"Naw, what are you doing?"

"I'm digging a damn hole, what do you think?"

"What for?"

"What for? You wait'll you see that dynamite go up and you'll know."

"This far away?"

"This far away."

Ben looked off to where we'd planted the explosives. "Good Lord!" he said.

Ben took over the shovel after a while, and we got a pretty good hole scraped out. Then I took the wooden box, set it down in the hole, and got the end of the wire. I bared it with my pocket knife, split the two wires, and attached one to one of the little screws and the other to the second screw. Then I tightened them down with the point of my jackknife. Of course, I'd made sure the handle was down.

"What happens now?" Ben asked.

"Nothing." I stood up and put my knife away. "The handle is down now. When I get ready to go, I pull the handle up and then push it down."

"And the dynamite lets go?"

"It better," I said. "Or we're in a hell of a mess."

We left things as they were and mounted up and rode to the top of the mound. I paused and looked south. Far off, maybe two miles, I could see the line of willows that marked Caney Creek. I'd halfway expected to see a cloud of dust that would announce the coming of the Mexican herd, but the horizon was unblemished.

I said, "Be handy if that cattle inspector was to suddenly show up—that range official."

"I want to see that dynamite go up," Ben said. "I never seen nothing like that before."

"Neither have I. But I'd as soon wait for another time," I said.

"It appears to me that we've got time to ride to the creek and water the horses," I told him. "Go down and tell Harley to have everybody cinch up. I'll be down below on this side. I want to lead them around where we got our wire stretched."

I let my horse ease his way down the slope. Then I waited until the others came around the side of the mound, and I led them around the left, far wide of our line of explosives, and we set off for the creek. Once there, we pushed through the willows and let the horses sink their muzzles in the slow-moving, cool water.

As we watered, I stared through the opposing line of willows toward the horizon. It seemed I could see a faint cloud of dust a few miles off. I watched careful. The dust became more apparent. When my horse raised his head, I urged him forward and crossed the creek and got on the other side of the willows for a better look. There was no doubt about it. It was the Mexican herd, and I guessed them to be no more than two miles away. Even as I strained to look, the dust became thicker. I turned my horse and crossed the creek back to Ben's side. A thought had been growing in my mind, even as we had been planting the dynamite. "I'm going to go have one last talk with Flood," I said.

Ben looked startled. "Like hell you are! Have you gone crazy?"

I shook my head. "Maybe he'll listen to reason this time. Anyway, it's worth a try."

"It's worth getting killed," Ben said heatedly. "We made our plans—let's stick to them. Have you forgotten what happened to Boyd and Charlie?"

"That's exactly the reason I'm going. There's already been too much killing. I've got to see if I can't stop it before any more happens."

"With that bunch? Justa, have you forgotten those are also stolen cattle? You don't think he's going to head them back to Mexico on your request, do you?"

"No," I said, "but he might turn them northwest and bypass us. I've got to try. I hate the idea of using that dynamite. And

I hate even worse a running gunfight. These cowboys of ours are inexperienced. Some of them are bound to get killed."

"Aw, shit!" Ben said disgustedly. "Then I'm going with you."

I shook my head. "No you're not. I need you here to run matters in case something happens."

Hays and Lew were in our little group, and they'd overheard our every word. Hays said, sort of swallowing as he did, "I'll go with you, Boss."

I half smiled. For some reason I didn't think his heart was in it, but I did appreciate the offer. I told him so but said, "Naw, I think you better stay here with Ben. If ya'll have to come get me, I reckon we'll need as much experience on this side as we can get."

But then Lew Vara said, quietly, "I'd like to come, Justa."

It surprised me. It wasn't his fight like it was ours. He was just working for wages, and there was no point in him taking any extra risks. "Lew, I might have stirred them up a little," I said slowly. "They may not be exactly friendly."

"That's all right. Besides, I want Clarence Wooley to know I'm still around. Me and him still have a little personal matter to settle."

I shrugged. "All right." I turned my horse and started back across the creek.

Ben called, "What do I do if something happens?"

"Do as we originally planned," I said. "Pull the lever all the way up and then push it down. Try to do it right in front of the lead cattle. Then, in all the confusion, charge. And shoot anything that's got a gun in its hand."

Lew and I rode out. We put our horses into a lope without saying anything. After about a mile, I could see the familiar sight of the black buggy on the left side of the herd, riding out a hundred yards or so and slightly to the front to avoid the dust. Lew and I veered in that direction. As we rode across the front of the herd, we could hear shouts from the drovers riding point, but we just ignored them and headed for the buggy. When we were still a hundred yards away Flood must have recognized us, because he pulled his buggy horse up and sat waiting with slack reins. We rode up to his left side. Lew was a little ahead of me. I pulled up where I was almost beside his buggy horse so I could talk straight on. "Mr. Flood," I said.

"Mr. Williams." He did not seem so genial or cheerful as he had on our last visit.

"I've come to dissuade you from your present line of march. You could always swing northwest and save both of us a lot of trouble. Not to mention a lot of bloodshed."

"Mr. Williams, my reply to you is the same I gave you the first time. We are taking this route because it is the best and most feasible. Now, you've already seriously endangered my delivery date, and I'm planning legal action on that matter in Houston. As for bloodshed, well, you began it, sir."

That angered me. "You were warned," I said. "You will shortly be guilty of trespass, and we'll see about the legality of that or how it might affect any civil suit you'd care to bring."

"Young man," he said. "I have no more time to banter words with you. We are going about our legitimate business."

"Legitimate business, hell! On top of everything else, these damn cattle are stolen."

His face flushed. "Are you calling me a thief?"

At that instant Clarence Wooley came riding up. He did as he had before, resting his arms on his big, Mexican-style saddle horn and staring at me with a little fixed smile on his face. I ignored him and said to Flood, "I'm calling you a damn fool if you don't divert this herd. You got my message about Caney Creek?"

"I received it," he said. "From my employee that you so brutally wounded he may never have the use of his right arm again. Not to mention the two that you murdered."

It made me hot. I started to reply about Boyd and Charlie, but I held my tongue. Inflaming tempers wasn't going to accomplish my purpose. "I suppose your men thought they were invited guests," I said. "With their torches. Look, Flood, I'm going to stop you. And the cost is going to be heavy. Think on that."

I was about to rein my horse around when I became aware of Clarence Wooley. In one smooth move he'd drawn his pistol and was holding it leveled on my chest. I let my reins go slack. He said, "You ain't gonna be stoppin' nobody, sonny boy, 'cause you ain't goin' nowhere. Now jest let yore revolver fall out of yore holster and hit the ground."

Then I heard Lew's voice: "Something else is going to hit the ground first, Wooley."

Wooley and I both looked at the same time. Lew had edged his horse closer to the buggy. Now, leaning slightly out of the saddle, he had his arm extended and the barrel of his revolver pressed right up against Flood's head. Flood's face was frozen. "Better tell him, Mr. Flood, to drop that weapon of his. That is, if you want to keep your head."

"Better put your gun away, Clarence," Flood said, through stiff lips.

For a second it was touch and go. I was watching Wooley, and I could see the indecision in his eyes. It appeared he'd rather shoot me and the hell with Flood. Lew said, as if he were aware of this, "You're right in my line of fire, Wooley. I wouldn't have to move this revolver more than two inches and you'd be the one with a hole in him."

"What about this'n here?" Wooley said, indicating me with his gun.

"I wouldn't know," Lew said. "But *you* know I ain't going to miss."

"Clarence, drop that revolver," said Flood, a little fear in his voice.

Another second passed, and then Wooley slowly reholstered his gun. He spit and said, "I ain't dropping my gun in the dirt."

I drew my revolver, covering Wooley in case he had second thoughts. Lew said to Flood, "Now you just pick up those reins and put your horse into a slow walk. Don't make no sudden movements. You are liable to jiggle my gun, and it could go off while it's pressed agin' yore head."

Flood flicked the reins and started forward, still with Lew holding the gun next to his head. I backed my horse, watching Wooley. He just sat there, his arms once more resting on his saddle horn.

"What are you doing to me?" asked Flood thickly.

"Nothing," I said. "We're just asking you to escort us out of your hospitality. We feel like the tomcat fucking the skunk: We ain't had all we want, just all we can stand."

We went slowly like that until Wooley had been left a hundred yards behind. By then we were in front of the herd. I could see some of the drovers looking over at us, but they made no move in our direction. The way Lew was positioned, the top and sides of the buggy hid his gun hand from most directions.

After a bit more, I told Flood to put his horse into a trot. A quarter of a mile of that and we were well clear of the herd and the drovers. I said to Flood, "You better think over what I told you. You can save yourself a lot of trouble by turning northwest."

"You're the one had better be thinking about trouble," he said.

"Let's go, Lew."

He suddenly jerked the reins out of Flood's hands, threw them over the traces, and then fired his pistol right beside the ear of the buggy horse. The horse jumped and then set off at a dead run, cutting to the right in front of the herd.

We raced away, laughing like hell. I looked back. Flood's buggy was still going in circles while he frantically tried to retrieve the reins. I could see several drovers coming to his aid, but it appeared to me the frightened horse was going to pull them into the herd before help could arrive.

We crossed Caney Creek and then dropped our horses to a walk. Ben had pulled the men back to Damon's Mound. I said to Lew, "I appreciate that."

"It's what I'm drawing wages for."

"But it was damn good thinking."

"I'd already figured Wooley was going to try somethin' like that," he said. "So I was ready."

There wasn't any point in saying ought else, so I didn't. But it did make me feel a little guilty about holding back the information from Lew that the sheriff was on to him. Well, I figured that if we both made it through the fight, I'd give him a little extra money and the information and speed him on his way and no harm would be done.

Ben was about fit to be tied. When I told him what had happened, he wound up even tighter. "It was a fool thing to do," he said. "What if you'd been killed? Or held prisoner? They could have just waltzed right through us. I wonder sometimes about you, Justa. You always calling me dumb. I swear."

I let him go on like that until it was out of his system and then said quietly, "It had to be done for my peace of mind, Ben. Now let it rest."

I figured the herd was still about two miles away from the dynamite, so I called for everybody to make a lunch from the grub we'd brought and rest themselves and their horses. While they were eating, I told them the plan. "I've laid a string of dynamite charges across the path they have to take," I said. "After I fire the dynamite, there ought to be considerable confusion on their side. That's when we're going to hit them. I'll be out in front, about a quarter of a mile. Ya'll will all be hidden behind this mound. As soon as that dynamite goes off, you are to come at a run. Ben, I can't have my horse with me, because there's damn little cover and they'd spot him. Besides, I reckon the explosion would spook him so bad he'd break his neck trying to get loose. So you hold him back here for me and bring him to me when we go after them."

The Cajun Kid asked, "What we do? We shoot to death?"

"They'll be shooting," I said. "I don't see where you have any choice. My idea is to run those cattle and those drovers as far back toward Mexico as we can. Use whichever you're best with from horseback—handgun or rifle. But the idea is to keep them on the run, not give them a moment's rest. Any questions?"

Ben said, "What about Flood?"

I shrugged. I didn't honestly know about Flood. "I've seen him twice, and neither time did he appear to be armed." I said to the men, "That's the owner of the herd. He's riding a buggy. If he shoots at you, he's fair game. Anything else?"

A young cowboy, obviously nervous, said in a high voice, "Yeah, is it too late to ask for the day off?"

They laughed, but I said, "No, it's not. I don't want anyone doing this whose heart ain't in it. You could get killed."

Another cowboy said, "I'm thinking about Boyd and Charlie." I recognized him as one who'd fetched in the bodies.

"So am I," I said. "This ain't just about range rights and diseased cattle anymore. These people have brought some fever up from Mexico, and it ain't got a damn thing to do with their cattle."

I got under what shade I could find and lit a cigarillo. Nobody came near me, so I was alone with my thoughts. We'd had plenty of trouble before, just like every other rancher in those changing times, but this appeared to be the worst of the lot. I knew it was the first time I'd ever risked the wholesale lives of my ranch hands in a fight. Usually it was a matter that Ben and I and a few selected friends could handle. I was sitting like that, thinking, when I became aware of two figures galloping across the plains toward us from the north. I got up and walked out from under the trees the better to see. After a little I could see that it was Tom Brown and another man. They pulled up as I walked forward. "Hello, Tom."

I was hoping he hadn't come to put up any objections, but he said, "I heard you was about to take some action. We'd like to help. You remember Grover, don't you?"

"Hello, Grover," I said. "I thought you got shot."

"I heals fast," he said grimly.

I could see he carried his left side kind of stiffly. I said, "Well, I'm glad to have you, Tom. But this one might get a little rough."

"That's fine with me." He and Grover dismounted. "I was just afraid we might have missed you. One of my hands saw you go by this morning, but he just got around to telling me. I remembered what you'd said about where you planned to stop them. What's the deal?"

I led them over under the trees and explained what we were going to do. "We can't just sit up here under cover and pick them off. They'd just fall back and wait. And we never would get them cattle driven back like that. So the only thing we can do is charge them. I'm hoping the confusion caused by that dynamite will give us time to get in amongst them before they can get orgainzed. It has to be a running fight."

"Suits me," Grover said flatly. He didn't act like a man who much took to being shot.

"Who's leading the charge?"

"You can if you want to, Tom." I smiled. "Naw, won't be no leader. We just all go and mix it up with them. My men got orders to shoot any man pointing a gun at them."

"Suits me," Grover said again.

I looked around at him. Tom said, "Grover is a mite put out."

"I noticed," I said. I stood up. "I reckon I better get to my station. They ought to be at Caney Creek by now."

I climbed up on the mound and looked through the last line of little trees that weren't much taller than the crown of my hat. Just as I had expected, I could see the first of the herd emerging from the willows. Well, I had warned Flood. It was on his head now. I heard a sound behind me, and I turned. It was Ben and Tom Brown. "Ya'll better get back down," I said. "I'm going down this side in just a minute."

"I just want to get this straight," Ben said. "If the dynamite don't fire, we still go?"

I nodded. "Do we have any choice? If it doesn't go, get everybody on top of the mound and have them hold off until the herd is almost here. Then fire a few volleys and charge. That would be the only change."

"All right." He turned and went to the back.

"I stopped by Smalley's and Osgood's," Tom said. "Neither one was home. They're both in town. Reckon they planned it that way?"

I smiled. "Does it matter?"

"Guess you're right. I doubt they'd been much help. Well, I better get to my horse."

I ducked down the front of the mound and then, stooping low in the high grass and bushes, made my way the quarter mile to the little clump of cedar where we'd left the detonator.

I crawled down in the hole and peered out through the bushes. The herd was now clearly visible, only a scant mile away.

And less than that from the line of dynamite.

I watched it coming on. There was something different about the drive, and I immediately recognized what it was: The drovers were pushing the cattle much harder now. They had them almost in a trot. I figured Flood had decided we'd hit him at or near the creek, and he wanted the cattle to have as much momentum as possible when we tried to push them back.

I looked at the detonator handle, praying silently that it would work. If it didn't, we were going to lose an awful lot of men.

They continued on at their fast pace. I could see it wouldn't be long. I was slightly amazed to see the black buggy of Flood's close to the herd and seeming to be helping with the drive. He was even up further than the point riders.

That disturbed me a little. If I could help it, I did not intend to take any of the men up in the blast. But if they got too far forward, there would be nothing I could do about it. I planned to set off the blast just as the lead cattle got about ten yards from my line of dynamite. I had it marked with a clump of purple sage right in the middle of the line.

They were getting closer. I slowly pulled the handle up, watching the cattle as they headed straight for the purple sage. The point riders were dangerously close to the front.

So was Mr. Flood.

And I had no idea how powerful the blast would be or how far reaching.

The cattle were rushing forward. I could see at least six riders, and Mr. Flood, up near the front, pushing the lead steers on. They were coming too fast.

In a panic, I thought I'd better blast. If I waited any longer, the riders would be right in the midst of the explosion.

I shoved the handle home.

Nothing happened. The herd swept on. Now the lead steers and some of the riders were at or near the blast line.

My heart sank. They'd be on me in nothing flat. I jerked the handle up and shove it down again.

Still nothing happened.

There was no choice for me now but to jump up and make a run for it. In a few minutes they'd be on me.

I was looking back toward Damon's Mound, judging the distance, when I heard a sound like being right in the middle of a rolling thundercloud. It was a BOOM that just went on and on and on.

I looked around to the front, toward the herd.

It was the damnedest thing I'd ever seen.

# CHAPTER
# 8

It looked like somebody had gotten grapple hooks and taken hold of a line of the prairie and jerked it about halfway up to the sky. It was just a solid wall of dirt and dust that seemed to rise straight up along the whole stretch of three hundred or so yards where we'd set the charges. I said, "My God!"

I'd known it was going to be big, but I'd never expected anything like it. Then, even as I looked, I felt a blast of hot wind hit me with the force of a hurricane blow, and a few seconds after that, I felt dirt and clods begin to rain down on me. I huddled down in the hole and put my arms over my head.

It had worked all right. Much better than I could have dared to hope.

When I heard the rumbling start to decrease, I peeked over the edge of my hole. The dirt was falling back to dirt, but the storm of dust was still rising in the air. It was so thick I couldn't see anything. I stood up, trying to get a better view.

Then, from behind me, I heard the thunder of hooves, sounding like nothing after the spectacle I'd just heard. I looked back. Ben was leading our men around the mound, heading straight for me. I stepped out of the hole and out of the cedar clump and waved my arms. They came dashing up to me, skidding to a halt.

I caught my horse's reins out of Ben's hand and swung aboard. But then I held up my hand. There was no use rushing into that tempest until we could see what we were doing.

Our hands, by now, had caught sight of the cloud of dust and the disturbed prairie. I heard a few exclaiming and carrying on. I doubted that many had ever seen dynamite or had any idea what it could do.

Certainly I hadn't.

Tom Brown came up alongside me. "Lordy!" he marveled. "Looks like you blowed up the whole prairie!"

Now the dust was clearing, so that I could see through patches of it and see movement, either men or animals or both. I raised my hand. It was time. "Let's go!" I yelled.

We went forward at a lope and then a gallop, alert to keep our horses under control in case we had to make certain sudden moves. I looked behind me. We were too bunched. I waved my arms to the right and the left. "SPREAD OUT!" I yelled. "SPREAD OUT! OUT! OUT!"

The men sheared off and branched out into what was a line abreast of riders. Within thirty seconds, we were in among the heaps and piles of clods thrown up by the blast.

Then came the dead cattle. At first they were scattered, some of them looking like they'd been blown apart and blown straight up. Then they started coming in clumps.

But after that came the men and the horses. Because of the haze of dust, I could only see those in my near vicinity, but I counted three drovers on the ground. They looked plenty dead.

We swept through the thinning cloud of dust and popped out on the other side. There were more dead cattle and several more bodies. I hadn't meant to blow up any of the drovers—or any of the cattle, for that matter; it had just occurred because of the speed with which they'd been coming on and the delay in the detonation of the dynamite.

Once we were clear of the dust and could see, I was amazed at how far ahead of us the herd was. They were running at stampede speed, with the drovers frantically trying to catch up and turn them. We put spurs to our horses and set off in pursuit at a dead run. When we got within a hundred yards we began to fire, admittedly without much hope of hitting anyone.

But they must have heard the bullets singing overhead, because a few of the drovers looked back and then urged their mounts to even greater efforts while they leaned down over the necks of their horses.

I was looking for Clarence Wooley, but I couldn't spot him. Neither was Mr. Flood in evidence. I figured he'd been left far behind by the stampeding cattle.

We slowly gained on them. I fired the last cartridge in my pistol, shoved it back in the holster, and took out the spare I was carrying in my saddle bag.

At one point three of the drovers on the right side of the herd suddenly pulled up and whirled around to make a stand. They'd pulled their rifles out of their boots, and they sat on dancing horses and aimed down on us. Almost together, we let go a single volley. One of the drovers fell out of his saddle, and another sagged and dropped his rifle. But I saw smoke blossom from the rifle of the third, and out of the corner of my eye, as we pounded down on him, I saw one of my men throw up his hands and tumble out of the saddle.

The drover fired again, but so did we. It was his last shot. The way his body jerked around, he must have been hit half a dozen times.

Now the other drovers, looking to be about seven or eight in number, began to be aware of how close we were getting. They were making half-hearted attempts to turn the cattle, but most of their attention was on us. They were strung out on the right and left side of the herd. From time to time, one would turn in his saddle and fire a hopeful shot in our general direction.

But our fire, by now, was so concentrated, on account of the way the drovers were lined up, that we were nearly all shooting at the same man.

The tail-end man on the left side fell. Then the man up from him. Seeing his partners fall and knowing he'd probably be next, the lead drover on the left side suddenly veered off and left the herd, spurring his horse toward a copse of cedar and post oak.

After that we concentrated on the drovers on the right side. We were within fifty yards of the four of them when they wheeled to the right, firing as they did. I saw another man go down, but again we were moving too fast to tell who it was. All I knew was that it wasn't Ben, because he was riding right beside me.

We fired in sporadic volleys at the four drovers, but they were riding away, cutting back to the southwest and not bothering to return fire anymore, just leaning low over their horses and lashing them with their quirts. I could not be sure, but it appeared to me that the lead rider was Clarence Wooley. I reined my horse to a stop, jerked my rifle out of the boot, and tried a shot. I aimed for the rider but was willing to hit his horse.

The range was too great. I fired three times without noticeable effect. Still watching the drovers growing smaller in the distance, I slowly put my rifle away. I had not intended for Mr. Wooley to continue to be at large.

Now we had the herd to ourselves. We ran them hard until I thought we were in danger of wearing our horses out. Finally I called a halt. We fired a few more shots to send them on their way and then turned back at a walk. I was anxious about our two men who had fallen, but the first casualty we came to was one of the drovers. One of my crew got down to check him over. He was dead.

As were the several others we came upon. There were loose horses running all over the place, trailing their reins. I had several cowboys catch them up and trail them along with us. Later I'd turn them over to Vic Ward, but I couldn't leave them saddled and bridled out on the prairie.

Then we came on the first of our men. With a shock, I recognized him as the Cajun, Joe Thibbedoux. It made me sad. He'd been an honest man, and now he'd caught an unlucky shot square in the middle of the chest and his gun days were over. I had his horse caught up, since it was one of ours, and had him loaded aboard, belly down across his saddle.

A little further on we came upon the outfit's chuck wagon. Apparently the cook had been trailing the herd, and he'd been caught right in the middle of the stampede when the herd had turned back from the explosion. The wagon was over on its side. One horse lay dead in a mass of tangled and twisted harness. Flour and beans were scattered all around. We found the cook on the far side, leaning up against the wagon canvas and looking dazed. He stared at us with vacant eyes. I asked him if he was all right. "What the hell happened?" he asked in a kind of stupor. "Was it lightnin' struck?"

"Sort of," I said.

We passed a few more of the drovers lying on the ground. One of them sat up as we approached. His left arm dangled loosely. He looked up at us from the ground and said, "I need help."

I pointed the few hundred yards to where the chuck wagon lay. "Your cook's right over there," I said. "He'll help you."

"My arm's busted."

"No shit?" I replied. "Would you rather it was your neck?"

"That's cold, Justa," Ben said. "Oughtn't we to take him back to the ranch?"

I looked at him. "How do you know that he isn't one of the ones that stabbed Boyd and Charlie to death?"

He didn't say anything else until we passed another body. Then he said, "Ain't we supposed to be burying these men?"

"Bury them if you want to," I said harshly. "I ain't running no funeral parlor."

"Justa, it's over. Can't we show a little charity?"

I still had the hot blood of battle in me. And I wasn't kindly disposed toward any of these men who'd caused me so much trouble and grief. And killed my men and threatened our livelihood. "Tomorrow I go into town and see Vic Ward and tell him what happened," I said. "I want things like they are. The burying is a matter for the county. I ain't asking my men to bury gunsels that were just trying to kill them."

Just then we came upon the first of our men to go down. With sadness I saw it was the young cowboy Slayton, the one who'd stood with me at the south corner of the branding corral.

I got down while Ben held my horse and knelt beside him. There was a flicker of life left in him. He opened his eyes for a second as I looked down in his face. His mouth opened, and for a second I thought he was going to speak. But then he closed his eyes and his mouth and ceased breathing. His horse was grazing nearby, and I caught him up and sadly helped a couple of the others to load him belly down across his saddle. It made me feel bad. I was seeing too many of my men riding a horse in that awful way.

On both sides of the dynamite line, the prairie was littered with dead cattle. I didn't know how many—maybe up to a thousand. Well, the crows and the buzzards and the wolves were going to have an early Thanksgiving.

Ben suddenly cried, "Look yonder!"

We were just walking our horses slowly, letting them blow. I looked in the direction he was pointing. Just a few yards short of one of the huge craters the dynamite had made, I could see something black. At first I couldn't make out what it was; then I recognized it as J.C. Flood's buggy. I put spurs to my horse and loped the hundred or so yards to where it lay, wrecked. The horse was dead in the traces. From the way he was wadded up, it looked like he'd been blown backward into the buggy. The buggy was on its side, the top half off and one wheel splintered. I saw a pair of legs sticking out from under the collapsed top. I got down and pulled the top back. J.C. Flood was sitting on the ground, his back up against the seat of the buggy. His face was dead white, and he was breathing in pants. He said, between gasps, "Ribs. Crushed. Can't breathe."

"I reckon I gave you fair warning, Flood. Don't ask me for help."

"Please," he said. "Hurt bad. You won. Never should have tried . . ."

I looked at him a long moment, debating. I was going to hate myself whichever way I went. I finally stood up. "Dammit!" I said. "Dammit to hell! And damn you to hell, Flood. You sonofabitch! I ought to shoot you right between the eyes. You caused the death of four of my men for your greed, and now

I'm supposed to do the charitable thing. You fucking bastard.
You chickenshit sonofabitch."

"Help me!" he said, gasping.

I turned around and said, harshly, "Harley, send a man into
town for a doctor. No, send five or six. Tell 'em to eat good
and drink all the whiskey and beer they can hold. In fact, you
go just to make sure they have a good time. Hell, take ten. It's
all over with here. And tell Sheriff Ward what happened."

A sort of thin, ragged cheer went up. I knew they'd all been
under a little more strain than they were used to. I guess they
were relieved to get away from it.

"What about our men on the horses?" Harley asked quietly.

It saddened me all over again. "Take them to the funeral
parlor," I said. "Ya'll stay in town tonight. Put up at the
hotel."

Tom Brown came up beside me. "Well, Justa, you done
what you set out to do." He looked down at Flood, who was
breathing with difficulty. "I reckon this one learned his
lesson."

"Him?" I leaned over and spit on the ground. "His kind
never learns. Next time he gets a chance to do something
crooked, he'll do it. He'll go on until somebody kills him."

Tom laughed slightly. "I never heard such a racket as that
dynamite made. I thought the world was coming to an end."

Where we were situated, we could look down the line at the
six huge holes, any one of which would have made a nice
watering tank for stock. "Well," I said, "if we were to get a
good rain, this part of the prairie might have some use."

We waited until Harley and the rest of our men rode for
town. From where we were, it was only about a five-mile trip.
We had the best part of fifteen miles back to the ranch.

There was nothing left for us to do. We left Flood moaning
and groaning and started back. We stopped briefly at Caney
Creek to water the horses and eat a little something ourselves,
and then we pushed on. After a mile or so, Tom Brown and
Grover veered off, headed for Tom's ranch. I thanked them for
their help and participation. "If you see Smalley and Osgood
before I do," I said, "tell them we sure missed them."

"Sure I will," said Tom. "Flood might could have used them more."

After they left, it was just Hays and Ben and Lew and I. We jogged slowly along, taking our time. Our horses had had a good hard day, and they'd be plenty glad to see the barn and the feed trough.

"Well, it's over," Ben said.

"You sure?" I said. "Wooley got away."

"Wooley was just a gunman. Flood was the boss. By the time he gets healed up—if he does—those cattle of his are going to be scattered from here to hell and gone."

I started thinking about Nora. It would be good to go in and see her without that ax that had been that Mexican herd hanging over my head. But then I looked back at the horses Hays and Lew were trailing and I felt bad. I said to Lew, "I never got to know that Cajun Kid fellow. Did you know much about him?"

He shook his head. "Naw. I'd heard of him; heard he was a pretty square fellow."

"Well," I said, "he's got money in his pocket and money coming. You know of anybody we could send it to? Any family or girlfriend?"

"His kind don't leave many tracks, Justa. Was I you, I'd put the money back in the safe or divide it up amongst them as he was riding with when he caught the unlucky one."

The unlucky one. That's really all it came down to. And it could have happened to me as easily as him. I wasn't wearing any bullet-proof shirt. It made one stop and think.

But if one wanted to get on with the business of living, it was best not to stop and think. All the thinking in the world wouldn't stop an unlucky bullet.

I knew I was going to have some bad feelings for a time about the men I'd blown up. It just hadn't been my style. But it also hadn't been something I could help. If the damn dynamite had gone off when it should have, those men that were killed might have been knocked out of the saddle by the blast, but they wouldn't have been blown into parts.

As we rode along, I took out my pocket watch and looked at

it. I was stunned to see it wasn't much past noon. It seemed that
hours and hours had passed since I'd set off those charges. The
way matters were going, we'd be home by midafternoon.

Lew was riding on the outside of the four of us, and I ducked
my horse around and pulled up alongside of him. I told him
that, if he wanted, he could get his money, leave his horse, and
take a fresh ranch horse and light out that very night. I said I
could get him some grub put up to take along.

He must have wondered why I was willing to see him on his
way so quickly, but I didn't enlighten him. He thanked me for
my offer but said he preferred to get a night's rest and some
food in him and make a fresh start in the morning. "I ain't in
that big of a hurry, now that I'm pretty sure where I'm
headed."

"Let me ask you something," I said. "You seem to know
Clarence Wooley. You reckon he's planning on letting matters
lie? Or you reckon he'd be fool enough to come back up here
out of revenge?"

"I wouldn't concern myself about that," he replied.
"Wooley don't do nothin' else they's money in it."

We rode on a bit further before I said, "I don't guess you'd
care to tell me why you said what you did. About you and
Wooley having a personal score to settle."

"No, I wouldn't," he said. "But I know where he's headed
now. That's why I'm not in such a hurry as I was this morning.
After I find him and get it settled, I may be in a position to tell
you."

I got the strong impression it had something to do with the
murder that Lew was accused of. Naturally, I didn't press the
matter.

I guess I should have been happy. We had effectively routed
the threat that had been posed to our cattle, but it had been a
very costly victory. I'd lost four good men; that was the biggest
price. But in addition, a wedge had been driven between us and
our neighbors, the Smalleys and the Osgoods. They'd acted out
of cowardice and timidity, but they wouldn't blame themselves
for that. They'd blame it on me and act with consequent

bitterness. That was human nature. You put a man in a position where he comes off looking bad, and he'll blame you.

On top of all that was the ranch. For a week we'd just let everything go while we fought Flood and Wooley. And on a ranch the size of ours, you get a week behind, it can take you a year to catch up. We were behind in our haying, we were behind in branding the late spring calf crop, and we still had five thousand cattle to move back from the coast.

And there wasn't a cowhand on the place that wasn't worn to a frazzle.

And we were short-handed now by four men.

I ain't normally given to that sort of thinking, but it wouldn't have hurt me any if Flood died a slow, lingering death while the doctor was coming to him.

A little after two o'clock we rode slowly into the quiet ranch yard. With all the hands away, the place seemed almost deserted. We dismounted at the horse barn, and I told Hays to tend to the horses and then turn them out into the corral. We kept what we called the house horses in that corral. These were horses that Ben and I and Norris and Harley used. The *remuda* for the working horses—the mounts the cowboys used—was a big, fifty-acre fenced trap about a mile behind the house. It was big enough that the horses could graze and wouldn't have to constantly be fed hay. We kept a few other horses in the house corral that the cowboys could use to catch up their mounts out of the big trap, but naturally it was empty now, since we'd used those horses in the attack.

I said to Lew, "Get your gear ready or whatever you want to do and then come up to the house in a few minutes and I'll have your money ready."

He nodded and went in the bunkhouse, while Ben and I walked toward the house. Ben said, "You know, Justa, I believe all this has been hard on Dad. I think that's why he's been doing kind of poorly lately."

"I have no doubt of that," I said grimly. "That's another reason I don't wish Mr. Flood well."

As we neared the house, we noticed a horse tied in front. It was an unfamiliar horse, but then I didn't know every mount on the place. "Wonder what that horse is doing there," said Ben.

"Likely Norris has him up just in case."

"In case of what?"

I laughed slightly. "I imagine Norris never gave up expecting us to send for him."

We mounted the steps and crossed the porch and walked into the relative coolness of the hallway. It felt mighty good after the heat of the prairie. We walked down the hallway and turned into the study. Ben was just saying something about how good a drink would taste. He never finished the sentence.

We stopped stock-still a step into the study. Sitting up against the far wall, facing us, were Norris, Vic Ward, and the young Hawkins boy. Hawkins appeared to be wounded. There was blood all over his left thigh, and he had his head back and his face grimaced in pain. Someone had tied a tourniquet around the leg above the wound.

"Wahl, glad to see you boys back. But it was damn sorry of ya'll not to leave us no horses caught up."

It was Bob Casey. He was sitting in my chair, drinking my whiskey and holding a gun steadily on Ben and I. Arnie Welch was in another chair in the corner, gun drawn. I looked quickly to my right, looking for Dad. He was in his accustomed chair. He smiled wanly as if to say it was a sorry homecoming and he wished he could do something about it. Buttercup was sitting beside him, up against the wall. His hands were tied, and there was a nasty-looking cut above his right eye. But he still looked like he was ready to fight a wildcat. Through the open door, I could see into the office and see that the safe door was standing open.

I said to Casey, "I see you have taken to hitting old men and shooting kids."

"Old man hell!" said Casey. "The sum'bitch jumped us. I had to hit him 'fore he could let off that cannon he was a-holding."

"I see you've stolen the money in the safe," I said. "Well, take it and get out."

"Whar's yore horses?"

"They're in the corral. The one by the barn." I didn't mention they were ridden down.

I looked at Vic Ward. "What are you doing here, Sheriff? You promised me a week."

"I didn't come to arrest Lew. I heard you'd bought a case of dynamite, and I came to see what you were going to do with it."

I had made a mistake and he'd made a mistake. I should never have asked the question, and he should never have answered it the way he did.

"So, you done come to arrest Lew," said Casey. "He'll be right interested to hear that."

"He ain't here," I said. "He's gone to town with the rest of the hands. Now you two get out. My father is not well. And that boy needs a doctor. Any fool can see he's bleeding to death. Norris, how long since you've loosened that tourniquet?"

"About five minutes. It gushed when I did." His eyes were down.

Casey said, "I reckon it's time fer you two boys to take a little weight off yore hips. Jes' with them two fangers. Unnerstan'?"

Ben and I slowly pulled our revolvers out of their holsters. There wasn't much else to do. It was certainly no time to play hero.

"Now, you'ns jes' lay them revolvers on the floor and kick 'em over to me and Mr. Welch."

We did as we were bade. I watched Casey carefully, wondering what their plans were. I knew there had been about fifteen hundred dollars in the safe. That was a lot of money for two such as them. I hoped they'd be content with that and leave. I was very worried about the effect all this might be having on Dad. I was also worrying about the Hawkins boy.

Casey was busy picking up our revolvers and adding them to the pile he had by his chair. He said to me, "Now, you say them hands went on into town?"

"Yes. To the doctor's. We had some wounded."

"When they be gettin' back?"

"Any time now," I lied. "At least the ones that weren't hurt. About eight of them."

Welch got out of his chair and came toward Ben and I. He waved his pistol at the wall to our left. "You two high mucky-mucks jes' set down there agin' the wall. An' you, Mr. Boss, you jes' turn yore wallet out."

I was looking down, taking my wallet out of my back pocket, when he swung. I never saw it coming. All I felt was the crash of his right fist catching me just on the left side of my face. It staggered me, but I didn't go down. I felt—more than saw—Ben start forward, and I jerked out a hand to stop him. "Don't!" I said.

I shook my head. I could taste blood in my mouth and feel a little trickling down my cheek, but I wasn't going to give Welch the satisfaction of knowing he'd hurt me.

Casey laughed. "Hell, Welch," he said, "you can't hit hard enough to break a winder pane."

"Bullshit!" he said. And he wound up and slugged me again, this time flush in the face. I felt my nose give a little crunch. I had sense enough this time, even though the force of the blow didn't warrant it, to stagger against the wall and slide to the floor. Welch turned to Casey. "Now wadda ya thank? Thank I can't hit? Damn near broke his fucking head."

"You sonofabitch," said Ben, his face livid.

Welch suddenly hit him a chopping blow across the face with the barrel of the gun he was holding in his left hand. A cut sprung up on Ben's cheek, spouting blood. Before he could react, I grabbed his belt and jerked him down on the floor beside me. Welch stood over us, jeering. "You two want some more? Big-shot sonsabitches. Reckon you like to hit more'n you like to git hit."

I didn't say anything; I just watched them. I glanced over at Norris. He wouldn't meet my eyes. I knew he was feeling guilty. I'd left him to protect the ranch, and he'd let these two slip up on him. But I don't know what he could have done. They'd probably come to the door with some plausible-sounding excuse and then got a gun on him. After that, it would have been easy to take Buttercup. Obviously, Vic Ward had come along at the wrong time and walked right into a trap. Of course, right then, I wasn't feeling too charitable toward him. He'd had no business coming to our ranch. He may have come to inquire about the dynamite, but he'd have arrested Lew just the same.

At that instant, a knock came at the front door.

Casey looked quickly at me. "Who would that be?"

"I don't know," I said. "Maybe the hands have come back."

"Call out to whoever it is to come in."

"I'll be damned if I will."

He leveled his pistol at me. "Call out."

"No."

He swung his aim toward Dad and looked at me.

I yelled out, "Come in!"

I heard the creak of the screened door as it opened and then the sound of boots coming down the hall. The door to the study opened inward, and Ben and I were far enough behind it that we couldn't see who it was until they stepped into the room. I was praying it wasn't Hays; he was perfectly capable of doing something dumb enough to get the whole room filled with bullets.

Then I heard Casey chuckle. "Wahl, here's ol' Lew. Come on in, pad'nuh. Got a shr'uff in here done come to arrest you."

I looked up. Lew Vera had walked in. He stood there looking around, looking bewildered. "What the hell's going on here, Casey?"

"Aw, nuthin' to speak of. Jes' squarin' a few accounts." Casey was chewing tobacco, and he paused to spit tobacco juice on the carpet. "Reckon you know 'bout squarin' accounts."

I saw Lew look at Vic Ward. "Sheriff," he said. "Have you come to arrest me?"

Vic didn't say anything.

Casey said, "You better reckon on it, pad'nuh." He indicated me with his gun. "An' I reckon yore asshole buddy knowed about it. They both let the cat outen the bag."

Lew turned and saw me for the first time. "Hell, Justa, they been beatin' on you?"

"Some." I wiped the back of my hand across my face. It came away smeared with blood.

He looked at me hard. "Did you know about this?" he asked. "About the sheriff?"

I wasn't going to lie to him, not after the way he'd backed me in the confrontation with Flood and Wooley. "Yeah," I said. "Sheriff Ward came out here three or four days ago. Right after I'd sent you to San Antonio. He said he'd just realized he had papers on you. But he promised me he'd give you a week."

"Justa, you ought not to be saying that!" said Vic. "It sounds like I ain't been doin' my duty."

I looked over at him. "And you being here today sounds like you were breaking your word."

"I told you, I come to warn you not to use that dynamite on that herd."

Ben laughed. "You're a little late for that."

I was going to tell Ben to shut up, but Lew was still looking at me intently. "Justa," he said, "you knew and you didn't tell me?"

There wasn't much I could do except admit it. "Lew, I was wrong," I said. "I should have told you. But I was in a bind and I needed your gun. I was afraid if I told you, you'd have taken off, not trusted Ward to wait a week. And as matters have turned out, you would have been right."

"That was the reason? Because you needed my help and you was afraid I'd run out on you?"

"Yes," I said. "I should have told you and taken my chances. But I thought it would be all right because Vic had promised me a week. That's why I offered you what money Ben and I had for you to go ahead and take off and I'd wire you the rest."

He thought about it for a moment, and then he shrugged. "Well, it ain't exactly your style, but I reckon you meant it for the best. You was in a bind. I might have done the same if I'da been you."

Welch said, "Say, what the goddamn hell is all this palaver? This ain't no family reunion. We got to figure out what to do."

Casey asked Lew, "Where's the Cajun?"

"He caught one," said Lew shortly.

"You with us?"

Lew looked over at Vic Ward. "Don't see where I got much selection."

"Lew, did you do murder?" I asked.

He came back to me and shook his head. "Naw, but I got blamed for it. Wooley done the killin'. Town near Dallas."

"Then stay here," I said. "I'll hire you the best lawyer money can buy. You run, and you'll be running the rest of your life."

Welch took a kick at me but only caught me a glancing blow on the shoulder. "Shut yore mouth! We want anythang outen you, we'll knock it out. An' what makes you thank you gonna live long enough to git anybody a lawyer?"

"Welch! Cut that shit out!" said Lew sharply. "You ain't killin' nobody. You understand?"

"Whatta you say, Lew?" said Casey. "Reckon we better get to makin' tracks? The big boss over there says the rest of the hands will be back from town pretty soon."

Lew glanced over at me. He knew the ranch hands were in town for the night, but he didn't say anything, except, "Yeah, we better get."

"They be horses in that corral?"

"Yeah," said Lew. "But they're rode down. The fresh horses are in a trap about a mile behind the house. Why don't you send Ben out to fetch us some fresh mounts. He can take one of the horses out of the corral and catch us up a string."

"Whyn't one of us go?" said Casey. "How we know he'd come back?"

"Don't be a damn fool," Lew said. "These ain't the kind of people to run out on their family. And I'm not going, because I don't want to see anymore of this gun-whipping people."

"All right." Casey motioned at Ben with his pistol. "Get us six horses. Bridle and saddle three and bridle three others."

"Ben," I said, "make it damn fast. We've got to get Hawkins some help before he bleeds to death."

For the first time, Lew seemed to notice the plight of the

young man. He said to Casey disgustedly, "What'd you have to shoot this kid for? Hell, he ain't even wearing a gun."

"Welch done it," said Casey in a sullen voice. "He taken us by surprise. What the hell you kere fer anyway?"

Lew crossed over and knelt by the boy. He loosened the tourniquet. Even from across the room, I could see the sudden flood of fresh blood. "You've hit a big artery," he said. "This boy is going to die if he doesn't get to a doctor."

Casey spit more tobacco juice on the floor. "Ain't nothin' we kin do."

Lew stood up. "We can send him to town. I'm going out and hitch up a buckboard."

Casey stood up. "Like hell you are. You want to bring trouble down around our ears?" He waved his gun at Ben. "Boy, run get them horses fer us. And make it damn snappy."

I tried to signal Ben with my eyes to warn Hays, but I reckoned I didn't have to.

Lew looked at Casey. "Are you pointin' that gun at me?" he asked.

"Now, Lew," said Casey, half whining, "I ain't pointin' nuthin' at you. I jes' sayin' we got to get outen here. When we be gone they kin take the boy in. An' we'll be gone quick's we git them horses. Listen," he said eagerly, trying to placate Lew because he was obviously afraid of him, "I taken close to two thousand dollars outen that safe. We got plenty of money."

Lew just shook his head. "I don't want any."

Casey stared at him. "Huh?"

"I ain't no thief." He stepped closer to Casey. "Let's you and I get something straight. I'm gonna ride with you because I ain't got any choice. But I don't like you. And I don't want none of your ways. And don't try no bullshit on me or I'll kill you."

Casey backed up a half step. "Looks to me like I'm holding a gun and yores is still in the holster."

Lew said evenly, "You might get off one shot into me before I drew, but then I'd get three into you before you could get off the next one. You just keep your mouth shut to me and leave these folks alone."

I didn't recall ever feeling so helpless, not even on an occasion when I'd been locked in a root cellar by some people who meant to kill me after they'd got me to confess to something I hadn't done. Mainly, it was because of Dad. I watched him closely. His heart had grown weaker and weaker ever since he'd been shot, and I was fearful that any undue commotion might be too much. For that reason I was even afraid to try and bait our captors into a mistake.

All I could think was thank God for Lew. Even though he'd thrown his hand in with theirs, he was still there to keep them from going to excess. I reckoned he was a little disappointed in me, but there wasn't ought I could do about that.

I did have one additional worry. Ben and I had both carried an extra revolver in our saddle bags during the attack. I was fearful he might elect to retrieve his, load it from his cartridge belt, and step through the door shooting. If he did, there was more than a good chance that enough lead would be flying that one might hit Dad or Norris or the sheriff. I knew he was fast, but there were three armed men on alert for just any sort of trick, and one of them was Lew Vara. He wouldn't want to shoot Ben, but if Ben was shooting he'd shoot back.

All I could do was hope that Ben would play it smart. I just wanted these men gone.

Arnie Welch was drinking whiskey at a pretty good rate. He held the bottle out to me. "Wan' a drink, big shit?"

I just looked at him.

He laughed and turned the bottle up. "Wadn't gonna give you none nohow. Wouldn't gimme no drank, ain't givin' you none."

From the study, you couldn't see out the front. Lew had gone into the office, which did look out into the ranch yard. When he came back he said, "I see a rider heading for town. Looks to be about a mile off. Would that be Hays?"

"Probably," I said. "I would imagine Ben sent him."

Welch lurched up and towered over me. "What's this?" he said. He raised his pistol threateningly as if he meant to cave the top of my head in.

Lew grabbed his arm. "Don't be a damn fool!" he said. "It's

nothing to us if he heads for town. The sheriff's here, and the ranch hands have probably already started this way. And he's on a tired horse."

"I owe the cocksucker a good lick," said Welch. "He shamed me the other day."

Lew said, "Welch, you're drunk. Give me that bottle. We've got a long ride ahead of us."

Welch sulked, but he wasn't about to challenge Lew. "Wahl, I owe him one."

"Appears to me you've already paid him," said Lew. "And you shot that boy. You'll swing for that if he dies. We need to be gone."

It seemed an eternity before Ben got back. Welch and Casey were becoming more and more uneasy, and the more jittery they got the more whiskey they drank. At one point Casey became convinced that we had more money hidden around the house, and he began threatening Norris and me, through Dad, to tell him where it was.

Norris said, in his businessman's voice, "Don't be a fool. In this day and time, no one leaves cash lying around. They put it in banks, where it can draw interest, or in investments, where it can make more money. The only reason we had that much is because it's near the end of the month and payday for the hands."

Casey just stared at him as if he were speaking a foreign language. I imagined that all Casey knew about banks was that they were hard to rob.

But Dad said, "Young man, quit waving that pistol under my nose. If you intend to shoot me, go ahead. You look like the kind that would shoot an unarmed man."

"Casey, you're making a damn fool out of yourself," warned Lew.

Then we nearly did have trouble when Welch ordered Buttercup to the kitchen to fix them a sack of grub. He said, "Gran'pa, you supposed to be cook around this outfit. Git yore ass out to the ki'chen and sack us up some grub. 'Nough fer two, three days."

Buttercup bridled up like a sore horned steer. "Who you

thank you callin' grandpaw, you young pup? Fer two cents I'd
git up offen this floor and whip yore cornbread ass until yore
watermelon mouth called for yore mama."

I didn't want any commotion to upset Dad. "Buttercup!" I
said sharply. "Do what he says. Get them some jerked beef and
some bacon and a big pot of beans. Throw in a cooking pot and
a coffee pot and some coffee. And be quick about it."

He gave me a resentful look, all the while glaring at Welch,
but he got up and did as he was bade.

Ten minutes after Buttercup was gone I heard the screen
door slam, and then Ben came walking into the room with his
hands over his head. "The horses are out front," he said.

Casey looked at him suspiciously. "They good horses?"

Ben gave him a sour look. "We ain't got nothing but good
horses. Damn the luck."

"Welch, go hurry that cook up," said Lew.

Casey was looking us over. "Reckon I'll go find some
rope," he said.

"What for?" asked Lew.

"Tie these sonofabitches up."

Lew gave him a disgusted look. "You don't have to tie them
up. We'll run all their horses off. You think they can catch us
on foot?"

"What about their guns?"

"Unload 'em and sling them out on the prairie. We'll be out
of range in five minutes."

"What about this cannon?"

Lew looked at me. "Throw that one the furtherest."

While Casey was disposing of our firearms out on the
prairie, I talked to Lew. "Well, Lew, I reckon you know what
you're doing. I think you're making a mistake, but if your stick
floats that way I ain't going to nay-say you."

"Don't see no choice, Justa. My only chance is to lay my
hands on Wooley and bring him back to tell the truth."

"Aw Lew, he ain't gonna do that. You'll have to kill him to
keep from getting killed yourself."

"Maybe," he said.

Sheriff Ward had to put his two bits in just then. "Lew, you got folks in town. It ain't going to make them look good, you runnin' off like this. I'm ordering you to disarm them other two and come back with me as my prisoner."

Lew stared at him, speechless.

"Shut up, Vic," I said. "You've caused enough trouble."

That startled him. I'd never talked to him like that before. He said to Dad, "Do you hear how your son is talking to the law?"

Dad said gently, "He was raised to keep his word. Don't blame him."

"Lew, will you leave us one horse?" I asked, and I nodded toward young Hawkins.

He considered. "Will you give me your word that you'll use it to take the kid to a doctor and not to round up your other horses?"

I nodded. "My word on it."

"All right." He gestured at Ward. "I'll leave you his horse. But I'm going to take the saddle and bridle off him. I'll throw a rope around his neck so you can lead him to the barn to harness him up."

About then we heard the sounds of a squabble from the kitchen, followed by a smack and a thud. I half rose, but Lew waved me back down. He stepped into the dining-room door, from where he could still see back into the study. "Welch!" he yelled. "Welch, leave that ol' man alone."

Welch came in looking triumphant, carrying a big cloth sack. "Ol' bastard was tryin' to short us on the coffee," he said. "I fixed him."

Lew just shook his head, as I would have done, in disgust. "Welch, you are some piece of work. Now get that grub loaded. We're leaving."

Casey came back, and Lew told him to get mounted. Casey said, "When'd you start givin' the orders?"

"When you turned out the way you did. Now get moving. And leave that horse that belongs to the sheriff alone. I'll tend to him."

Casey left, with Lew following. He stopped in the door and turned to me. "Justa," he said, "I'm going to ask you not to track us. And don't stick your head out of the house while we're scattering your horses. I won't shoot at you, but I don't know if I can stop the other two."

"We'll stay put until you're good and gone," I said.

He looked sad and ashamed. "I know you don't think much of me for going off with those two."

I shrugged and just looked at him. The truth was I didn't, but I didn't see, as he said, where he had much choice.

He said again, "I wish you wouldn't come after us. I know you will, but I wish you wouldn't."

"You've been talking about not having any selection. You see where I got any?"

He shook his head. "No, I reckon not. But you know I'll have to protect myself."

I nodded. "So will I."

I said to him, "You could split off from those two. They're who I'm going to really be after."

He shrugged. "I ain't sure I'm any better than they are."

"I think you are."

He tipped me a little salute. "Well, adios. I'd wish you good luck, but I ain't real sure I want you to have any. Not in the near future." Then he glanced over at Hawkins. "But I hope the boy makes it. I hope I won't be seeing you."

Then he was gone. After a moment we heard loud voices raised. I imagined it was Casey and Welch arguing with Lew about leaving us a horse. But then the talk subsided and I heard the sound of hoofbeats. I was pretty sure Lew had won the argument, but I still rushed to the door as soon as I heard them depart. The sheriff's horse was still there, tied with a rope as Lew had promised.

I went back into the study. Everyone was getting to their feet. I went to Dad. "How do you feel?" I asked him.

There was the slightest hint of a twinkle in his eye. "Appears the Williams family is losing the biggest part of the arguments here lately," he said.

I thought of what we'd done to Flood and his herd. "Not all of them."

"What do we do?" asked Norris.

"You take the sheriff's horse out to the tack barn," I said, "and hitch him up to the buckboard. We've got to get that kid to a doctor."

"Hadn't we ought to use him first to catch up at least one horse?" Ben asked.

I turned around and stared at him in amazement. He ducked his head. "Sorry."

"You better go see about Buttercup." Then I changed my mind. Ben was better with horses than I was. In fact, he had several that sometimes would come to his whistle. "No," I said, "you better get outside and see if you can whistle up a horse. I'll go see about Buttercup."

I went out into the kitchen. Buttercup was sitting at the table with a cup of coffee and a bottle of whiskey. He was cussing steadily. There was a small lump on the side of his face. "Cussing ain't going to do any good," I said. "They're out of earshot."

Having an audience sent him off into a fresh spasm. When I finally got him calmed down, I asked, "What'd he hit you for?"

"Aw," he said, "I was tryin' to fix the bastards. I dumped this morning's grounds in a can for fresh coffee, but the sonofabitch caught me at it and whomped me up the side of the head. I'd jes' like to have that sonofabitch in my rifle sights, that's all. Just once in them sights. Don't kere about the range. Jes' one shot, that's all I ask."

"I'll run catch them and bring Welch back and tie him to a stake out in the pasture and you can take one shot at him every morning until you hit him. How will that suit you? Say, set up at about a thousand yards and move him in fifty yards a shot."

"Wouldn't take but one mornin'," he said grumpily.

"You got more things to do than sit around here cussing and drinking coffee with whiskey in it," I said. "You pack us enough grub and gear for at least three days, maybe four. Make it four. And put in some canned tomatoes and peaches and whatever else you got to relieve the beef and beans. And a couple bottles of my whiskey."

"Whiskey!" he said. "You be a-goin' on a manhunt, not a social. Want to addle yore brains?"

"Is that what's the matter with you?" I said.

I went out in back and made a vain search for where Casey had thrown our handguns. But it was obvious he'd walked out into the tall grass and flung them in all directions. I spent a fruitless ten minutes searching and then gave up. We'd find them next winter when the grass died down.

I did find Buttercup's old Sharps rifle. It had landed muzzle down, and the barrel was choked with dirt. I took it back in the kitchen and told him about it. That set him off anew, so I slipped out quietly and went outside. Just as I was walking toward the tack barn to see how Norris was coming along and to see what guns might be in the saddle bags that we'd used that morning on the attack, Ben came riding up bareback on one of his favorite horses, a big chestnut that would go all day and help you make camp that night.

"That was quick," I said.

He slid down and tied the horse. "Damn fool is a glutton for oats. Rattle a little in a bucket, and he can hear them a mile away. Let me get him saddled and I'll fetch in a few more. What do you want to ride?"

"That big black of mine," I said. "And that roan I like for an alternate. And we'll need a pack horse."

"Just be the two of us?"

"Yeah."

He whistled. "That is really going to piss off Norris."

"He'll just have to be pissed off," I said. "We're going to be moving fast and hard. And I have the feeling they'll fall in with some of those drovers we ran off."

"You figure they're heading south, then?"

"I know they're heading south. Or I know Lew is. He's going after Wooley, and that's the way Wooley ran. I expect the other two will stick to Lew like leeches. They think he'll be protection. Which is where they are wrong."

Just then Norris came out of the barn, leading the buckboard horse. "We've got to get in a hurry," he said. "What are you two doing standing around gabbing?"

"No hurry, Norris," I answered. "Only hurry is to get that kid into town. Take the buckboard on over to the house and I'll be along to help. Ben, you better get busy. Norris said for us to hurry."

While Ben was saddling his horse, I looked in the saddle bags that Ben and I had used. Sure enough, my extra gun was in mine. Ben's was in his, along with the extra long-barreled revolver Thibbedoux had carried. I held it up and said, "Where'd you get this?"

He was cinching up the girth on the chestnut. "It was laying by him. Didn't see no point in it going to waste. I also took the hundred dollars out of his pocket. What shall we do with that?"

I shrugged. "Donate it to the school fund, I guess. Lew said to divide it up among the men that was riding with him. You might do that."

Our rifles were still in place in their boots. After reloading my spare revolver, I shoved it down in my holster. Then I pitched Ben his. "Don't dally," I said. "When they're all saddled and bridled, bring them to the front of the house."

I walked on back to the house and got there just in time to help Norris and the sheriff load young Hawkins in the buckboard. Norris had stripped a mattress off somebody's bed and fixed it up as a pallet in the bed of the buckboard to make the rough trip a little easier on the kid. We got him laid down, got a pillow under his head, and then covered him with a blanket. The kid was conscious but terribly weak. I didn't give him much chance of making it to town alive. I said to the sheriff, "Vic, you better get going. And don't forget to loosen that tourniquet every fifteen minutes."

He jerked his head back like he'd been slapped. "I ain't goin' to town," he said. "I'm goin' after them outlaws. I'm the sheriff here."

I sighed. I'd expected an argument out of Norris but not out of Vic. "Vic, by tonight they'll be out of your jurisdiction. And we damn sure ain't going to catch them by then. In fact, we'll be damn lucky to catch them this side of the border."

He said stubbornly, "Then I'll be a private citizen after they get out of my county. But they ain't takin' my gun and setting me up against a wall. No, sir!"

"Vic, you've already got more of a problem on your hands than you know about," I said. "There's a lot of dead men out there on that prairie. Flood's men. Between Damon's Mound and Caney Creek. You need to get into town and organize a party, maybe including a preacher and the undertaker, and get out there and see what's what. And there's a lot of dead cattle and horses. You don't get out there tomorrow as early as you can, that place is going to smell so bad you won't be able to get near it. Now get in that wagon seat and get this boy into town!"

"You used that dynamite, didn't you?" he said.

"We'll discuss it some other time, Vic."

"Like hell we will." He took a step back. "Norris can take this boy in."

"Norris has got to stay here and look after Dad and the ranch."

"Oh yeah?" he said. He gave Norris a glance as if to say "You mean like he did last time?"

It made me angry, and I was already none too pleased with Sheriff Ward. I said, "Get going, Vic."

"No," he said. "You're coming with me. I'm getting up a posse right now as I am duly authorized to do, and you and Ben is sworn in. We're going after them three, and we'll take a look at what mischief you done with that dynamite as we pass through."

Norris had been standing quietly by. He hadn't even reacted when Vic had flung his snide insinuation. But now he said quietly, "Vic, you'll be coming up for reelection in less than a year. You've always had money and support from us in the past. I don't believe you can get elected without it. Especially if we run someone against you."

It stopped him in his tracks. He looked at Norris, and then he looked at me. I nodded slowly and said, "That's about the way it falls out, Vic. Now unless you got another way of making a living or got a bunch of money saved up, I reckon you better get to driving this wagon."

He said, a little anguish in his voice, "But I been sheriff for twenty years."

"We know," said Norris. "Could be it's time for a change."

He glanced at us one more time and then, without a word, picked up the reins and climbed into the seat. Just before he slapped the horse into motion, he said to me, "But you still going to have to account to me about using that dynamite on people."

"Get going, Vic," I said.

We watched him as he pulled away. I was conscious of Norris standing beside me. I knew in a moment I was going to have to argue with him. But he surprised me by saying, "I ain't going to ask to come along, Justa. I reckon you are right about me. It was my fault those two got in the house and robbed us and hurt you and Ben. It wouldn't have happened to you or Ben."

"What happened?"

"Nothing much," he said. "They came to the door and said they'd left some stuff in the bunkhouse and could they get it. Next thing I know, I've opened the door to watch what they took and I'm looking at drawn pistols. You can guess the rest. They made me open the safe by threatening Dad. Then Vic came up and I had to let him in. Same reason. Then Hawkins tried to be a hero. He'd been watching the house and seen them go in and figured something was wrong. So he snuck in through the kitchen and came through the dining room and came rushing in the study with that old rifle of his. It misfired, and they shot him in the leg. He's lucky Welch isn't a better shot. Thing was, they didn't have to shoot him. He'd already put his gun down. Welch shot him out of meanness. Anyway, I fucked up and I know it."

I looked at him a long moment, considering. Even on the ranch, Norris dressed in his town clothes. He was wearing a white seersucker suit, though he'd gone without the string tie he usually wore. But he had on city shoes. I said, "You better get dressed and get your guns and plenty of ammunition."

"Dressed?"

"Well, change your clothes. You ain't exactly fitted out for the chase."

He stared at me. "You mean I can go?"

"Ain't you mad as hell the way you got treated?"

"Of course."

"Don't you want to make it clear you won't stand for such abuse?"

"Certainly."

"Then don't stand around here. We're leaving within the hour."

I went in to see Dad. He actually didn't look any the worse for the ordeal. In fact, I got the hazy opinion he might have enjoyed some of it. He was glad to hear I was taking Norris. He said, "You and I both know he ain't got no business going. But it hurts him to be left out of such matters. It makes him feel unworthy."

"And him smarter than all of us put together."

"That's just the way of it," said Dad. "Let him have his chance here. But keep a close eye on him."

"I know."

After that I told him about the fight that morning and about how well the dynamite had worked. It brought a smile to his face. "Good for you, Son."

"It was your idea," I said. "Scared the hell out of me, but it blowed the hell out of them."

"That was the idea," he said. "Listen, Justa, I'm proud you gave that Flood man one last chance. You warned him plenty. But when it comes down to it, there ain't no point in trying to teach a mad dog table manners. It'll just git you bit. You finish them off is what you do. And that's what you did."

"Vic Ward seems a little upset about the matter. I think he plans to take me to task about it."

He smiled slightly. "I wouldn't worry too much about Vic Ward. You leave him to me and Norris."

"Norris already got his attention once," I said. "I guess he can do it again."

I'd been sitting on the couch next to his rocking chair. I got up and said, "I've got to go out and tell Ben to get Norris up a couple of horses. I didn't know then I was going to take him."

Brownsville, the town on the Texas side of the border, was a little under two hundred miles away. I desperately wanted to catch up with them before they could find sanctuary in Mexico, but it was going to be a race. As we set out, sundown wasn't that far off, and they had a good four-hour head start. I asked Ben, as we rode, what kind of horses he'd given them. "Justa, you ought to know yourself, unless you ain't been paying any attention. It's what I told them—we ain't got any bad horses. They may not be as good as what we're straddling, but they'll run anything else in the country into the ground. You can just forget their horses playing out on them."

I'd worried a little about leaving Dad with just Buttercup to care for him, but I knew Hays would get to town, and Hays and the rest of our hands would be back at the ranch before the night was out. I hated to do the men out of their good time, but there was nothing could be done about it. We were still in a fight. I'd just made the mistake of sending them to celebrate a little soon.

Norris was riding along grimly, not saying a word. I was hoping he wouldn't take the position he had something to prove. That kind of an attitude can lead to taking risks, and Norris wasn't good enough to get away with many risks.

"How we going to go about this?" asked Ben.

"Simple. Follow them until we catch them."

"It's a big prairie," he said. "They could be off to either side and we could ride right past them."

I shook my head. "Lew is going to head for Brownsville as direct as a crow can fly. We'll do the same. Wooley has got about the same head start on Lew as he does on us. Except Wooley don't know there is anyone chasing him. Lew knows we'll be hot behind him. If he catches Wooley before he can cross into Mexico—which is what I know he's trying to do—it might slow them up enough for us to catch up."

"Who's going to be shooting at who?" asked Ben.

I thought about it and smiled slightly. "It might get a little confusing. Casey and Welch will be shooting at us. So will Wooley. We'll be shooting at them. I figure Lew won't bother with us unless we get in his way. So he'll be shooting at Wooley and . . . Hell, Ben, what do you want to ask such tomfool questions for?"

The moon was on the wane, but there was still light enough to ride by. We pressed on until nearly nine o'clock and then made a cold camp, eating some beef and cold beans and sucking down a can of apricots apiece. I hadn't wanted to make a fire for fear our quarry might be near enough to spot it and be able to gauge our progress. We each had a drink of whiskey and then turned into our bed rolls and settled down for the night. I looked up at the star-filled sky and thought about Nora. I wondered how long she'd be content to be patient. She would, by now, have heard that I'd settled Flood's hash and run his cattle off. By rights, she'd figure that I was through with the job I'd said I had to do and that I ought to be showing up pretty soon.

Except I was out on the prairie in pursuit of more trouble. And this trouble she wouldn't know about, and there'd be no way for me to get word to her.

And I might be gone a good long time, leaving her to wonder why I didn't come or send word. And that Kansas City drummer had said he was coming back to get her.

And me out on the prairie. I tell you, it made me restless and made sleep hard to come by. I could only comfort myself with the thought that if she really cared for me, she'd understand and be content to wait, albeit in the dark.

Some comfort. Some small comfort.

# CHAPTER
# 9

Early the next day we passed Damon's Mound and then came on the site of the dynamite blasts. Evidently, the undertaker or somebody had been out because all the human bodies were gone, including Mr. Flood. His dead horse and wrecked buggy were still there, but someone had taken him off.

But the dead cattle were still scattered around. They hadn't yet begun to bloat, but they would soon under that relentless June sun. I was surprised to see several parties of people dressing out steers. They appeared to be townsfolk and I guessed they'd come out to get some free meat.

I couldn't say that I blamed them. We waved but didn't dally. Just kept riding. I'd thought that some of them might be from Blessing, and I toyed with the idea of swerving over and sending a message to Nora. But they were a quarter of a mile away, and that would have meant spending a lot of time that I didn't want to spend. I was on the chase, and that was all that was holding my attention.

I was angry, but it wasn't showing. That's one of my oddities: The madder I get, the calmer I get. I wanted Welch the worse, mainly for shooting the young Hawkins boy but also for hitting Ben and me. But I wanted them both for violating our house and putting our father through such an ordeal. I didn't care about the money, though I intended to recover every cent or get the equivalent amount out of their hides. I just didn't like their presumption that they could rob the Williams family and threaten them and steal their horses and beat up on them and get away with it.

Norris had been against hiring them from the first. But thus far, he had foregone saying I told you so. Which was a sagacious attitude on his part.

When we made our nooning, Ben told me that he'd had a hell of a time making Hays go into town. Hays had wanted to come into the study, guns blazing, and rescue us all. Ben said, "It took a lot of convincing to make him understand some people besides Casey and Welch might get hit, and that was no way to run a rescue."

"Ray is loyal to a fault," I said, "but Lord, I wish he'd think once in a while."

"He finally rode off, but he was bitching all the time. Said we didn't have no real appreciation of him."

"Hays would bitch if he was hung with a new rope," I said.

"Harley and the rest should be back at the ranch by now," added Norris. "Maybe matters will be getting back to normal."

We had a little fire going to warm up the beans and make coffee. The people dressing the cattle had had several fires burning, so I'd figured our little bit of smoke against the sky wouldn't be noticed. I reached over and opened the coffee-pot lid to see if it was boiling. It wasn't quite up to bubble. I said to Norris, "What makes you think this ain't normal? I can't remember a time when there wasn't trouble of some kind."

"It'll take a week's work to drift those cattle back to their regular range," said Ben. "And I hate to think how much flesh they lost, eating that salt grass down there on the coast."

"That right there," I said, "is enough to make me hope we find Clarence Wooley before Lew does."

Norris looked up from fiddling with the fire. "We're not after Wooley. Our business with him is done."

Ben looked at him and said coolly, "We run across him, you might find out he figures to still have business with us."

Something had been bothering me ever since we'd passed through the hordes of dead cattle. I was almost sure I'd seen a few with Smalley's brand on them. I told Ben and Norris what I'd seen.

Norris said, "Yeah, and I'm almost certain I saw a couple with Osgood's brand on them."

"What do you reckon?" I said. "They just got mixed in? Though they were at least five miles off their ranch range in Osgood's case and seven or eight in Smalley's? I guess we'll have to pay for 'em. I imagine they'll suddenly all turn out to be seed bulls and high priced as hell."

Ben was in the process of taking the coffee pot off the coals, using his hat for a pot holder. He poured out three cups, handed them around, and then said, "Tom Brown told me he thinks that they sold their cattle to Flood."

"What!"

"Yeah, to make the herd look more legal. They figured, I guess, that they were going to lose them anyway, so they took a short price and drove them down country and in with his Mexican cattle."

"Uh oh," said Norris. "That means you blew up some cattle that he had a perfect right to be moving over the range. That puts us in the wrong."

I mulled that over for a moment. "But ninety percent of that herd was illegal," I said. "Anybody could see through a fast one like that."

"Doesn't matter," said Norris. "Using that dynamite was questionable at best. The law doesn't take kindly to using explosives to blow people and property up."

"What would have been the difference if we'd used guns?"

"Self-defense. Protection of life and property. Guns are a traditional defense. Dynamite is not. Not much a man can do if you bushwhack him with a load of dynamite."

"Shit!" I got up and went to my saddle bags and brought back a bottle of whiskey and poured some in my coffee. Then I passed it around. I took a sip, thinking. "Some neighbors we got," I said. "You think Flood will try and bring legal action over this?"

Norris shrugged. "What's he got to lose?"

Ben said, "Maybe the sonofabitch won't make it. He looked pretty bad all hunched up there against his buggy."

"He'd have to admit he was bringing an illegal herd in," I said.

"No he won't," said Norris. "He can disclaim ownership. He can say he was only acting as an agent."

"But he said in front of the sheriff that they were his cattle."

"An expression open to interpretation. An agent would say they were his cattle."

"Shit!" I said again. I finished my coffee and stood up. "Let's get going. We've got to make some time today."

"Oh, I reckon they ought to be slowing down about now," said Ben.

I looked at him. "What's that mean? You said you gave them good horses."

"I did. They are good horses."

"You mean maybe they didn't take any grain along? Like we did."

Ben gave me a pained expression. "They didn't ask me for any, but I loaded them some on one of their spare horses."

"What did you do that for?"

"Hell, Justa, they're our horses. You reckon I was not gonna see they got fed right?"

"Then what do you mean by they ought to be slowing up?"

He shrugged and said, "Let's wait and see. I can't be sure."

We rode hard all the rest of that day, alternately walking and loping the horses. By now we'd changed to our second mounts, giving our first horses' backs a rest. Occasionally we were coming across little remnants of the Mexican herd. But since they were drifting south, we paid them no mind.

But mostly the prairie was empty. I judged us to be some forty miles from the ranch, but already the vegetation was beginning to change. The lush grass was giving way to more and more spotty patches of brush and little mesquite clumps. I knew that the further south we went the worse would be the grazing. Where our range was, you could damn near figure one head of stock per acre. The country we were entering, it would take two or three acres for every cow. And it would only get worse the further we went until finally, after Corpus Christi, a man would need ten to twenty acres for every head.

The terrain plainly showed the passage of the herd. What grass and weeds hadn't been grazed down had been trampled flat. It was as good as a highway for us. Now and again we'd come across some cow that had weakened and fallen out and laid down to die. Enough time had passed so that the crows and coyotes and buzzards had left nothing but clean-picked bones, shining white in the sun.

I could only guess how far ahead our quarry was. They'd be traveling like us—getting the most out of their horses, stopping only when they absolutely had to, making cold camps so as to not show any smoke, changing horses as often as need be, riding as far into the night as they could.

I didn't figure we were gaining, no matter what Ben said. Casey and Welch might not have sense enough to know how hard I'd be after them, but Lew Vara would and he'd drive them. With his fists or with his will or with a gun, if need arose. But probably his biggest threat would be to leave them.

Then late that afternoon, we came across a horse limping toward us. We pulled up. I saw with some surprise that the horse, a bay gelding, wore our brand. Ben got down and, without a word, went to his saddle bags and took out a pair of pincers. Then he took down his lariat, shook out a loop, and caught the horse. I got down to help him. While I held the horse, Ben took the pincers and pulled all the horseshoe nails, leaving him barefooted. Then he took the rope off, whacked the horse on the rump, and watched him go galloping off across the prairie.

To my questioning look he said, "That's just one."

"What?"

"I loosened two shoes on three of the horses. Well, I didn't really loosen the shoes—I clipped the top off the nails where they come up through the hoof and get bent over. I figured it would take about a day for them to work loose."

"So they're going to be down to three horses pretty soon."

"I reckon," Ben said. He coiled his lariat, hung it back over his saddle horn, put the pincers away, and climbed back in the saddle. "I'm ready," he said.

Norris was not much of a one to talk very much, unless he was secure about his subject. He could talk business or books all day long, but he didn't know a great deal about a manhunt so he mostly kept his mouth shut. But that night, after we'd bedded down, he said, "Justa, if we take those two alive, I want five minutes with that Welch fellow."

I was astonished. My bookish brother? "What are you going to do?" I said. "Bore him to death by reading him a financial statement or a prospectus for municipal bonds?"

Ben laughed.

But Norris said, through clenched teeth, "I'm going to beat him half to death."

Ben said, "Half? Now Norris, you know what Dad taught us: Don't start a job you don't intend to finish."

"Norris," I said, "what's this all about? I never heard you talk like that. What's going on? Why Welch and not Casey?"

There was silence for a moment, and then Norris said, "Because Welch kicked me in the balls."

I succeeded in smothering a laugh, but Ben couldn't control his. To make it worse, he said, "I didn't know you had any."

"By God!" Norris said. He suddenly sat up. "I don't have to take that. Especially from my own brother." He stood up. "Just get up, Ben. I'll practice on you."

Ben was laughing so hard he couldn't answer. I had to climb out of my blankets and head Norris off. "Ben," I said, "now shut up! I mean it! And apologize to Norris. Right now!"

But Ben was still laughing and he had a hard time getting the words out. Finally he wheezed out, "Didn't . . . mean . . . Norris. Sorry."

I said, "Now, that's enough of that. Get back to bed, Norris. We're only taking four hours' sleep tonight. Let's don't have anymore of this foolishness, or I'll send both of you back."

But after everything was quieted back down, Ben said, "Norris, I was just joshing. It just come into my head and popped out my mouth. Just an easy thing to say. I know you got balls." Then he paused. "Though I don't know what you want with 'em, considering the size of your pecker."

Norris didn't get upset. He said quietly, "All right, Ben. I'll get you for this."

I said, "Will you two schoolboys go to sleep, dammit! Next one opens his mouth is going to stand guard the rest of the night."

Which was something I had been thinking about. Lew would know that the horseshoes on the bay gelding had been tampered with. And he would probably figure that we were gaining. He was smart enough to double back on his trail and catch us unawares at night and maybe run our horses off or put us out of commission in some other way.

Next morning we came across the second of our horses. Ben got down and repeated his procedure of the day before. As far away as we were, there was no way of telling if the horses would make it back to the ranch, but we had no choice but to turn them loose. We already had more horses than we could comfortably handle. More would have just slowed us down. But they'd either make it back to the ranch or wander up to some other ranch and we'd eventually get word, since our brand was known up and down the coast.

I said, "They've lost two."

"And should lose a third," added Ben.

"That means they are having to take it slower or stop earlier in the day because they can't change horses. Doesn't matter about the third horse. They can't go any faster than their slowest man."

"We should be gaining on them, then," said Norris.

"Probably."

"How far you figure to Brownsville?"

"Less than a hundred miles, I would reckon," I said. "Maybe a little more."

Ben said, "About three more days, if they push it."

I was thinking. "I've got an idea Lew is going to leave them," I said. "I think he'll take the two best horses and push on."

"Aw, Lew wouldn't do that," said Ben.

"Yes he would," I argued. "Just as I would if I were in his place. He doesn't think any more of Casey and Welch than we do. And he wants Clarence Wooley awful bad. If they go to slowing him up where he thinks we might catch up or Wooley might get away, he's going to cut them loose."

"Then if that happens," said Norris, "it becomes a question of what we do, doesn't it? It's Welch and Casey we want, not Lew Vara."

Ben said to me, "You don't want Lew, do you?"

"No. But I want Wooley. And to get Wooley, I might have to take on Lew. I hope not. Anyway, enough of this talk. Let's get riding."

We pounded hard all that day and on into the night. I figured we'd made the best part of forty miles. But the horses were showing signs of wearing down, and we weren't doing so well ourselves. But that night, making a cold camp, it seemed I could see the faint glimmer of a small fire well down the prairie. I sat up in my blankets, studying it. Being on the prairie is a lot like being on the water: The stars come down so low that they seem to be more a part of the earth than the heavens. But the more I studied the light, the more convinced I was it was a campfire. I pointed it out to Ben and Norris.

"What do you reckon it means?" asked Norris.

"If it's their campfire, it means that Lew has pulled out on them," I said.

"Why?"

"Because Lew has got more sense than to make a fire at night."

"So what do we do now?"

"We get real careful. Norris, you take a watch for two hours. Then call me. Ben can have the dawn watch."

By the afternoon of the next day, I was convinced I could see little specks moving across the prairie in front of us. They could have simply been loose cattle or some other party, but the timing was right for it to be our quarry. Unfortunately, we couldn't push any harder than we had been. The horses were really beginning to show signs of hard use. I hated to think how rode down Welch's and Casey's mounts were with no alternates to change off on.

There is one advantage to being in the catch party pursuing across the coastal plains: Your quarry can't double back on you, and there's no place for him to fort up and take you unawares in a bushwhack. By noon of the next day, we could plainly see our adversaries. And they could see us. We topped a little rise and paused to give the horses a chance to blow and study the situation. We saw them pause also, and it appeared as if they turned in the saddle and looked back at us. We could clearly see it was two riders trailing one extra horse.

"It's them," I said. "Lew has cut them loose and gone on ahead."

But Ben was more concerned about the extra horse. "Them sonofabitches are jerking along a lame horse," he said.

I said, "They're just using it for a pack animal, Ben. He ain't got no weight on him."

Ben was angry as hell. He considered all our horses as belonging to him, and he couldn't stand to see one mistreated. I'd seen him give one of our cowboys a whipping he wasn't likely to forget just because he'd brought a horse in with whip welts on his rump. Now he was incensed at seeing them dragging a horse that should've been set adrift. "Maybe all four shoes came off," I said.

"I only loosened two," he said. "Damn them!"

The way to cripple an animal, or to slow him down, is to loosen just one or two shoes. You don't want to loosen all four, because he'd soon kick them off and go on barefoot. And on our soft prairie, that wasn't any hardship on an animal.

I said, "Well, quicker we get to them, the quicker we can make matters right." I urged my tired horse forward.

As soon as we started moving, we saw the party ahead take off. We could see them urging their horses to greater speed, but from their gait, I could tell the animals didn't have much more to give. We gained steadily. After an hour, I estimated we were only a little over a mile behind. I said, "In half an hour, we'll switch to our other horses and make a run at them."

Ben was looking at the sun, shading his eyes. "Not much more than an hour of good daylight left. Be sundown pretty soon."

"That's why I want to catch them quick," I said grimly. "They might find someplace to hide after dark."

Though I didn't know where. The country had turned rough. It was now mostly rock and sand and cactus and saw grass and tumbleweeds. The only trees were stunted post oak and mesquite that had taken a permanent list to one side from the sea breeze that blew steadily inland. But none of these trees were grouped together enough that they would make much cover.

We pushed on hard. We could plainly see their efforts to distance themselves, but their horses were just rode down. Finally, not too long before dark, we saw them pull up. For a few minutes we couldn't figure what they were doing. There wasn't a bit of cover near them. Far off I'd been able to see a tiny copse of cedar, but I'd known we'd catch them before they could reach that. They must have also.

"What the hell are they doing?" Ben said. "They're in the middle of the bald-ass prairie. Reckon they are going to surrender?"

"No," I said. I knew what they were about, but I didn't want to tell Ben. He'd see soon enough.

They got off their mounts and then one of them, I couldn't tell which, took the animal they were using as a pack horse and positioned him between us and them. The horse had already started to fall by the time the sound of the shot reached us.

Ben jumped up in his stirrups. "Goddamn them!" he raged. "Did you see that? They shot that horse!"

"What did you expect them to do?" I said. "Fight in the open with no cover?"

"I'll skin them for this," he said. "Don't you dare kill 'em, Justa."

Now they were only half a mile away. As we came on, we could see them take the saddles off their worn-out mounts and throw them on the dead animal for more cover. Then one of them drove the two horses off. I reckoned they planned to take

care of us and then make use of our mounts. But as tired as
their animals were, a child could have caught them up. I
figured they were just getting them out of the way of the
gunfire in case they needed them later.

We kept on. At a quarter of a mile, we saw them flop down
behind the dead horse with their rifles. I saw the puff of white
smoke as they fired, and then we heard the whistle of the
bullets over our heads and then the faint crack of the shots.

If they expected to hit anything at such a range they were
kidding themselves, but they might get lucky. "Spread out!" I
said. "Ben, you go to the right. Norris, you stay in the center.
I'll swing to the left."

They fired a few more times, but then I reckoned they saw
it was futile and they held off and saved their ammunition. At
two hundred yards, I called for Ben and Norris to let go of the
spare horses and the pack animal they were trailing. After that,
I called for them to dismount and proceed on foot.

Ben had swung way out to the right and I had done the same
on the left. Since their only cover was dead on, their flanks
were exposed. I yelled for Norris to hold his position some
hundred yards away and keep up a steady rifle fire on them.
"Don't let them raise their heads!" I yelled.

Now I was on the ground, creeping along with my rifle. It
was terribly rough going, what with every inch of ground
covered either with thorny brush or cactus or sharp stones.
Within ten yards, both of my hands were bleeding. I didn't
expect Ben was faring much better.

They tried a few shots in my direction, but I was so low and
there was enough small clumps of weeds and briers that they
couldn't get a clear shot. And by now, I'd turned their flank
and was on their quarter to such a degree that they had to
forsake the cover of their dead pack animal to take a shot at me.
I was about fifty yards away when I peeked around a
good-sized saragousa cactus and could just make out a pair of
legs sticking back from the dead horse. I could see the man's
legs from about the hips down. I aimed carefully and squeezed
off a shot. I heard a yell and saw him jerk his legs up toward
his belly. I didn't know if it was Welch or Casey. I also wasn't

certain I'd hit him. I heard Ben fire from the other side. Norris
was keeping up a sporadic fire from dead on. I hoped he was
holding his position and not exposing himself. But I knew he
felt he had something to prove. He was far enough away—or
at least I'd told him to go to ground far enough away—that he
shouldn't be too exposed.

But that line of thinking went straight out of my mind as a
bullet suddenly plowed into the dirt not six inches from my
face, spraying me with sand and sharp slivers of rock. I
immediately rolled to my left and kept rolling until I'd fetched
up behind a tumbleweed that was anchored on the thorns of a
pear cactus. The cactus was growing out of a crack in a little
shelf of rock that rose up six or eight inches and came as near
to being cover as anything around. Sighting under the tumbleweed, I could now see two pairs of legs from my new
position. I fired and knew that I'd hit, because I saw the near
leg jerk convulsively and heard a yelp. At the same instant Ben
fired, and I saw Welch, who was on the far side, half rise to his
knees. Then he fell back. I fired again at the legs on my side,
which belonged to Casey. But he had drawn them up so that all
I succeeded in doing was shooting the heel off one of his boots.

I began working my way farther around to my left so as to
almost be behind them. Their position was indefensible, and
they were soon going to learn it. Within a few more yards I was
going to be in a position to shoot the ass off both of them.

As I worked my way around, I was gratified to hear the
steady fire from Norris. That meant he was still all right and
keeping them occupied.

I chanced to glance to my right just in time. Casey had
wheeled and, lying flat on his belly, rifle in position, caught me
crossing a little open patch. I snapped off a shot, firing with
one hand, and rolled over and over. The bullet from his shot
struck a bare foot behind me. I ended up behind a bramble
thicket, rammed my rifle through, and fired at what little I
could see of him. He let out a cry. At the same time Ben fired,
and there was an answering yell from Welch.

I was trying to work my rifle barrel around in the bramble

thicket to get a clean shot when Casey yelled, "We give! We give! Don't shoot no more, we give!"

"Throw out your guns and stand up!" I yelled back.

"We are shot to pieces," he said. "I don't know if we can stand up."

"Then throw out your guns and crawl out into the open. If you don't do it in a hurry, we'll start shooting again."

"We're coming!" he yelled. "Hol' yore far, fer God's sake."

I waited and then raised up cautiously, my rifle at the ready. Both men had crawled out from behind the dead horse and were now collapsed on their bellies. I got up and started forward, watching for any movement from either man. Ben was converging from the other side and Norris had started in from the front.

"Don't either of you even twitch," I said. "Or you'll just think you were shot to pieces."

We came up to them. Ben turned them over. They both had their eyes open and there was color in their faces, but they were showing a lot of blood, especially on their pants legs.

"Check them for weapons," I told Ben. "They might have a hideout gun."

Ben jerked their boots off. He found a knife in Welch's boot but no gun.

They were moaning and groaning and calling for water. I said to Norris, "Catch up a horse and bring them a canteen."

"To hell with them," he said.

"Now, Norris," I said, "that ain't a Christian attitude."

"Well, dammit!" But he went off in search of a canteen.

Together, Ben and I got the britches off both of them because it was clear they'd been hit in the legs. Welch wasn't wearing any underwear, and Casey had on a pair of dirty, cut-off long johns.

Casey had been hit three times in the legs—once in his left calf, which wasn't too serious, but twice in the upper right thigh. In addition, the little toe on his left foot had been shot clean off. Since it was on Ben's side, I figured it was his work.

Welch had been hit twice in the left lower leg. One of the bullets had broken the bone. He'd also caught one in the left hand. The bullet had gone all the way through and lodged in the forearm of his right arm. Casey had been hit high on the right shoulder. I figured that was the shot I'd snapped off one-handed.

Norris came back leading all of the horses, including the pack horse. The poor animals were so worn out they'd just stayed, heads hanging, where we'd left them. Ben took their bridles and saddles off and just tied a short picket rope to the halter of each animal. They wouldn't be wandering far. Norris had refused to give them the canteen, so I went over and gave each of them a drink. They sucked it down like water was going out of style.

Ben came over to help me dress the wounds. "I'm only doin' this," he said, "so as to get them well so I can beat the shit out of them for shooting one of my horses."

Norris had a clean white shirt in his saddle bags. I got it out and tore it into strips. He just watched. I could tell he wasn't going to help.

Then I got the bottle of whiskey. Welch said, "Lord, gimmee a drank."

"This ain't for drinking." Then I poured it onto the bullet wounds in his legs. Lordy, he nearly rose off the ground and screamed to wake the dead. It did my heart good to see him hurt so bad. After that, I bound up the wounds with the bandages I'd made from Norris's shirt. I knew the slug was still in his forearm, but that wasn't a job for the likes of us. That would have to wait for a doctor.

After that, I went to work on Casey and got nearly as good a response from him as I had from Welch. I didn't know what to do about his shot-off toe. The wound was so clean it looked like it had been done with an ax.

"You ought to cauterize that," said Ben. "Be the only way to keep it from bleeding."

"We ain't got an iron."

"Use a knife."

"Build a little fire while I look at his shoulder."

Casey raised his head slightly. "What are ya'll gonna do?"

"You don't want to know," I said.

With difficulty, I got the shirt off him. The shoulder wound appeared to be more than I could handle. The bullet seemed to have entered from the front, traveled on until it hit the shoulder blade in the back, and broke that. There were no signs of it coming on through. All I could do was pour in some whiskey and tear off a strip of cloth and use it as what I'd heard called "a tent." What you did was stick a small strip of cloth down in the bullet hole. That was supposed to keep the wound draining and keep it from healing outside in. A doctor had once told me a wound had to heal inside out; if it went the other way, you were likely to get an infection.

When I was through, I said to Casey, "You two sonofabitches are stupid. Didn't you know we'd work around behind you? Why didn't you kill the other two horses and use them for cover?"

"We was scairt of being afoot out here," he said.

I looked across the prairie where their horses were standing, too tired to even graze. "You were already afoot," I said. "I take it Lew took the best two horses and lit out."

"Yeah." Casey licked his lips. "I shore could use a drank of whiskey."

Ben was standing over him. "You bastard," he said, "you ain't getting any whiskey. All you're getting is rough treatment. Shooting my horse."

"Hell, he was lame," Casey whined. "He was nearly crippled. It were an act of kindness."

"The horse wasn't lame," said Ben. "I loosened shoes on three of them. You idiots didn't have sense enough to notice."

"Well, damn," Casey said tiredly. "I should have knowed. Damn the luck."

Just then I noticed that Norris had come up and was standing over Welch. His face was set and angry. "Get up, Welch," he said.

Welch looked puzzled. "I cain't. I'm shot."

"Get on your feet or you'll get shot again."

"Cap'n, I cain't. I tell you, I'm hurt bad."

"Get up!"

"Hell, Norris, don't do that," I said.

"Welch, stand up, damn you," he said again.

"Norris, the man is hurt. It's not fair."

"I don't give a damn," he said. His face was set and determined. He'd vowed he was going to kick Welch in the balls and, dead or alive, he was going to do it.

Ben got up from the little fire he'd built to heat the blade of Welch's knife. "I'll help," he said. He went around and got Welch by the shoulders and lifted him to his feet.

Welch cried, "Here! What are you doin'! Stop this here foolishness!"

Ben got him on his feet and Welch stood there, tottering uncertainly. Ben said to Norris, "You better hurry."

I was disgusted. Without warning, Norris kicked Welch squarely and with maximum force right in the crotch—his naked crotch with his balls hanging down. Welch let out a scream and collapsed to the ground, moaning and holding himself. Norris leaned down and yelled in his face, "That's what it feels like! Maybe you won't be so quick to go around kicking people in the balls the next time."

I just shook my head. "You two are children," I said. "Ben, is that knife ready?"

"Starting to glow. Be red in just a second."

Welch just thought he'd had the best of the party. When I laid the blade of that red-hot knife to the stump of Casey's toe, I think Casey would have swapped out right then and there for a kick in the balls. He literally rose up in the air, and his scream was probably heard in some parts of Houston.

But the cauterization certainly stopped the blood, and he'd been losing quite a bit. I told him, but he didn't seem to appreciate the information; he just kept moaning and carrying on.

"These boys act like sissies," Ben said. "You'd think anybody that could shoot a kid and threaten a sick old man ought to be tougher than that. Hell, they just a couple of pussies."

I wet a scrap of cloth and hung it over the cauterized stump. I said to Casey, "You decide to ride the owl-hoot trail, you've got to expect these little inconveniences ever so often."

It was growing dark. There wasn't much we could do for the horses. Ours had had a good watering early that afternoon at a little creek we'd crossed. I assumed that Casey and Welch had done likewise.

Ben got what feed we had left and went out and gave each horse a little bait to go with the dry grass they were already starting to tentatively graze on. They wouldn't get much help from it, but I was glad to see them eating. A horse that will try to eat is not going to lay down and die on you, and I'd seen horses so rode down that you could have put a barrel of sweet oats under their noses and they'd have ignored them and just went down and never got up again.

We started getting ready for the night. Norris went out and got a load of wood, and I got Welch's and Casey's bed rolls and got them in them. I didn't expect any help with the wounded prisoners from either Norris or Ben, but for different reasons. Of course, they didn't know what good news I was going to give them later that night.

For supper we had beef and beans and canned tomatoes. I gave each prisoner a plate, but they only picked at their food. I said, "You better eat up and get your strength back. You've got a hard ride tomorrow."

Casey flung his arm over his face and moaned. "Cap'n," he said, "we're shot to pieces. I cain't even move."

"Fine with me," I said. "Then you can lay out on this prairie and die."

"We need a couple days to rest up."

"When did Lew leave?" I asked.

"Yestiday mornin'. Right after cawfee, he taken an' put a gun on us an' said we was to saddle his horse and put another on lead. Then he taken the best part of the grub and lit out."

"He say where he was goin'?"

"Brownsville, I reckon. Ain't nothin' else in that direction. An' he taken off due south."

"You're sure he was heading south?"

"Course. We could see him there, four miles off, an' he never flinched from south."

"You think Clarence Wooley's in Brownsville?"

His face got blank. "I don't know nuthin' about no Clarence Wooley."

"You want a drink of whiskey?" I asked him.

His face got eager. "Hell, yes!"

"Then answer my question about Wooley."

His face went dead again. "Told ya. Don't know nuthin' 'bout no Clarence Wooley."

From my left, Welch suddenly said, "He's a-lyin'. He's jes' scairt of Wooley. You give me a drank of whiskey an' I'll tell you."

"Tell me first," I said.

Casey said, "You better keep yore mouth shut. You'll get us both kilt."

"Gimmee the whiskey," said Welch.

"Tell me."

He considered. But I could see in his face that he was dying for a drink and that the whiskey was going to win out. He said, "Wooley headquarters in Brownsville an' San Antone. If he ain't on a job, he's in one place er the other'n. Vara is gonna find him, 'cause he said so. And if Vara says he be gonna do somethin', he'll do it. You stay after Vara and you'll find Wooley. Myself, I wouldn't want to find him. An' anybody with a lick o' sense wouldn't neither."

I got up and poured him out half a tin cup full of whiskey. He had it drunk as soon as it hit his mouth. He held the cup back out. "I got to have more, Cap'n."

"Why don't you ask one of my brothers for more?"

"Aw," he said. "You a gen'lman, Cap'n. Help a poor man out."

Casey said, "What about me? I didn't get none."

"And you didn't talk none, either."

I went back to the campfire and sat down. I got out my pocket watch and looked at it by the light of the fire. It was nearly eight o'clock—nearly time to turn in. I planned to be on the move by five the next morning.

But I still had to give Ben and Norris the news.

I waited until they'd mellowed down with a little coffee and whiskey, and then I said, "I'll be pushing on in the morning."

"Where we heading," said Ben, "Brownsville?"

"You ain't going," I said.

He looked shocked. "You ain't taking Norris, surely!"

Norris said, "And why not?"

Ben began to sputter, but I said, "I'm not taking either one of you. You've got to get those two to a doctor and a sheriff, and it's not a job for one man. That's why you've both got to go."

"But, Justa," argued Ben, "you may run into Lew *and* Clarence Wooley. Them ain't good odds."

"Lew is not going to be shooting at me," I said. "He may try to stop me from killing Wooley, but I'm not interested in killing Wooley. I'm interested in bringing him back for the murder of Boyd and Charlie. That'll serve Lew's purpose as well as mine. Lew knows I understood he had to take off with Welch and Casey. He didn't have any choice. If he'd've stayed, Vic Ward would have arrested him."

Norris said, "I am against you going on by yourself. It's a dangerous trip, and I'm going to tell you what you're always telling me: The ranch couldn't function without you. You've got responsibilities to the ranch and to the family."

"Oh, hogwash, Norris," I said. "Ben and Harley could run that ranch without me and you know it. Don't come that game on me. My only use to this family is to make it clear to folks who want to mess with us that it ain't a real good idea. That's why I can't let Wooley get away with anything. Somebody else might get the idea we're easy. Getting a little money and being well off ain't all that hard. But staying well off is. Too many people want what you got. My job is to discourage them."

"I wish you'd take one of us along," said Ben.

"You've got jobs. Ben, yours is to get back and pitch in with Harley and get the ranch to operating back to some semblance of normal. Norris, you've got to get into Blessing and see what Vic Ward is up to about this dynamite business. See how Flood is and see what action he may plan to take. If it looks like it might get serious, you might want to contact our Houston attorneys. Joe Bloom in Blessing is a good man, but this might be over his head."

"That's just what I'm talking about," said Norris. "You have a much greater responsibility to the family and to the ranch than just with your gun. You are the boss. You are always saying that you can't risk me because I know all of our business affairs. You can get another bookkeeper, which is what I am, but you don't get another boss that easy."

Ben said, "He's right, Justa."

"He may be," I said. "And you may be. But the one clear theme that has been declared here is that I'm the boss. And the boss says you are taking these boys back tomorrow and I'm going on."

They groused and complained, but in the end, they gave in. "We ain't taking them all the way back to Blessing, are we?" asked Ben.

"Not unless you want to bury them along the way. No, I figure Kingsville is only about forty miles northwest of here. You won't make it tomorrow night, but you should get there day after tomorrow. Get them to a doctor and go to the sheriff and have him wire Vic Ward. That ought to get them held until Vic can extradite them from one county to another. I don't know how that works, but I figure he's mad enough at them holding a gun on him that he'll find a way."

Norris wanted to know if I wanted him to pack me up some supplies. I shook my head. "I'll just take a little meat. I figure to make Brownsville by late afternoon or early evening. It can't be more than twenty miles. Even taking it easy, it should be a pretty short ride. Ben, which horse is in the best shape?"

"My chestnut," he answered. "I'll give her a little extra oats before I turn in. She ought to be in pretty good shape by the time you leave in the morning."

"When you get your business done in Kingsville," I said, "I want you to load yourselves and the horses on the train to Houston. If they'll stop for you in Wharton, you'll only have a thirty-mile ride to the ranch, and the horses ought to have picked up by then."

Kingsville was the site of the huge King ranch, and the railroad—just as they'd done for us—had run a spur line down to accommodate them, even though there wasn't a blessed thing for a hundred miles.

"I hope you'll be careful, Justa," said Norris.

I started to say I would, but Ben said, "Shit, he don't know how. He calls me wild. Hell, he's crazy."

We were a family that always said the best of each other.

We went to sleep that night to the moans and groans of Casey and Welch. I'd figured they were too bad hurt to be dangerous, but Ben insisted on tying their hands together with leather tongs.

He was a mean sonofabitch in some ways. But he was my brother. For better or worse.

# CHAPTER
## 10

As I rode out the next morning, it was still a good hour to dawn. I let the chestnut just shamble along, picking her way in the dark over the rough country. Ben had fed her the last of the grain and that had pepped her up a little, though I reckoned her to be pretty sore from four days of hard riding.

But I had plenty of time. I figured to ride for about three hours, then stop and make some coffee and eat a little beef and let the chestnut graze and rest. Not too many people know that a man walks faster than a horse. A man can walk four miles an hour, but a horse, just slacking along, will only do a little better than three. You've got to push a horse up to a fast walk to bypass that four-mile-an-hour clip. Of course in a lope, a horse can knock off six or seven miles an hour and keep it up all day for at least a couple of days. But then you're back down to that slow walk and not making any time. In the chase we'd just been on, we'd been averaging better than forty miles a day for four days, and that will take it out of a horse. Even horses as well cared for and conditioned and fed as ours were. The chestnut I was riding, like all our horses, had a strain of thoroughbred blood in her. Some years back, Ben had started

breeding back all our quarterhorse mares to some damn
expensive thoroughbred studs. The result had been a string of
horses with that quick speed of the quarterhorse but with the
staying power of the thoroughbred.

And Lew Vara was riding one of our horses and leading
another. Both with our brand on them. I reckoned we'd be able
to reach an understanding without too much trouble. Horse
stealing, in our part of the country, is reckoned to be a pretty
serious offense, ranking just below cheating at cards and just
above murder.

I figured he had a half-day start on me, but that didn't
amount to much. It would take him better than a day or two to
slip quietly around Brownsville and get on to Clarence Wooley's whereabouts.

My plan was to find Lew and get him to throw in with me.
After all, our aims were the same: to bring Wooley to justice,
though for different crimes. I had originally intended to kill
Wooley because I didn't figure I'd be able to prove he'd been
on the raid when Boyd and Charlie had been murdered. But
now Lew was in the way, and I didn't want to fight Lew to get
at Wooley. So my only choice was to take him back alive
somehow and work to get him convicted. I figured to perjure
myself and claim I saw him on the raid and saw him participate
in the deaths of Boyd and Charlie. I wouldn't feel bad about
doing such a thing, because if he hadn't actually been on the
raid he'd ordered it, and it amounted to the same thing.

Dawn came and we began making better time, since the
chestnut could see where she was putting her feet. I figured she
was pretty sore, but she was going along strongly, driving
forward with her big, powerful rear hams and reaching out with
her front legs. She had a very nice gait. You could have drank
a glass of whiskey on her back and never bumped your teeth
with the rim or spilled any.

After a while I got to smiling, and then I laughed out loud.
I was thinking about my mild-mannered, bookish brother and
his insane determination to kick Welch in the balls, wounded or
not. It really hadn't been all that out of character. Norris had a
bulldog quality about him, and once he'd set his mind to do

something he was going to do it, no matter what. Welch could have been gasping his last and Norris would have still propped him up and kicked him. You did not mess with Norris's private person. I knew that, but Welch hadn't. I once hit Norris when I was about eighteen and he was sixteen. I had hit him a good lick, one that had knocked him unconscious. From then on it was fight at first sight. I finally got so tired of whipping him that I begged him to call it off. But that wouldn't do. He was going to pay me back that lick if it killed him. And it damn near did. He was cut and bruised about the face and had black and blue marks all over his ribs where I'd taken to hitting him in the body to keep from marking up his face anymore. Our mother had still been alive then, and she was getting plenty tired of Norris showing up for supper with a split lip. Of course he couldn't fight for sour apples, but that didn't make any difference. He was going to get in that last lick to pay me back for the first one. Finally I let him catch me a good one on the mouth, and I went down and stayed there. It nearly scared Norris to death. He thought he'd killed me. When he ran for a wet rag, Dad came by. He'd seen the whole thing and he'd said, "Get up from there and quit scaring your brother. Ain't you got any sense? You don't have to play at being dead, holding your breath. Way you work I sometimes think you've passed on with a hay fork in your hand."

I never hit Norris again. It was just too much work.

And now Lew Vara lay ahead. Another determined man. I knew that from the fight we'd had. I'd knocked him down enough to have settled the hash for half a dozen men. But he'd kept getting up. Well, I was going to have to find some way to reason with him without fists or guns involved.

About ten in the morning we struck a little creek shaded by some oak and mesquite and palm trees. When you got down near the border, you commenced to run into palm trees. I had been all along the coast of Mexico and even down into Central and South America, so I was familiar with the species. Still, it was strange to see such an exotic plant sticking up out of the arid plain.

I pulled in at the creek and unsaddled the chestnut. I took the bits out of her mouth so she could water and then graze on the green grass that was growing along the creek bank.

I built a little fire and made some coffee and then had a lunch of beef and biscuits. After I'd washed up and put the fire out, I lay back against my saddle, smoking and thinking. I'd figured to lay up for about two hours and give the chestnut a good rest. I figured the morning's walk had worked the soreness out of her, so now all she needed was a little rest and she'd be as good as new. I was just thinking of grabbing myself a little catnap when I heard the distinct sound of a shod hoof striking against stone. And it wasn't the chestnut because she was still down on the creek bank grazing on the soft grass.

I came immediately alert. The sound had come from my left, but I didn't turn that way. Instead I slowly eased my revolver out of its holster and held it in my hand by my right side so that it was out of sight.

The sound of two horses came nearer. I heard the creak of saddle leather. I kept my eyes half slitted so that they looked closed. The horses were very near. I heard them stop. Then a man's voice said, "Okay, tramp, up an' on yore way. Yo're on private propity an' you be trespassin'."

I opened my eyes and looked to my left. Two men sat a-horseback not five yards from me. They were a rough-looking pair, unshaven and dirty. Their horses were no great shakes either. One of them, the one on my right, appeared to be about half Mexican or maybe more. The other was just ordinary work-a-day common trash. He had a red kerchief around his neck.

"That ain't very friendly," I said. "I'm just passing through. Stopped to water my horse."

"Well, keep passing," Red Kerchief said. "Sling your saddle."

I eased over on my left elbow but still kept my right hand behind my back, holding my revolver. I said, "Look here . . . My horse is rode down and needs a blow. She ain't drinking that much water."

Red Kerchief said, "I got to tell you agin?"

"I been on this range plenty of times before and I ain't ever been treated so rudely. What the hell is going on?"

"You're going on," he said. "Now."

The Mexican-looking one said, "You geet, meester. Or chou one sorry hombre."

"Just whose ranch is this, they don't want any company?" I asked.

Red Kerchief said, "Thet wouldn't be none o' yore business. Yore business is gettin' up off yore ass an' gettin' the hell outen here."

I yawned.

The Mexican said, "I theenk I kill me one gringo." His hand made a motion toward his gun.

Before he could even touch the butt, they were both looking at the open mouth of my .44/.42. "Be real still," I said.

They froze.

I said, "Now, you two get off your animals," I ordered. "Do it real careful and keep both your hands where I can see them. I guarantee you I can get two in each one of you before you can even think of getting a gun in your hand. Now move!"

They were watching me warily, calculating, gauging me. For a second they didn't budge. I came up on one knee and pointed my revolver straight at the chest of the Mexican. I said softly, "You first."

Without taking his eyes off me, he slowly swung his leg around and dismounted. I switched to Red Kerchief. "Now you."

He did as the Mexican had. When they were both standing beside their horses, I said, "Now, using just your left hand, unbuckle your gun belts and let them fall. Do it carefully. Ya'll have done made me nervous, and this Colt of mine has had the trigger release filed down to a hair."

They dropped their gun belts and I told them to take two steps forward. "I wouldn't want ya'll to get tempted to bend over and grab. I'd have to shoot you in the head, and that would be messy. Now, just what the hell is this all about? When did folks in this part of the country start running strangers off the range? Passing strangers?"

"It's our boss," said Red Kerchief sullenly. "Man owns the ranch. He don't like strangers poking about."

"And who would be the man that owns this ranch?"

The question seemed to embolden Red Kerchief. "He's a man you'll damn shore whisht you hadn't fucked with. That's who he be."

"Does he have a name?"

"Damn right. It's Mr. Flood. Mr. J.C. Flood. And it'll be a sorry day fer you thet you throwed down on a couple of his riders."

I couldn't help myself, and I laughed out loud. It all came pretty plain then. "Stolen any Mexican cattle lately?" I asked.

Red Kerchief jerked his head back. He began to sputter. "You be callin' us cattle thieves?"

"Damn right," I said. "And now I can understand why Mr. Flood doesn't want anybody poking around. By the way, I've been passing bunches of your cattle for the last forty miles. They ought to be drifting in any day. Better catch them as they pass, because I think they're heading for home. Which is across the Rio Grande."

They both stared at me. The Mexican finally said, "Chou know Meester Flood?"

I laughed again. "He's probably the only man I ever blew up in a buggy. With dynamite."

They looked at each other. Then they came back to me. Red Kerchief said, "He ain't . . . Is he kilt?"

I shook my head. "Worse luck. But I reckon you boys can take the next couple of weeks off. Now, I want you to tell me where Clarence Wooley is. Is he here on the ranch?"

I swear they both went pale, which was a pretty good trick for the Mexican. They didn't say a word. "Well?" I said.

Red Kerchief said, "I don't know nothin' 'bout no Clarence Wooley."

"I've heard that before," I said dryly. "Now come on, let's have the truth. I'm gonna get it out of you one way or the other."

"Doan' know nuthin'," said Red Kerchief.

I took his hat off with one shot. He jumped, but he settled

down immediately when he realized he hadn't been hit. He turned slightly and looked behind him at his hat, which now bore a neat hole in the front.

"Be much cooler that way in the summer," I said. I cocked my pistol. "I'm gonna take you in the kneecap with the next one. Be a long time before you do any walking. Might even be a cripple."

"Wait a minute!" he said. "Jest a damn minute!"

"Well?"

He stared at the ground. "He ain't here."

"Where is he?"

He looked up at me defiantly. "Onliest reason I'm tellin' you is 'cause I hope you find him. Then we'll see who's sorry. He's in Brownsville. Er that's whar he lit out fer."

"Where does he stay?"

"Damn if I know. And thet be the truth."

I figured he wasn't lying and that I wasn't going to get much more out of these two prairie gophers. "Well, that's fine," I said. "Now you two gentlemen unsaddle and unbridle your horses."

That got me another staring. Red Kerchief said, "What fer?"

I said, "Cat fur to make a pair of kitten britches. Now get at it before I take you off at the legs."

Reluctantly, sullenly, they did as they were bid. When they were through, I waved them away and then I went over and yelled at their horses and slapped them and fired my pistol in the air. Both animals, not being of the best breeding, took off for the wilds. Red Kerchief was almost apoplectic. "Here! What the hell you done! You leavin' us afoot out here?"

"Exactly," I said. "Take off your boots."

I had to threaten them again, but they eventually did as they were told. I was enjoying myself. Mr. Flood's whole plan of operation had become quite clear. The herd we'd run off was probably just the first of many. He used his ranch as a holding ground while his crew raided into Mexico and brought back small lots of cattle. Then, when he had enough to make the drive to Houston, he set out. Some specimen, Mr. Flood. Well,

I was going to bust his whole operation up. Starting with these two fine specimens. "Start walking," I said.

"You be joshing!" protested Red Kerchief. "It's six miles to ranch headquarters."

"That being the case, I reckon you better get started."

He started in to whine about how rough the country was and what it would do to their feet. I put a shot within six inches of his right foot, and he hopped straight up. I reckoned some little sharp rock splinters had gotten through his grimy socks.

I cocked my pistol and just looked at them. They finally started walking, but they glared back at me with every halting step they took. By the time they'd gone fifty yards they were both limping. Red Kerchief yelled back at me, "I hope to hell you find Clarence Wooley. He'll fix yore wagon proper."

They were certainly a bad-tempered pair.

I watched them until they were perhaps half a mile away, and then I caught up the chestnut, slipped the bit back in her mouth, and saddled her up and stepped aboard. By the sun I figured it was near on to noon and I figured I couldn't be much more than nine or ten miles from Brownsville. With the mare stepping right out, that would be no more than a two-, two-and-a-half-hour ride.

I hit the outskirts of the town, by my pocket watch, at a little after three. I headed straight for a livery stable and got the chestnut mare bedded down in a stall with plenty of hay and oats. She looked like she was glad to see a barn again. I reckoned she was as sick of the prairie as I was, especially that last fifty miles.

I got my saddle bags that still contained a clean change of clothes and headed for the nearest hotel. Brownsville, like most border towns, wasn't exactly at the forefront in civilized living, and the hotel was as good an example as any. I took the best room they had and inquired about a bath. The desk clerk, who seemed to be taking a nap even while I was talking to him, said he could have a tub brought up to my room and some boys would fetch up pails of water. He said it would cost me a dollar. I said I thought I could stand it. I had taken the money back off Casey that he had stolen out of the safe. I had also taken back the money I'd paid him on the good grounds that he hadn't earned it. I'd done the same for Welch. They'd squealed, but I'd explained that where they were headed, the state would see to their needs and they wouldn't need any money. They'd been a hundred and fifty dollars short of what they should have had, but Casey said that Lew had taken that. Casey had said that Lew had said he had it coming, and I suppose he did.

I went up to my room. It featured one of those kind of beds where the mattress sags so badly that everything rolls to the middle. I threw my saddle bags on the bed and then walked to the window and looked out on the dusty street. Brownsville was a town that was sort of shaped like a T. The leg of it was the main street that ran down to the Rio Grande. The top of the T was the part that stretched up and down the banks in front of the international bridge that crossed into Mexico. I reckoned it to be a pretty big town, with something like five thousand inhabitants. It damn near had as many saloons, which was going to make it a job of work to comb either Lew or Clarence Wooley out of the hair of the place.

I started with the livery stables, hunting through them for the two Half-Moon horses that Lew had departed with. I figured the horses would be easier to find than him. I finally found them down in a little stable that was attached to a hotel. I figured Lew wouldn't stable the horses at one place and stay at another, but then you never knew. There was a saloon across from the hotel, and I got a table by the window and settled down to wait. I figured I'd find Lew sooner or later, but the trick was to catch him off guard and get the drop on him, so as to have time to talk before he could either shoot at me or run.

So I sat, sipping slowly at a glass of whiskey and smoking. Lew had to be afoot, unless he'd hired or bought another horse, so that meant he was just walking around, looking for Wooley. By six o'clock I'd sat there for better than an hour, and I was drawing some attention from the other patrons, who were a pretty seamy-looking lot. The border is not exactly famous for the quality of its gentry. You can make one of either two observations of any man you meet along the border: He is either being chased or he is chasing someone. Most outlaws don't like to stay in Mexico because, sooner or later, they are likely to run afoul of the Mexican authorities, and I've heard there is nothing worse than falling into the hands of the Mexican law. For that reason, you'll find a standing army of scoundrels and renegades perched for flight somewhere near the Rio Grande. And the problem with any social contact with such is that most of them already have so many crimes on their heads that one more is just another raindrop in a storm.

I had been aware that a big hombre with damn near no neck and arms about the size of my thighs had been eyeing me from the bar for some time. He wasn't a pretty sight. He'd gone nearly bald and he had a badly squashed nose and two or three scars about his face. His gun wasn't exactly set up like that of a gunfighter, so I figured him to be a saloon brawler, one that preferred his fists or a knife. In either case, I didn't need trouble with him. But of course, it wouldn't be the first time in such a place. I couldn't recall ever being down in a border town in which I didn't have trouble of some kind.

After a time of drinking and brooding and staring at me, he finally decided the time was right. He pushed away from the bar and came straight to me. He stood there, looking straight into my face. I said, "Yeah?"

"Lissen, how long you a-gonna set there a-usin' my table?"

I looked around. There were four or five empty tables, including one just behind me that looked out on the street through an identical window. I said, "I didn't know these tables came with names on them."

"Wahl, you're a-talkin' mighty high and mighty fer a nimrod ain't none of us ever seed before."

With my boot I shoved out the chair across from me. "If this is your table, then sit down. I'll buy you a drink."

He wiped a hand, about the size of a bear's paw, across his nose. He said, "Whatta you reckon I'd a-wanna be drankin' with the likes of you?"

"Well, it's a choice," I said. "If you don't have a drink, you're going to work yourself up to where you're either going to take a swing at me or pull a knife. If you try it, I'll shoot you before you can do either one. About three times. So that's your choice. You can either have a drink or get real dead. Which is it to be?"

He stared at me, dumbstruck. "You a-meanin' to tell me you'd up and kill a man over a damn table?"

I shook my head. "Not over the table. You've been eyeing me for the last half hour, trying to figure out the best way to get me in a fistfight. I haven't got the slightest intentions of fighting somebody like you. So I'd shoot you to keep from getting beat to death. Not over a table."

He looked at me hard for a second, and I thought he really was going to swing. I shifted in my chair a little, so as to clear my holster. I had no intentions of being beat half to death by somebody like him.

Then he suddenly laughed. "Why, yo're a good ol' boy." He clapped me on the back, nearly knocking my face into the table. "Yeah, you had me figgered prezactly. But I didn't know I was a-gonna run into no hornets' nest. Yeah, I'll have that drank."

He sat down opposite, and I signaled the bartender for two more whiskeys. While the whiskey was coming, he looked at me suspiciously. "You ain't the law, are you?" he asked.

I shook my head. "No. I'm a rancher."

He brightened. "Es thet a fact! Say, you lookin' to buy some Mexican cattle?" He leaned across the table and said, confidentially, "I kin git you some dirt cheap. How many ya want?"

"I don't want any Mexican cattle. I don't have the time or the money to hold them in quarantine."

"Hell, buddy, they is ways 'round thet. You ain't got to worry 'bout no quarantine. An' I'm talkin' dirt cheap, too."

"Naw, I reckon not," I said. "I've come to see a man has a ranch little north of town. He's got some cattle he says he's looking to unload. They're Mexican cattle, but they've been quarantined."

His eyes narrowed. "Who would you be talkin' 'bout? This here man got cattle to unload?"

The bartender brought our drinks, and I paused while he set

them down. When he was gone, I said, "Fellow name of Flood. J.C. Flood. I'm going to see him in the morning."

"Shiiit!" he said. "J.C. Flood! Why thet hombre is the biggest crook in six counties. He ain't got no quarantined cattle! Them cows of his is still so green they got to be fed tamales. J.C. Flood my ass!"

"You know him, then?"

"Know him? Why that crooked sonofabitch has done me out of mor'n a few dollars. An' iffen he didn't always go around with that damn gunsel of his, I'd a-settled him a long time ago."

"I suppose you mean Clarence Wooley?" I said innocently.

He slapped the top of the table with the palm of his hand. I thought the legs would collapse. "The very one!" He narrowed his eyes at me. "Say, you wouldn't be no friend of his, would you?"

"Other way around," I said. "Him and I are due to get something settled between us. You wouldn't happen to know where he is, would you?"

My friend took a huge gulp of his whiskey and then wiped his mouth with the back of his paw. "Big Tom knows ever'thang goes on in this town."

"You being Big Tom?"

"Hell, yes," he said. "Seen enybody bigger?"

"And you know where Wooley is?"

"Not prezactly, but I reckon I could find him. He's 'round town. Seen him yest'idy."

All the while we'd been talking, I'd been staring across the street. It was coming dusk, and I was fearful Lew would slip by me in the dark. But just at the instant I'd asked Big Tom if he could find Wooley, I saw Lew Vara's unmistakable profile come down the street and turn into the little hotel.

"So you could find him?" I said.

"If I wanted to."

"What would it take to make you want to?"

He looked at me shrewdly, calculating how much I was good for. "Ten dollars," he said.

I went into my pocket. I had a little roll of greenbacks for show, but the majority of the nearly two thousand dollars was in my boot. I peeled off a twenty, shoved the rest of the money back in my pocket, and then tore the twenty in half. I handed Big Tom half of the bill. He looked at it, perplexed. "Thet ain't my idear of a ten-dollar bill. Feller, are you crazy?"

"I'm going to give you twenty." I told him the name of my hotel and said, "You find Wooley without letting him know that anyone's looking for him. Then you come to my hotel and tell me. I'll want to know tonight or as early in the morning as I can." I waved the other half of the bill. "Then you get the other half of this. Take it to the bank, and they'll give you a brand new one to replace it."

"Wahl, if that don't beat all!" he said. "I never heered of sich a thang. But look here, iffen I don't find him, we is both out twenny dollars."

"Make a try. You look like an honest man. I'll just bet you find him."

"You shore you ain't no frien' of this Wooley's?"

"You sure you aren't? I don't want him to know I'm looking for him."

He said, "Ef I could ever ketch that cocksucker with his back turned er when he didn't have that damn gun, I'd show you what good frien's we is. I'd get him in a bear hug and break his fuckin' back."

I stood up. Lew would have had time to get to his room and get settled down. I dropped three silver dollars on the table. "Have a couple of more drinks on me," I said.

"Why, thankey kindly. Yo're a real gent."

"Sorry I couldn't give you a fight," I said.

He waved a huge hand, dismissing it. "Aw, thet's all right. Somebody else'll come along. I'll probably see you tonight. Say, who do I ast fer?"

"Oh, 'Bill' will do. I'm in room four. If I'm not there, it'll just be because I'm out for a bite of supper."

I left Big Tom holding half a twenty-dollar bill and scratching his head. I expect he was trying to decide if I was crazy. Tearing money in half probably didn't strike him as the proper way to treat the stuff. But soon enough he'd figure out that it had been done to make him try harder, and try harder he would.

I crossed the street and entered the lobby of the hotel I'd seen Lew go in. It was about on a par with the one I was staying in; at least the desk clerk on duty must have been the twin of the one at my hotel. I went up to the counter and said, "Hey!"

He looked up, a fat, heavy-cheeked, semi–North American. "A man came in here about thirty minutes ago." I described Lew. "What room is he in?"

The clerk shrugged his fat shoulders. "Who can say?" he said. "Thees es a beeg hotel. We have meeny guests."

If the joint had over twelve rooms I was cross-eyed. I took a five-dollar bill out of my pocket and laid it on the desk. The clerk eyed it. It was probably close to a week's pay for him. "Think real hard," I said. "Maybe you'll remember."

He pursed his lips. "Maybe eet comes back to me. Chess, maybe I see that señor chest a few meenites ago. Maybe eet es room tin."

I put another five-dollar bill on the desk. "I'm going to need a key for that room."

He looked hard at the money. Then he swallowed again. That was a lot of money to have fall out of the sky for a man like him. Probably he had a señora at home and six niños. He hesitated. "Chou don't do no chooting."

"No chooting," I said, mocking him. "Choust a leetle friendly visit. The hombre in ten is mi amigo. Big surprise. Comprende?"

"Oh, chure," he said. "Surprise. Amigo. Chure."

"Joke," I said.

He was all smiles now, or whatever it was that passed for a smile when he got through moving his fat face around. "Choke," he said. "Bromo."

"Chure," I said. "Bromo. Choke."

I think we could have gone on like that all night, I guess, but he got impatient for his money and I got impatient for my key. We swapped, finally, and I went and sat in one of the two chairs that the lobby contained. The chair was up against the back wall near the hall that led to the first-floor rooms and the stairs to the second floor. I figured number ten would be on the second floor. But I was so positioned that Lew wouldn't immediately see me when he came out of the hall. He'd have to turn around, and I'd already have a gun leveled on him. But, of course, I was hoping he wouldn't come out. My thinking was that he'd come back to the hotel, it being after seven o'clock, to grab a couple of hours' sleep and then to go to hitting the saloons again when they started warming up around nine or ten o'clock.

The desk clerk was puzzled by my sitting down in the lobby, now that I had the key. I made a sleeping motion by putting my two hands together and laying them against my tilted head. Then I touched my finger to my lips. "Beeg choke," I said.

His face lit up again. "Chure! Choke!"

Ain't nobody loves a "choke" more than a fat desk clerk.

At ten minutes after eight, I judged Lew had settled down for a nap. It was dark outside, so I'd be able to tell if he had a light on in his room. I got up, entered the hall, and went up the stairs. As I got to the top, I pulled my revolver. Number ten was the first room on the right. I squatted down by the door, being careful not to get in front of it, and, as softly as I could, inserted the key. There was no light showing from the inside—not from under the door or around the side cracks.

But I wasn't taking any chances. Not with Lew Vara. I turned the key, wincing at the slight sound it made. Then, still hunkered down and mostly protected by the wall, I turned the handle and gave the door a slight shove. For the first foot it swung freely. Then the rusty hinges bound up, and it went the rest of the way with a quiet, slow *creeeeaaaak*.

A gun shot, lit by a bright orange flame, suddenly thundered out, and a bullet tore through the space I'd have been in if I'd been standing in the door. I cocked my pistol, the sound loud in the silence after the shot. My eyes were accustomed to the dark, and I could see his outline sitting up in bed. But I knew that he was temporarily blinded from the flash of his own gun. "Lew, don't move," I said. "It's Justa Williams. Now you just let that gun drop. I ain't here for harm."

"Justa?"

"Yeah. I want to talk to you, but I don't want you holding no damn gun while I do. Drop it or I'll put one in your right arm and put you out of commission for six weeks."

"Have you come to take me back? If you have, go ahead and shoot."

I knew I didn't have but a few more seconds before he could see. Still, I was crouched behind the hallway wall and he was a sitting target. I said, "No, I've come to make a deal with you about Wooley. Now quit stalling and drop that damn gun. Now! Or we'll have the whole damn hotel around our ears."

I saw the revolver fall from his hand. It landed on the bed.

"Now light that oil lamp."

He leaned to his left, where a lamp was sitting on a little bedside table. I heard the match scratch and then the flame. I scuttled into the room as fast as I could, jerking the door closed behind me. The lamp caught, and I reached the bed and scooped up his revolver. Lew turned around and stared at me. He was wearing just his jeans. He'd taken off his shirt and socks and boots. "I figured you'd come huntin' me," he said. "You get them other two?"

"Yes." I pulled up a chair, turned it backward, and sat down. I was to his left and almost to the foot of the bed—well out of reach in case he tried to jump at me. "How come you had to leave them?"

"I had business," he said. "An' they was slowing me up. Two or three days traveling with a couple of damn fools like Casey and Welch is near about all a man can stand. You kill 'em?"

"Shot 'em up pretty good. They won't be dancin' for a while." I didn't exactly have my pistol pointed at him, but it wasn't that far off. "But I didn't run you down about them."

"Like I told you," he said, "if you've come to take me back, you might as well go ahead and shoot. I'm not going back. I told you I was regretful of what I was doing to you and your family, but I couldn't do ought else."

"I understood that. And that ain't why I'm here. You didn't even take any more money than you had coming when you had the chance. I don't believe you're a thief. Or a murderer. But

I've got to reach an agreement with you because you're in my way. We both want Wooley. I want him because he caused the death of two of my cowboys in a murderous fashion. So I want him dead. Or alive long enough to get dead at the end of a rope. You want him alive so he can clear you, though I'm damned if I can see how you're going to get a man to put his head in the noose to save yours. You take him back, he ain't going to admit anything."

"I got to try," said Lew grimly.

"We've got to come to an agreement. We can't both be hunting him. If you think I'm about to kill him, you'll try and stop me. I can't have that."

"And I can't have you killin' him," he said. "Not yet. The problem is that you want vengeance and I want to clear my name of doing murder. I think I got first call."

"Let's throw in together, and I'll do my best to help you bring him back. If . . ." I let that big *if* hang in the air.

"If what?"

"If you can show me how you're going to get him to go back to a courtroom and admit to a murder you're charged with."

He swung his feet around to sit on the side of the bed, and he began pulling on his socks. Just as he reached for his boots I said, "Lew, you better not have a hideout gun in one of those boots. I'm aiming right at your shoulder, and you'll never get around with it."

He laughed softly and picked up a boot by the heel. He swung it around over the bed and turned it upside down. A Derringer fell out. He said, "You mean that little ol' pop gun?"

"That little ol' pop gun," I said.

He finished putting on his boots and then crossed the room to a sideboard and picked up a bottle of whiskey. He poured himself a drink and then offered it to me. I shook my head. He leaned back against the sideboard, sipping whiskey and thinking. Finally he shook his head. "I can't see it, Justa. You'll kill him sure as hell. Wooley ain't about to let you get close enough to him to take him alive. But he might just me. I ain't real sure he knows I got blamed for that murder. I been huntin' him all day, but he ain't in his regular hangouts. I got to say no deal."

I sighed. "Well, I didn't want to do this, but I'm going to holler downstairs for the desk clerk to get the sheriff. Don't you make no sudden moves."

He said, his face darkening, "I thought you said you wasn't going to take me back. Hell, ain't your word worth nothin'?"

"I'm not taking you back," I said. "But I'm going to put you on ice until I can get Wooley. I should have him within twenty-four hours."

"How you gonna put me on ice?"

"You rode in here with two Half-Moon horses, and you ain't got no bill of sale. And I own those horses. I'm going to charge you with horse theft."

"You sonofabitch!"

I shook my head. "No I'm not. I'll drop the charges as soon as I get Wooley. You ought not to be in jail more than a day."

"You are a sonofabitch," he said. "A smart sonofabitch, but still a sonofabitch."

"Want to change your mind?"

He spread his hands. "I don't see much choice."

"There's not any. We work together? My way?"

He shrugged.

"Yes or no?"

"Yes." But he didn't look happy.

"Your word on it?"

"Yes, dammit!"

I pitched him his pistol. "Get dressed and let's go over to my hotel. I got a man out looking for Wooley. He knows him well. When he finds him, he's going to report to me at the hotel."

"I don't believe it's going to be that easy," said Lew. "The man probably works for Wooley."

"I don't think so."

As we walked to my hotel, I told him about my encounter on the Flood ranch. I said, "I figure Wooley is waiting to hear from Flood about what to do. I don't reckon he'll make a move until he gets word from his boss. But it could be he's over in Mexico for the time being."

"It's funny—you mainly think of cattle being stolen in Texas and driven into Mexico," said Lew. "You never think of it the other way around."

"Used to be that way," I said. "That's why all the ranches within a hundred miles of the border dried up. It cost you so much to protect your cattle, you couldn't afford to raise them. Now it looks like they've gone the other way around. I reckon it's a lot easier to steal cattle in Mexico."

"But harder to market them."

"Not if you have a slaughterhouse in, say Houston. And I'd bet dollars to doughnuts that Flood has some sort of arrangement to dispose of his cattle, even if it's just a way to consign them out to northern markets."

We neither one had eaten, so we stopped off in the cleanest-looking cafe we could find and ordered up some steaks and potatoes and fruit. They had papayas and mangoes and plenty of oranges. Whenever I was on the border, I always took the opportunity to take on a load of that fresh fruit. It was the only thing about the border I liked.

I had told Lew about blowing up our neighbors' cattle and Norris's worry about what Flood might do. He asked me what I planned.

I just shook my head and said I had no idea. Which I didn't. "But that ranch of his only ten miles from the border is going to mitigate against him," I said. "Especially since I didn't see a cow on the place."

"Maybe they hadn't stole any lately."

"Maybe that's where Wooley is right now."

Lew shook his head. "No. Not yet. We busted up his crew—or you did, with that dynamite. It'll take him time to put another one together."

We made a few saloons on the way, just on the off chance we'd see Wooley. But as I'd told Lew, I hoped we wouldn't see him. "We run across him in a saloon," I said, "and you know damn good and well it's going to mean a gunfight. And he might have plenty of help with him. We've got to take him unawares or alone. I much rather have somebody else looking for him—like that Big Tom I told you about."

We got back to my hotel about ten-thirty. I went up to my

room and got a couple of glasses and a bottle of whiskey, and we sat in the lobby, drinking and waiting for my bird dog.

While we waited, Lew told me about the trouble he'd gotten into. He told it slowly and with discomfort. It was obviously an embarrassment to him. At one point I tried to get him to leave it alone, but he said I not only ought to know, I had a right to know. He said that he'd been up in Waxahachie, working as a night guard in the railroad marshaling yards. He said it was a good job, paying sixty dollars a month, and he was happy with it. "Then one day," he said, "this Pinkerton detective showed up. They check out everybody that works for the railroad. You may not have known that, but they do. Sometimes it takes them awhile, but they get around to it."

It seemed that some three or four years previous, Lew had been up in Oklahoma and had fell on hard times. He said, "It ain't no excuse and I ain't proud of it, but I was broke and just a kid and I fell in with a bunch and we went to using a running iron on other folks' calves. Wasn't long before some of the bunch got caught. I managed to get away, but they named me. Well, it was just small-time stuff. I bet we didn't steal more than twenty head, so there wasn't no big to-do about it. I went on back to Blessing and fooled around there for a while, doing what I could. That's when me and you had that fight. After that I lit out and went up around Fort Worth and Dallas. I didn't want to get near any cattle work for fear of being connected to that business in Oklahoma, even though that was long past. So by then I'd gotten pretty good with a gun, and the railroads had been having a lot of trouble with theft, so they were hiring pretty rough ol' boys. Which I was qualified for. Then the Pinkertons got around to checking into my background, and they run across that old stuff in Oklahoma. They didn't have enough to jail me, but they had enough to get me fired. So there I was, broke, out of work, and angry."

He drew on his cigarillo for a second. "Of course, I didn't have brains enough to be angry at myself for that foolishness I'd gotten myself in. I was angry at everybody else. Couldn't have been my fault."

"I know the feeling," I said dryly.

He blew out smoke. "Anyway," he continued, "I knew about this big poker game that was played in the railroad hotel there. In fact, I'd guarded it one night. It was a regular bunch—a couple of railroad big shots and three or four wealthy ranchers. Played every Friday night as regular as clockwork. Big game. Real big game. I'd seen pots for as much as two thousand dollars when I was guarding it. So I figured there had to be at least ten or twelve thousand dollars in the game."

"Lot of money," I said.

"A hell of a lot of money," he said.

"Right then it looked like all the money in the world." He paused to pour himself out another drink. "Well, I knew I couldn't do it by myself and I didn't know of any help around Waxahachie, but I'd known Clarence Wooley from that bunch in Oklahoma. He was the oldest of us, and I knew he was a hardcase. I'd heard he was in San Antone, so I hopped a train and went down there and looked him up and explained what I had. Well, he liked the idea, and he gathered up another hardcase name Kid White and we went on back to Waxahachie and pulled the job. Except it went all wrong from the first."

"What happened?"

"We went busting in the room, and the guard was nowhere in sight. Naturally we were wearing handkerchiefs over our faces. They probably wouldn't have recognized Wooley or Kid White, but they'd sure as hell known me. Anyway, while Wooley was busy gathering up all the money, the guard came busting out of a closet and let loose with a shotgun. Blowed Kid White nearly in half. Wooley shot him. Then a guy at the table jumped up and made a grab at my mask. I hit him with my gun and knocked him down. He fell on the floor." Lew stopped and looked off. "Wooley shot him. For no reason. Then we got the hell out of there. I understood the guard, but I damn sure didn't understand the man on the floor."

"Is that it?"

"Not quite. We got away and rode out of town a good piece. Wooley had managed to gather up about six thousand dollars. We stopped to divide up the money. I wasn't so much interested in that, as I was in taking him to task for shooting that defenseless man on the floor. We quarreled and guns got drawn and he shot me." He touched his left shoulder, just under the collarbone. "Took all the money and left me for dead."

I had seen the scar, slight though it was, when we'd been in his hotel room and he'd been shirtless.

"What I don't understand," I said, "is if they knew you, why ain't you named on those papers Vic Ward has? It's just a description and the name Lew Walters."

Lew nodded. "Whenever I went off to work, I always used another name. They is a prejudice against Mexicans, and I look Mexican a little and my last name sounds Mexican, so I mostly used names like Walters."

I looked at my watch. It had gone past midnight by a quarter of an hour. I said, "And you figure if you can run Wooley down, you can get him to go back and confess to killing a helpless man?"

"I can take him back up there and have the men in that poker game look at the both of us and testify as to who fired that shot."

I shook my head. "Lew, you are dreaming. There'd already been a shotgun blast. That's a lot of smoke in a closed room. Then Wooley shoots the guard. I got to figure there's more confusion than a triple wedding ceremony. Those men would have been ducking under the table. And you and Wooley standing side by side? How they going to testify which of you shot? You hit the man. He was at your feet."

"I got to try," he said doggedly.

"I believe you, because I know you and I know that ain't your style. But how are members of a jury going to get to know you in the day or two your trial will take? You'll swear it was Wooley and Wooley will swear it was you. All that will happen is you'll both swing. Hell, let me finance you out of this country for a while. Or move to California. I'll loan you a stake."

"No." He shook his head. "I'll make Wooley tell the truth. I'll tell you, Justa, when I threw in with you it was for my own benefit. As soon as you described the man with Flood, I knew it was Wooley. I was just biding my time. You surprised the hell out of me with that dynamite, but I wasn't worried. I knew he'd heard you warn Flood not to cross that creek and I knew he'd be in the back of the herd. I figure he lit out south as soon as the first bunch of dynamite went up."

I was going to argue with him some more, but just then Big Tom came huffing and puffing through the front door. He pulled up in front of us like a steamboat making a docking. He had sweat on his face, and he looked like he'd been running. He said, "Bill, I done what I could. But I lost him. I follered an' follered the man, waitin' fer him to light long enough I could git back here and tell you. But the sonofabitch never stayed still long enough. He went in his hotel an' I thought I had him shore. But then he popped back out with a valise in his han'."

"A valise?"

Big Tom nodded solemnly. "A carpetbag valise. Went straight to the railroad station and tuck the midnight train to San Antone."

"Shit!" said Lew.

Big Tom looked at him. "Friend of ours," I said.

"Wadn't no time to git back here an' tell you," Big Tom continued. "Sonofabitch stepped aboard jes' as the damn train was pulling out."

I frowned. "When's the next one?"

"Not till noon tomorrow. They runs ever' twelve hours. Worst luck."

"Shit!" Lew said again.

I dug in my pocket and came out with the other half of the twenty-dollar bill. I handed it to Big Tom. "Here you go. You did your part. But you are sure that was Wooley that got on that train?"

"Sure as shootin'," he said.

"Well, that would be what it would come to if you was sending us on a wild goose chase."

He looked from me to Lew and then back to me. "Ain't no call fer them kind of words. When I werk fer a man I werks fer him. And it's like I told you between me and Wooley."

"Didn't mean to offend," I said.

"No offense taken," he said. "I'll be around in the mornin' to see if they's anymore he'p I can give you."

"You do that."

When he was gone, Lew asked, "Do you believe him?"

I shrugged. "I guess so. Why? Did you want to call him a liar?"

Lew chuckled softly. "Not likely." He stood up. "I'm headin' for bed. I'll see you around eight o'clock."

# CHAPTER
# 11

I didn't go straight to bed. Instead I walked down to the railroad depot, which was right near the railroad bridge at the river. There was only one ticket agent on duty, and I went up to his window and gave him a description of Wooley and asked if such a man had bought a ticket for the midnight train to San Antonio. The agent was an old man with a gray handlebar mustache and rimless glasses perched on his nose and a green eye shade. He said, "Listen, young man, I'm in the railroad business, not the business of spying on other people. Now unless you're the law or somedody who's got a damn good reason to know, I ain't got no information fer you."

"I'm not the law," I said, "but I have good reason to believe that the man I'm describing loaded out a horse. And I don't think he just bought a ticket to San Antonio; I think he might have bought a through ticket to Houston. And the reason I'm interested is because I'm pretty damn sure that horse he ladened out is wearing our brand. Now, has the railroad gone into the business of shipping stolen livestock?"

He gave me a good long study. Fortunately, I was pretty presentable. I'd had a bath and a shave and had put on clean

229

clothes. After a long minute he said, "Tell me about that feller again."

I did, though my description had to be sketchy at best. There was no way to describe that flat, mean look on Wooley's face, and he didn't have that many distinguishing marks. What was more, I wasn't really sure how tall he was, since I'd never seen him except on horseback.

The agent listened to me and then he thought a moment. "I'll check."

He was gone for a few minutes. When he came back he said, "Didn't sell no through tickets to Houston. They was three gents bought tickets tonight and all was to San Antonio. Only one comes close to the man you're a-talking about was the only one ladened out a horse."

I said, "He didn't ask for a special stop at Wharton?"

The old man was chewing tobacco, and he turned and spit. "Wouldn't a done him no good if he hadda. He's got to request that out of San Antonio. That's a different line outta there to Houston. Ain't nothin' to do with us."

"You got a telegrapher on duty tonight?" I asked.

He spit again. "You're lookin' at him, bub."

"I want to send a wire. To Blessing, Texas."

He shoved a blank through the window cage to me, and I took it and went over to a little table where they had pencils picketed on pieces of string so you couldn't steal them. I wet the lead and addressed the wire to Norris:

URGENT STOP URGENT STOP URGENT STOP MUST KNOW IF BLACK BUGGY HAS SENT OR RECEIVED ANY WIRES LAST TWO DAYS STOP ESPECIALLY TO CW ON BORDER STOP WIRE ME HERE SOONEST OR SAN ANTONIO STOP BE THERE TOMORROW NIGHT STOP

We had a code for our telegrams that the telegrapher in Blessing knew about. URGENT meant within the day. URGENT STOP URGENT meant get it to the ranch as soon as possible. Three URGENTS meant to pay whatever it cost to get someone to take it to the ranch immediately.

Of course, Norris was going to have to get the telegrapher in Blessing to reveal confidential information to him. But it wouldn't be the first time he'd done it. We were well aware that it was an abuse of power and we tried to only use it when we had no choice and when we felt like it served the purposes of justice.

I took the blank back to the old man and asked him to get it off right away. He consulted a book. "Blessing key ain't on duty after six P.M."

"Look," I said, "would you go ahead and send it? Bradley has a room right off the telegraph office. He might hear the key clicking and pick up. He's done it before."

The old man shrugged. "Yore money. But it costs you every time I hit this key."

I put down a ten-dollar bill. "Try him several times."

He looked at me and he looked at the money. "Must be a damn good horse," he said.

"It is."

"All right, young fellow," he said. "I'll keep sending long as I'm on duty. When my relief comes on at six, I'll pass it along if I ain't reached that Blessing key."

"Thank you," I said.

I left and went back to the hotel, but I didn't sleep good. Nobody but a dead man could have slept good in that bed.

At breakfast I told Lew about my visit with the ticket agent and what he'd said. Lew said, "You reckon Wooley is just going to San Antonio? That is one of his hangouts. Or you reckon he's headed toward Blessing to see about Flood?"

"We ought to know in a couple of hours. Either way, we need to get the horses down to the station and bill them out for San Antonio. You've got to bill them out two hours in advance of train time."

We were eating ham and eggs and drinking coffee with a little whiskey in it. Neither one of us was overloaded on sleep and we both needed a little pickup. We finished up and paid the bill, and then Lew took off for his hotel and I headed for the stable where I'd left the chestnut. I'd already paid up at the hotel and had my saddle bags with me.

The mare was glad to see me when I came into her stall. She was one of those rare horses that genuinely liked to work and got impatient when they were cooped up in a stall too long. She'd been glad to see it when she was fagged out, but now she had a bunch of travel in her and was ready to go. I saddled her up and paid out and then swung aboard. I ran into Lew just as I hit the top of the T and turned right for the railroad station. He was riding a bay that I recognized and leading another horse with a pack sack over his back. "Good-looking horses you got there," I said.

"Yeah," he said dryly, "picked them up cheap off a real dumb ol' boy. Say, you wouldn't have really sicked the sheriff on me, would you?"

"You know the answer to that."

We got to the station and located the stockmaster. He led us down to a car that only had one other horse in it. We led the animals up the ramp and tied them off with their reins, taking the bits out of their mouths first. Then we tied the stirrups on the two riding horses over the saddles so they wouldn't swing around and agitate the animals. The railroad provided hay, so we pitched a good bit up to the end of the car where our animals were tied, made sure they had water, and then got our chit from the stockmaster and went on up to the ticket office.

Norris's telegram was waiting for me:

BLACK BUGGY WIRED CW ON BORDER TWO DAYS AGO STOP MESSAGE SAID URGENT HE COME TO AREA STOP SAID BRING HELP STOP SAID ON THE SLY STOP BB RECOVERING STOP NO MORE DETAILS NOW STOP YOU BE CAREFUL STOP

I showed it to Lew. "Looks like he's on his way," he said. "According to your pet bear, he boarded the train by himself, but that doesn't mean he couldn't have sent some help ahead. But my guess is he's going to look for it in San Antonio."

"What in the world do you reckon they are up to?" I asked.

Lew gave me a look. "Your brother says for you to be careful. If I was him, I'd take care to be careful himself. People like Flood and Wooley don't take a whipping without trying to get back at you."

"You think they'd hit the ranch?"

"Wooley will hit anything if he gets paid enough. And I would reckon Flood's got the money for a little vengeance."

I thought about wiring Norris back to put him on his guard but decided not to. If he couldn't figure that Wooley wasn't coming into the area to nurse Flood back to health, he needed more help than I could give. Just the very way Flood had worded the telegram was a giveaway. He hadn't said come to Blessing, he'd said come to the area. In other words, don't ride down main street advertising your presence. And he'd said come on the sly.

I decided I'd wait until we got to San Antonio to decide what to do. "If Wooley is going to recruit men in San Antone, it's going to take him awhile. We may be able to catch up to him there."

"Maybe," said Lew. "But there's a bunch of trains out of San Antonio. Especially toward Houston. I don't know how many men he's looking for, but it won't take him long to round up a bunch in San Antonio. Not if Flood is paying the right kind of money."

Train time came and we found us seats in the chair cars. It was about a six-hour ride to San Antonio, but we had whiskey and smokes and I reckoned we could stand it.

We'd been riding about an hour, watching the dry countryside go by, when Lew said, "Justa, you told me you didn't believe I was a murderer. Or a thief. But I told you last night that I had robbed and stole."

"You figure to do it again?"

He shook his head. "No, I reckon I have had my fill of that. I wish I could claim I done it because I was young and dumb. Or because I was hungry. But the truth is I done it because it was the easy way. Or it looked like it at the time."

"Then I reckon you can count yourself not being a thief. A

thief is a body like Flood or Wooley. They won't ever quit until somebody kills them. And I reckon somebody will, sooner or later."

We were twelve hours behind Wooley. I didn't know if that would give him time to hire men and catch a train or not. And I couldn't know if he'd go on to Houston and then double back or be able to persuade the railroad to make a stop at the little town of Wharton, which, on that line, was the closest stop to Blessing. Normally the train would pause to let a passenger down, but they'd seldom stop and wait while a man unloaded just one horse. They'd do it for a bunch of horses because that was good business but not just for a few.

We pulled into San Antonio about six that evening. While Lew unloaded the horses, I immediately went to the ticket office and inquired about anyone answering Wooley's description buying a ticket. The line from San Antonio to Houston was owned by the same railroad that had run the spur line to Blessing, so I knew some of the officials and had some influence. But all that was worth naught, as the agent just shook his head and said he hadn't heard of or seen anyone like I'd described. The last train for Houston had left at two that afternoon and the agent had been on duty at the time.

I was considerably troubled because I didn't like the way the train times worked out. Lew came up leading the horses, and I told him what I'd found out. I said, "Now we know for sure, according to the way Flood worded his telegram, that Wooley ain't going to Houston and then to Blessing by train. He's not going to arrive in the middle of Blessing, especially getting off a train. So does he go to Houston and then set off on horseback? It's damn near eighty miles. That's a hard two-day ride or an easy three. He might be able to arrange to get off at Wharton, but that will mean he's got plenty of men and horses with him. I don't know whether we ought to watch this train station or try and track him around town."

"We could do both," said Lew. "One of us stay here and watch and the other one scout around town."

I gave him a look. "You're wanting me to trust you? Out of my sight?"

He shrugged. "How do you want to do it? I gave you my word I'd play it your way."

I considered. "Well, it does make some sense. I tell you what. You stay here. I'll go on into town and have a real careful look around. I don't reckon Wooley will be very easy to take in this town."

Lew nodded. "He's got friends in every saloon in this town."

"Friends?"

He smiled slightly. "Folks that have the same interests he does."

"The next train leaves at ten," I said. "That means he'd have to be here with his horse, or horses, by eight. You hang around, and if you spot him I'm going to be looking around Commerce Street. If ten o'clock comes and goes, come to the Del Prado Hotel. I'll be in the lobby."

The Del Prado was an elegant old hotel, one that I didn't figure Wooley's ilk would frequent.

"What's the next train after this one tonight?" asked Lew.

"I think it's ten tomorrow morning. But it's the express, I think. If it is, they'd never stop in Wharton."

We had set ourselves a hard task. We wanted Wooley, but we didn't want him in San Antonio. It was a town that contained too many resources for him. We wanted him on the prairie, but to do that we'd have to be right behind him. And we couldn't take the same train.

I rode slowly downtown, put the chestnut mare up in the livery stable of the hotel, booked a room with two beds, and then went across the big military plaza down to Commerce Street and the seedier side of town, where all the saloons were located.

San Antonio was a rowdy town, a mixture of some of the toniest people in Texas and some of the worst. It was said that the criminal elements could operate so freely because the law had been corrupted to the point of nonexistence. On a previous visit I'd even heard some talk of vigilante committees to be formed by some of the more respectable folks. For that reason I was cautious in scouting. It wouldn't have been any great trick to have found trouble in any one of those saloons on Commerce Street, but calling attention to myself was the last thing I wanted. Mostly I contented myself with looking in windows. When I did go in for a drink I did it as quietly as I could, hunching up my shoulders and pulling down my hat over my face.

There was no sign of Clarence Wooley. Naturally, I didn't dare ask questions, but I must have surveyed twenty saloons, a number that didn't mean anything. Nobody had ever counted the saloons in San Antonio because, as somebody said, nobody was ever sober long enough to count that high.

I went back to the hotel about nine-thirty and sat out in the lobby. A waiter from the bar fetched me out a large brandy, and I sat there sipping it and waiting on Lew. It really didn't matter that we hadn't located Wooley. What we really wanted was him on a train and us right behind him.

And knowing where he was going to get off. That was the important fact to locate.

The trains ran often enough that the most of a lead he could have on us would be six hours and I knew ways to cut that down. If he were heading for the Half-Moon we'd be there first.

Because he was going to have to go into Blessing first and confer with J.C. Flood. Get his orders. And I had no doubt they'd be murderous.

I sipped my brandy and thought. I wasn't all that worried about Wooley when it came to the ranch, but it didn't solve Lew's problem and he damn sure had one.

He came in a few minutes after ten and sat down in one of the big, Spanish-style chairs next to mine. For a minute he didn't say anything; he just looked around. The lobby of the Del Prado was two stories high, with big marble columns and good-quality rugs on the floor. I reckoned it to be the most elegant hotel in the South, outside of one I'd stayed at in New Orleans.

"Pretty swank," said Lew. "Never been here before."

I said, "I didn't have any luck. Of course, I didn't expect to."

"Neither did I," he said. "If Wooley got on that train he was wearing a skirt, because they wasn't but two women boarded it. And no horses. Train didn't even have a cattle car."

"I didn't expect him to take that train. It's only a five-hour run to Houston, and that would put him in there at three in the morning—earlier than that if he could get off at Wharton."

"You were right about the train in the morning," said Lew, "except it goes at nine. But it is an express and don't stop. Next one goes at two. It's what they call a local. Stops at every crossroads."

"That'll be the one," I said. "That gives him time to round up his ruffians and have a good night on the town."

Lew was silent for a moment, then said, "Justa, you ain't exactly treating me square. When I saw Wooley when they were driving that Mexican herd, he was surrounded by his men and I knew I couldn't get at him. But when you busted them up, I figured I could run him down in Brownsville. And I might have, too, if you hadn't come along. Now he's back surrounded by another bunch, and it's going to be hell for me to cut him out. I got to have him alive, Justa."

I lit a cigarillo. "I been thinking about that, Lew. Don't worry. We'll find a way to take him. I don't know exactly how yet, but we'll find a way. I'll think of something."

He gave me a look that said he wasn't exactly convinced.

We watched the passengers loading on the nine o'clock express, but, as I'd expected, there was no sign of Wooley. We were in the stationmaster's office. I'd made myself acquainted with him, and he knew of my father and our ranch and our connections to his railroad. He'd promised me full cooperation.

"Handy bein' rich, ain't it?" said Lew laconically.

I let it pass.

We went on back to the hotel for lunch and to wait for the two o'clock train. I'd made arrangements with the stationmaster that we could load our horses at the last moment, and he'd passed the word on to the cattlemaster to save us space in a car.

"Well, we've done all we can," I said. "He could have slipped by us somehow, but I don't see how."

"Why don't we get down there early," suggested Lew. "Maybe see them buying their tickets. At least we'll get a close look at them. They won't be able to see us in your partner's office, the head honcho."

"All right."

We finished our lunch, picked up a bottle of whiskey for the ride, paid out of the hotel, and then went down to the depot. We came at it from the back, away from where the passengers loaded. Once inside the stationmaster's office, we settled down to wait. The windows in his office had some kind of green tint on them where you could see out right easy, but folks outside couldn't see in. I figured it worked on the same principle where you could see into a lighted room at night, but you couldn't see into the dark out of one—us being in the dark behind them tinted windows.

One-thirty came and went and there was no sign of Wooley. I said, "Of course he'd have loaded his horses beforehand. Could have done it any time."

"Can't you find out?"

"Doesn't make any difference. We'll see him get on the train. That's all that counts. I'm still planning on us taking that later train. I think it would be way too risky to get on the same train as he does."

"Then why did you make arrangements to load our horses?"

"Lew," I said, "we got to be ready for anything. We're chasing a man we ain't seen in a week."

Then it was two o'clock and the last of the passengers were aboard. The train was crowded because it was a local and would be making stops all down the line. I went up to the ticket agent and asked, "Are you dead certain that nobody like I've talked about bought a ticket? Or three or four tickets? Maybe five?"

"I'm sure, Mr. Williams."

"Damn!" I said. "I don't understand. He *had* to take this train. It would have put him into Wharton about six this evening, enough time to ride a couple of hours before dark and make the next day an easy ride to Blessing."

"Maybe he just wasn't ready to go," said Lew.

The cattlemaster came in and I questioned him about the stock cars. He just shook his head. "Didn't load but one horse, an' that belonged to some old cowboy I been seein' on this line for ten years. Rides in the cattle car with the horse."

"Damn!" I said again. I turned to Lew. "I don't know what to do."

Just then the ticket agent said, "You know, they could have rode out to Eula and taken the train there. It stops for half an hour to take on water. We ain't got water here. All the north-bound trains water at Eula."

"Quick," I said, "telegraph down there and see if they are loading there."

"I ain't exactly supposed to do that, Mr. Williams."

The stationmaster came in. When I told him what I needed, he nodded. "Do it."

The agent went to his key and tapped out a message asking the agent in Eula to wire back a description of all passengers and animals being loaded.

After that, all we could do was sit back and wait. Time passed—maybe half an hour. The stationmaster said, "Takes about forty-five minutes, Mr. Williams. You'll get your answer."

It seemed a long time, but then the key began to click. The agent went over and wrote the message out. He handed it to me. I read it, and then I said to Lew, "It's them. They bought tickets to Wharton. There's six of them, and they loaded six horses. The train will stop for them in Wharton. I've made a mistake, Lew. We can't wait until that night train. They could go on through the night and be there in the morning. We've got to chase them right now."

Lew said, "How? A-horseback? A hundred and fifty miles?"

I turned to the stationmaster. "Mr. Cawley, I've got to have a special. Just an engine and a stock car is all I need."

He gawked. "Good Lord, Mr. Williams, that's a pretty expensive proposition you're talking about."

"I don't care." I mentioned the name of a high official of the railroad in Houston who was a friend of Dad's. "Wire him," I said. "He'll tell you we're good for the money."

"I ain't denying your ability to pay, Mr. Williams. Though a special from here to Wharton is likely to run two or three thousand dollars."

"I don't care," I said.

Mr. Cawley said, "I don't even know if the track is clear for that amount of time." He looked at his agent.

The agent said, "Yessir. It's clear for the next six hours, and then we got a freight coming through. The special can be shunted off in Wharton 'till the freight passes an' then back on back here."

Mr. Cawley took out a big bandanna and wiped his brow. It was obvious he didn't get such requests every day, and he wasn't quite certain what to do. "All I got in the yard is two little switching engines. They can't pull much," he said.

"I told you," I said, "just a stock car. An engineer and a fireman. You don't even really need a fireman: Me and my friend can fire the boiler."

He shook his head. "I'll see what I can do. Damn unusual. I'll say that, by God."

It was an impatient wait. Lew said, "They'll be clear out of the state at this pace."

I didn't say anything. Instead I busied myself composing a telegram to Norris, warning him that Wooley might be in the area the next day and to take all precautionary measures. I added that we were coming with all speed. I sent it URGENT URGENT URGENT.

The stationmaster came back in, still mopping his brow. He said, "I've got you fixed up, but it'll take about an hour. We've still got to switch a string of freight cars, and I've sent for a fireman."

"I told you we could shovel coal," I said.

He looked at me. "Was you coming back?"

"Oh," I said. "I never thought."

"How much of a lead will they have on us?" asked Lew.

Mr. Cawley peered at him over his spectacles. "I shouldn't reckon they'll have any lead. That there local is gonna stop ever'whar. Ya'll can just highball it. Wouldn't be surprised if you din't ketch 'em 'fore they got to Wharton."

Of course we didn't want to do that, but I didn't say anything. Instead I studied a map of the track route that was tacked to the wall. Out of San Antonio, it ran almost due north until just before it got to Wharton. Then it started curving right around to the east as it headed for Houston. It gave me an idea. I said to Lew, "See to our gear. I'll be right back."

"Where you going?"

"Nearest mercantile."

I jumped on the chestnut and rode for the center of town. It wasn't but a few blocks before I found a big enough mercantile to accommodate me. I ordered two hundred feet of one-inch rope and a dozen sticks of dynamite with blasting caps and the same amount of six-inch fuses.

The man asked me, cautiously, if I were familiar with the handling of dynamite. "I'm famous for it," I said.

Then I left the store and loped back to the depot. The dynamite was in my saddle bags, so Lew couldn't see that, but he looked questioningly at the rope.

"It might come in handy," I said. "I don't know."

Then our private train was pulling into the station. The little switching engine wouldn't run as fast as a regular locomotive, but we weren't pulling anything but two horses and a cattle car. And we weren't stopping for anything except to take on water.

Lew and I decided to ride in the cabin with the engineer and the fireman. It would be plenty hot, but we wanted to be able to see ahead.

Mr. Cawley, looking slightly embarrassed, said, "Mr. Williams, I have figgered this out and this trip is gonna cost you $2463.50. Do you want to check my figures?"

I shook my head. "Just put it on our regular ranch account."

He said, "You understand we got to bill you fer the cost of brangin' the locomotive back to the yard. See, this ain't like you buy yoreself a ticket to a destination. See, you be takin' the whole train."

I told him I understood. "I just want to thank you, Mr. Cawley. You've been mighty obliging."

We boarded and went pulling out of the station, the engine making chuffing sounds as it picked up speed. The engineer's name was Stringer, and the fireman was someone called Shorty. Mr. Stringer said, "Wahl, yo're the boss. I'll run her as fast as you say."

"Pour on the coal," I said.

"Got to stop fer water in Eula. Won't take a min'it."

"Do what you have to do."

We made the water stop, Shorty climbing up on top of the engine to open the cover to the boiler and then the big spout coming over and letting down a flood of water.

Then it was done and we were on our way. Within two miles we were running at better than forty miles an hour. Mr. Stringer yelled, over the engine noise, "This is just about all she'll do until we hit a downgrade about fifty mile up the track. Then we'll pick up a little more speed."

I was excited, and I could see by Lew's face that he was excited too. For the first time in a long time, I felt like I was finally coming to grips with my real enemy. I didn't know how I was going to defeat him, but I figured I'd find a way.

Lew must have been thinking the same thing, because he yelled in my ear, "Six to two. Those ain't real good odds."

"I know," I yelled back. "We've got to figure out a way to even them up."

"Maybe let them get to your ranch and then take them from the back."

I gave him a look. "No! They're not getting anywhere near the ranch."

Mr. Stringer was a menace. He chewed tobacco and he spit out the window. It didn't take us long to realize that standing behind him wasn't the most ideal place to be in the cab.

Once Shorty yelled in my ear and asked if I owned the railroad. I gave him a puzzled look. He said, "I never knowed of nobody havin' they own train less'n they was the president of these here United States. I figured you owned the blame thang, an' I was gonna hit you up fer a raise."

It made Lew laugh. But I was too deep in thought to pay much attention. I was trying to formulate some sort of plan to, as Lew hoped, even up the odds. We could bushwhack them with rifles, but there was so little cover in that country that it was doubtful we could get more than two before we revealed ourselves and then they could make it plenty hot for us. I had the dynamite, but I had no clear idea what I was going to do with it. And I had the rope, but the use of that would be dictated by the conditions of the terrain. I knew the country between Wharton and Blessing but not real well. I had been trying to visualize a bushwhack location ever since we'd boarded the cab of the locomotive, but I couldn't think of one clearly for the life of me. It could be we were about to have a tiger by the tail, and we might get more interested in getting loose from it than catching it.

Lew said, in my ear, "How much longer, you reckon?"

I'd seen mile signs by the side of the tracks. They came every ten miles. We'd come some sixty miles and were now running a shade over forty-five miles per hour. Shorty was keeping the fire roaring, and Mr. Stringer was keeping the steam needle just below the red. We blew for crossings and for the little towns we whistled through, but we weren't slowing up for anything. I said, "I think it's about seventy, eighty miles to Wharton, but I'm not sure. About another hour and a half." I pulled out my pocket watch and looked at it. It was four-thirty. "It's gonna be close. That local is due in Wharton at a quarter after six. I'm going to stop us two miles short, and we're going to cut crosscountry and try and get out ahead of them and set up some kind of a trap. But it's gonna be close."

"Can't we go no faster?" he asked.

I shrugged. "Ask Mr. Stringer."

I saw him go up to the engineer and yell in his ear. For answer Mr. Stringer spit tobacco juice out the window, barely missing me on the backdraft, and tapped the pressure gauge. The needle was hovering dangerously close to the red area. He yelled something at Lew. All I heard was ". . . blow up."

Lew came back to me. "I think we're going as fast as we can," he said.

We watched the countryside fly past and tried to keep the smoke and cinders out of our eyes. I'd left the whiskey in my saddle bags back in the cattle car, so there was no relief in that direction. I'd been wearing a white shirt when we'd started the journey, but it wasn't white anymore. I leaned over to Lew's ear and said, "Don't try and convince anybody you ain't a Mexican right now. You look like a black Mexican."

"Don't talk to me," he said. "You look like tar baby."

We were starting into the long curve that pointed the tracks east when I got a glimpse of a train a few miles ahead of us. I put my mouth up to Mr. Stringer's ear and asked him what train it was.

"One you're a-lookin' fer," he said.

"How far are we from Wharton?"

" 'Bout ten mile."

I said, "I want to stop two miles short. Will they be able to see us?"

"Not 'less they got real good eyes. Track curls around. You don't want to go slam on into Wharton?"

"No. Two miles. And we'll be getting off in a hurry, so stop her fast. I'll say much obliged now." I shoved two ten-dollar bills in his pocket, one for each of them.

"I'll spot her at the two-mile mark," he said. "Won't be off a foot."

I said to Shorty, "I'll see about your raise."

Then Mr. Stringer was venting steam and pulling back on the throttle and gently applying the brakes. The other train had disappeared around the bend, but I could hear it blowing and ringing its bell for Wharton.

Mr. Stringer said, "Here she be. The two-mile mark. I wish you boys good luck, whatever it is you are about."

We jumped from the cab before the train had come to a full stop. Without a word, we raced back to the cattle car and threw open the door and climbed in. While Lew was wrestling the ramp out the door and to the ground, I was busy with the horses, tightening cinches, untying stirrups, getting the bits back in their mouths.

We led them down the ramp as fast as they'd go. Shorty had come back to help with the ramp. "You boys go on," he said. "I'll tend to this."

We gave him a thank you and then turned and spurred off

across the prairie. This was not a time to save the horses. They'd all three had plenty of rest and were full of run.

I was leading us on a course that I thought would intercept the line that Wooley and his gunsels would have to take from Wharton to Blessing. Lew got up aside me and said, "What's the plan?"

I just shook my head. I had a lot of hope but no plan. "Don't know," I said. "Play it as it comes. Right now we got to get in front of them."

I figured they wouldn't rush unloading their horses and might even take time to buy a few extra supplies. But either way they wouldn't be running their horses as we were, because they'd have no reason. They had thirty miles to go, and with dark a scant two hours away they'd just be looking for a good place to make camp for the night.

And I thought I knew such a place. Or at least I hoped I did. It was a small pond where cattle watered, with a pretty good little grove of post oak just off to its north side. It was only about three or four miles from the depot at Wharton and, if I was remembering right, on a dead line to Blessing.

The grass was nearly belly high to the horses and made it hard going for them. It also concealed many a pitfall. This wasn't the time to have a horse break a leg. After we'd gone about a mile, I pulled us down into a lope and then, after another half mile, a fast walk.

Fifteen minutes later I said, "There it is."

"What is?" asked Lew.

I pointed. We had just topped a little rise, and far off, maybe a mile and a half, I could see the scraggly branches of the post oaks and the sheen of the sun shining off the pond water. "There. That's where we ambush them. But we've got to hurry."

"How you know they'll come that way?"

"They have to," I said. "It's the only water around. They'll be near enough that their horses will smell it even if they don't see it."

We kicked the horses up into a gallop. The horse that Lew

was trailing was still so fresh that he didn't have to be led—he ran along right beside us.

I looked to my left, toward Wharton, but didn't see any sign of anyone. The country was rolling, rather than flat. They could have been just beyond the next rise.

But we rode into the oak copse without sign of anyone. It was cool and pleasant after the heat of the locomotive cab and then the hard ride under the sun. Both Lew and I looked like we'd been working in a coal mine. I jumped down from my horse and then took the big, heavy coil of rope and slung it over my shoulder. "Lew," I said, "tie the horses and stick a feed bag on their noses so they don't nicker. Then come join me. Bring both rifles and all the ammo we got."

I undid the ties holding my saddle bags and slung them over my shoulder and then started running out of the oak grove. There was one single oak tree about seventy yards away on the Wharton side. I struggled through the thick grass and got to its base. I took the coil of rope down and tied one end about two foot up the little oak. Then I started off backward, playing out the rope as I went. I'd stop every ten yards or so and gauge whether or not I was bisecting the line I expected them to take to the pond.

But hell, it was just a guess. The two hundred feet of rope had seemed like so much in the mercantile, but now, out here on the broad prairie, it seemed a pittance. It was foolhardy, I thought, to expect them to come through that narrow little two-hundred-foot space. But it was the best idea I could come up with.

When I reached the end of the rope I hunkered down in the tall grass, taking off my hat to make myself less visible. The line of my rope was about a hundred yards from the pond and was stretched across the bottom of a gentle little rise.

I saw Lew come out of the oaks, a rifle in each hand and running bent over. I stood up and waved a hand. He veered in my direction. In a moment he had slumped down beside me. "This ain't the best cover I've ever seen," he said. "Don't you reckon we'd do better in the trees?"

I showed him the rope and pointed to the little tree where it was anchored on the other end. "Oh," he said.

"True, we got better cover from those trees, but I don't think we'd get but one shot. We might get two of them, but then the other four would surround us. We've got to find a way to bring all of them down at once."

"And you think clotheslining them is the way?"

"I ain't going for the riders. We're going to try and trip the horses."

He looked at me doubtfully. "I don't see another tree around here."

"We're the tree," I said.

He cocked his head to one side and looked at me like I'd lost my mind. He said, "Two or three, maybe four horses are going to hit that rope at the same time, and me and you are going to hold it?"

It sounded pretty foolish, even to me. I admitted it. "But it's all I can think of. If they scatter, Wooley will damn sure get away. That is, unless you want to knock him out of the saddle with a rifle bullet."

He grimaced. "You know I can't do that, Justa. But hell, this damn rope is gonna jerk the arms right off us."

I said, looking off into the distance, "We're gonna soon know."

# CHAPTER
# 12

I had seen them about a mile off just as they'd topped a little swell in the prairie. Then they'd disappeared again as a swimmer might between the troughs of a wave. "What makes you think they'll come between us and that tree?" Lew asked.

"I don't *think*," I said. "I *guess*. And *hope* and *pray*. I'm hoping their horses will head them for it. They will have had a five-hour ride without water and then a three-mile gallop. I'm hoping they'll smell it."

Lew wet a finger and held it up. He looked at me with a sour expression on his face. "Wind's in the wrong direction."

"It's swirling," I said. "Look at that grass."

"It's blowing in more than it's blowing out."

"Dammit!" I said irritably. "Will you quit being a Jonah? What do *you* reckon we ought to do?"

"All right," he said. "The wind's in the right direction."

I turned around and pulled my saddle bag to me. The mercantile clerk and I had already prepared the sticks of dynamite. I handed Lew three sticks. "Boy, you gettin' fond of this stuff," he said. He handled it gingerly, like he wasn't certain how to hold it. "We going to heave this at them?"

"If we can get close enough," I said. "Trouble with that stuff is if you can't throw it far enough, you are likely to do yourself more harm than the other party."

"What do you do with it?"

"If this rope trick works and we get them down, we'll try and work close enough to pitch a little in amongst them. But first we've got to stop them."

They topped another rise and we could see they were much closer. What we couldn't tell, peering through the high grass, was whether they were on a route that would bring them to our rope.

We watched. My heart was pounding. I'd been waiting many a day for this. If I didn't pull the last of Flood's teeth right here and now on this grassy prairie, he might be a thorn in our side for years to come.

They rose with the prairie again. Now they were only a short quarter of a mile away, still coming at a lope.

Lew said tensely, "I don't think they're coming right. They look to be going on the other side of that tree."

"You can't tell yet," I whispered.

But then they cut the distance in half, and I could see that Lew was right. They were making straight for the oak grove, a route that would take them on the other side of our anchor tree. Well, it had been a fifty-fifty guess and I'd guessed wrong. I watched as they came within seventy-five yards, then fifty of our line. There was no mistake: They were going the wrong way.

Suddenly Lew went scrambling away. I looked around in amazement, wondering what he planned. Then I saw him suddenly pop up out of the grass some twenty yards away. He yelled, "Hey!" and waved his hand. Then he dropped back into the concealment of the tall grass.

I watched in wonder as the six riders suddenly veered in his direction. They didn't slacken speed; if anything, they touched their spurs to their mounts and came on faster. They were coming inside the tree. As fast as I could, I took a turn of the rope around my waist and then grasped it with both hands and dug my boot heels in. They were twenty yards away from the rope.

Just before they hit, Lew got behind me and reached around my waist and got hold of the rope with his two hands. I watched them. When I calculated the lead horse was only a few yards from the rope, I said, "Now!" and surged backward, stretching the rope until it ran straight to the tree, two feet off the ground.

The shock jerked Lew and I forward into a jumbled mass. Just as he'd said, I thought my arms were jerked out of their sockets, and the loop I'd taken around my waist had almost cut me in two.

But we scrambled to our knees as fast as we could to see what damage we'd accomplished. Only one horse was in sight, and he was riderless. He was going back toward Wharton, bucking and kicking and occasionally stepping on his bridle and jerking his head down.

We watched, rifles at the ready, able to see but exposing only the top half of our heads. Another horse popped up and went running off. Then another. A man stood up and made a grab at the horse's bridle. The animal shied and the man took a step toward him. Lew fired an instant before I could stop him. I wanted several of them up at one time. But by the time I put out my hand, the crack of the rifle had sounded and the man had gone tumbling backward, shot clean in the chest.

We immediately hunkered down. "I've done it now," said Lew.

"Yes, you have," I said.

"I never thought."

"That's obvious. Now work your way around to the right. Those fuses work out to about twenty seconds after you light one. So don't hold it too long. Try and get in between them and the little oak grove. They get in there, we'll never rout them out."

I began working my way to my left. I crawled carefully, trying not to disturb the grass so as to give away my position. I figured they were about sixty yards away. That was way too far for me to throw a stick of dynamite, so I began slowly crawling their way. Every so often I'd take a quick look over the grass. There was nothing in sight, except I could see where the grass sort of ended at the spot where they'd trampled it down as they'd been spilled into a heap. After I'd made about ten yards in their direction, I chanced a quick look and saw a man doing the same. It wasn't Wooley. He saw me just as I got my rifle up. I fired into the grass where I'd seen his head disappear, but there was no yowl of pain.

When I figured I was forty yards away, I decided to see what a stick of dynamite would do to their general feeling of well-being. They were certainly quiet. I hoped Lew hadn't let them slip up on him in the tall grass.

I lit a cigarillo and got it drawing good. Then I took a stick of dynamite, shifted into the best throwing position I could get in without exposing myself, and applied the coal of the cigarillo to the end of the fuse. It started sputtering almost immediately. I watched to see how fast it burned, let it go two inches of its six, and then heaved it in the general direction of Wooley's party. Ten seconds went by, and then came this godawful explosion. As soon as its rolling thunder had died down, I upped on my knees for a quick look. There was plenty of dust and smoke, but I could see where the stick had lit. It had blown a hole in the prairie and flattened the grass all around, but it had been a good fifteen yards short of the mark.

You can't throw a stick of dynamite very far when you are laying on your belly.

But as I watched, I saw a stick come sailing from where I figured Lew would be. It too was short, but it would have caught anyone crawling through the grass trying to make the oak grove.

It caught one. I saw him rise up from the ground at almost the same place where Lew's stick had fallen into the grass and start frantically back to where he'd come from. He'd taken two steps when the dynamite went off. The blast just picked him up and hurled him into the air. He came down on his head and disappeared into the brush and grass. If he wasn't dead, he'd had most of the life blowed out of him.

I wormed my way ahead for another five or six yards and

then tried another throw. I dared to get up a little and conse- quently got off a good one. It went high and long and blew up before it hit the ground. I stayed on one knee, watching. The force of the blast hit me in the face, blowing my hair back, but it was no stronger than hurricane winds I'd faced on the coast. When the dynamite went off it was like seeing the lightning inside a thundercloud. There was a hell of a bright light that was suddenly surrounded by all the black smoke. The blast blew the grass flat, and I saw a horse suddenly rear up and go racing away. Someone had been holding him down.

All of a sudden a voice yelled out. "Williams? Is that you, Williams?"

"Who wants to know?" I yelled back.

"This is Clarence Wooley. What the hell you want?"

"Want you," I said. "How'd you know it was me?"

"You the onliest one I know is chickenshit enough to fight with dynamite instead of a gun like a man. What's the matter, can't you shoot a gun?"

"Come out and find out."

"How many of ya'll is they?"

"Enough," I said. "More than you."

"You got yore brothers with you?"

"And some others."

"Lew Vara?"

"I wouldn't know," I said.

"Well, what do you want with me? You done won the range war with yore fucking dynamite. What else you want? I'm jes' on my way to collect Mistuh Flood."

"Takes six gun hands to collect one old crook?"

All of a sudden I heard Lew yell, "Justa!" In that instant it struck me that Wooley had never been that much of a talker. On the sound of Lew's voice, I rolled over and over to my left. Just as I made my first turn, a rifle cracked and a bullet tore into the ground where I had been lying. Wooley had kept me talking to zero in on where I was.

For answer, I lit another stick of dynamite and heaved it. This one was closer. As it went off I raised my head cautiously over the top of the grass. I could see I'd only been three or four yards short of landing in the big middle of them. As it was, I heard a man yell and then let out a string of cuss words. If there had been rocks in the ground I could have killed the whole bunch of them with that one stick, but as it was, in the soft dirt, I figured all I was doing was giving them a good bruising and maybe an ear ache.

When the noise of the blast had died down and some of the dust and smoke had cleared, there suddenly came a burst of revolver and rifle fire from Wooley's party. They were sweeping the area, firing in a semicircle and firing about six inches off the ground. The bullets came whipping through the grass with a whining, ripping sound as they plowed through the grass. I hugged the ground, getting as low as I could. Several slugs came within feet of me and one almost passed over my head, but that was as close as they came. They were firing blind, just hoping to hit something. I was pretty sure Wooley didn't realize it was just Lew and I. I worried about Lew, afraid a blind bullet might have found him, but then, through the top of the grass, I saw a stick of dynamite go arcing toward Wooley's position in a sputtering tumble. It, too, exploded just short. But the explosion caused a man to suddenly get up and start running. He was running low, trying to stay as close to the grass as he could. I tracked him with my rifle and squeezed off a shot just as he got to the top of the rise. The bullet took him in the side of the chest and knocked him rolling.

There was another fire of survey, only lessened by the loss of their third man. I had moved my position until I was almost on their quarter. The odds were getting much closer to even.

Wooley yelled out, "Williams!"

I didn't answer.

"Williams! You out there? Williams!"

"I ain't biting again, Wooley." I immediately crawled a few yards away from where I'd been.

He said, "Look here, we got us a Mexican standoff. We can't get away and you can't get away. What say we call it a draw and pull back at the same time?"

"You got it wrong, Wooley," I yelled. "We don't want to get

away. And I ain't going to let you get away." I switched positions again.

There was real puzzlement in his voice when he said, "Look here, what you got such a hard-on fer me for? What the hell, I was workin' for Flood."

"Were you working for Flood when you killed two of my men?"

"Hell, you killed plenty of mine."

"Not in cold blood. Not stabbed to death. Not after they'd surrendered."

He was silent for a moment, and then came a sudden fusillade of shots near the area I'd been in. For the hell of it, I let out an "Oooooh!" and rolled away. Immediately, more shots poured in. But they were shooting blind, lying on their stomachs and firing where they thought I ought to be.

But it had been a mistake. Lew yelled out, "Justa! You all right?"

I should have realized that it would have fooled Lew also. I yelled back, "I'm all right. Keep quiet."

After a moment I heard Wooley yell out, "Is that you, Vara? Is Lew Vara out there?"

I tried a few shots through the grass myself. On the third shot, I heard a distinct thud and a low moan. I had hit someone; how bad I could only guess.

I sighted up at the sun, calculating how much daylight was left. Not much, I figured. No more than half an hour. Under cover of darkness, Wooley was more than likely to escape. I didn't know if he had a horse left, but he'd be able to slip out through the grass and be a mile away before we'd have any idea he was gone. If we were going to flush him, it would have to be done soon. I started crawling to my left and forward, working my way closer to Wooley's position. When I judged I was no more than twenty-five yards away, I got out two sticks of dynamite. I lit one, watching as the fuse burned down two inches. Then I lit a second one off the first. Lying on my side, I heaved the first one in a kind of side-armed arc. When it exploded I jumped to my feet, covered by the smoke and dirt and dust, and heaved the second straight at Wooley's position. Then I dropped to the ground.

I heard somebody yell out, "Gawda'mighty damn! We're dead!"

Somebody else yelled, "Throw it out! Grab—"

The stick exploded.

For a long time after, there was a silence. They could have all been dead, but I wasn't going to walk up to see. I waited, watching the sun get lower and lower.

After ten minutes I yelled, "You want another one? I'll give you thirty seconds by my watch."

After a pause I heard Wooley's voice. It was weak. "Hold up! We're beat. My arm's broken."

"How many left?"

"Two of us. Me and Billy Spurl. But he's hurt, too."

I said, "Stand up! Hands over your heads!"

"I tol' you, my left arm's broke."

"Then put your right arm up!"

There was a pause. "What you plannin' on doin' when we stands up?"

"That depends on you."

"You ain't shootin' us down, are you?"

"That's your style, Wooley. Your thirty seconds are near about up. You want another stick of dynamite to suck on?"

"Hold on! We're a-comin'."

I waited ten seconds and then cautiously raised my head. Twenty yards away, Wooley and one of his henchmen were standing up, hands raised. Or the henchman had his hands raised. Wooley's left arm was dangling by his side, looking longer than it should have.

"Lew!" I yelled. "Keep them sighted in. I'm going to stand up. Fire if either one of them so much as flinches."

They were a pretty sorry-looking sight. Both of them were covered in dirt, and besides Wooley's arm, he had a cut across his chest you could see through his torn shirt. I guess that dynamite had found rocks or guns or other hard objects and sent them winging. The henchman had a bloody face and a bloody thigh. He didn't look too steady on his pins.

I held my rifle at the ready and started forward. When I was within ten yards I said, "Come on, Lew. It's all over."

I could see where they'd first gone to ground. It was surrounded by holes the dynamite had made. There were parts of two horses lying all over the place. It made me slightly ill.

I stood where I was until Lew had come up to me. He was to my right. Clarence Wooley was right in front of him. "Hello, Clarence," said Lew. "I been looking for you. Want you to take a trip with me."

"That can wait, Lew," I said.

"What you mean to do with us?" asked Wooley.

"I mean to take you back to Blessing and charge you with murder." I motioned with my rifle at the one he'd called Billy Spurl. "I don't know about this one. Has he been working for you long?"

"I don't know nothin' 'bout no murders," said Wooley.

"Yes you do," I said. "You knifed two of my men to death. Now, lest you get any wrong ideas, I reckon you better unbuckle those gun belts and let them drop. You won't be needing them for quite some time."

The one called Billy Spurl started down with both hands. I said, "Ah, ah! Just use one hand. That's all ol' Clarence has got. Ain't fair outdoing a cripple."

"I'm hurtin' like hell," said Wooley. "I need to sit down."

Lew raised his rifle. "Drop that gun belt, Wooley. And be damn quick about it."

My big fear had been that a third man might have been lurking in the grass, waiting to ambush us. But there was no sign of anyone else alive. I could see two dead men toward the back of the trampled-down grass. Then Lew had blown one up and I'd shot another.

We had them. I glanced over at Lew. "Well, we done it," I said.

Wooley was taking an uncommon long time to get his buckle undone. Billy Spurl had already dropped his, though his holster had been empty, as was Wooley's. I was thinking vaguely what a big, solid belt buckle Wooley had. It was huge, maybe four or five inches long and four inches wide. It appeared to be silver, with some kind of mother-of-pearl inlay. I was just thinking that I'd seen one like it before when his right hand came away with a Derringer magically appearing in his palm. Before I could even blink, he'd fired. By the sound Lew made beside me, I knew he'd been hit. But I didn't have an instant. I fired my rifle from the hip. The bullet took Wooley in the stomach and he fell over backward, the second shot from the twin-shot Derringer firing into the sky as he fell.

I swung left. Billy Spurl was going for his boot. I levered in another shell and shot him in the top of the head as he bent over. He collapsed in a heap.

# CHAPTER
# 13

I dashed forward. Before I could see to Lew, I had to make sure
Wooley was harmless. I got to his side. I'd hit him just about
the navel. He was breathing hard, but his eyes were open. I
jerked the Derringer out of his fist and threw it into the grass.
Then I pulled off his boots to make sure he didn't have any
more concealed weapons. They were empty.

I took a brief glance at his belt buckle and cursed myself. I
had known of that trick. The belt buckle was a big, concave
affair. It was standing open. A man could secret a Derringer in
there, snap it shut, and have a gun ready to hand at any time.
And damn few would know it was there. I'd last seen one in
Mexico, and I cursed myself for being so slow to recognize it.
If I'd been faster, Lew wouldn't have been shot.

I kicked Billy Spurl over. He was good and dead. Then I
went to Lew.

He was lying on his back, gasping. The bullet had caught
him just at the base of the throat. It appeared to have broken his
collarbone as it had plowed through. As gently as I could, I
lifted his head enough to see the back of his neck. The big .44
caliber bullet had made a hell of a hole when it had exited, but

it had missed his vertebra. If it had hit his neck bone, it would have been all over.

But as it was, he was having trouble breathing and he was losing a hell of a lot of blood. I didn't have a piece of cloth on me clean enough to make a bandage. I jumped up and raced to the oak grove and ran up to the pack horse. I got a bottle of whiskey and then jerked out a half-clean shirt of mine. There was some Spanish moss hanging down from the tree, and I jerked down a big handful of that. I ran back and knelt by Lew.

He was conscious enough that he gave a big jerk when I poured whiskey into the wound. He moaned and said, "Damn."

But it didn't come out like his voice. It came out like a hoarse croak. I figured the slug must have hit his vocal cords or maybe his voice box. A big slug like that can do considerable damage. I figured Wooley had been shooting for his chest but the gun had bucked on him and the bullet had gone higher. The only lucky part was that it hadn't gone six inches higher. If it had, I would have been treating Lew with a shovel and not a whiskey bottle.

I couldn't reach around to the back to pour any whiskey on the wound, so I ripped my shirt up into strips, made one into a pad, soaked it with whiskey, and then held it against the wound. Lew give another quiver and kind of gurgled.

After that I took a wad of the Spanish moss, soaked it as much as I could with whiskey, then put it on the pad and placed it behind his neck. I did the same for the front wound, where the bullet had entered. Then I took some of the strips and wound them around his neck like bandages to hold the pads in place. I'd been told that Spanish moss would help stop bleeding by assisting in coagulation. But I figured whoever had told me that was talking about a cut or a puncture wound and not a half-inch hole a big-caliber bullet had made.

And with the wound where it was, there was no chance to get any kind of tourniquet on it. The only thing that would shut down the bleeding on such a wound was a doctor with a needle and thread.

Lew said, in that hoarse croak, "S'bad?"

There was no use lying to an old hand like Lew. He knew he was on his back from the force of a bullet and he knew he was still stunned and that something bad wrong had happened to him. "It ain't good," I said. "You are losing a lot of blood. I got to get you into Wharton."

"Wooley?"

It really wasn't the way it came out of his mouth, but I knew what he meant. I said, "He's gut shot. I don't think he's dead yet."

"Talk'm."

"You want me to talk to him?"

He tried to nod, but the effort was too painful.

"You want me to get him to admit he killed the man in Waxahachie?"

He tried to nod again.

"Lew," I said, "we ain't got a hell of a lot of time. It's three miles or better to Wharton, and you ain't got much spare rope."

He frowned at me with his eyes.

I got up. "All right, but I ain't going to make a job out of it. We got to get moving."

I went over and knelt by Wooley. The light was fading fast and his face seemed to be in shadow. He'd had his eyes closed, but they fluttered open as I leaned over him. He looked at me, but there was nothing in his eyes. They were just flat, uninterested. His shirt was soaked with blood all the way down to his trousers.

"Wooley," I said, "Lew Vara is wanted for a killing you did. At that poker game in Waxahachie. Why don't you tell me now you did it? It could get him off."

He looked at me without blinking and didn't say anything.

"Look here, Wooley, you are gut shot and you are dying and you know it. You got maybe half an hour and there's not a damn thing I can do for you. You know it as well as I do. Why don't you do one square thing in your life? Lew Vara is a good fellow. Why get him hung for something you done?"

He said, moving his lips slowly, "Whiskey."

You weren't supposed to give a man that had been gut shot

anything to put in his stomach. But I reckoned that only applied to them that had a chance to live. And Wooley didn't have any chance. We could have been next door to a hospital and he wouldn't have made it.

So I jumped up and went back to Lew, where I'd left the bottle. As I leaned down to pick it up, I could hear the sound of Lew's breathing. I didn't like it. It was a harsh, rasping sound. It sounded like some of the blood was getting down in his lungs. If such was the case, he could drown.

One of the dead horses was lying nearby, and I jerked the saddle off him and lifted Lew's legs and jammed the saddle in under his butt. I waited half a minute and it seemed as if his breathing steadied and got smoother. Then I went back over to Wooley. I knelt by his side and lifted his head up with one hand and poured whiskey in his mouth with the other. He took two or three gulps and then gasped and coughed. I quit pouring but held the bottle ready.

He breathed for a moment more and then said, "Hit me."

I poured him out a couple more gulps. When he gasped again, I corked the bottle and leaned it against his side. "All right, you've had your whiskey," I said. "Now how about telling me you killed that man in the poker game and not Lew."

He rolled his eyes around at me. "Fuck you," he said.

I stood up so I could stare down at him. "Wooley, I can't believe even you are that much of a bastard. You are going out. What have you got to lose? You might even save a little of your soul. If you got one."

"Go preach on another corner," he said.

"Lew's hit bad," I said. "He might not make it either. But I'd like to clear his name. Hell, you shot him. Ain't that enough for you?"

He laughed. Or he tried to laugh. But he was getting so weak it came out as a weak, wavering gurgle. He said, "Was aiming at you. Damn Derringers ain't worth a shit over a yard."

What he said made sense. I'd been wondering why he'd gone for Lew instead of me. But a Derringer is really a belly gun—one you shove in somebody's belly and pull the trigger.

At ten yards, which was the distance we'd been, one was about as accurate as spitting.

"You and your fucking dynamite," he said.

I couldn't waste much more time. "Wooley, I can offer you a bullet in the head or I can let you lay here and suffer it out. It ain't going to hurt any less until you're dead. But you don't get that bullet unless you tell me who shot that poker player in Waxahachie."

I could see him knotting the muscles in his jaws against the pain; clenching and unclenching his fists. But all he did was look at me with those flat eyes and say, "Fuck you. You and your fucking dynamite. I wisht I'd killed you."

"That your last word?"

"Gimme whiskey."

"Get it yourself," I said.

"Arms won't work."

I figured my bullet must have hit a big nerve of some kind. I said, "That's too damn bad."

I walked away. He didn't call after me.

I checked on Lew and then hurried to the oak grove and got the horses. Night was nearly on me. I spent a full half an hour rigging a kind of sledge for Lew. I took both of our bed rolls, put them together, and then punched holes at each of the upper two corners. Then I got the rope we'd used to trip up Wooley and his men and cut off a couple of twenty-foot lengths. I ran each length through a hole, tied them off, then backed up two of the horses and put a loop around each horse's neck. One of them was the pack horse, the other was the horse Lew had been riding.

After I got the sledge ready, I got Lew under the shoulders and dragged him onto the bed rolls, his feet toward the horses. That would keep them higher than his head, because the pull of the ropes tended to lift that end of the sledge.

Then I wrapped the bed rolls around Lew and tied him and them together with a lariat rope. Otherwise he would have just slid on off the sledge when the horses started pulling it.

When I had him in place, I asked how he felt. It had gotten

too dark to see much of his face, but he sort of fluttered his hand as if to say he was doing all right.

Well, I knew that wasn't so, and it was going to be a whole lot less so if we didn't get some help and Johnny quick.

Lew said, "Tu'ty."

I figured he was saying he wanted a drink of water. I frowned. I didn't know if he ought to have any. But he said it again, and I got the canteen. I knelt down and poured a little in his mouth. I said, "Don't reckon you ought to swallow that, Lew. Just let it lay in your mouth and then trickle out the sides."

He turned his head and let the water run out. Then he came back to me and said, "W'lly?"

I patted his shoulder. "Everything is fine. Don't worry. We've got to get moving."

I had tied the lead rope of the pack horse to the bridle of Lew's horse. I had done it in such a way that they would have to pull Lew's sledge evenly. I mounted the chestnut and took the makeshift harness of the pulling horses and started us off. Within a few strides, I was beside Wooley and looking down at him. His head had fallen to one side and his eyes were closed. He wasn't breathing. He'd gotten out cheaper than he should have. If I'd had my way, he'd have suffered the whole night and then died just as the sun was coming up.

I touched spurs to the chestnut and urged her gently forward, tugging, at the same time, on the pulling horses' rigging.

Now I could appreciate that sea of grass, because that makeshift sledge just slid across it like I was dragging it over ice. I glanced back from time to time. Lew seemed to be doing all right, thought I couldn't really see his face as dark as it was. I wanted to hurry, but every time I tried to speed the horses up, the pack horse and Lew's horse, neither one of which was used to pulling a load, would get all out of gait and go to tugging unevenly on the sledge. Consequently, I had to hold our pace down to a sedate walk, which seemed to make the passing of every mile an eternity.

The moon finally came out, and it allowed me to see better. By its light I took a look at my pocket watch and was amazed to see it was ten o'clock. More time had been spent patching up Lew and rigging his sledge and dallying with Wooley then I had realized.

As we traveled, I thought of all that had happened in the past weeks. It seemed much longer than that, though, since Ben had come into my office demanding I do something about some Mexican herd. Much longer; maybe a year.

But now it was nearly over. Wooley was dead, the Mexican herd was scattered and on its ways back to Mexico, and Nora was back.

Only J.C. Flood was left to deal with. Well, if he wanted to go to the law we could do that. I figured we could hire more and better lawyers than he could, and we'd fight him on any civil action if we had to go to the supreme court of the state. I'd spend a million dollars before I'd give him one.

Of course there was still the little matter of Vic Ward and me and the dynamite. Well, we could make a landmark case out of that one, too. I'd exploded that dynamite on public land in order to protect our deeded grazing range. Ward could make all the trouble he wanted; it wasn't going to change a thing for me.

And Nora. Well, it was going to be a pleasure to have time to see her and visit and see what kind of an understanding we could come to. Thinking about her made me feel good inside, but just then I heard a moan from the sledge. I pulled up my chestnut, got down, and went back. Lew's face was all over sweat and he was panting. I could tell he was getting weaker. I knelt down by his side. "Lew. You got to hold on. It ain't much further."

He licked his dry lips. It appeared to me he was starting to run a fever. I went to my horse and got the canteen and let a little trickle into his mouth. This time he swallowed it. I waited, but it seemed to do down all right and stay. I said, "Can you hold on a little longer?"

He nodded his head just the slightest. I patted his shoulder and then went to my horse and swung aboard.

It took us another hour to reach the outskirts of Wharton. Getting the sledge across the tracks was a painful maneuver for Lew, but there was nothing I could do about it. It would have hurt him worse if I'd tried to pick him up and carry him across. But we were finally near the little depot. It was dark, as I'd expected, but there was a little shack just behind it and I figured that's where the station agent lived. I pulled up in front, dismounted, and then banged on the door until I saw a light glow in the window. An old man came to the door, bearing a shotgun. "Who the hell you be and what fer you makin' sech a racket?" he demanded.

I told him who I was.

He peered at me. "You be that feller that hired thet special?"

"Yes. And I own part of this railroad and I've got a wounded man out here that needs help."

He said, "Why shore, Mistuh Williams. Whyn't you say so?"

He opened the door, and together, we got Lew into the house. The place wasn't very big, but they had a big dining table, and we laid Lew on top of that. He was terribly pale and not looking well at all.

The old man, whose name was Jenkins, said, "I'll roust out my ol' woman. An' they's a boy here. My grandson."

"What we need is a doctor," I said.

He shook his head. "Ain't no doctor here."

My heart sank. I knew it was a small town, but I'd prayed—hoped, really—that they might accidentally have one.

Jenkins said, "We got us a vet. He sometimes works on folks if it ain't too ser'us."

"Get him," I said.

The old man went to a door and yelled through it. "Jamie! Jamie! Git in here!"

Then he went to another door and yelled for his "ol' woman" to get up. The boy was out first. He came into the light, still wearing his nightshirt, but with a pair of jeans on underneath. He was rubbing the sleep out of his eyes with both fists. Jenkins said, "Jamie, you light out and fetch Mr. Purvis Martin. Tell him we got a gunshot wound over here. You be right smart about it, too."

The boy left, and then Jenkins's wife came in wearing some

sort of robe that had once seen service as a bedspread. Without a word, she started making coffee and frying bacon.

You'd have thought she got up in the middle of the night every day to take in desperate strangers the way she went about it.

I had untied the rope from around Lew, and now I sat at the table by him. I just flat didn't like the waxen color of his face. He turned his head slightly and looked at me. He didn't try to speak. I figured by then his throat was too sore to attempt talking. I tried to reassure him. "You are going to be all right, Lew. Help is on the way. We'll see you through this."

He half nodded his head.

I said, "I'm sorry as hell I didn't realize what Wooley was doing. The thing of it is, I'd seen one of those buckles before. Dammit!"

He frowned at me as if to say I was getting it wrong. Then he croaked out, "Me."

Or something that sounded like it. I said, "All right, you was stupid too. You should have caught it yourself and blowed the sucker down. So it's only right that you got shot."

That made him try to smile. Which made me feel better. It wasn't much of a smile, but at least he had strength enough to try.

I said, "You want a really good laugh, let me tell you what Wooley told me. He wasn't even aiming at you. He was aiming at me. That's a Derringer for you at ten yards. Thank my stars he wasn't aiming at you."

But it didn't make him smile. The mention of Wooley had brought a frowning question to his eyes. I knew what he wanted to know, but I didn't think it was exactly the right time for complete honesty. I said, "He told me the whole story. Deathbed confession. You ain't got a thing to worry about."

Relief showed in his face. To get his mind off the subject— because I'm not a real good hand at lying—I said, "Good job you got shot in the throat, Lew. You was getting to where you talked way too damn much."

Which made us both smile.

Then the boy was back with the veterinarian.

Purvis Martin was a nice young man with a gentle touch. He undid my bandages and approved of my use of the Spanish moss. While he examined the wounds, Mr. Jenkins told me proudly that Purvis had studied "animal doctorin'" at the Agricultural and Mechanical College in Bryan. He said, "It's a wonder what he kin do with a sick cow or horse."

But we didn't have a sick cow or horse. We had a man with a gunshot wound. Purvis said, "Mr. Williams, I could stitch up the outside, but that wouldn't do much good. Most of the bleeding is going on inside, and that means you got to cut in there to put in stitches. That's way over my head. You need a doctor. And not next week, neither."

"Where's the nearest one? A good one?" I asked.

He shrugged. "Houston."

I whirled on Jenkins. "What's the fastest we could get a special here?"

"Best bet is that ten o'clock train out of San Antone." He pulled out his big railroad watch. "Be here in 'bout two hours."

Purvis said, "I can clean the wounds with carbolic acid to reduce the chance of infection. Though infection ain't the big worry here. But I might could put some tents in each hole and get the blood to drain out, rather than going down his gullet. And I've got some clean dressings. But the most important thing right now is to get his strength up." He looked down into Lew's face. "You reckon you could swaller some beef broth? It'll hurt like hell, but it'll help you a good deal."

Lew nodded. I'd been watching his face while Purvis had talked. Even when the vet had said we didn't have much time, Lew hadn't shown the slightest bit of emotion. You lead a rough life and you've got to be ready to bear the consequences.

Purvis asked Mrs. Jenkins. "Would you be able to make him any beef broth?"

"It's already on," she said. "We had a roast fer supper, an' I cut a chunk off that and set it to boilin'."

"Then I'll get about disinfecting the wounds." Purvis went into his bag and came out with a sinister-looking bottle and some bandages. He said to me and Jenkins, "You might want to take hold of him. This stuff does bite a little."

But Lew shook his head, and I said, "Won't be necessary, Doc. He ain't happy unless he's hurting."

Purvis poured on the carbolic acid, but Lew never flinched. Then he put in the tents and bandaged him. He shut his bag. "Well, that's about all I can do," he said. "But I'll set with you until the train comes."

I appreciated that. He was the nearest thing to a medical man and he must have known that his presence was a comfort, even if there wasn't anything else he could do.

So we waited. Young Jamie was standing over in the corner, goggle-eyed and interested. I figured him to be about ten years old. I took a silver dollar out of my pocket and flipped it through the air to him. He caught it with one hand and then looked at it, his eyes getting even bigger.

Jenkins said, "Now here, don't you go a-spoilin' that boy."

"Just paying him for his work."

Jenkins said, "We don't need pay fer he'pin' folks. Glad to do it."

"And I'm glad to pay him," I said.

The broth finally started boiling. I went out to the saddle bags and came in with a bottle of whiskey. I was expecting a frown from Mrs. Jenkins, but none was forthcoming. Instead, she set a glass on the table for me. I said to Purvis and Jenkins, "Ya'll care for a drink?"

Purvis shook his head, but Jenkins said, "Don't mind if I do."

*That* got a frown from Mrs. Jenkins. Mr. Jenkins kind of mumbled around and said, "Well, train *is* comin' in. Reckon I better hold off—'fficial duties, you know."

Lew looked at the bottle longingly. I asked Purvis what he thought. He shrugged and said he didn't have the slightest idea. "Most of my patients don't drink."

"Maybe it would disinfect it on the inside a little," I suggested.

He shrugged again. "I don't see where it could hurt."

I held the bottle to the corner of Lew's mouth. "Now, get

you a mouthful first, but don't swallow it right away. Just let a little trickle down your throat and see if you can handle it."

I poured in a little. We watched, and it was easy to tell when Lew let a little down into his throat. He was trying not to show that it hurt, but his legs would twitch every time he swallowed.

I got about a tumblerful down him, and I couldn't see that it did him much good one way or the other. He still didn't have any color in his face, and he looked drawn and weak. Purvis took his pulse and then backed away to where Lew couldn't see him and shook his head.

I looked at my watch. The minutes were creeping by. There was still half an hour to go before the train was due to arrive.

If it wasn't late.

The broth got done and Mrs. Jenkins set to work, pouring it from one cup to another to make it cool faster. Naturally, Lew wouldn't be able to tolerate anything hot on the torn flesh inside his throat.

When the broth was cool enough, Purvis and I helped Lew up into a sort of sitting position, while Mrs. Jenkins fed it to him with a big spoon. At first it was hard going, but then he got into it and was able to take it down in pretty good style. I figured she'd got better than a pint down him. When we let him back down, he kind of sighed. I figured he'd swallowed a lot of blood, and that will make you sick to your stomach. I figured the broth gave him some relief.

After we got Lew settled, Mrs. Jenkins set in and fixed us all a big plate of bacon and eggs. Until I took the first bite I hadn't realized how hungry I was. I couldn't even remember when was the last time I'd eaten. I cleaned my plate and poured a little whiskey in my coffee, and then I sat back and relaxed for the first time. Lew was even looking better. The broth had done better than the whiskey. Some little color was coming back into his face, and his eyes had lost some of their hollow look. If he could just hold on for a few more hours, he might yet pull through.

But Purvis took his pulse again and didn't look happy.

With the train due at any time, Jenkins went out to a shed behind his house and came back with two long hoe handles.

We rigged those into the bed rolls to make a sort of stretcher so we could carry Lew onto the train.

Jenkins went out to set the stop signal. Ordinarily, the night train didn't stop unless it had a passenger to pick up or one to let off, and if the engineer didn't see a signal he'd just blast right on through.

I thanked Mrs. Jenkins for her help and left a five-dollar bill under my plate that she would find after we'd left. Then I got on one end of the stretcher and Purvis and Jenkins on the other. Jamie held the door open, and we carried Lew outside. We took him around to the front of the station and set him on a baggage cart. Then I went over to the track and put my ear to a rail. I listened a second and then said, "It's coming. No more than a mile off."

"I can see the light," said Jenkins. "She's rounding the curve."

Then the train was slowing and coming to a stop, chuffing and hissing steam and squealing her brakes. After the engine had stopped, you could hear the rest of the cars taking up the slack in their couplings.

The conductor got off, and Jenkins ran down to tell him what we needed. We'd already decided that the best place to stretch Lew out would be in the baggage car. The conductor came down the line of cars to where we were waiting, complaining about it being against company policy to let passengers ride in the baggage car. I mentioned a couple of names to him, and he suddenly got very cooperative.

We got Lew loaded and settled as well as we could. Then I got off and thanked Jenkins and Purvis. I gave each of them twenty dollars. Purvis didn't want to take his, claiming he hadn't done that much.

"You must have," I said. "He's more alive than he was."

To Jenkins I said, "Take out of that for the tickets. I'm much obliged and I won't forget your help." Then I jumped into the baggage car before either one of them could say anything. I called to Jenkins, "You'll load my horses?" He nodded.

The baggage clerk was sitting at his little desk, watching us curiously. He asked, pointing at Lew, "What's the matter with him?"

"Nothing," I said.

"Then how come his throat is all bandaged up?"

"It's sore."

"What from?"

I gave Lew a wink. "Singing too loud in Sunday school."

Lew tried to smile, but it didn't come off too well.

It was going to be a long ride to Houston. It didn't help that there was a casket over in one corner of the car.

It was a near thing. We got into Houston a little before four in the morning. I sent around to the hospital for them to hurry around with an ambulance. When we got to the hospital, a doctor was there. He'd just been called out, but he took Lew on. After a while he sent for another doctor, and they worked on Lew for the balance of the night. A little after dawn, one of the doctors came out and told me Lew was going to be all right. He said, "I don't know how he stayed alive, but he did. He's sewed back together. Not it's just a question of a lot of rest and getting his strength back." He looked at me curiously. "How'd he get that wound?"

"Accident," I said. "Cleaning his gun."

"Doesn't look like the sort of fellow who'd try to clean a loaded gun," said the doctor.

"You mean you ain't supposed to?"

He gave me a slight smile. "I'll let him get better before I inquire into the matter. Police here are interested in such things, you know."

"Happened a long way from Houston," I said. "We came in on the train."

He shrugged. "Then I guess it's none of our affair."

When I was sure there was nothing more I could do, I went around to a good hotel and checked in and ordered up a breakfast of steak and eggs and a bottle of whiskey. When I was done with that the stores had opened, and I went out and bought a new pair of jeans and a couple of shirts and some socks. What I had on my back and in my saddle bags needed to be shot and buried deep.

Then I went to a barber shop and had a shave and a haircut and had my boots polished. From there I went back to the hotel and had one of the longest baths I'd ever taken. It was hot, too, in spite of the weather, but I was trying to soak the soreness out of my muscles and the weariness out of my bones. I couldn't count the number of days I'd been on the go, and I was too tired to even try.

I turned in and slept until early afternoon. When I woke up I washed my face and then went over to see about Lew. He was conscious but weak and wasn't allowed no visitors. I was told to come back the next morning.

I'd left the horses on the train, knowing the railroad would put them in their livery stable. Since I'd been concerned with Lew and getting him settled in the baggage car, I hadn't seen to their loading and I was worried they might not have been properly looked after. But I saw them in the depot stables and they looked fine. I went in the office and arranged for them to be loaded on the ten o'clock train the next morning, the one I intended to take.

I didn't do much that night. I went to a variety show but got restless about halfway through and went back to the hotel, where I worked on the bottle of whiskey until I got sleepy enough to go to bed.

In the morning I packed my saddle bags, checked out of the hotel, and went over to see Lew. I was restless to get home. All I could think of were all the little details that needed to be wrapped up.

Including Nora.

I was tired of the trail and anxious to get back to business.

Lew could see me, but he couldn't talk. To my eyes he looked as drawn down as a spavined horse, but the doctor assured me again he was going to be all right.

The doctor said, "You wouldn't look so good yourself if you'd been shot and then spent four hours on an operating table. All his vital signs are good."

I didn't know what that meant, but I could see a glimmer in

Lew's eyes when he sighted me. He put up a weak hand and we sort of shook. I said, "I've got to be getting on back, Lew. I'll leave money to cover your hospital bill. Wire me a day in advance of when they turn you loose, and I'll meet the train in Blessing. I want you to come back to the ranch and rest up until you decide what you want to do."

His mouth worked, and I could see he wanted to say something. The doctor held up his hand. "Don't try to talk," he said.

"Just save it, Lew. We'll have plenty of time later." Then I gave his hand another shake and was gone.

The train wouldn't go fast enough to suit me. It was a two-and-a-half-hour trip to Blessing, and I spent most of it walking up and down the aisle of the chair car. It could be said that I walked to Blessing.

When we finally got there and I got my horses unloaded, I toyed with the idea of going by to see Nora. But then I gave that pleasure up. The most important matter was to get back to the ranch and see how conditions stood.

I pushed the chestnut and pulled the other two horses. She was full of run, and it was a pretty short trip. I rode up to the barn and dismounted. A cowboy was standing there, so he got the pleasure of seeing to the horses while I went straight into the house. I passed down the hall and turned into the study. Dad and Ben and Norris and a middle-aged man I didn't know were all there, just sitting around.

Norris said coolly, as I walked in, "Just in time, Justa." He made a motion with his hand. "This is Mr. Ernest Boyle. He's a range inspector for the Texas Cattlemen's Association. Fully empowered."

I looked at Mr. Boyle. He was sitting with his hat balanced on his knee; clean, pressed, and fresh.

And about a week late.

"Howdy, Mr. Boyle," I said. "Hope you didn't kill your horse getting here."

# CHAPTER
# 14

It took some little telling to fill everybody in on what had happened since I'd left. By the time I was finished, it was suppertime. Mr. Boyle was staying over, so he'd be eating supper with us. For his sake, and for the sake of just how fast he'd answered our call for help, I was hoping that Buttercup would be cooking.

But such wasn't the case. Dad had promoted him and his rifle to the full-time job of night watchman, though what he was going to watch out for was anybody's guess. I reckoned Dad had done it because I was away and not there to be tormented by the meals Buttercup massacred.

"Well, Justa," said Ben, "you could have let them six come on. We got your telegram in plenty of time and was laying in the gate for them. We'd've give them a pretty warm welcome."

They were sorry about Lew but glad he was going to make it. Norris said, "And you say that Clarence Wooley confessed to killing the man Lew is supposed to have shot? Before he died?"

"Listen," I said, "let's get off the subject. I'm off the trail and I'd like to forget it for a time. What about those Houston municipal bonds? Did you buy them?"

"Bought something else. Better return."

"What?"

"Tell you later."

Norris and Ben had made it into Kingsville all right with their prisoners. They'd taken them to the sheriff, and he'd wired Vic Ward and then held them. They didn't know if they'd been transferred to Blessing or not.

"We been kind of busy around here," said Norris. "Haven't had much time to go frolicking into town to see about a couple of high-handers you never should have hired in the first place."

I said, "Well! There, it's out! Don't you feel better? I don't see how you held it in this long, waiting to tell me you told me so."

Norris said to Mr. Boyle, who was looking understandably confused, "He hired a couple of outlaws to rob us. And he's the boss."

"What about Flood?" I asked.

Norris shook his head. "Don't know. He stays holed up in the hotel."

"*Our* hotel," Ben said, and he laughed.

"Sends a lot of telegrams but doesn't seem to do much besides that. I hear he's still stove up and walking with a limp. Somebody said the doctor said he had four broken ribs."

"But he hasn't taken any legal action?"

Norris shook his head. "He hasn't gone to any lawyers in Blessing. But then he wouldn't."

After supper I had a private talk with Mr. Boyle. I found it very enlightening. Nobody had said anything about Nora, and I didn't bring her name up. Ben and Norris, now that most matters seemed settled, were only too eager to have something to rag me about. I'd expected more fire and smoke from Norris about leaving him and Ben to take Welch and Casey in while I went on, but he didn't have much to say. Harley came in just before bedtime and gave me a report on the cattle. So far as we could tell, nobody had seen the slightest sign of tick fever in either our cattle or Tom Brown's. Osgood and Smalley had not been heard from. I doubted that we would hear from them until a lot of dust had settled.

Next morning Ben and Mr. Boyle rode out to the site of the dynamiting. He wanted to cut some brands off the cattle and verify that none of them had been trail branded.

I went in to see Vic Ward.

He was cordial enough, getting up to shake my hand. I went straight to the point. "Vic, before I took out after Casey and Welch, you were making noises about causing me some trouble over that dynamite. You still got that in mind?"

He put his hands behind his head and leaned back in his wooden swivel chair. "Talking about making noises—Norris was talking about ya'll not supporting me for reelection. You going to support me?"

"No," I said.

He stared at me for a second and then slowly took his hands down and put them on his desk. "Why not?"

"I could say it's because I think you're over the hill. But that wouldn't be true. I don't think you ever started up the hill. Thinking back, I can't recall a single bit of law business— serious business—that you ever handled. It seemed like most of the ranchers handled it themselves."

He twiddled his thumbs for a time and then said, "Well, reckon I will have to look into that dynamite business. That was on public lands."

"And out of your jurisdiction," I said. "But something else you might find interesting: the Texas open-range law of 1882. It says a rancher can use any means—any means, Vic—to protect his cattle from the incursion of an illegal herd. That covers public lands, Vic. Open-range law applies to public lands."

He said, "Yeah, but they be talking about cattle. It wasn't only cattle you blowed up. Think about that, mister."

"We've got a range inspector at the ranch," I said. "I'll finish what the law says. It says a rancher has a right to protect his cattle from the incursion of a foreign or illegal herd and to protect it from any implements used to further that herd's passage. Now Vic, what do you reckon those drovers were, sightseers? Or you reckon we could call them *implements*?" I stood up. "Now you just try us on for size on this one and we'll make you look like a damn fool."

He stopped me at the door. I turned. He looked bitter; bitter and defeated. "Who you planning on running against me?" he asked.

"Lew Vara," I said. "As soon as he's well enough."

"Lew Vara!" His face lit up. "Lew Vara is in the hospital in Houston. And when he gets out, the only thing he'll be running for is a rope to put around his neck!" He laughed out loud.

I just shook my head. "Vic, it's amazing how you can know a man as long as I've known you and still not know him. I guess it takes a little trouble to bring out a man's best or worst. The worst, in your case."

I left to see Nora. Her welcome took the bad taste out of my mouth that talking to Vic Ward had caused.

After that I didn't get a chance to see much of her for a time. We were busy trying to get the ranch back to normal, whatever that was. It took a solid week to get all the cattle hazed back to their regular range. And then for two more weeks we were busy patrolling our southern boundaries and making sure none of the Mexican cattle decided they wanted to see the sights in Houston.

Then one day, just as we were sitting down to lunch, Ray Hays came in and said, "Boss, they's a man settin' out there in a black buggy wantin' to see you."

"What man? What's his name?"

He said, "Wahl, jus' how many men you know sets around in a black buggy?"

"Hays, one of these days I'm going to kill you for your smart-aleck ways."

"Boss, you cain't do that," he said promptly. "Law is clear on the matter. You kin fahr me, but you can't kill me."

"Let's go," said Norris. "But give me a moment to go in the office."

It was J.C. Flood, all right. He was sitting in a new buggy, pulled right up to our steps. He had that same genial smile on his face. As we came out onto the porch, he said, "Howdy, gents. Just came by to tell you that I'd be willing to settle out of court for those cattle of mine that you blowed up and the bodily damage and mental anguish you caused me."

"That's damn fine of you, Mr. Flood," I said.

"No call to go the law over such a matter," he said. "All going to court does is make the lawyers rich."

"You want us to pay for the cattle you stole?" I asked.

He laughed heartily. "Oh, indeed, Mr. Williams. That's a good joke. But I got bills of sale, gentlemen. And a quarantine certificate."

"Which you know won't hold water. Smalley and Osgood going to join you in this matter?"

"Never can tell," he said cheerfully.

"Sounds like you are threatening us with a nuisance suit, Mr. Flood."

That brought a good-natured laugh from him. "Well, either way," he said, "it will cost you money. I'll take twenty-five thousand dollars for my end and call it quits. What do you say? Never have to worry about any more Mexican herds from me."

Norris stepped forward. He had a paper in his hand. "Mr. Flood, if we were to give you twenty-five thousand, you'd still be ten thousand dollars short. Have you got it in hand?"

The genial smile was replaced by puzzlement. "I don't understand you."

Norris held the paper out in front of him. "This is the note on your ranch. We bought it through our bank from the First State Bank in Brownsville. They were glad to get rid of it. Seems you lied about some of your assets. We got it discounted ten cents off the dollar. Seems you are two payments behind, Mr. Flood, which makes the note a demand note. You are herewith notified to pay up. You got the money?"

Flood looked at us. All the smile had gone out of his face. He said, "Well, this puts a different complexion on the matter. I reckon I had better get busy and raise you your money. Wouldn't want to get in bad with my mortgage holders." He snapped the reins on his horse's back and wheeled the buggy around. "Good day, gents."

I looked in amazement at Norris. I said, "What do you want to shoot at people with a gun for? You're more dangerous with that paper than with any six-gun. I never scared Flood, dynamite and all, as bad as you did just waving that piece of paper."

He looked quite satisfied with himself. "He'll never get the money up in time, and that land is soon going to be worth twice what we paid for it."

"Is it a better investment than Houston municipal bonds?" I asked.

"Oh, quite."

Six weeks later, Lew Vara went on trial in Waxahachie for murder. I took the train up there and perjured myself by testifying that Clarence Wooley had admitted to me, with his dying breath, that he had killed the guard and the other man in the poker game. Lew was acquitted, and he came back to the ranch to work until it was time to run for sheriff. He was very grateful to me, but I hadn't forgotten what he'd done when Wooley had tried to hold me. But he did question me sharply about Wooley admitting to such a thing. "That don't sound like him," he said. "If he was going to the devil, he'd rather take somebody with him."

I said, "You know he done it and I know he done it. Let's let it rest at that."

"Are you satisfied I didn't do it?"

"Yes. You heard my testimony."

"You didn't do it to square accounts?"

I shook my head. "No. Like you said, it was what you were drawing wages for, what you done that day."

But I was still slightly troubled about the matter. Perjury is not a thing to be taken lightly. I met with Dad privately and told him the whole story. "Did you tell Lew that you'd see him through the matter?" he asked.

"Yes," I answered.

"And you believed he was innocent?"

"Yes."

"Then when you tell a man *yes*, be sure in your own heart that you don't mean *maybe*."

I felt better after that.

I finally got Nora out to the ranch. In the cool of the evening, we walked out to where I'd laid plans for the house for she and I to occupy. It was set on a broad little rise about half a mile from the ranch house. It was nothing more than stakes drove into the ground to mark off the different rooms. It was going to be a big house for two people—eight rooms with a big dining room. I'd planned to build it out of limestone and wood with a Spanish-tiled roof.

We stood there, looking at it. "I was just about ready to start the foundation when you ran off on me," I said. "I'd planned on bringing you out here and showing it to you once I got the foundation set. It was going to be my way of proposing."

She turned to me, pressing her soft breasts against my body and tilting up her face. She said, in that cool way of hers, "What if I'd said no?"

I shrugged. "Well, I guess I could have turned it into a barn, or Norris might have used it. He's courting a belle lives in Austin."

She reached up and kissed me lightly. "What are you going to do now?"

I kissed her long and deeply. Then I said, "That's what I brought you out here to ask. What should I do?"

She kissed me again. "Pour the foundation," she said.

We kissed for a long moment. I could feel the passion rising in my throat. Then she pulled back and said, "If I change my mind, you can always turn it into a barn."

## ABOUT THE AUTHOR

Giles Tippette is a Texan by birth and by choice. He has earned his living as a writer since 1966. Prior to that he was a venture pilot, a mercenary, a diamond courier, and a bucking event rodeo cowboy. In addition to his books, he has written over 500 articles for such magazines as *Time, Newsweek, Sports Illustrated, Esquire,* and *Texas Monthly.* He presently lives in San Angelo, Texas.